A Dance to the Music of Time
# Temporary Kings

ANTHONY POWELL was born in London in 1905. Son of
a soldier, he comes from a family of mostly soldiers or
sailors which moved from Wales about a hundred and fifty
years ago. He was educated at Eton and Balliol College,
Oxford, of which he is now an Honorary Fellow.

From 1926 he worked for about nine years at
Duckworths, the publishers, then as scriptwriter for
Warner Brothers in England. During the Second World
War he served in the Welch Regiment and Intelligence
Corps, acting as liaison officer with the Polish, Belgian,
Czechoslovak, Free French and Luxembourg forces, and
was promoted major.

Before and after the war he wrote reviews and literary
columns for various newspapers, including the *Daily
Telegraph* and the *Spectator*. From 1948–52 he worked on
the *Times Literary Supplement*, and was literary editor of
*Punch*, 1952–8.

Between 1931 and 1949, Anthony Powell published five
novels, a biography, *John Aubrey and His Friends*, and a
selection from Aubrey's works. The first volume of his
twelve-volume novel, *A Dance to the Music of Time*, was
published in 1951, and the concluding volume, *Hearing
Secret Harmonies*, appeared in 1975. In 1976 he published
the first volume of his memoirs, *To Keep the Ball Rolling*,
under the title *Infants of the Spring*.

In 1934 he married Lady Violet Pakenham, daughter of
the fifth Earl of Longford. They have two sons, and live
in Somerset.

*Books by Anthony Powell*

*Novels*
Afternoon Men
Venusberg
From a View to a Death
Agents and Patients
What's Become of Waring
Oh How the Wheel Becomes It

*A Dance to the Music of Time*
A Question of Upbringing
A Buyer's Market
The Acceptance World
At Lady Molly's
Casanova's Chinese Restaurant
The Kindly Ones
The Valley of Bones
The Soldier's Art
The Military Philosophers
Books Do Furnish a Room
Temporary Kings
Hearing Secret Harmonies

*To Keep the Ball Rolling (Memoirs)*
Volume I: Infants of the Spring
Volume II: Messengers of Day
Volume III: Faces in My Time
Volume IV: The Strangers All Are Gone

*General*
John Aubrey and His Friends

*Plays*
The Garden God *and* The Rest I'll Whistle

Anthony Powell

# Temporary Kings

*A Novel*

FLAMINGO

Published by Fontana Paperbacks
by agreement with Heinemann

# FOR ROLAND

First published by
William Heinemann Ltd 1973
First issued in Fontana Paperbacks 1974
Seventh impression April 1983

This Flamingo edition first published
in 1983 by Fontana Paperbacks,
8 Grafton Street, London W1X 3LA

Copyright © Anthony Powell 1973

Printed and bound in Great Britain by
Richard Clay (The Chaucer Press) Ltd,
Bungay, Suffolk

# ONE

The smell of Venice suffused the night, lacustrine essences richly distilled. Late summer was hot here. A very old man took the floor. Hoarse, tottering, a few residual teeth, arbitrarily assembled and darkly stained, underpinning the buoyancy of his grin, he rendered the song in slower time than ordinary, clawing the air with his hands, stamping the floor with his feet, while he mimed the action of the cable, straining, creaking, climbing, as it hauled upward towards the volcanic crater the capsule encasing himself and his girl, a journey calculated to stir her ungrateful heart.

> Iamme, iamme, via montiam su là.
> Iamme, iamme, via montiam su là.
> Funiculì funiculà, via montiam su là.

A first initiatory visit to Italy, travelling as a boy with my parents, had included a week at this same hotel. It overlooked the Grand Canal. Then small, rather poky even, its waterfront now extended on either side of the terrace, where, by tradition, the musicians' gondola tied up. Near-tourist outfits replaced evening dress antique as the troupe itself, in other respects the pattern remained unaltered, notably this veteran and the 'business' of his song. Could he be the same man? A mere forty years – indeed three or four short of that – might well have passed without much perceptible transmutation in a façade already radically weathered by Time when first observed. The gestures were identical. With an operatic out-thrust of the body, he intimated the kingdoms of the earth ranged beneath funicular passengers for their delectation.

> Si vede Francia, Procida, la Spagna,
> E io veggo te, io veggo te.

The century all but within his grasp, the singer might actually recollect the occasion for which the song had been composed; on that great day, as the words postulated, himself ascended Vesuvius accompanied by his inamorata, snug together in the newly installed spaceship, auspicious with potentialities for seduction. Had a dominating personality, the suggestive rotations of the machinery, Procida's isle laid out far below, like a girl spreadeagled on her back, all combined to do the trick? The answer was surely affirmative. Even if marriage remained in question – conceivably the librettist's deference to convention – at least warmer contacts must have been attained.

The stylized movements of the hands were reminiscent of Dicky Umfraville at one of his impersonations. He too should have harnessed his gift, in early life, to an ever renewing art from which there was no retiring age. To exhibit themselves, perform before a crowd, is the keenest pleasure many people know, yet self-presentation without a basis in art is liable to crumble into dust and ashes. Professional commitment to his own representations might have kept at bay the melancholy – all but chronic, Frederica and his stepchildren complained – now that Umfraville had retired from work as agent at Thrubworth. Sometimes, after a day's racing, for example, he might return to the old accustomed form. Even then a few misplaced bets would bring the conviction that luck was gone for good, his life over.

'Christ, what a shambles. Feeling my back too. Trumpeter, what are you sounding now? – *Defaulters,* old boy, if your name's Jerry Hat-Trick. You know growing old's like being increasingly penalized for a crime you haven't committed.'

'Which ones haven't you committed?' said Frederica. 'You've never grown up, darling. You can't grow old till you've done that.'

Sufferance, as well as affection, was implied, though Frederica had never tired of Umfraville, in spite of being often cross with him.

'I feel like the man in the ghost story, scrambling over the breakwaters with the Horrible Thing behind him getting closer and closer. There hasn't been a good laugh since that horse-box backed over Buster Foxe at Lingfield.'

As a rule Umfraville disliked mention of death, but the legend of Buster Foxe's immolation under the wheels of a kind of Houyhnhnm juggernaut, travelling in reverse gear, was the exception. It had resolutely passed into Umfraville myth. Captain Foxe's end (he had been promoted during the war) was less dramatic, though certainly brought about by some fatal accident near the course, terminating for ever risk of seeing an old enemy at future race-meetings. It would be worth asking Umfraville if he had his own version of *Funiculì-Funiculà*, an accomplishment by no means out of the question.

The present vocalist to some extent controverted Frederica's argument, supporting more St John Clarke's observation that 'growing old consists abundantly of growing young'. The aged singer looked as if thoughts of death, melancholy in any form, were unknown to him. He could be conceived as suffering from rage, desire, misery, anguish, despair; not melancholy. That was clear; additionally so after the round of applause following his number. The clapping was reasonably hearty considering the heat, almost as oppressive as throughout the day just passed. Dr Emily Brightman

7

and I joined in. Acknowledgment of his talent delighted the performer. He bowed again and again, repeatedly baring blackened sporadic stumps, while he mopped away streams of sweat that coursed down channels of dry loose skin ridging either side of his mouth. Longevity had brought not the smallest sense of repletion where public recognition was in question. That was on the whole sympathetic. One found oneself taking more interest than formerly in the habits and lineaments of old age.

In spite of the singer's own nonchalance, the susceptive tunes of the musicians, the gorgeous dropscene, the second carafe of wine, infected the mind not disagreeably with thoughts of the evanescence of things. At the beginning of the century, Marinetti and the Futurists had wanted to make a fresh start – whatever that might mean – advocating, among other projects, filling up the Venetian canals with the rubble of the Venetian palaces. Now, the Futurists, with their sentimentality about the future, primitive machinery, vintage motorcars, seemed as antiquely picturesque as the Doge in the *Bucentaur*, wedding his bride the Sea, almost as distant in time; though true that a desire to destroy, a hatred and fear of the past, remained a constant in human behaviour.

'Do you think the soubrette is his mistress, or his great-granddaughter?' asked Dr Brightman. 'They seem on very close terms. Perhaps both.'

From our first meeting, at the opening session of the Conference (when friendly contacts had been achieved by mutual familiarity with *Borage and Hellebore,* my book about Burton, and her own more famous work on The Triads), Dr Brightman had made clear a determination to repudiate the faintest suspicion of spinsterish prudery that might, very mistakenly, he supposed to attach to her circumstances. Discreetly fashionable clothes emphasized this total severance from anything

8

to be thought of as academic stuffiness, a manner of dress quietly but insistently smart. One of her pupils at the university (our niece Caroline Lovell's best friend) alleged a reputation of severity as a tutor, effortless ability to reduce to tears, if necessary, the most bumptious female student. Dr Brightman, it was true, was undoubtedly a little formidable at first impact. We touched on the Dark Ages. She spoke of her present engagement on Boethius, in a form likely to prove controversial. The male don of her name, known to me when myself an undergraduate, appeared to be only a distant relation.

'You mean Harold Brightman, who played some part in organizing a dinner to celebrate the ninetieth birthday of that old rascal Sillery? He's a cousin of some sort. There are scores of them engaged in the learned professions. We all stem from the Revd Salathiel Brightman, named in *The Dunciad* in connection with some long forgotten squabble about a piece of Augustan pedantry. He composed *Attick and Roman Reckonings of Capacity for Things Liquid and Things Dry reduced to the Common English Mensuration for Wine and Corn*. I believe the great Lemprière acknowledges indebtedness in preparation of his own tables of proportion at the end of the *Bibliotheca Classica*. Salathiel is said to have revolutionized the view held in his own day of the cochlearion and oxybaphon, though for myself I haven't the smallest notion of how many of either went to an amphora. Speaking of things liquid and things dry, shall we have a drink? Tell me, Mr Jenkins, did Mark Members persuade you to come to this Conference?'

'You, too?'

'Not without resistance on my own part. I had planned a lot of work this long vac. Mark positively nagged me into it. He can be very tyrannical.'

'I resisted too, but was in difficulties about a book. It seemed a way out.'

9

To say that was to make the best of things, let oneself down gently. Writing may not be enjoyable, its discontinuance can be worse, though Members himself must by then have been safely beyond any such gnawings of guilt. By now he was a hardened frequenter of international gatherings for 'intellectuals' of every sort. He had been at the game for years. The activity suited him. It brought out hitherto dormant capabilities for organization and oratory, neither given a fair chance in the course of an author's routine dealings with publishers and editors; nor for that matter — Members having tried reversing the rôles — trafficking with authors as editor or publisher. The then ever-widening field of cultural congresses pleased and stimulated his temperament. At one of them he had even found a wife, an American lady, author and journalist, a few years older than himself, excellently preserved, not without name and useful connections in her own country. She was also, as Members himself boasted, 'inured to writers and their inconsequent ways'. That was probably true, as Members was her fourth husband. The marriage still remained in a reasonably flourishing condition, in spite of hints (from the critic, Bernard Shernmaker, chiefly) that Members had dropped out of the Venetian rendezvous because another, smaller conference was to include a female novelist in whom he was interested. A reason for supposing that particular imputation unjust was that several other literary figures had thought the rival conference more tempting. These differed in this from Members only insomuch as he had played some part in organization of the Venetian gathering at the London end. That was why, to avoid becoming vulnerable in his own apostasy, he had to find, at short notice, one or two substitutes like Dr Brightman and myself. He brushed aside pretexts that I never took part in such activities.

'All the more reason to go, Nicholas, see what such meetings of true minds have to offer. I should not be at all surprised if you did not succumb to the drug. It's quite a potent one, as I've found to my cost. Besides, even at our age, there's a certain sense of adventure at such jamborees. You meet interesting people – if writers and suchlike can be called interesting, something you and I must often have doubted in the course of our *via dolorosa* towards literary crucifixion. At worst it makes a change, provides a virtually free holiday, or something not far removed. Come along, Nicholas, bestir yourself. Say yes. Don't be apathetic.

> Leave we the unlettered plain its herd and crop;
>   Seek we sepulture
> On a tall mountain, citied to the top,
>   Crowded with culture!

It's not sepulture, and a tall mountain, this time, but the Piazza San Marco – my patron saint, please remember – and a lot of parties, not only crowded with culture, but excellent food and drink thrown in. There's the Biennale, and the Film Festival the following week, if you feel like staying for it. Kennst du das Land, wo die Zitronen blühn? Take a chance on it. You'll live like a king once you get there.'

'One of those temporary kings in *The Golden Bough*, everything at their disposal for a year or a month or a day – then execution? Death in Venice?'

'Only ritual execution in more enlightened times – the image of a declining virility. A Mann's a man for a' that. Being the temporary king is what matters. The retribution of congress kings only takes the form, severe enough in its way, I admit, of having to return to everyday life. Even that, my dear Nicholas, you'll do with renewed energy. Like the new king, in fact.

Here upon earth, we're kings, and none but we
Can be such kings, nor of such subjects be.

That's what the Venice Conference will amount to.
I shall put your name down.'

'Who else is going?'

'Quentin Shuckerly, Ada Leintwardine. They're certain. Not Alaric Kydd, which is just as well. The new Shuckerly, *Athlete's Footman,* is the best queer novel since *Sea Urchins.* You ought to have a look at it, if you've got time. You won't regret the decision to go to Venice. I'm *désolé* at not being able to attend myself. Unfortunately one can't be in two places at once, and I have a duty to make myself available elsewhere. There will be a lot of international figures there, some of them quite distinguished. Ferrand-Sénéschal, Kotecke, Santos, Pritak. With any luck you'll find a very talented crowd. I'd hoped to hear Ferrand-Sénéschal on the subject of Pasternak and the Nobel Prize. His objections – he will certainly demur at the possibility – will be worth listening to.'

In suggesting that the international fame of several foreign writers liable to attend the Conference was not to be entirely disregarded in assessing its attractions, Members was speaking reasonably enough. To meet some of these, merely to set eyes on them, would be to connect together a few additional pieces in the complex jigsaw making up the world's literary scene; a game never completed, though sometimes garishly illuminated, when two or three unexpected fragments were all at once coherently aligned in place. To addicts of this pastime, the physical appearance of a given writer can add to his work an incisive postscript, physical traits being only inadequately assessable from photographs. Ferrand-Sénéschal, one of the minor celebrities invoked by Members, was a case in point. His thick lips, closely set eyes, ruminatively brutal expression, were familiar enough from newspaper pictures or publishers' catalogues, the man himself never quite defined by them. I had no great desire to meet Ferrand-Sénéschal – on balance would almost prefer to be absolved from the effort of having to talk with him – but I was none the less curious to see what he looked like in person, know how he carried himself among his fellow nomads of the intellect, Bedouin of the cultural waste, for ever folding and unfolding their tents in its oases.

There was another reason, when Members picked Ferrand-Sénéschal's name out of the hat as a potential prize for attending the Conference, why a different, a stronger reaction was summoned up than by such names as Santos, Pritak, Kotecke. During the war, staff-officers, whose work required rough-and-ready familiarity with conditions of morale relating to certain bodies of troops or operational areas – the whole world being, in one sense, at that moment an operational area – were from time to time given opportunity to glance through excerpts, collected together from a wide range of correspondence, inspected by the Censorship Department. This symposium, of no very high security grading, was put together for practical purposes, of course, though not with complete disregard for light relief. The anonymous anthologist would sometimes show appreciation of a letter's comic or ironic bearing. Ferrand-Sénéschal was a case in point. Scrutinizing the file, my eye twice caught his name, familiar to anyone whose dealings with contemporary literature took them even a short way beyond the Channel. Ferrand-Sénéschal's letters were dispatched from the United States, where, lecturing at the outbreak of war, he had remained throughout hostilities. Always a Man of the Left (much in evidence as such at the time of the Spanish Civil War, when his name had sometimes appeared in company with St John Clarke's), he had shown rather exceptional agility in sitting on the fence that divided conflicting attitudes of the Vichy Administration from French elements, in France and elsewhere, engaged in active opposition to Germany.

Cited merely to illustrate the current view of a relatively well-known French author domiciled abroad through the exigencies of war, Ferrand-Sénéschal's couple of contributions to the Censor's digest deftly indicated the deviousness of their writer's allegiance. No doubt, in one sense, the phrases were intended precisely to achieve that, naturally implying nothing to be construed as even covertly antagonistic to the Allied cause. Whatever else he might be, Ferrand-Sénéschal was no fool. Indeed, it was his own appreciation of the fact that his letters might be of interest to the Censor – any censor – which provoked a smile at the skill shown in excerpting so neatly the carefully chosen sentences. In addition, personal letters, even when deliberately composed with an eye to examination, official or unofficial, by someone other than their final recipient, give a unique sense of the writer's personality, often lacking in books by the same hand. They are possibly the most revealing of all, like physical touchings-up of personal appearance to make some exceptional effect. In the case of Ferrand-Sénéschal, as with his portraits in the press, the personality conveyed, not to be underrated as a force, was equally not a specially attractive one.

Avoidance, during this expatriate period, of all outward participation, even *parti pris,* in relation to the issues about which people were fighting so fiercely, turned out no handicap to Ferrand-Sénéschal's subsequent career. Not only did he physically survive those years, something he might easily have failed to do had he remained in Europe, but he returned to France unembarrassed by any of the inevitable typifications attached to active combatants of one sort or another. Some of these had, of course, acquired distinction, military or otherwise, which Ferrand-Sénéschal could not claim, but, in this process, few had escaped comparatively damaging sectarian labels. In fact, Ferrand-Sénéschal, who had worked hard during his exile in literary and academic spheres in both American continents, found himself in an improved position, with a wider public, in a greatly changed world. He now abandoned a policy of non-intervention, publicly announcing his adherence to the more extreme end of his former political standpoint, one from which he never subsequently deviated. From this vantage point he played a fairly prominent rôle in the immediately post-war period of re-adjustment in France; then, when a few years later cultural congresses settled down into their swing, became – as emphasized by Members – a conspicuous figure in their lively polemics.

Remembrance of these censored letters had revived when I was 'doing the books' on *Fission*. A work by Ferrand-Sénéschal turned up for review. Quiggin & Craggs had undertaken a translation of one of his philosophico-economic studies. Although the magazine was, in theory, a separate venture from the publishing house producing it, the firm – Quiggin especially – was apt to take amiss too frequent disregard of their own imprint in the critical pages of *Fission*. I should in any case have consulted Bagshaw, as editor, as to whether or not a Quiggin & Craggs book might be safely ignored. Bagshaw's preoccupations with all forms of Marxism, orthodox or the reverse, being what they were, he was likely to hold views on this one. He did. He was at once animated by Ferrand-Sénéschal's name.

'An interesting sub-species of fellow-traveller. I'd like to have a look myself. Ferrand-Sénéschal's been exceedingly useful to the Party at one time or another, in spite of his heresies. There's always a little bit of Communist propaganda in whatever he writes, however trivial. He also has odd sexual tastes. Political adversaries like to dwell on that. In America, they allege some sort of scandal was hushed up.'

Bagshaw turned the pages of Ferrand-Sénéschal's book. He had accepted it as something for the expert, sitting down to make a closer examination.

'You won't find anything about his sexual tastes there. I've glanced through it.'

'I'll take it home, and consider the question of a reviewer. I might have a good idea.'

By the following week Bagshaw had a good idea. It was a very good one.

'We'll give Ferrand-Sénéschal to Kenneth Widmerpool for his routine piece in the mag. It's not unlike his own sort of stuff.'

That was Bagshaw at his best. His editor's instinct, eccentric, unguarded, often obscure of intent, was rarely to be set aside as thoughtless or absurd. He reported Widmerpool as being at first unwilling to wrestle with the Ferrand-Sénéschal translation (having scarcely heard of its author), but, on reading some of the book, changing his mind. The article appeared in the next issue of *Fission*. Widmerpool himself was delighted with it.

'One of my most successful efforts, I think I can safely aver. Ferrand-Sénéschal is a man to watch. He and I have something in common, both of us intellectuals in the world of action. In drawing analogy between our shared processes of thought, I refer to a common denominator of resolution to break ruthlessly with old social methods and outlooks. In short, we are both realists. I should like to meet this Frenchman. I shall arrrange to do so.'

The consequences of the Ferrand-Sénéschal article were, in their way, far reaching. Ferrand-Sénéschal, who visited London fairly often in the course of business – cultural business – was without difficulty brought into touch with Widmerpool on one of these trips. Some sort of a fellow-feeling seems to have sprung up immediately between the two of them, possibly a certain facial resemblance contributing to that, people who look like one another sometimes finding additional affinities. In the army, for example, tall cadaverous generals would choose tall cadaverous soldier-servants or drivers; short choleric generals prefer short choleric officers on their staff. Whatever it was, Widmerpool and Ferrand-Sénéschal took to each other on sight. As a member of some caucus within the Labour Party, Widmerpool invited Ferrand-Sénéschal to meet his associates at a House of Commons luncheon. This must have gone well, because in due course Ferrand-Sénéschal returned the compliment by entertaining Widmerpool, when passing through Paris on his way back from Eastern Europe, touring there under the banner of a society to encourage friendship with one of the People's Republics.

This night-out in Paris with Ferrand-Sénéschal had also been an unqualified success. That was almost an understatement of the gratification it had given Widmerpool, according to himself. Either by chance or design, his comments on the subject had come straight back to the *Fission* office. That was the period when Widmerpool, deserted by his wife, was keeping away from the magazine. Not unreasonably, he may have hoped, by deliberately building up a legend of high-jinks with Ferrand-Sénéschal, to avoid seeming an abandoned husband, unable to amuse himself, while Pamela lived somewhere in secret with X. Trapnel. That could have been the motive for spreading broadcast the tidings of going on the Parisian spree; otherwise, it might be thought, an incident wiser to keep private. Certainly highly coloured rumours about their carousal were in circulation months after its celebration. Apart from other considerations, such behaviour, anyway such brazenness, was in complete contrast with the tone in which Widmerpool himself used to deplore the *louche* reputation of Sir Magnus Donners.

This censure could, of course, have been a double-bluff. When we had met at a large party given for the Election Night of 1955 – the last time I had seen him – Widmerpool deliberately dragged in a reference to the weeks spent together trying to learn French at La Grenadière, adding that it was 'lucky for our morals Madame Leroy's house had not been in Paris', words that seemed to bear out, on his part, desire to confirm a reputation for being a dog. That was early in the evening, before Pamela's incivility had greatly offended our hostess, or Widmerpool himself heard (towards morning, after Isobel and I had gone home) that he had lost his seat in the House. In *Fission* days, Bagshaw had been sceptical about the Paris story, without dismissing it entirely.

'I suppose some jolly-up may have taken place. The brothels are closed nowadays officially, but that wouldn't make any difference to someone in the know. I'm not sure what Ferrand-Sénéschal is himself supposed to like – being chained to a crucifix, while a green light's played on him – little girls – two-way mirrors – I've been told, but I can't remember. He may have given Kenneth a few ideas. I shall develop sadistic tendencies myself, if that new secretary doesn't improve. She's muddled those proofs of the ads again. I say, Nicholas, we've still too much space to spare. Just cast your eye over these, and see if you've any suggestions. You'll bring a fresh mind to the advertisement problem. It's a blow too we're not going to get any more Trapnel pieces. Editing this mag is driving me off my rocker.'

In the light of what I knew of Widmerpool, the tale of visiting a brothel with Ferrand-Sénéschal was to be accepted with caution, although true that he had more than once in the past adopted a rather gloating tone when speaking of tarts, an attitude dating back to our earliest London days. Moreland used to say, 'Maclintick doesn't like women, he likes tarts – indeed he once actually fell in love with a tart, who led him an awful dance.' That taste could be true of Widmerpool too; perhaps a habit become so engrained as to develop into a preference, handicapping less circumscribed sexual intimacies. Such routines might go some way to explain the fiasco with Mrs Haycock, even the relationship – whatever that might be – with Pamela. That Ferrand-Sénéschal, as Bagshaw suggested, had been the medium for introduction, in middle-age, to hitherto unknown satisfactions, new, unusual forms of self-release, was not out of the question. By all accounts, far more unlikely things happened in the sphere of late sexual development. Bagshaw was, of course, prejudiced. By that time he had decided that Widmerpool was not only bent on ejecting him from the editorship of *Fission*, but was also a fellow-traveller.

'He probably learnt a lot from Ferrand-Sénéschal politically, the latter being a much older hand at the game.'

'But what has Widmerpool to gain from being a crypto?'

Bagshaw laughed loudly. He thought that a very silly question. Political standpoints of the extreme Left being where his heart lay, where, so to speak, he had lost his virginity, the inquiry was like asking Umfraville why he should be interested in one horse moving faster than another, a football fan the significance of kicking an inflated bladder between two posts. At first Bagshaw was unable to find words simple enough to enlighten so uninstructed a mind. Then a lively parallel occurred to him.

'Apart from anything else, it's one of those secret pleasures, like drawing a moustache on the face of a pretty girl on a poster, spitting over the stairs – you know, from a great height on to the people below. You see several heads, possibly a bald one. They don't know where the saliva comes from. It gives an enormous sense of power. Like the days when I used to throw marbles under the hooves of mounted policemen's horses. Think of the same sort of fun when you're an MP, or respected civil servant, giving the whole show away on the quiet, when everybody thinks you're a pillar of society.'

'Isn't that a rather frivolous view? What about deep convictions, all the complicated ideologies you're always talking about?'

'Not really frivolous. Such spitting itself is an active form of revolt – undermining society as we know it, spreading alarm and despondency among the bourgeoisie. Besides, spitting apart, you stand quite a good chance of coming to power yourself one day. Giving them all hell. The bourgeoisie, and everyone else. Being a member of a Communist *apparat* would suit our friend very well politically.'

'But Widmerpool's the greatest bourgeois who ever lived.'

'Of course he is. That's what makes it such fun for him. Besides, he isn't a bourgeois in his own eyes. He's a man in a life-and-death grapple with the decadent society round him. Either he wins, or it does.'

'That doesn't sound very rational.'

'Marxism isn't rational, Nicholas. Get that into your head. The more intelligent sort of Marxist tells you so. He stresses the point, as one of its highest merits, that, like religion, Marxism requires faith in the last resort. Besides, my old friend Max Stirner covers Kenneth – "Because I am by nature a man I have equal rights to the enjoyment of all goods, says Babeuf. Must he not also say: because I am 'by nature' a first-born prince I have a right to a throne?" That's just what Kenneth Widmerpool does say – not out loud, but it's what he thinks.'

Bagshaw had begun on his favourite political philosopher. I was not in the mood at that moment. To return instead to sorting the *Fission* books was not to deny there might be some truth in the exposition: that Widmerpool, conventional enough at one level of his life – conventional latterly in his own condemnation of conventionality – might at the same time nurture within himself quite another state of mind to that shown on the surface; not only desire to re-shape the world according to some doctrinaire pattern, but also to be revenged on a world that had found himself insufficiently splendid in doing so. Had not General Conyers, years ago, diagnosed a 'typical intuitive extrovert'; cold-blooded, keen on a thing for the moment, never satisfied, always wanting to get out to something else? In one sense, of course, the world, from a material assessment, had treated Widmerpool pretty well, even at the time when Bagshaw was talking. On the other hand, people rarely take the view that they have been rewarded according to their deserts, those most rewarded often the very ones keenest to be revenged. Possibly Ferrand-Sénéschal was just such another.

Whatever Ferrand-Sénéschal's inner feelings, the meeting with him in Venice was not to be. Not even a glimpse on the platform. His death took place in London only a few days before the Conference opened. He suffered a stroke in his Kensington hotel. The decease of a French author of international standing would in any case have rated a modest headline in the papers. The season of the year a thin one for news, more attention was given to Ferrand-Sénéschal than might have been expected. It was revealed, for example, that he had seen a doctor only a day or two before, who had warned him against excessive strain. Accordingly no inquest took place. Death had come – as Evadne Clapham remarked, 'like the book' – in the afternoon. Later that evening, so the papers said, Ferrand-Sénéschal had been invited to 'look in on' Lady Donners after dinner – 'not a party, just a few friends', she had explained to the reporters – where he would have found himself, so it appeared, among an assortment of politicians and writers, including Mr and Mrs Mark Members. Social engagements of this kind, together with a stream of acquaintances and journalists passing in and out of his suite at the hotel, had evidently proved too much for a state of health already impaired.

The London obituaries put Léon-Joseph Ferrand-Sénéschal in his sixtieth year. They mentioned only two or three of his better known books, selected from an enormous miscellany of novels, plays, philosophic and economic studies, political tracts, and (according to Bernard Shernmaker) an early volume, later suppressed by the author, of verse in the manner of Verlaine. This involuntary withdrawal would make little difference to the Conference. Well known intellectuals were always an uncertain quantity when it came to turning up, even if they did not suddenly succumb. Pritak, Santos, Kotecke, might equally well find something better to do, though not necessarily meet an unlooked-for end. I made up my mind to ask Dr Brightman, when opportunity arose, whether she had ever encountered Ferrand-Sénéschal; if so, what she thought of him.

The youngest and best-looking of the troupe, the one Dr Brightman had called the Soubrette, took a plate round for the collection. The rest burst *en masse* into *Santa Lucia*. The programme came to an end. Preparations began for moving on to another hotel. Before they got under way, the old singer, in participation with the Soubrette, surreptitiously examined the takings, both gesticulating a good deal, whether with satisfaction or irony at the extent of the offering was uncertain.

'To sing Neapolitan songs in Venice is rather like a Scotch ballad in Bath,' said Dr Brightman. 'Naples is unique. Even her popular music doesn't export as far north as this. A taste for Naples is one of the divisions between people. You love the place, or loathe it. The character of the traveller seems to have no bearing on the instinctive choice. Personally I am devoted to the Parthenopean shore, although once victim of a most unseemly episode at Pompeii when younger. It was outside the lupanar, from which in those days ladies were excluded. I should have been affronted far less within that haunt of archaic vice, where I later found little to shock the most demure, except the spartan hardness of the double-decker marble bunks. I chased the fellow away with my parasol, an action no doubt deplored in these more enlightened days, as risking irreparable damage to the responses of one of those all too frequent cases of organ inferiority.'

She briskly shook the crop of short white curls cut close to her head. They looked like a battery of coiled wire (like the Dark Lady's) galvanizing an immensely powerful dynamo. The bearing of the anecdote brought Ferrand-Sénéschal's name to mind again. I asked if she had ever met him.

'Yes, I once was introduced to Ferrand-Sénéschal in the not very inviting flesh. He told me he despised "good writing". I praised his French logic in that respect. As you doubtless know, his early books are ridiculously stilted, his later ones grossly slipshod. I was at once hustled away by his court of toadies. Certain persons require a court. Others prefer a harem. That is not quite the same thing.'

'Some like both.'

'Naturally the one can merge with the other – why, hullo, Russell.'

The young American who had come up to our table seemed to be the only one of his countrymen at the Conference. He was called Russell Gwinnett. We had sat next to each other at luncheon the day before. He had explained that he taught English at a well-known American college for women, where Dr Brightman herself had spent a year as exchange professor, so that they had known one another before meeting again at the Conference.

'How are you making out, Russell? Have you met Mr Nicholas Jenkins? This is Mr Russell Gwinnett, an old friend from my transatlantic days. You have? Come and join us, Russell.'

The serious business of the Conference, intellectuals from all over the world addressing each other on their favourite topics, took place at morning and afternoon sessions on the island of San Giorgio Maggiore. To re-animate enthusiasms imperilled by prolonged exposure to the assiduities of congress life, extension of the syllabus to include an official luncheon or dinner was listed for almost every day of our stay. These banquets were usually linked with some national treasure, or place of historic interest, occasions to some extent justifying the promise of Members that we should 'live like kings'. They gave at the same time opportunity to 'get to know' other members of the Conference. Through the medium of one of these jaunts, which took place at a villa on the Brenta, famous for its frescoes by Veronese, Gwinnett and I had met.

He was in his early thirties, slight in figure, with a small black moustache that showed a narrow strip of skin along the upper lip above and below its length. That he was American scarcely appeared on the surface at first, then something about the thin bone formations of arms and legs, the sallowness and texture of the skin, suggested the nationality. The movements of the body, supple, not without athletic promise, also implied an American, rather than European, nervous tension; an extreme one. He wore spectacles lightly tinted with blue. His air, in general unconformist, did not strongly indicate any recognizable alignment.

I had not sat next to him long the previous day before unorthodoxy was confirmed. Having invoked the name of Dr Brightman, Gwinnett (like herself) created the usually advantageous foundation of good understanding between writers – one by no means always available – by showing well-disposed knowledge of my own works. That was an excellent start. He turned out to hold another ace up his sleeve, but did not play that card at once. In showing control, he began as he went on. After the gratifying, if subjective, offering made in the direction of my own writing, he became less easy. In fact he was almost impossible to engage, drying up entirely, altogether lacking in that reserve of light, reasonably well-informed social equipment, on the whole more characteristic of American than British academic life. This lapse into a torpid, almost surly reluctance to co-operate conversationally suggested an American version of the least flexible type of British don, that quiet egotism, self-applauding narrowness of vision, some-times less than acceptable, even when buttressed with verified references and forward-looking views. If Gwin-nett showed signs almost of burlesquing a stock academic figure, he was himself not necessarily lacking in interest on that account, if only as a campus specimen hitherto unsampled; especially as he seemed oddly young to have developed such traits. Even at the outset I was pre-pared for this diagnosis to be wide of the mark. There was also something not at all self-satisfied about him, an impression of anxiety, a never ceasing awareness of impending disaster.

At table he had messed about the food on his plate, a common enough form of expressing maladjustment, though disconcerting, since the dishes happened to be notably good. He refused wine. It might be that he was a reprieved alcoholic. He had some of that sad, worn, preoccupied air that suggests unquiet memories of more uproarious days. Above all there was a sense of loneli-ness. I talked for a time with the Belgian writer on my other side. Then the Belgian became engaged with his neighbour beyond, leaving Gwinnett and myself back on each other's hands. Before I could think of anything new to say, he put an unexpected question. This was towards the end of the meal, the first sign of loosening up.

'How does the Veronese at Dogdene compare with the ones on the wall here?'

That was a surprise.

'You mean the one Lord Sleaford's just sold? I've never been to Dogdene, so I haven't ever seen it in anything but reproduction. I only know the house itself from the Constable in the National Gallery.'

The Sleaford Veronese had recently realized at auction what was then regarded as a very large sum. The picture had always been a great preoccupation of Chips Lovell, who used often to grumble about his Sleaford relations never recognizing their luck in ownership of a work by so great a master. Lovell, who agreed with Smethyck (now head of a gallery), and with General Conyers, that the picture ought to be cleaned, was also in the habit of complaining that the public did not have sufficient opportunity to inspect its beauties. In those days admission to Dogdene was about three days a week throughout the summer. After the war, in common with many other mansions of its kind, the house was thrown open, at a charge, all the year round. Even so, the Veronese had to be sold to pay for the basic upkeep of the place. In spite of the publicity given at the time of the sale, I was impressed that Gwinnett had heard of it.

'I've been told it's not Veronese at his best — *Iphigenia*, isn't it?'

That had been Lovell's view in moods of denigration or humility. Gwinnett seemed more interested in the subject of the picture than whether or not Veronese had been on form.

'That's an intriguing story it depicts. The girl offering herself for sacrifice. The calm dignity with which she faces death. Tiepolo painted an Iphigenia too, more than once, though I've only seen the one at the Villa Valmarana. There's at least one other that looks even finer in reproduction. It's the inferential side of the myth that fascinates me.'

Gwinnett sounded oddly excited. His manner had altogether altered. The thought of Iphigenia must have strangely moved him. Then he abruptly changed the subject. For some reason speaking of the Veronese had released something within himself, made it possible to introduce another, quite different motif, one, as it turned out, that had been on his mind ever since we met. This matter, once given expression, a little explained earlier lack of ease. At least it suggested that Gwinnett, when broaching topics that meant a lot to him, was not so much vain or unaccommodating, as nervous, paralysed, unsure of himself. That was the next impression, equally untrustworthy as a judgment.

'You knew the English writer X. Trapnel, Mr Jenkins?'

'Certainly.'

'Pretty well, I believe?'

'Yes, I was quite an authority on Trapnel at one moment.'

Gwinnett sighed.

'I'd give anything to have known Trapnel.'

'There were ups and downs in being a friend.'

'You thought him a good writer?'

'A very good writer.'

'I did too. That's why I'd have loved to meet him. I could have done that when I was a student. I was over in London. I get mad at myself when I think of that. He was still alive. I hadn't read his books then. I wouldn't have known where to go and see him anyway.'

'All you had to do was to have a drink at one of his pubs.'

'I couldn't just speak to him. He wouldn't have liked that.'

'If somebody had told you one or two of his haunts — The Hero of Acre or The Mortimer — you could hardly have avoided hearing Trapnel holding forth on books and writers. Then you might have stood him a drink. The job would have been done.'

'Trapnel's the subject of my dissertation — his life and works.'

'So Trapnel's going to have a biographer?'

'Myself.'

'Fine.'

'You think it right?'

'Quite right.'

Gwinnett nodded his head.

'I ought to say I'd already planned to get in touch with you, Mr Jenkins — among others who'd known Trapnel — when I reached England after this Conference. I'd never have expected to find you here.'

After the statement of Gwinnett's Trapnel project, relations might have been on the way to become easier. That did not happen; at least easing was by no means immediate. For a minute or two he seemed even to regret the headlong nature of the confession. Then he recovered some of the earlier more amenable manner.

'You did not go on seeing Trapnel right up to his death, I guess?'

'Not for about four or five years before that. It must be the best part of ten years now since I talked to him — though he once sent me a note asking the date when some book had been published, the actual month, I mean. He went completely underground latterly.'

'What book was that — the one he wanted to know about?'

'A collection of essays by L. O. Salvidge called *Paper*

*Wine*. There had been some question of Trapnel reviewing it, but the notice never got written.'

'Where was Trapnel living when he wrote you?'

'He only gave an accommodation address. A newspaper shop in the Islington part of the world.

'I want to see Mr Salvidge too when I get to London.'

'As you know, he contributed an Introduction to a posthumous work of Trapnel's called *Dogs Have No Uncles.*'

'It's good. Not as great as *Camel Ride to the Tomb,* but good. What a sense of doom that other title gives.'

In contrast with the passing of a prolific writer like Ferrand-Sénéschal, Trapnel's end, in spite of aptness of circumstances, took place unnoticed by the press. That was not surprising. He had produced no 'serious' work during his latter days. Throughout his life he had been accustomed to 'go underground' intermittently, when things took an unfavourable turn; the underground state becoming permanent after the Pamela Widmerpool affair, her destruction of his manuscript, return to her husband. That was when Trapnel disappeared for good. I knew no one who continued to hobnob with him. He must have made business contacts from time to time. His name would occasionally appear in print, or on the air, in connection with hack work of one kind or another. This was usually radio or television collaboration with a partner, a professional, safely established, to whom Trapnel had passed on a saleable idea he himself lacked energy or will to hammer out to the end. In these exchanges he must have inclined to avoid former friendly affiliations, reminders of 'happier days'. It had to be admitted Trapnel had known 'happier days', even if of a rather special order.

Bagshaw was a case in point of Trapnel deliberately rejecting overtures from an old acquaintance. As he had himself planned after the liquidation of *Fission*, when such fiefs were comparatively easy to seize, Bagshaw had carved out for himself an obscure, but apparently fairly prosperous, little realm in the unruly world of television. Now he was known as 'Lindsay Bagshaw', the first name latent until this coming into his own. I never saw much of him after the magazine ceased publication, though we would run across each other occasionally. Once we met in the lift at Broadcasting House, and he began to speak of Trapnel. Even by then Bagshaw had become rather a changed man. Success, even moderate success, had left a mark.

'I'd have liked Trappy to appear in one of my programmes. Quite impossible to run him to earth. I caught sight of him one day from the top of a 137 bus. It wasn't so much the beard and the long black greatcoat, as that melancholy distinguished air Trappy always had. I couldn't jump off in full flight. It was one of those misty evenings in Langham Place. The lights were shining from all the rows of windows in this building. Trappy was standing by that church with the pointed spire. He was looking up at those thousand windows of the BBC, all ablaze with light. Something about him made me feel very sad. I couldn't help thinking of the Scholar Gypsy, and Christ-Church hall, and all that, even though I wasn't at the university myself, and it wasn't snowing. I thought it would have been a splendid shot in a film. I wondered if he'd agree to do a documentary about his own failure in life — comparative, I mean. About a month later, I ran into one of his understrappers in a pub. He was going to see Trappy later that evening. I sent a note, but it wasn't any good. No answer.'

There was also the occasional Trapnel story or article to appear, nothing to be ashamed of, at the same time nothing comparable with the old Trapnel standard. This submerged period of Trapnel's life could not have been enviable. He abandoned The Hero of Acre, all the other pubs where he had been accustomed to harangue an assemblage of chosen followers. The roving intelligentsia of the saloon bar – cultural nomads of a race never likely to penetrate the international steppe – professional topers, itinerant bores, near-criminals, knew him no more. They were thrown back on their own resources, had to keep themselves instructed and amused in other ways. Where Trapnel himself went, whom he saw, how he remained alive, were all hard to imagine. Probably there remained women to find him still passable enough even in decline; more or less devoted mistresses to maintain survival of a sort. As Trapnel himself might have insisted – one could hear his dry harsh voice speaking the words – a washed-up condition is not necessarily an unattractive one to a woman. That had also been one of Barnby's themes: 'Ladies like a man to rescue. A job that offers a challenge. They can annex the property at a cheap rate, and ruthlessly develop it.'

Trapnel may have been annexed by a woman, not much development feasible, minimum financial security about the best to be hoped. That in itself was after all something. Gwinnett agreed the plausible assumption, after the collapse of Trapnel's hopes, was personal administration taken over by a relatively prudent wage-earning mistress; even a good-hearted landlady, whose commonsense regulated money matters, such as they were, warding off actual destitution. That is, Gwinnett had nothing else to offer. His accord was not enthusiastic. Comparative reluctance to accept that a woman might have kept Trapnel going, made me wonder whether Gwinnett were not homosexual. He might be a homosexual as well as a redeemed drunk; the former state, possibly repressed, seeking outlet in the latter. Then he brought back the subject of women himself.

'I'd like to ask you about this girl—the castrating one.'

'Pamela Widmerpool?'

'I've been spun so many yarns about her.'

The stories he had been told were, on the whole, garbled in a manner to make the true circumstances of Trapnel's life all but unrecognizable. It was in any case a field where accuracy was hard to come by. At the same time, if Gwinnett's information had percolated through misinformed sources, he himself showed unexpected flashes of insight. Enormous simplifications were possibly necessary to carry a deeper truth than lay on the surface of a mass of unsorted detail. That was, after all, what happened when history was written; many, if not most, of the true facts discarded. Besides, what could be called unreservedly true when closely examined, especially about Trapnel? The stories told to Gwinnett became notably blurred in their inferences about Pamela Widmerpool. Trapnel's relationship with her emerged as little more than a love affair that had gone wrong, something that might have happened to anybody. Naturally, in one sense, it *was* a love affair that had gone wrong, but subtlety was required to express the unusual nature of that love affair, its start, progress, termination. All these had been conveyed with such lack of finesse that no kind of justice was done to the exceptional nature of those concerned: Pamela: Widmerpool: Trapnel himself. For Gwinnett, too, there existed the seldom remittent difficulty of translating the personalities and doings of English material into American terms.

The impression these reports had left with him was of a man's luck—Trapnel's luck—having suddenly, meaninglessly, taken a turn for the worse. From being, in his way, a notable writer, a promising career ahead of him, Trapnel had been suddenly, inexorably, struck down by misfortune, although leading much the same sort of life as he had always led, with girls not so wholly different from Pamela, before he had linked himself to her. Sometimes Gwinnett hedged a little, but that main interpretation was the one he was prepared, even if unwillingly, to accept.

'Trapnel's crack-up is easy for an American to understand. If you don't mind my saying so, to find a writer of even your age on his feet, and working, is not all that common with us.'

'Some of the violent consuming nervous American energy was characteristic of Trapnel too.'

'He'd no American blood?'

'Not that I know of.'

'I'd like to think he had.'

'His father was a jockey in Egypt. If Trapnel had written about that we'd have a completer picture.'

'Completion was one of the things Trapnel aimed at, you said – the idea of the Complete Man. Did he achieve some of that? I think so.'

'Vigny says the poet is not a sport of nature, his destiny is the human predicament.

'And the concept was challenged by this girl – as it were invalidated.'

Gwinnett thought about that for a moment, almost as if he were hoping to rebut his own conjecture. Then he laughed, and changed his tone.

'It was the god Hercules deserting Antony.'

'As a matter of fact the god Hercules returned in Trapnel's case. There was music in the air again, though only briefly.'

Gwinnett had heard more misleading accounts. The best in existence was probably Malcolm Crowding's. It was at least first-hand. No doubt Crowding's story had been a little ornamented with the passage of time, no worse than that. The basic facts were that Trapnel had found himself in possession of a hundred pounds. No one argued about that, a fact in itself sufficiently extraordinary. What was additionally astonishing, almost a miracle, was the sum being in notes. A cheque might have brought quite different consequences. Where opinion chiefly differed was in the provenance of the money. It was usually designated, rather pedestrianly, as payment for forgotten 'rights', which had finally borne fruit in some medium functioning in long delayed action, possibly from a foreign country. Alternatively, more picturesquely, the hundred pounds was said to be a legacy left to Trapnel's father, the celebrated jockey, as one of the items in the eccentric will of a grateful backer of the winning horse, ridden by Trapnel *père,* at a long forgotten Egyptian race-meeting. By slow but workmanlike processes of the law, the bequest had in due course been deflected to Trapnel himself as heir and successor, the sum delivered to him. If the latter origin were true, the whimsical testator must either have had a long memory, or omitted to overhaul his will for a great many years. In either case, almost equally surprising, Trapnel was traced, the money handed over in cash. The only colourable explanation was that Trapnel, improbable as that might seem, having found his way personally to the inter-mediary – lawyer, accountant, publisher, agent – by his old skill induced whoever was in charge to accept a receipt for notes. If so, that final mustering of Trapnel's long dormant forces proved dramatically, in a sense appropriately, fatal.

Were the hypothesis of the female guardian a correct one (situation reminiscent of Miss Weedon curing Stringham of drink), she would in the normal course of things certainly intercept any money Trapnel might earn, or, more credibly, derive from 'public assistance'. Even in his less calamitous days, there had been interludes in the past of signing on at 'the Labour' – the Labour Exchange – though what trade or vocation Trapnel claimed at such emergencies was never revealed. When, so transcendentally, the hundred pounds in cash materialized into his hands in the manner of a highly proficient conjuror, Trapnel (like Stringham) must have evaded his keeper, reverted to type in the traditional manner, decided, now the money had come his way in this utterly unforeseen manner, to squander it gloriously in The Hero of Acre.

Malcolm Crowding's account of Trapnel's apotheosis in The Hero was likely to be the most reliable. He had been there in person. Besides, his own works proclaimed him a writer of little or no imagination. He could never have invented such a story. By that time he had ceased to publish verse, and was lecturing on English literature at a newly-founded provincial university, in fact spending the night in London in connexion with the editing of a textbook. He approached the subject of Trapnel, like his own academic work, in a spirit of the severest literary puritanism. On impulse, a wish to call up old times, he had dropped in that night to The Hero.

'I expect he hoped to pick up a boy-friend,' said Evadne Clapham. 'The Hero was full of queers when I was taken there last. It was much against my will in any case. They were all standing round wide-eyed watching that old wretch Heather Hopkins giving an imitation of John Foster Dulles in his galoshes.'

Whatever Malcolm Crowding's original intention, Trapnel's arrival in The Hero offered something worth while; in fact supplied a story to become, ever after, Crowding's most notable set-piece.

'It was Lazarus coming back from the Dead. Better than that, because Lazarus didn't buy everyone a drink — at least there's no mention of that in Holy Writ.'

Somebody present — probably Evadne Clapham again, bent on disorganizing the side-effects of Crowding's story — suggested that free drinks were to be inferred on the earlier resurrectionary occasion from Tennyson:

'When Lazarus left his charnel-cave . . .
The streets were filled with joyful sound.'

Crowding refused to allow his narrative to be obstructed
by inconclusive pedantry of that sort. He merely increased the vibrant note of his rather shrill voice.
Evadne Clapham, or whoever else it was interrupting,
ceased to argue. Crowding, feeling the Tennysonian
phrase appropriate enough for Trapnel's sojourn in
outer darkness, developed new metaphor in the direction of Shelley.

'The charnel cave was put behind him. It was Trapnel
Unbound.'

There were present in The Hero old stagers who
had endured in that spot since Trapnel's own great
days, when, tall, bearded, loquacious, didactic, draped
in his dyed greatcoat, toying with the death's-head
swordstick, he had laid down the law on literature,
commanded the price of a drink (though never as now),
dominated the length of the saloon bar. His arrival
was a thunderbolt. Even the most complacent of The
Hero's soaks were jolted by it from their evening's
drinking. Crowding never tired of telling the story.

'X. started in at once – Wodehouse and Wittgenstein,
Malraux and the Marx Brothers – it was just like the
old days, though never before had The Hero known
a night like that for free drinks.'

Unlike the mourners of Lazarus – to accept Crowding's apprehension of the incident, rather than Evadne
Clapham's – the mourners of Trapnel, as, on the strength
of his resurrection, they were soon to become, were
stood round after round. The Hero, one of those
old-fashioned pubs in grained pitchpine with engraved
looking-glass (what Mr Deacon used to call a 'gin
palace'), was anatomized into half-a-dozen or more
separate compartments, subtly differentiating, in the
traditional British manner, social subdivisions of its

clientèle, according to temperament or means: saloon bar: public bar: private bar: ladies' bar: wine bar: off-licence: possibly others too. Customers occupied in these peripheries were all included in the Trapnel largesse, no less than those in the saloon bar, where he had manifested himself. Swept in, too, were several birds of passage, transients buying half-a-bottle in the off-licence. The fountains ran with wine, more precisely with bitter and scotch. News of this boundless munificence got round immediately, not only emptying The French-polishers' Arms opposite – according to Crowding, lately a serious rival to The Hero in draining off a sediment of discontented intellectuals – but also considerably reducing numbers in The Marquess of Sleaford round the corner, where intellectuals were virtually unknown. Not only were these two latter pubs practically cleared of customers, but what Crowding called a 'thirsty concourse' poured into The Hero from The Wheelbarrow (at the time of Bagshaw's first marriage, his last port of call on the way home, owing to staying open until eleven), auxiliary drinkers from other taverns being all hospitably received by Trapnel, if they could only get near enough to him. Crowding, telling the story, would here shake his head.

'X. looked dreadfully ill. As near the image of Death as the knob of that stick he used to carry round, before he threw it into the Grand Union Canal. His face was even whiter.'

Trapnel had been at the height of his old form, talking at the top of his voice, laughing, shouting, contradicting, laying down the law about books and writers, films and film stars, giving prolonged imitations of Boris Karloff; in general reconstructing in its most intrinsic aspects his own persona of years gone by. Not only Crowding, but many others, agreed The Hero had never known such a night. That could not go on for ever. An end had to come. Finally, inexorably, closing time was announced. This moment always represented the peak of Crowding's narrative.

'X walked through the doors of The Hero like a king. There was real dignity in his stride. It was a royal progress. Courtiers followed in his wake. You can imagine – free drinks – there was quite a crowd by that time, some of them singing, as it might be, chants in a patron's praise. X stopped outside, and they all stood round. He waited for a moment by the kerb. Everyone kept back somehow, as if they didn't dare be too familiar. X gazed up the street, then down it, in that proud way of his. He must have been looking for a taxi. He hadn't said yet where he wanted to go. I noticed for the first time that his beard was turning grey. Suddenly he gave a start, remembering something. He wrung his hands, rushed back, tried to get into the pub again through the outer doors, which they were barring up. They wouldn't let him back. He gave a loud cry.

' "I've forgotten my stick. I've lost my stick. My death's-head stick.'

'Of course they wouldn't let him in again after closing time. Somebody told him he hadn't brought a stick with him. Whoever it was couldn't have known about the sword-stick. X didn't take that in for a second or two. When he did, he began to laugh. He laughed and laughed, like one of his own impersonations of a horror film – and it was pretty horrible too. He went on laughing for some minutes, walking slowly back to the edge of the pavement. People close said his look was quite frightening.

' "No," he said. "Of course I haven't got a stick any longer, have I? I sacrificed it. Nor a bloody novel. I haven't got that either."

'Then he heeled over into the gutter. Everybody thought he was drunk.'

At this point in the narrative Crowding would pause,

his face apt to twitch so violently that the most sensitive of his listeners had to turn away. He would then slow up the tempo of the narrative for its termination.

'Drunk? They were sadly in error. I watched Trapnel the whole time we were in the saloon bar together. He consumed exactly one bloody double Three Star in the course of the whole bloody time he was in The Hero.'

After adding this comment as a kind of tailpiece to his chronicle, Crowding always stopped, and glared round like a man expecting contradiction of the most vigorous kind. Contradiction never came. Even Evadne Clapham was silent. Whether that was owed to the force of Crowding's recital, or because most of the audience usually knew Trapnel had never been a great drinker, was uncertain. The surmise that alcohol in itself played no great part in his final collapse was no doubt correct, though he may have allowed himself that night an unwise admixture of drink and 'pills'; simply too many pills. Either could have resulted from finding himself unexpectedly in funds. An inner fatigue, utter moral exhaustion, had to be taken into consideration too. He was removed from the street in due course, to a hospital, dying an hour or two later. By the time the ambulance arrived, the near-criminal potential of the traditional Trapnel entourage had extracted from his pockets all remnants, if such there were, of the hundred pounds. He died quite penniless. At that particular juncture, he appeared to be living alone. That probably explained getting his hands on the money. Crowding never mentioned this last fact, but he would change his tone, from pub crony to academic critic, as he drew to an end.

'I respected the man more than his work. He became a legend in his own lifetime. He often said so himself, and with truth. Sometimes my students ask me to tell them about him – and did you once see Trapnel plain?

I reply "I did", and often stopped and spoke with him. At the same time I am put in a quandary. These young people find the intellectual climate of *Camel Ride to the Tomb* unsatisfying. I cannot in all fairness blame them. Where, they say, is the social conscience? I have to reply, they look in vain.'

At the time of his death, Trapnel's *œuvre,* so far as I knew, consisted of *The Camel*; the selection of short stories published as *Bin Ends*; a fair amount of additional stories, never yet collected, some dating back to his early days as a writer before the war (when he had kept himself alive by all sorts of odd employments); a miscellany of occasional pieces, criticism (some of it quite good), articles, parodies, stuff written for papers like *Fission,* and never brought together; finally the *conte* (unpublished in Trapnel's lifetime on account of some legal battle over 'rights') *Dogs Have No Uncles.* A work in Trapnel's liveliest manner, almost long enough to be called a novel, its posthumous appearance with Salvidge's Introduction had done something to prevent Trapnel's reputation from slumping too severely after his death. All this did not constitute a large aggregate of work, but, together with what was available in other material, should make a respectable critical biography. In any case, Trapnel's was still an unexplored period. Gwinnett added another item.

'Did you know he kept a *Commonplace Book* during his last years?'

'Where is it?'

'I have it myself.'

Gwinnett seemed for a moment uncertain as to what he was prepared to say on the subject. Then, after this hesitation, described how the librarian of his university, knowing about Gwinnett's interest in Trapnel, had drawn attention to an English bookseller's catalogue, which listed, among other manuscripts offered for sale, certain papers of Trapnel's come on the market. The price was not high, the College authorities uninterested. Gwinnett acquired these odds and ends himself. None of them turned out of startling interest, even the *Commonplace Book*, though there was enough there to make its purchase worth while to a potential biographer. That was Gwinnett's own account.

'I'll show you the book. Some of the notes – they're all abbreviated, almost a code – are surely about the castrating girl. You say she's married to – is the name Widmerpool?'

'Yes, she's still married to him.'

That was strange enough. In the course of a dozen years or more of the Widmerpools' married life many stories had gone round, the least of them lurid enough to imply the union could scarcely persist a week longer, yet it had persisted. They remained together; anyway to the extent of living under the same roof. That phrase did not, in fact, define the situation realistically. Each was usually under the different roof of one or other of Widmerpool's two places of residence. There was the flat in Westminster (one of a large block near the River), and his mother's former cottage in the Stourwater neighbourhood, which (Widmerpool mentioned when we met) had been 'enlarged and improved'. Stourwater Castle was now a girls' school; rather a fashionable one. The Quiggin twins, Amanda and Belinda, were being educated there.

The existence of these two separate Widmerpool establishments was sometimes offered as explanation of a capacity to remain undivorced, which certainly required elucidation. Pamela would disappear now and then with other men, behaviour apparently accepted by Widmerpool himself, so that it became, as it were, accepted by everyone else, a matter of comparatively little interest. People recently returned from abroad would report that Pamela Widmerpool had been seen in Spain with an ambitious journalist; among the islands of the

Ægean with a fashionable don; that one of the generals at a NATO headquarters had fallen out with another senior officer, when she was staying with him; that her visit to an embassy in Asia had resulted in a reshuffle of diplomatic personnel; that the TUC had been put in a flutter one year at their conference by her presence with a delegate at a local hotel. A Pamela Widmerpool anecdote might stop the gap in a languishing dinner-table conversation, but, unless highly spiced, was by now unlikely to hold the attention of the company for long.

'My wife loves travel,' said Widmerpool. 'She likes seeing how other people live.'

No convincing answer had been offered to the question why she did not leave him for one of her many, if soon disillusioned lovers; nor why Widmerpool himself never chose his moment to divorce her. For some reason the *status quo* seemed to suit both. Trapnel, alleging the Widmerpool marriage to exclude sexual relationship (scarcely even tried out), had also spoken in a few tortured sentences of the frustration, agony, alienation, inspired in himself – though he loved her – by Pamela's blend of frigidity with insatiable desire. People who went in for more precise ascriptions in such matters, especially far-fetched or eccentric ones, explained this matrimonial paradox by the theory that Widmerpool actually took pleasure in his wife's infidelities, derived masochistic satisfaction, at the very least felt flattered, by the agitation she inspired. Pamela too, so these amateurs of psychology concluded, on her own side luxuriated no less in enjoyment of a recurrent thrill at being unfaithful. Another husband, less tolerant, could prove less satisfactory. Such hypotheses, if not widely accepted, remained comparatively unchallenged by more convincing speculation. At least they attempted to make sense of an otherwise inexplicable situation. They even offered a dim outline of a genuine, if macabre, bond of union; one very different from Trapnel's enslavement. Even Dicky Umfraville's comment had a certain force.

'Anyway they've remained married. Took me five attempts, even if I placed the right bet in the end.'

Loss of his seat in the Commons did not prevent Widmerpool from remaining a fairly prominent figure in public affairs, though there was some surprise when (a few weeks before the Conference opened in Venice) he was created a Life Peer. This advancement, proceeding through the medium of a Conservative Government, must undoubtedly have been conferred after consultation with Labour sources of authority, then in Opposition. Roddy Cutts, who held a minor post in the Tory administration, agreed that Widmerpool's elevation to the Lords had aroused adverse comment on both sides of the House. At the same time, Cutts was sure the recommendation must have been cleared with the Leader of the Opposition, in spite of his reputed dislike for Widmerpool himself. Cutts was inclined to dismiss talk, such as Bagshaw's, of Widmerpool's fellow-travelling.

'After all, if you're on the Left, you have to take a Leftward line in public. That doesn't necessarily mean you're a Communist. Widmerpool may have had leanings in that direction once – certainly his own side thought so – but after all he's not the only one. Personally I'm inclined to think all that's over and done with. There was a story about his being mixed up with Maclean and Burgess. I can't remember which. It was even said he lent a hand in tipping them off. Somebody did, but I'm sure it wasn't Widmerpool. Besides, I don't believe the man's a bugger for a moment. Labour peers had to be created. It wasn't at all easy to settle on suitable names. Not everyone wants to be kicked upstairs to the Lords. Widmerpool lost his seat. He'd made himself very useful on the financial side at one time or another, no matter what the talk about fellow-travelling. Yes, I mean contribution to Party funds. Why not? The money's got to come from somewhere. Probably undisclosed inner workings of the Labour Party machine played a rôle too. Patronage? Might be. These things happen. No different to ourselves in that respect. A political party has to be operated. The PM would never have gone over Hugh's head. When Widmerpool arrived in the House I found him abrasive about marginal issues. Latterly we've got on pretty well. We may be opponents, that's no reason why one should doubt his sincerity. What is true – probably played a part in the peerage – is the active manner Widmerpool's promoted East-West trade, naturally a sphere where some community of political thought, anyway outward acceptance of the other fellow's point of view, is likely to oil the wheels. Whatever he did in that direction had, of course, the blessing of the Board of Trade. He must have made a packet too. Do you ever drink that wine from round the Black Sea? We don't at all despise it at home. Tastes a bit sultry at times, but has the merit of being cheap. Kenneth Widmerpool's got to do something to bring the pennies in with a wife like that. I dare say he wanted the peerage to induce her to stay.'

This last supposition was unconvincing. It was possible to accept Bagshaw's theory, up to a point, that Widmerpool dreamed of revenging himself on the world; in addition, that his marriage was one of the areas where that mood might seem to some extent justified. The notion that a Life Peerage would impress Pamela was improbable; typical of the unimaginative side of Roddy's nature. That was one's first thought. Then, reconsidering the evidence, the view emerged as one Widmerpool himself might easily hold. Pamela was unlikely to be interested, one way or the other, in whatever prestige might be supposed to attach to that transmutation. She had never shown the smallest inclination to reach out towards more considerable aggrandizements for herself. They were reported, according to good authority, to have been on offer from lovers at different times. Her disregard for anything of the kind, provided its active expression remained within not too outrageous bounds, was one of his wife's few characteristics potentially advantageous to Widmerpool's public life. He could convincingly point to her behaviour as embodiment of contempt for 'The Establishment', an abstraction increasingly belaboured by him in speeches and articles. In fact, considering the Life Peerage in the light of Pamela's past conduct, so far from its creation – as Cutts put forward – assuring an irreducibly solid foundation for a marriage often rocked by upheaval, the reverse appeared more likely, similar landmarks in her husband's career having been emphasized in the past by proportionately augmented scandals. A Life Peerage, as an extreme example of Moreland's conviction that matrimonial discord vibrates on an axis of envy, rather than jealousy, could even portend final severance.

To explain all that, even a small part of it, to Gwinnett, in hope of enlarging his view of the Widmerpools in relation to Trapnel, was not easy; certainly not within the time allotted for sitting under the Veroneses. Nothing about the Trapnel story was simple. Although Gwinnett was quick to grasp things, nothing about his own personality was simple either. He was an altogether unfamiliar type. He himself seemed almost painfully aware of our mutual difficulties of intercommunication. That made things no easier. There was an innate awkwardness about him. Now, for instance, he stood by the table, unable to make up his mind whether or not to accept Dr Brightman's invitation to sit with us.

45

'What will you drink?'

Without answering, he caught a passing waiter and ordered a citronade. On such a night nothing was more natural than to prefer a cooling soft drink to something stronger, yet again one speculated for some reason about the possibility of an alcoholic past. Something about him suggested rigid control, concealment, an odd way of life. He had the air of punishing himself, possibly for his own supposed social inadequacies. When he sat down, all Dr Brightman's briskness was required to dispel the threat he brought of damped conversation. He had been carrying a newspaper under his arm, which he laid on the table. It was French, the name folded out of sight.

'We were talking of courts and harems, Russell,' said Dr Brightman. 'Those who need them. I'm sure you must have experienced friends like that.'

Gwinnett smiled, but did not comment. The relationship between himself and Dr Brightman appeared good, the best yet, so far as observable. There was none of the coyness that might be suggested by the idea of a distinguished female professor becoming friends with a young academic colleague of the opposite sex. You felt they liked each other, had perhaps learnt from each other, would not for a second hesitate to be tough with each other, if required by circumstance. There was no suggestion of sentimental feelings, a kind of mother/son relationship, just because Dr Brightman had been far from home, Gwinnett something of an oddity in his own surroundings.

'Talking of harems,' she said, 'the owner of the Palazzo we're invited to visit tomorrow bears the famous name of Bragadin, and claims to be descended from Casanova's patron, though not, of course, in the legitimate line.'

Gwinnett showed no great interest in that. I asked

which of the several Bragadin palaces this was. I had not studied the extra-mural programme carefully, preferring these excursions to come as a series of bracing surprises.

'One never open to the public. Our Conference is greatly favoured. There's a Tiepolo ceiling there on which I've longed to gaze for years. In fact the hint that Conference members might gain access was the chief weapon of Mark Members in overcoming any hesitation in agreeing to attend.'

'It's the Jacky Bragadin one reads about in gossip columns?'

Dr Brightman nodded,

'The Palazzo wasn't inherited. All sorts of people have lived there at one time or another. Jacky Bragadin – though I've no right to speak of him in this familiar manner – bought it just after the war.'

Gwinnett, who had been looking about him without paying much apparent attention to what Dr Brightman was saying, joined in at that.

'Jacky Bragadin's mother's was one of the big American fortunes of the last century. She was a Macwatters of Philadelphia. That's where the funds for the Bragadin Foundation come from.'

'Which have been of good use to most of us in our time,' said Dr Brightman. 'My knowledge of the benefactor, like that of Mr Jenkins, derives chiefly from gossip columns. His well publicized personality remains, all the same, for me an elusive one, beyond an evident taste for entertaining persons as rich as himself. Remarkable that he should have found time enough from that hobby to have given birth to a Foundation.'

'He's not married, I think?'

'Do you imply the Bragadin Foundation is illegitimate too? A case of parthenogenesis, I expect. In any case, I am more concerned with his Tiepolo.'

Tiepolo ranking with Poussin as one of my most admired Masters, I asked the subject of the ceiling, the very existence of which was unknown to me. The bare fact that members of the Conference could visit the Palazzo had been announced, knowledge of its contents no doubt taken for granted in an assembly of intellectuals.

'One of the painter's classical scenes — *Candaules and Gyges*. The subject, thought to have some contemporary reference, caused trouble at the time the ceiling was painted. That's why the tradition of playing the picture down, keeping it almost a secret, has persisted to the present day. The owner is in any case said to be more than a little neurasthenic in approach to his possessions, and much else too.'

Gwinnett knew about the ceiling.

'I've been told it's not unlike the Villa Valmarana *Iphigenia* in composition,' he said. 'The owner won't allow it to be photographed.'

He turned to me.

'Speaking about the *Iphigenia* again made me think of what we were talking about at that luncheon.'

He picked up from the table the paper he had brought with him, opened it, folding back a page. It was *Détective, Ici Paris,* or another of those French periodicals that explore at greater length cases, usually already reported, which through expansion promise more pungent details of crime or scandal. Gwinnett singled out two sheets, the central spread. He was about to hand them over, but Dr Brightman, catching the name under a photograph, intercepted the paper.

'Good gracious,' she said. 'That ugly little man? I should never have thought it.'

I looked over her shoulder. The headline ran along the top of both pages.

L'APRES-MIDI D'UN MONSTRE?

Two large cut-out photographs stretched across the type-face, the story, whatever it was, fitting round their edges. In spite of Dr Brightman's lack of principle in appropriating the letterpress to herself, and although I was not close enough to read the sub-titles, the likenesses of the two persons portrayed were immediately recognizable. Both photographs had manifestly been taken some years before, ten at least. In fact that of Ferrand-Sénéschal made him look a man in early middle-age. He had been caught on some public occasion, mouth wide open, hands raised above his head in a passionate gesture, almost as if he, too, were singing *Funiculì-funiculà*, miming the ascending cable. No doubt he had been snapped addressing a large audience on some political or cultural theme.

The other photograph, also far from recent, though less time-expired than Ferrand-Sénéschal's, was more interesting. It was of Pamela Widmerpool. Her hair-do suggested the end of the war, or not long after. The picture could have dated from the year of her marriage to Widmerpool, possibly even taken at the moment of emergence from the ceremony. In spite of heavy touching-up on the part of the blockmaker, the expression was resentful enough for that. This touching-up had added a decidedly French air to her appearance. That could have been acquired not only from the cupid's bow mouth, brutally superimposed on her own, but, more universally, from the manner in which photographic portraiture in the press automatically assumes the national characteristics of whatever country has processed the blocks, fabricated their 'screen'; an extension of the law that makes the photographer impose his personal view of them on individuals photographed. Dr Brightman scrutinized carefully both pictures.

'Lady Widmerpool? A very bedworthy gentlewoman, I understand. But Ferrand-Sénéschal? I am frankly surprised. I should never have guessed . . . assoiffé de

49

plaisir . . . dévoré de désir . . . terrible obsession . . . How unchanged remains the French view of English life – phlegmatic, sadistic aristocrats, moving coldly and silently from one atrocity to another through the fogs of le Hyde Park and les Jardins de Kensington.'

I tried to peer over Dr Brightman's shoulder at what was written. Clutching the paper obstinately, she refused to surrender an inch of its surface.

'The implication is that Lady Widmerpool visited Ferrand-Sénéschal in his luxurious hotel suite – accommodation Sardanapalus would have found over-indulgent – only a few hours before the Reaper. Even that is chiefly my own assumption. Nothing definite is even hinted.'

Gwinnett laughed abruptly, rather uncomfortably. His laugh was high and nervous. He addressed me again.

'Isn't that the lady we talked about – Trapnel's girl?'

'Certainly.'

'The implication is she was in bed with this Frenchman after he was dead.'

'Is that how you read it?'

Dr Brightman disregarded our exchange, too engrossed to hear, or because Trapnel's name meant nothing to her. From time to time she read out a phrase that took her fancy.

'Fougueuse sensualité . . . étranges caprices . . . amitiés équivoques . . . We never seem to get anything solid. Odieux chantages . . . but of whom? Situation gênante . . . Then why not tell us about it? Le scandale éclate . . . It never seems to have done so. I am still not at all sure what happened, scarcely wiser than after reading the headline.'

She handed the paper over at last. Reservations about its interest were more than justified. As usual in such journalism, promise was far short of performance. There was a hint that some scandal about Ferrand-Sénéschal had been hushed up in France fairly recently, no details given, only pious horror expressed. That social engagements since arrival in London sufficiently explained taking an afternoon's rest, even between sheets, in the light of medical advice, was altogether ignored. References to Pamela – called 'Lady Pamela Widmerpool' – were even less specific. Indeed, they were written without serious attempt to fit her into the Ferrand Sénéschal story, such as it was. Nothing whatever was alleged against her, except that she – apparently other persons too – had visited the hotel suite at one time or another. By implication, Ferrand-Sénéschal's habits so notorious, that visit in itself was damaging enough. Her own pranks were touched on only vaguely, not very accurately, though more directly than the law of libel would have allowed an English paper. Widmerpool was treated simply as a great nobleman of the Old School.

'One of my maiden aunts – a social category no longer extant – used to live permanently in that hotel,' said Dr Brightman. 'I'm sure she had no idea things like that were going on there. The place did not at all suggest gaiety. She would have been surprised. Rather thrilled too, I think.'

The respectable, unpretentious style of Ferrand-Sénéschal's hotel disavowed the *grand luxe* attributed to his two-room suite. It was only a few streets away from the former Jeavons residence in South Kensington, converted by Ted Jeavons after the war into several small flats, one of which he inhabited himself. The fact that Ferrand-Sénéschal was on his way to the Conference later on found no place in the *Détective* story, probably regarded as a banal detail likely to prejudice inferences that he had come to London with the sole purpose of participating in an orgy. Dr Brightman reached out for the paper again. She examined the picture of Pamela.

51

'I can add my own small contribution to the bulletin,' she said. 'The lady in question is in Venice at this moment.'

Gwinnett, who had been sitting silent, chewing at his thumbnail, shifted forward.

'She is, Emily? You've seen her?'

This time he sounded quite excited. Dr Brightman made a gesture to indicate she had enjoyed no such luck.

'I was so informed by a French colleague, who is also attending the Conference. We normally correspond about Gallo-Roman personal names, with special reference to Brittany. On this occasion I fear we descended to gossip. My friend must be unaware of the reference here to Lady Widmerpool, or I'm sure he would have mentioned it. He had witnessed what he described as an extraordinary incident at the French Embassy in London, where Lady Widmerpool, quite deliberately, broke the back of a small gilt chair during supper. That made such an impression, he immediately recognized her profile seen at Quadri's.'

'I'd give something to meet that lady.'

Gwinnett did not sound hopeful. Dr Brightman and I assured him there should be no difficulty in arranging that.

'You've just got to sit in the Piazza long enough. You see everyone in the world, if you do that.'

'But I don't know Lady Widmerpool.'

'I'll introduce you.'

That was said in the heat of the moment. Afterwards, immediately afterwards, it was to be seen as a rash offer. I hoped she would not walk into the hotel at that moment. The very idea of her being in Venice made Gwinnett restless, a state alternating in him with a kind of torpor. He rose from the table, then paused for a moment, again unsure what he wanted to do. He came to a decision.

'I'll take a stroll in the Piazza right now. Do you mind if I retain this journal?'

That could not be refused, since it belonged to him, though I had not yet studied the piece thoroughly. He folded it again, stood in thought for a moment, said good night. We said good night to him in return. It was not impossible that he might see Pamela Widmerpool in St Mark's Square. Perhaps he hoped to pick up someone there in any case. A girl? A man? One felt rather ashamed of these speculations, as earlier of wondering whether he was an ex-alcoholic. He had shown no sign whatever of seeking in Venice any sort of dissipation. The notion that he was bent on some such goal, no doubt quite unfounded, attached to his withdrawn mysterious air, a little uncommon in an American, anyway in Gwinnett's form. As soon as he was gone, Dr Brightman, without any prompting, began to speak of him.

'Let me tell you about Russell Gwinnett.'

'Please do.'

'He is a small fragment detached from the comparatively extensive and cavernous grottoes of gothic America. He is part of an Old America – the oldest – yet has become in some respects the New America. I hardly know how to put it.'

'Halfway between Henry Adams and Charles Addams?'

'Not bad. In fact alpha plus, insomuch as Henry Adams says that true eccentricity is in a tone, and only the conventional approach loves to assume unconventionality. Russell is unconventional by nature, not by choice. Even then, only in certain respects. He is good at such sports at racquets, skating, skiing. If there is a superfluity of Edgar Allan Poe brought up to date, there is also a touch of Edwin Arlington Robinson.'

'You outrun my literary bounds.'

'But you can at least understand that Russell is

at once intensely American, yet allergic to American life. That, in itself, can be paralleled, though not quite in Russell's terms. To quote Adams again, he is not one of those Americans who can only assert or deny. I did not use the comparison of the two poets recklessly. Russell, too, hoped to be a poet. He was sufficiently self-critical to see that was not to be. He also draws quite well. Almost always portraits of himself. We saw a lot of each other when I was over there. He is a nice young man, cagey in certain moods.'

'You know he is writing a book about X. Trapnel. That's why he wants to meet Pamela Widmerpool.'

'Trapnel is only a name to me. One of my pupils used to rave about his books. If Russell does that, he will do it well. He is industrious, in spite of his singularities, perhaps because of them. Had he been an English undergraduate, his rooms would have been equipped with black candles, skulls, the odour of incense. He likes Death. That atmosphere is not the American tradition. The taste has told against him, notwithstanding the significance of his name. There was also some kind of a tragedy in his early college days. He was friendly with a girl who committed suicide – at least she seems to have committed suicide. Perhaps it was an accident. He was not in the smallest degree to blame.'

'Why is his name significant?'

'He is descended – collaterally, I understand – from what is known as a "Signer", one Button Gwinnett, who set his name to the Declaration of Independence. Both halves of the name are of interest to persons like oneself, "Gwinnett", of course, "Gwynedd", meaning North Wales – the Buttons, a South Wales family, probably *advenae*. A small piece of topographical history nearly established by nomenclature.'

'I don't know how these things are looked on in America.'

'Like so much else, the attitude is ambivalent. In

general, anyway in the right circles, to be descended from a Signer can be highly regarded, even if many such have passed into obscurity. Some Americans will, of course, deny any interest whatever in such trivial matters.'

'Kind hearts are more than Cabots?'

'And simple faith than Mormon blood. This is something of a paradox in that the transgression – crime perhaps – of America has been to reject Classicism for Romanticism. The national distaste for moderation – to which Henry Adams referred – inevitably leads to such a choice. Russell himself is far from immune, though you might not guess that from outward bearing. Profound Romanticism is bound in due course to dilate towards its gothic extremities. In his particular case, family history may have helped.'

'It is often pointed out that one form of Romanticism is to be self-consciously Classical, but what you say accords with Gwinnett's choice of Trapnel as a subject. Let's hope he treats Trapnel's own Romanticism in a Classical manner.'

'Naturally the terms are hopelessly imprecise. That does not make them valueless. Baudelaire and Swinburne have Classical statements to make – more than many people are aware who regard them as pure Romantics – but their gothic side is equally undeniable. Underneath Russell Gwinnett's staid exterior I suspect traces of an American Byron or Berlioz. I spoke of Poe, the preoccupation with Death. When there was trouble about this girl, it was because he had broken into the place where her body was. Some found it deeply touching . . . others . . . well . . .'

'Were there a lot of girls?'

'Apparently none after that. No one seems to know why. Again, some look on that with admiration, others deem it unsatisfactory.'

'As to Byron – what you said about Button Gwinnett

— was this Gwinnett brought up in a similar tradition of high descent, I mean in American terms?'

'His grandfather was a fairly successful lawyer, the father some sort of a bad lot, alcoholic, spendthrift, deserted Russell's mother at an early age. He is still alive, I believe. There were money difficulties about going to college, and so on. But we will talk more of Russell Gwinnett, and American gothicism, another time. Now I must go to bed. Fatigue comes on one suddenly here, delayed action after listening to all those speeches in demotic French about the Obligations of the Intellectual. I shall bid you good night. Tomorrow we meet under the Tiepolo ceiling.'

Not long after that I turned in too. The night had become a trifle cooler. Through the window of my bedroom the musicians' refrain was to be heard in the distance. Perhaps the songs were no longer theirs, cadences wafted now synthetically from the radio. For a while I tried to read in bed, *The Castle of Fratta,* a translation brought with me as appropriate. Nievo's view of Bonaparte's invasion of Italy was an antidote to Stendhal's. The novel might make a good film in the epic manner. I rather regretted not staying on for the Film Festival, more since I had never attended a Film Festival than because of anything very exciting on offer. A German picture about a prostitute who blackmailed her clients aroused a faint sense of curiosity. Then there was a British one, much recommended, adaptation of a Thomas Hardy story, in which Polly Duport was playing the lead.

I had seen Polly Duport act quite often, never again met her, since the day when we had travelled back to the War Office, with her mother and stepfather, Colonel Flores, in his official car, after the Victory Day Service at St Paul's. Then she had seemed charming, well brought up, a beauty too, with that unfledged look of a young, shy, slender animal. Now she was quite a famous actress. Her gifts had turned out to be for the Theatre, rather than everyday life, public rather than private. Anyone immersed in the English Theatre would undoubtedly put her among the three or four of her age and sex at the top of the profession. It was, so it seemed to me, not a very 'interesting' talent, though immensely 'finished'. She had been married for a time to a well-known actor. They had separated. Far from given to love affairs, she lived almost as a nun, it was said, devoted to the stage and its life. This was unlike her mother, whose voice and gestures Polly Duport sometimes recalled on the stage, without any of the mystery Jean had once seemed to exhale. Possibly something of her father's business ability, in one sense, taste for work, accounted for his daughter's serious approach to her profession, lack of interest in private life. The Hardy part was a new line for her. She was said to excel in it anything she had done before. That estimate might be consequence of an energetic publicity campaign.

Musings about the past shifted to the time when I had stayed in this hotel as a boy, to that eternal question of what constitutes experience. A close examination of what happened at any given period in itself provokes an unnatural element, like looking at a large oil painting under a magnifying glass, the over-all effect lost. Nievo, for example, was an over-all effect writer, even when he dealt with childhood. I tried to reconstruct the earlier visit. We had come to Venice because my father liked spending his 'leave' in France or Italy. However much they might be wanting in other respects, he approved of the Latin approach to sex and food. That did not mean he was always at ease on the Continent, but then, in any fundamental sense, he was rarely at ease in his own country. His temperament, a craft of light tonnage, borne effortlessly into heavy seas no matter how calm the weather on setting sail, was preordained to violent ups and downs in foreign waters. Language, currency, timetables, passports, cabmen, waiters, guides, touts, all the paraphernalia and hubbub incidental to travel, were scarcely required for the barometer to register gale force. He was, at the same time, always prepared to undertake any expedition, intricate, or arduous, in the interests of sightseeing – or ingenious economy, like sitting up on a station platform for a special train in the small hours – though not necessarily displaying a tolerant spirit while such excursions were in progress. His aesthetic tastes were varied, sometimes comparatively daring, sometimes stolidly conventional, but, once he had taken a fancy to a work of art, monument, building, landscape, that another critic might set a lower value on it than himself was altogether beyond his comprehension. He never stood in front of the Mona Lisa without remarking that, in the eyes of trivial people, the chief interest of Leonardo's masterpiece was to have once been stolen from the Louvre; thereby – as with much else in life – managing to have his cake and eat it, taste the sweets of banality, while ostensibly decrying their flavour.

My mother, too, liked these Continental trips. She enjoyed sightseeing, to which she brought a good deal of general knowledge, wholly untouched by intellectual theory; except possibly as provided by a much earlier, almost pre-Victorian tradition of upbringing. Garlic apart, she too was well disposed to the menus of France and Italy, so far as she ever allowed herself any self-indulgence; except perhaps indulgence of an emotional kind, even that rather special in expression. More important, for this last reason, was the manner in which foreign travel, at least in theory, offered relaxation to my father from a pretty chronic state of tension about his career, health, money, housing, hobbies, everything that was his; an innate fretfulness of spirit that seemed automatically to generate good reason to fret.

To emerge from a bank in Rome, notecase filled a moment before with the relatively large sum drawn to settle a week's hotel bill for three persons, and buy tickets for the return journey to England, then have your pocket picked while standing on the outside platform of a crowded tram, is a misadventure to fall to anyone's lot. On the other hand, for a French porter's carrying-strap to split asunder as he mounted the gangway of a Channel steamer with two suitcases across his shoulder, precipitating both into Dieppe harbour, was likely to befall only a traveller in a peculiar degree subject to such tribulations. It was additionally characteristic that the submerged suitcases (home forty-eight hours later in the immutably briny condition of a sea-god's baggage) contained not only a comparatively new dinner jacket (then a feature of Continental hotels), but also the two volumes of Pennell's *Life of Whistler*. Whistler was a painter my father admired. He had bought the books in Paris because his old friend Daniel Tokenhouse reported the French edition to have the same illustrations as the English, the price appreciably cheaper. To recall that was a reminder that I must make an effort to see Tokenhouse before I left Venice.

My father had few friends. The cause of that was not, I think, his own ever smouldering irascibility. People put up surprisingly well with irascibility, some even finding in it a spice to life otherwise humdrum. There is little evidence that the irascible, as a class, are friendless, and my father's bursts of temper may, for certain acquaintances, have added to the excitement of knowing him. It was more a kind of diffidence, uncertainty of himself (to some extent inducing the irascibility) that also militated against intimacy. Whatever the reason, by the time he reached later life, he had quarrelled with the few old friends who remained, or given them up as a matter of principle. Daniel Tokenhouse hung on longer than most, possibly because he too was decidedly irascible. In the end a row, brisk and rigorous, parted them for good.

Tokenhouse, going back to earliest days, had been a Sandhurst contemporary, though friendship, from the first tempered by squabbles, took root in the years after the South African War. The relationship had some basis in a common leaning towards the arts, a field in which Tokenhouse was the more instructed. It was strengthened by a shared taste for arguing. Those were the similarities. They differed in that Tokenhouse – like Uncle Giles – complained from the beginning that the army did not suit him, while my father, addicted to grumbling like most professional soldiers, never seriously saw himself in another rôle. Tokenhouse had specific ambitions. My father put them in a nutshell.

'For reasons best known to himself, Dan always hankered after publishing picture books.'

At the outset of the 'first' war, Tokenhouse, serving with the Expeditionary Force, contracted typhoid. He remained in poor health, through no fault of his own, doing duty in a series of colourless military employments, which took him no further than the rank of major. Whether or not he would have remained in the army had not some relation died, I do not know. As it was, he was left just enough money to be independent of his pay. He resigned his commission, taking immediate steps to gratify the aspiration towards 'picture books'. Tokenhouse did that with characteristic thoroughness, learning the business from the beginning, then investing his capital in a partnership of the kind he had in mind, a firm trafficking not only in 'the fine arts', but also topography and textbooks. One consequence of this was that I myself spent several years of early life in the same business, Tokenhouse my boss. We got on pretty well together. He had an unusual flair for that sort of publishing, making occasional errors of judgment — St John Clarke's Introduction to *The Art of Horace Isbister* one of the minor miscalculations — but on the whole a mixture of hard work, shrewdness, backing his own often eccentric judgment, produced successful results.

When it came to being hasty in temper, idiosyncratic in conduct, my father and Tokenhouse could, so to speak, give each other a game, but, acceptable as a brother-officer less successful than himself, Tokenhouse became gradually less admissible as a very reasonably prosperous civilian; more especially after my father himself was forced to leave the army on account of ill health. Minor skirmishes between them began to take on a note of increasing asperity.

'Dan would have been axed anyway,' said my father. 'Just as well there was a trade to which he could turn his hand, and money enough to buy his way into it. Dan would never have wriggled himself through the bottleneck for officers of his type and seniority. You know, as a young man, old Dan seriously thought of going into the Church. It was touch and go. Then some bishop made a public statement of which he disapproved, and he decided for the army, which his family had always wanted.'

Whether or not that was true, there could be no doubt Tokenhouse's nature included an inveterate puritanism, which army life had by no means decreased. Having abandoned the idea of taking Holy Orders, he developed an absolutely fanatical hatred for religion in any form, even the association of his own forename with a biblical character, thereby suggesting involuntary commitment, becoming a vexation to him. This puritanism also showed itself in dislike for any hint of sensuality in the arts, almost to the extent of handicapping a capacity for making money out of them. Even my parents, who knew him well, admitted that Tokenhouse's sex life had remained undisclosed throughout the years. Not the smallest interest in women had ever been uncovered; nor, for that matter, in his own sex either. He seemed quite unaware of the physical attributes of those he came across, though perhaps an unusually good-looking lady would just perceptibly heighten his accustomed brusqueness. That was my own impression after working for several years in the same office, a condition that can reveal a colleague, especially a superior, with an often devastating clarity.

This apparent non-existence of sexual partiality could have been due to the fact that Tokenhouse was aware of none. General Conyers (had they met, which never happened) might have hazarded a favourite solution, 'a case of exaggerated narcissism'. The peculiarities of Tokenhouse's subsequent conduct may have had their roots there; reaction perhaps from too rigid control, physical and emotional. The only personal relaxation he ever allowed himself, so far as was known, consisted in fairly regular practice of sparetime painting. Otherwise he was always engaged in business, direct or indirect in form.

Painting was a hobby of long standing. The pictures, if a school had to be named, showed faintly discernible traces of influence filtered down from the Camden Town Group. Rising to no great heights as masterpieces of landscape, they did convey an absolutely genuine sense of inner moral discomfort. A Tokenhouse canvas possessed none of the self-conscious professionalism of Mr Deacon's scenes from Greek and Roman daily life, flashy in their way, even when handled with notable competence. Tokenhouse, on the contrary, took pride in being an amateur. He always made a point of that status. It was therefore a surprise to his friends -- matter of disapproval to my father -- when he announced that he was going to retire from publishing, and take up painting as a full-time occupation. That was about six months before 'Munich'. By that time I had left the firm for several years.

For some little while before taking that decision, Tokenhouse had been behaving in rather an odd manner, having rows with publisher colleagues, laying down the law at dinner parties, in general showing signs of severe nervous tension. This condition must have come to a head when he exchanged publishing for painting; being simultaneously accompanied by a comparatively violent mental crisis about political convictions. No one had previously supposed Tokenhouse to possess strong political feelings of any sort, his desultory grumblings somewhat resembling those of Uncle Giles, even less coherently defined, if possible. To invoke Mr Deacon again, Tokenhouse had never shown the least sign of leanings towards pacifist-utopian-socialism. In making these two particular comparisons, it should equally be remembered that neither Uncle Giles nor Mr Deacon had ever showed any of Tokenhouse's sexual constraint.

Whatever the reason for this metamorphisis, the final row between Tokenhouse and my father took place on the subject of 'Munich'. It was an explosion of considerable force, bursting from a substratum of argument about world strategy, detonated by political disagreement of the bitterest kind. They never spoke again. It was the final close of friendship, so that by the time of the Russo-German Pact in 1939 – when Tokenhouse suffered complete breakdown and retired to a psychiatric clinic – there could be no question of going to visit him. There he stayed for the early part of the war, emerging only after the German invasion of the USSR. When I ran across him buying socks in London, not long after I came out of the army, Tokenhouse said he was making preparations to live in Venice.

'Always liked the place. Couldn't go there for years because of Mussolini. Now they've strung him up, it may be tolerable again. Better than this country, and Attlee's near-fascist Government. Come and see me, if you're ever there. Ha, yes.'

Although he had long since shaved off the scrubby toothbrush moustache of his army days, the ghost of its bristles still haunted his upper lip, years of soldiering for ever perpetuating in Tokenhouse the bearing of a retired officer of infantry. He must have carried out this migration expeditiously and in good order. Not long after our meeting, letters with a Venetian address began to appear in the papers, especially the weeklies, excoriating American foreign policy, advocating the 'Nuclear Campaign', protesting about the conduct of British troops in occupation of Germany, a great many kindred subjects too, signed 'D. McN. Tokenhouse, Maj (retd)'. Once he sent me a roneo-ed letter of protest about several persons imprisoned in South America for blowing up a power station. Since then we had lost touch with each other.

Before coming to Venice, I had felt that I should see Tokenhouse for old times' sake, at least speak with him on the telephone. We had not met for twenty years or more, so that any such renewal of contact would require tactful handling. In short, I had thought it best to send a note announcing date of my arrival. The telephone, even if Tokenhouse had installed one, might seem too much like holding a pistol to his head. He had always been a man to treat with caution. A note gave time to think things over, make an excuse, also by letter, if he did not wish the matter to be carried further. The Conference he was likely to view with irony, if not open laughter. He had always affected to find the goings-on of self-styled 'intellectuals' ridiculous, although not wholly detached from appertaining to that category himself. I reckoned that Tokenhouse must be in his middle to late seventies. One thought of the ancient singer. If he were really the same man, he was much older than that, still going strong enough. His voice or another's echoed on the summer night.

Iamme, iamme, via montiam su là.
Iamme, iamme, via montiam su là.
Funiculì funiculà, via montiam su là.

## TWO

The Bragadin Palace was approached on foot. Gwinnett and I walked together. Shared acquaintance with some of the circumstances of Trapnel's life had not made Gwinnett's behaviour less reserved. If anything, he was more farouche than before. Possibly he felt that to speak of the *Commonplace Book* had been indiscreet. Although he had emphasized that Trapnel's 'remains' contained little of interest, many researchers in Gwinnett's place might have kept the fact of its existence to themselves. In that respect he could not be called 'cagey', as Dr Brightman had characterized him at times. This lack of response was something less crude than 'caginess', almost suggesting terms like 'alienation' or 'withdrawal.' No doubt he was merely one of those persons, not so very uncommon, with whom every subsequent meeting after the first entails a fresh start from the beginning. The anxious air always remained. I should have liked to probe his views on the Ferrand-Sénéschal article, no more than skimmed, but something about Gwinnett's manner made this not the moment.

'Did you run across anyone you knew when you reconnoitred the Piazza last night?'

'How do you mean?'

'See anyone from the Conference?'

Gwinnett wriggled his neck.

'No.'

He drawled out the negative, making it sound as if he thought the question in itself uncalled for, a trifle intrusive. I asked if he knew what the Palazzo would be like. Gwinnett was more responsive to that. He began to speak of Venetian architecture, of which he evidently knew something, going on to recommend the book written about Venice by William Dean Howells when American consul here. Then he abandoned porticos and pediments, and fell into a long silence, suggesting a mood to be left alone. We made our way through narrow calles towards an area beyond the Accademia. I wondered how best we could disembarrass ourselves of each other's company without too blatantly seeming to do so. Suddenly Gwinnett came out of his dream with a sort of jerk, one of his characteristic nervous movements, which were not necessarily resentful. He spoke now as if referring to a matter he had been pondering for some little time, using that habitually low tone often hard to catch.

'It seems Louis Glober is house-guest at the Palazzo.'

'The publisher?'

'Glober was that one time. He's been a heap of other things too.'

'When I met him years ago he was in publishing. That's why I think of him as a publisher. I was in a firm that produced art books myself. He came to see us.'

'Glober's been more associated with pictures.'

'Paintings, you mean, or films?'

'Movies. I guess he owns some sort of a modern picture collection too.'

'He was keen on paintings thirty years ago. He wanted my firm to do a series on the Cubists. That was when we met. It was quite a funny occasion. I wonder whether he remembers. Do you know him?'

Gwinnett shook his head.

'I just saw a paragraph about him in the Continental *Herald-Tribune*. It said the well-known playboy-tycoon Louis Glober was here for the Film Festival, and was staying with Mr Jacky Bragadin.'

'I thought Glober an amusing figure. Since then

I've never done more than read about him in the paper in his playboy-tycoon capacity. I suppose he's a typical Jacky Bragadin guest. Did the *Herald-Tribune* name any others?'

'Just Glober. It seems he's come on here from the German Grand Prix.'

'Racing?'

'Automobile racing. World Championship.'

'He's in that game too?'

'Sure.'

To the eye of a fellow American I saw Glober must present a very different outline to that of my own remembrance. If not exactly the daily meat of the columnist, Louis Glober was a reasonably tasty snack, always available on the back shelf of the larder, where public personalities of a minor sort are stored in case of need. He was neither dished up too often to cause surfeit, nor left too long on ice to become stale. Contradictory features hampered his definition. The *Herald-Tribune* had termed him playboy-tycoon, this type-casting to cover publisher, film-producer, sportsman, 'socialite', a lot of other more or less news-valued labels, most with some basis in fact. The last photograph I had seen of Glober had been driving a vintage car. Gwinnett thought activities like sailing or motor racing had latterly taken the form of promotion, rather than too laboriously personal a rôle. That did not prevent Glober from still figuring as a noted rider, shot, golfer, yachtsman, or whatever else was required by the context. A taste for amusing himself had not inhibited making money, though again Glober was said to lose fortunes as easily as win them.

'The point I remember about Glober was that he seemed rather intelligent.'

'Ah-ha.'

The answer was non-committal, possibly disapproving, either because Gwinnett thought such a judgment, even if favourable, impertinent to pass on another human being, or because he was himself reluctant to allow the laurels of intelligence to decorate a brow of Glober's type. As not seldom when Americans utter that sound, hard to transliterate, I was uncertain. We talked of some of the reputed exploits; the blazing Hollywood restaurant from which Glober had carried shoulder-high down a ladder a famous film star – Dietrich, Hepburn, Harlow – neither of us was certain of the heroine; the methusalem of champagne that burst celebrating the return from Europe of Texas Guinan; the fight (almost won) in some night-club with an ex-middle-weight champion of Australia. A reporter never seemed far away to chronicle these vignettes of Glober as a picturesque or glamorous figure, his own clear-cut sense of the dramatic occasion endearing him to press and public wherever he went. Even in England, where he was not much known, editors instinctively printed the intermittent Glober item, compressed into a couple of lines on the back pages. I mentioned that.

'Would they report him today?'

'Perhaps not.'

'Glober must be about washed up.'

'What is he? In his sixties? Just about.'

Gwinnett gave the impression of not greatly caring for the idea of Glober, at the same time granting some respect to a romantic so unusually successful at giving public expression to his romanticism; showing ability too, even if a fluctuating one, in making a success of financial ventures. My own memory of Glober was far from unsympathetic, even if he now sounded rather different – though not all that different – from the young American first set eyes on. The mere fact that he was staying with Jacky Bragadin for the Film Festival, that he had been car-racing in Germany, argued survival powers of a sort; resilience not always found in characters of his type.

'Who's he married to now?'

Glober's wives had always been beauties. Once, very briefly, he had been husband of a world-famous film star. These unions lasted only a few years before being dissolved; soon renewed in similar fashion to the accompaniment of further widespread exudations of publicity in the appropriate quarters.

'No one, so far as I know. His last wife died quite a long while ago. They'd been wed only a very short time. It was leukemia, I think. Glober was photographed kneeling at her grave. There was a blanket of lilies, and, on a card written large enough to read in a newspaper picture, a message: *Farewell, Fleurdelys, farewell, fair one.*'

'Fleurdelys was her name?'

'It looked almost as if Glober was lying in the grave.'

Gwinnett spoke with an odd sense of excitement. He stared at me hard. I did not know quite whether he were criticizing Glober, or applauding him, expressing irony or admiration. The thought of what Dr Brightman had said about the dead girl came back.

'He was in a different mood when I met him.'

That had been towards the end of the nineteen-twenties. Glober had arrived in London as representative of a recently founded New York publishing house. Even before he landed, his name went round among the London publishers as a young American colleague with a head full of bright new ideas; by no means an unqualified recommendation to that particular community. Glober came to call on my own firm. He saw Daniel Tokenhouse. One of the bright ideas was the Cubist series. The suggestion was to produce generously illustrated, cheaply produced studies of these painters, blocks to be made in Holland or Germany by some newly devised process. Apart from the fact that the Cubists were still very generally regarded as wild men, if not worse, certainly unwise to encourage, transactions that included overseas production always entailed risks not every publisher was prepared to take. That was where Tokenhouse came in. Tokenhouse did not mind an element of risk. His predisposition for certain forms of rebellion against a humdrum approach to life was one of his unexpected sides. He also derived pleasure from the thought of how much the series would annoy other publishers, not to mention booksellers. Then, at quite an early stage, something went wrong in connection with the issue of the series. I did not remember exactly what upset the project, but it never went forward. There had been rather a row, money and tempers lost. I was in too subordinate a position at the time to be concerned, or greatly interested, except so far as being well disposed to 'modern art'. There were other things to think about, better ones, it then seemed, the business aspects forgotten among elements more memorable.

Tokenhouse was still occupied when Glober arrived for his appointment. Negotiations on the matter of St John Clarke's Introduction to *The Art of Horace Isbister* had just begun. St John Clarke was still haggling about payment. He was too well known a novelist to be dismissed out of hand, so Glober could not be received. The manager, with whom I shared a not over-luxurious office, was wrangling with a binder in the firm's waiting-room, a cubicle from its austerity in any case unsuitable for reception of another publisher, especially an American one. Tokenhouse rang through on the house-telephone with instructions to hold Glober in play for the further few minutes required to dislodge St John Clarke. The room where the manager and I passed our days, its walls grimly lined with file copies, was almost as comfortless as the waiting-room, but Glober was shown in. From the moment he entered, there was no need to provide distraction from the frugality of the surroundings. Glober himself took charge. In a matter of seconds we seemed already on the friendliest of terms. That was Glober's speciality. I made some apology for this delay after an appointment had been made.

'Don't worry. It's great to draw breath. There's a lot of running round in London. I didn't get to bed till late last night.'

He sat down in the collapsed armchair, and looked about him.

'You've got a real Dickensian place here.'

'*Bleak House?*'

Glober laughed his quiet attractive laugh.

'*The Old Curiosity Shop,*' he said. 'In the illustration.'

I supposed him thirty, possibly a year or two more, to my own twenty-two or twenty-three, but his self-confidence, maturity of manner, separated us by several decades. Unusually tall, incontrovertibly good-looking, Glober's features – in the later words of Xenia Lilienthal – were those of a 'young Byzantine emperor'. One saw what she meant. It showed she had taken in that aspect of him, in spite of her bad cold. His quietly forceful manner suggested a right to command, inexhaustible funds of stored up energy, overwhelming sophistication, limitless financial resource. At that age I did not notice a hard core of melancholy lurking beneath these assets. Perhaps in those days that side of his nature was better concealed. The instinct he so essentially possessed was getting on the right terms with everybody, no matter how transiently encountered. This intuitive impulse caused him to move from illustrating Dickens to pictures in general, the fact that he himself wanted to buy an Augustus John drawing before he left England. The gallery handling John's work had shown him nothing he fancied. Had I any ideas? I suggested direct approach to the painter himself, all the time feeling there was some quite easy answer, which Glober's flow of questions had put from my head.

'John's out of the country. If I could meet some private person that had a drawing he was willing to trade.'

Then I remembered such an opportunity had been announced the previous week. The Lilienthals were trying to sell a John drawing for Mopsy Pontner. Moreland had mentioned the fact. Moreland had been searching for a secondhand copy of *The Atheist's Tragedy* in the Lilienthals' bookshop, and Xenia Lilienthal had told him that Mopsy Pontner — more correctly, Mopsy Pontner's husband — had an Augustus John drawing to sell. The Lilienthals were accustomed to take books off Mr Deacon's hands, when included in miscellaneous 'lots' acquired by him at auction to add to his stock of antiques. Mr Deacon was not above marketing the odd volume of *curiosa* — eroticism preferably confined to the male sex — but did not care to be bothered with the sale of more humdrum literary works. The Lilienthals' shop was just around the corner. They were familiar with his quirks, like the Pontners, frequenters of The Mortimer, though not regularly.

Moreland (these were days before marriage to Matilda) always commended Mopsy Pontner's looks, but was a friend of Pontner, who was musically inclined in a manner Moreland could approve, a qualification by no means common. Moreland tended to keep off his friends' wives. Pontner, who knew several languages pretty well, earned a living by translating. He also bought paintings and drawings, when he could afford them, partly because he had a taste for pictures too, partly as a speculation. I ought to have thought of that when Glober raised the subject. This must have been a moment when money was required to tide over a financial crisis, take a holiday, or, as likely as either, invest in another work of art, which Pontner considered a better bet for a rise on the market. Pontner was older than his wife. The fact that Moreland found Mopsy attractive, liked talking about her, probably accounted for his passing on the information. At that time I had never met her, though knew she was reputed quite a beauty in her way. Suddenly remembering about this drawing, I told Glober it had been on offer a week or more before.

'Do you think it's still unsold?'

'Shall I make inquiries?'

'Go ahead. This is great. Mr Jenkins, we just had to meet.'

Glober was full of enthusiasm. He must have recognized one of his own characteristic situations taking shape before his eyes. His next reaction was that everyone must come to dinner with him to discuss the deal. By now he was certain the drawing remained unsold. Its existence revealed, it was now his by law of nature. Before the matter could be gone into further, Tokenhouse appeared in the doorway, having disembarrassed himself of St John Clarke, who could be heard coughing painfully, in a disgruntled manner, as he made his way down the stairs. Tokenhouse uttered his characteristically rather brusque apologies for the delay. Before they disappeared together Glober took my hand.

'Call me up at the hotel between four and five this evening, Mr Jenkins. Even suppose the drawing is sold, I'd like to have you dine with me.'

Tokenhouse heard that a shade suspiciously. He was jealous of outside contacts, not least American ones. Glober stayed for about an hour. I did not see him when he left. In the course of the day I made several telephone calls, finding the Augustus John drawing still available, Pontners and Lilienthals delighted to scent a buyer, I informed Glober.

'And they'll all have dinner with me?'

'Of course.'

Everyone was pleased with the idea. The party took place in Glober's sitting-room on one of the upper floors of the hotel, an old-fashioned establishment (pulled down a couple of years later) in the Curzon Street neighbourhood. It was a favourite haunt at that period of the more enlightened sort of American publisher. The place was just Glober's mark. When I arrived, he was inspecting the table laid for dinner.

'Good to see you, I've asked quite a crowd.'

Mopsy Pontner, bringing the drawing with her, arrived alone. At the last moment her husband had been prevented from coming by another engagement, arisen at short notice, having professional bearing on one of his translations. Pontner rightly judged his wife fully competent to negotiate the business of the drawing on her own. There were a dozen or more guests by the time we sat down. The Lilienthals arrived late, and rather drunk, having had a long session at The Mortimer with a customer who could not make up his mind whether or not to buy a Conrad first-edition in their catalogue. Xenia Lilienthal, small, with ginger corkscrew curls and a beseeching expression, was suffering from a heavy cold in her nose. Lilienthal, his mind on business, kept fingering the hairs of his sparse black beard. Glober had roped in another American publisher and wife, met the previous day in London, both hitherto unknown to him. They were on their way to the scuth of France. He wanted them to deliver by hand a present to a friend they had in common, who was staying at Antibes. A young man with a lisp and honey-coloured hair, come to the hotel earlier in the evening to sell Glober a Georgian silver tankard, had been asked to stay for dinner. This young man told the Lilienthals he had once met them with Mr Deacon, to which they assented without much warmth. There was a lesbian called 'Bill' (apparently lacking a surname), seen much at parties, who admitted soon after arrival that she was uncertain as to how firm her invitation had been to this one. Old Mrs Maliphant was present, who had been on the stage in the 'seventies. She was alleged to have slept with Irving; some said Tree; possibly both. Glober had encountered her at the house of one of the several publishers to whom she had promised her Memoirs. Moreland, to some extent responsible for the whole assembly, arrived in poorish form, absent in manner, probably weighed down with a current love affair gone wrong. Other guests, now forgotten, may also have been entertained. If so, their presence did not affect what happened.

The years invest the muster-roll of Glober's dinner-party with a certain specious picturesqueness, if anything increased by being a shade grotesque. At the time, at least on the surface of things, the evening turned out heavy going. That was Glober's fault only so far as he had been over-reckless in mixing people, always risky, sometimes fatal. In this particular venture, he had, as an American, under-rated the intractable strain in English social life, even at this undemanding London level, an easy thing to do for anyone not conversant with its heterogeneous elements, their likes and dislikes. Food and drink were both reasonably good. Conversation never got properly under way. Something was lacking.

Glober bought the Augustus John drawing on sight. He made no demur about the price, a fairly steep one in the light of the then market. It was a three-quarter length of a model called Conchita, a gipsy type Barnby, too, sometimes employed. Glober's own demeanour, as when he had visited the office, was enormously genial, but even he did not appear to find the going easy with Mopsy Pontner, whom he had placed next to himself at table. He sat between her and the American publisher's wife, a statuesque lady from Baltimore. Mopsy, with dark straggling hair and very red lips, perfectly civil, was uncommunicative in manner. She made Glober do all the talking. He probably did not mind that, but had earned the right to a little more notice than he seemed to be getting. He had also to work hard with the Baltimore lady, though not because she did not talk. The trouble was her anxiety about reservations on the Blue Train the following day. She continually returned to this preoccupation. When Xenia was not snuffling, she and Lilienthal exchanged second-hand-book chat across the table. The young silver salesman and 'Bill', recognizing no harmony in common, did not communicate with each other at all. Mrs Maliphant rambled on in a monologue about old Chelsea days, saying 'Wilde' when she meant 'Whistler', and 'Sargent' for 'Shannon'. Moreland left early. I left early too; early that is in the light of the sort of party intended, and the fact that my flat in Shepherd Market was only a few yards away. Glober said an effusive goodbye.

'Call me up when you're next in New York, Mr Jenkins. I'd like to have you meet James Branch Cabell.'

That was the last I saw of Glober. His firm fell into liquidation the following year. Several go-ahead American publishing houses went bust about that time. The fact was regarded as an amelioration of whatever row had taken place about the Cubists, indicating our own firm was well out of the commitment.

Glober's character was further particularized when, also about a year later, I came to know Mopsy Pontner better. It appeared that the evening at the hotel, anyway the latter part of it, had been less prosaic than might have been supposed at the time. Mopsy herself gave me an account of its consummation; no vague term in the context. She had, so she related, stayed on after the rest of the party had gone home. Glober, it seemed, had been more attractive to her, far more attractive, than outwardly revealed by her demeanour at dinner. In admitting that, she went so far as to declare that she had greatly approved of him at sight, as soon as she entered the room where we were to dine. Glober must have felt the same. The natural ease of his manner concealed such feelings, like Mopsy's exterior reserve. Later that night mutual approval took physical expression.

'Glober did me on the table.'

'Among the coffee cups?'

'We broke a couple of liqueur glasses.'

'You obviously found him attractive.'

'I believe I'd have run away with him that night, if he'd asked me. I was all right a day or two later, quite recovered. The affair stopped dead there. In any case he was sailing the next day. Some men are like that. Isn't it funny? One rather odd thing about Glober, he insisted on taking a cutting from my bush – said he always did that after having anyone for the first time. He produced a pair of nail-scissors from a small red leather case. He told me he carried them round with him in case the need arose.'

'We all of us have our whims.'

Mopsy laughed. So far as Glober was concerned, I do not put her conquest unduly high, though no doubt she was quite a beauty in her way. To exaggerate Glober's achievement would be mistaken, lacking in a sense of proportion, even though Mopsy was capable of refusal, having turned Barnby down. Barnby made a good story about his failure to please on that occasion, which was one way of dealing with the matter. Such sudden adventures as this one of Glober's can be misleading, unless considered in their context, time and place (as Moreland always insisted) both playing so vital a part. Nevertheless, this vignette, taken at an early stage of his career, suggests Glober's vivacity, liberality, wide interests, capacity for attack; Mopsy's footnote adding a small touch of the unusual, the exotic. These were no doubt the qualities that had carried him advantageously through the years of the Depression; New York to Hollywood, and back again; lots of other places too; until here he was at Jacky Bragadin's Venetian palace. I inquired about Glober's background. Gwinnett gave a rather satirical laugh.

'Why do the British always ask that?'

'One of our foibles.'

'That's not what Americans do.'

'But we're not Americans. You must humour our straying from the norm in that respect.'

Gwinnett laughed again.

'Glober's people were first generation Jewish emigrants. They were Russian. They took a German name to assimilate quicker, or so I've heard. Glober was from the Bronx.'

'What we'd call the East End?'

'His father made a sizeable pile in building. Glober himself didn't begin on the breadline.'

'You mean there was plenty of money before he started his publishing and film career?'

'He made plenty more. Lost plenty too. Money is no problem to Glober.'

Gwinnett spoke with conviction. The comment that Glober was a man to whom money-making was no problem recalled Peter Templer having once spoken the same about Bob Duport. Duport, of course, had always been on a smaller scale financially than Glober, also without any claims to newspaper fame. I felt that side of Glober, the newspaper fame, was not without a certain fascination for Gwinnett, even if he hesitated to approve of Glober as an individual. An idea suddenly struck me.'

'Does he write?'

'Does Glober write?'

'Yes?'

'Sure – did he refuse to sign his name to a contract you showed him in London on the grounds he couldn't write? I'll bet it wasn't true, and he can.'

Gwinnett was unbending a little.

'I meant books. It's always a temptation for a publisher to have a go at writing a book. After all, they think, if authors can do that, anybody can.'

'Glober's withstood the temptation so far.'

'What I was leading up to is Glober having something of Trapnel about him – a Trapnel who brought off being a Complete Man. Of course if Glober can't write, the comparison ceases to be valid, unless you accept as alternative Glober's experience as entrepreneur in the arts. That might to some extent represent Trapnel's literary sensibility.'

Gwinnett seemed unprepared for a comparison of that kind.

'I just can't imagine Trapnel without his writing,' he said.

'Certainly in his own eyes that would be a contradiction in terms. But all the beautiful girls, all the publishing and movie triumphs of one sort or another, all the publicity – yet the implied failure too. Experience of the other side of fortune. Losses, as well as gains, in money. Sadness in love, implicit in the changes of wives. In business, changes of interests. Nothing fails like success. Surely all that's part of being complete in Trapnel's eyes? Why shouldn't Glober be Trapnel's Complete Man at sixty?'

Gwinnett thought for a moment, but did not answer. The concept, even if it possessed a shred of interest, did not please him. He smiled a little grimly. There was no point in pressing the analogy. In any case, we had now reached the campo, along one side of which stood the palace to be visited; a Renaissance structure of moderate size, its exterior, as Gwinnett had explained on the way, severely restored in the eighteenth century.

In the Venetian manner, the more splendid approach was by water, but it had been found more convenient to admit members of the Conference through the pillared entrance opening on to the square. We passed between massively sententious caryatids towards a staircase carpeted in crimson. Dr Brightman drew level.

'This Palazzo is not even mentioned in most guidebooks,' she said. 'I've ascertained the whereabouts of the Tiepolo, and will lead you to it. Follow me, after we've made our bow.'

At the top of the stairs, supported by a retinue of the Conference's Executive Committee, and civic officials, Jacky Bragadin was receiving the guests. The municipality had helped to promote the Conference, in conjunction with the Biennale Exhibition, which fell that year, as well as the Film Festival. A small nervous man, in his fifties, Jacky Bragadin's mixed blood had not wholly divested him of that Venetian physiognomy, noticeable as much in the contemporary city as in the canvases of its painters; somewhat as if most Venetians wore Commedia dell'Arte masks fashioned in the Orient, only a guess made at what Europeans look like. Into such features Jack Bragadin had fused those of his American ancestry. He did not appear greatly at ease, fidgeting a good deal, a scarcely discernible American accent overlaying effects of English schooldays. The more consequential members of the Conference, after shaking hands, paused to have a word, or chat with the entourage, standing about on a landing ornamented with baroque busts of Roman emperors. The rest moved forward into a frescoed gallery beyond.

'Come along,' said Dr Brightman. 'The ceiling is in an ante-room further on, not at all an obvious place. These Luca Giordanos will keep most of them quiet for the time being. We shall have a minute or two to inspect the Tiepolo in peace.'

Gwinnett, preferring to go over the Palazzo at his

own speed, strolled away to examine the Roman emperors on their plinths. He may also have had an interest in Luca Giordano. I followed Dr Brightman through the doors leading into the gallery of frescoes. We passed on through further rooms, Dr Brightman expressing hurried comments.

'These tapestries must be Florentine – look, *The Drunkenness of Lot*. The daughter on the left greatly resembles a pupil of mine, but we must not tarry, or the mob will be upon us again.'

She also disallowed for inspection a rococo ball-room, white walls, festooned with gold foliage and rams' heads, making a background for Longhi caricatures, savants and punchinellos with huge spectacles and bulbous noses.

'How much they resemble our fellow members of the Conference. The ante-room should be at the far end here.'

We entered a small almost square apartment, high ceilinged, with tall windows set in embrasures.

'Here we are.'

She pointed upward. Miraculous volumes of colour billowed, gleamed, vibrated, above us. Dr Brightman clasped her hands.

'Look – *Candaules and Gyges*.'

At our immediate entry the room had seemed empty. A second later, the presence of two other persons was revealed. The unconventional position both had chosen to assume, for a brief moment concealed, as it were camouflaged, their supine bodies, one male, the other female. In order the better to gaze straight ahead at the Tiepolo in a maximum of comfort, they were lying face upwards, feet towards each other, on two of the stone console seats, set on either side of the recess of a high pedimented window. The brightness of the sun flowing in had helped to make this couple invisible. At first sight, the pair seemed to have fainted away; alternatively, met not long before with sudden death in the vicinity, its abruptness requiring they should be laid out in that place as a kind of emergency mortuary, just to get the bodies out of the way pending final removal. Dr Brightman, noticing these recumbent figures too, gave a quick disapproving glance, but, without comment on their posture, began to speak aloud her exposition on the ceiling.

'As Russell Gwinnett said, one is a little reminded of Iphigenia in the Villa Valmarana, or the Mars and Venus there. The usual consummate skill in handling aerial perspectives. The wife of Candaules – Gautier calls her Nyssia, but I suspect the name invented by him – is obviously the same model as Pharaoh's daughter in *Moses saved from the water* at Edinburgh, also the lady in all the Antony and Cleopatra sequences, such as those at the Labia Palace, which I was once lucky enough to see.'

To make no mistake, I took another swift look at the couple lying on the ledges under the window. There was no mistake. They were sufficiently far away to convey quietly to Dr Brightman that we were in the presence of her 'very bedworthy gentlewoman', heroine, by implication, of 'L'après-midi d'un monstre'. The horizontal figure on the left was certainly Pamela Widmerpool; the man on the right, lying like an effigy of exceptional length on a tomb, was not known to me. Dr Brightman as usual kept her head. Adjusting her spectacles, so as to make a more thorough survey of Pamela when the moment came, she continued to gaze for a few seconds upwards, her tone, at the same time, showing the keen interest she felt in this disclosure.

'Lady Widmerpool? Indeed? I'll curb my aesthetic enthusiasms in a moment in order to scan her surreptitiously.'

She concentrated for at least a minute on the Tiepolo, before making an inspection in her own time and manner. Leaving her to do that, I crossed the floor to where Pamela had brought her body into almost upright position in order to cast a disdainful glance on whoever had entered the room. As I advanced she gave one of her furious looks, then, without smiling, accepted that we knew each other.

'Hello, Pamela.'

'Hullo.'

Much of the beauty of her younger days remained in her late thirties. She had allowed her hair to go grey, perhaps deliberately engineered the process, silver tinted, with faint highlights of strawberry pink that glistened when caught by sunlight. She looked harder, more angular in appearance, undiminished in capacity for putting less aggressive beauties in the shade. Apart from the instant warning of general hostility to all comers that her personality automatically projected, an unspoken declaration that no man or woman could remain unthreatened by her presence, she did not appear displeased at this encounter, merely indifferent. Even indifference was qualified by a certain sense of suppressed nervous excitement, suggesting tensions almost compliant to interruption of whatever she was doing. Usually her particular form of self-projection excluded conceding an inch in making contacts easier, outward expression, no doubt, of an inner sexual condition. She was like a royal personage, prepared to converse, but not bestowing the smallest scrap of assistance to the interlocutor, from whom all effort, every contribution of discursive vitality, must come. Now, on the other hand, she unbent a little.

'Jacky didn't mention you were staying. I suppose you arrived in that ghastly middle-of-the-night plane. Who's the old girl? One of Jacky's dykes?'

That was about the furthest I had ever heard Pamela go in the way of taking conversational initiative, for that matter, in showing interest in other people's doings.

I explained that neither Dr Brightman nor myself was the latest addition to the Bragadin house-party; for fun, subjoining a word about Dr Brightman's academic celebrity. Pamela did not answer. She had the gift of making silence as vindictive as speech. Dr Brightman continued to examine the ceiling, while at the same time she moved discreetly in our direction. When she was near enough I introduced them. Dr Brightman's manner was courteously firm, Pamela in no way uncivil, though she did not attempt to name the man with her. He, also risen from the flat of his back, had now manifestly put himself into an attitude preparatory for meeting strangers. Evidently he was familiar with Pamela's distaste for social convention of any kind, in any case well able to look after himself. After giving her a statutory moment or two to make his identity known, he announced himself without her help. The intonation, deep and pleasant, was American.

'Louis Glober.'

He held out a large white hand, much manicured. The voice came back over the years, the tone just the same, quiet in pitch, masterful, friendly, full of hope. Otherwise hardly a trace remained of the smooth dominating young man who had interviewed Tokenhouse about the Cubist series, given the dinner-party for the John drawing, 'done' Mopsy Pontner on the dinner-table in the private suite of that defunct Mayfair hotel. He was still tall, of course, no less full of assurance, though that assurance took rather a different form. It was in one sense less flowing – less like, say, Sunny Farebrother's determination to charm – in another, tougher, more outwardly ruthless. What Glober had lost, physically speaking (a good deal, including, naturally enough, all essentially youthful adjuncts), was to a certain extent counterbalanced by transmutation into a different type of distinguished appearance. The young Byzantine emperor had become an old one; Herod the Tetrarch was perhaps nearer the mark than Byzantine emperor; anyway a ruler with a touch of exoticism in his behaviour and tastes. What was left of Glober's hair, scarcely more than a suggestion he once had owned some, was still black – possibly from treatment artificial as Pamela's – his handsome, sallow pouchy face become richly senatorial. Never particularly 'American' in aspect (not, at least, American as pictured by Europeans), now he might have come from Spain, Italy, any of the Slav countries. A certain glassiness about the eyes recalled Sir Magnus Donners, though Glober was, in general, quite another type of tycoon. Before I could reintroduce myself to him, Dr Brightman went into attack with Pamela.

'Tell me, do tell me, Lady Widmerpool, where did you get those quite delectable sandals?'

Pamela accepted the tribute. They went into the question together. I explained to Glober how we had met before.

'Do you remember – the Augustus John drawing?'

He thought for a moment, then began to laugh loudly. Putting a hand on my shoulder, he continued to laugh.

'This warms me like news from home. Is it really thirty years? I just don't believe you. The charming Mrs Pontner. It was a privilege to meet her. How is she?'

'No more with us, I'm afraid.'

'Passed on?'

'Yes.'

Glober shook his head in regret.

'Was that recently?'

'During the war. I hadn't seen her for ages, even by then. She'd married Lilienthal, the bookseller with the beard, who came to your party too. When Pontner died, Mopsy went to help in the bookshop. Then

Xenia went off with an Indian doctor, and Mopsy married Lilienthal.'

'Mrs Lilienthal was the little redhead with the bad cold?'

Glober certainly possessed astonishing powers of recall. I could hardly bring his guests to mind myself, the facts just offered having come from Moreland a comparatively short time before. Otherwise, I should never have remembered (nor indeed known about) most of what I had just related. Whenever we met, which was not often, Moreland loved to talk of that period of his life, days before marriage, ill health, living with Mrs Maclintick, had all, if not overwhelmed him, made existence very different. On that particular meeting, he had dredged up the story of Mopsy Pontner's sad end; for sad it had been. Glober shook his head, and sighed.

'Mrs Pontner, too. I recall her so well.

> The forehead and the little ears
> Have gone where Saturn keeps the years.'

'You didn't produce that extempore?'

'Edwin Arlington Robinson.'

I was glad to hear a representative quotation from a poet named by Dr Brightman as contributing a small element to Gwinnett's makeup, and wondered how often, when obituary sentiments were owed in connection with just that sort of personal reminiscence, Glober had found the tag apposite. Frequently, his promptness suggested. The possibility in no manner abated its felicity. We talked for a minute or two about other aspects of that long past London visit of his. I told him Tokenhouse now lived in Venice, but Glober did not rise to that, reasonably enough. The strange thing was how much he remembered. This conversation did not please Pamela. Abandoning an apparent amicable chat about footgear with Dr Brightman, she now pointed to the ceiling.

'You haven't explained yet what's happening up there.'

When she addressed Glober, the tone suggested proprietary rights. One of the paradoxes about Pamela was a sexuality, in one sense almost laughably ostentatious, the first thing you noticed about her; in another, something equally connected with sex that seemed reluctant, extorted, a possession she herself utterly refused to share with anyone.

'What's happening? That's what I want to know.'

She stood, legs thrust apart, staring upward. White trousers, thin as gauze, stretched skintight across elegantly compact small haunches, challengingly exhibited, yet neatly formed; hard, pointed breasts, no less contentious and smally compassed, under a shirt patterned in crimson and peacock blue, stuck out like delicately shaped bosses of a shield. These colours might have been expressly designed – by dissonance as much as harmony – for juxtaposition against those pouring down in brilliant rays of light from the Tiepolo; subtle yet penetrating pinks and greys, light blue turning almost to lavender, rich saffrons and cinnamons melting into bronze and gold. Pamela's own tints hinted that she herself, only a moment before, had floated down out of those cloudy vertical perspectives, perhaps compelled to do so by the artist himself, displeased that her crimson and peacock shades struck too extravagant a note, one that disturbed rather than enriched a composition, which, for all its splendour, remained somehow tenebrous too. If so, reminder of her own expulsion from the scene, as she contemplated it again, increasingly enraged her.

'Can't anybody say anything?'

Glober, half turning in her direction, and smiling tolerantly, parodied the speech of a tourist.

'Oh, boy, it sure is a marvellous picture, that Tee-ay-po-lo.'

All of us, even Dr Brightman, fixed attention once more on the ceiling, as if with the sole object of producing an answer to Pamela's urgent inquiry. There was plenty on view up there. Pamela's desire to have more exact information, even if ungraciously expressed, was reasonable enough once you considered the picture. Dr Brightman took up her former exposition, now delivered to a larger audience.

'The Council of Ten made trouble at the time. Objection was not, so many believe, to danger of corrupting morals in the private residence of a grandee, so much as to the fact that the subject itself was known to bear reference to the habits of one of the most Serene Republic's chief magistrates, another patrician, with whom the Bragadin who owned this palace had quarrelled. The artist has illustrated the highspot of the story's action.'

The scene above was enigmatic. A group of three main figures occupied respectively foreground, middle distance, background, all linked together by some intensely dramatic situation. These persons stood in a pillared room, spacious, though apparently no more than a bedchamber, which had unexpectedly managed to float out of whatever building it was normally part – some palace, one imagined – to remain suspended, a kind of celestial 'Mulberry' set for action in the upper reaches of the sky. The skill of the painter brought complete conviction to the phenomena round about. Only a sufficiently long ladder – expedient perhaps employed for banishing Pamela from on high – seemed required to reach the apartment's so trenchantly pictured dimension; to join the trio playing out whatever game had to be gambled between them by dire cast of the Fates. That verdict was manifestly just a question of time. Meanwhile, an attendant team of intermediate beings – cupids, tritons, sphinxes, chimaeras, the passing harpy, loitering gorgon – negligently assisted stratospheric support of the whole giddy structure and its occupants, a floating recess perceptibly cubist in conception, the view from its levels far outdoing anything to be glimpsed from the funicular; moreover, if so nebulous a setting could be assigned mundane location, a distant pinnacle, or campanile, three-quarters hidden by cloud, seemed Venetian rather than Neapolitan in feeling.

'Who's the naked man with the stand?' asked Pamela.

An unclothed hero, from his appurtenances a king, reclined on the divan or couch that was the focus of the picture. One single tenuous fold of gold-edged damask counterpane, elsewhere slipped away from his haughtily muscular body, undeniably emphasized (rather than concealed) the physical anticipation to which Pamela referred, of pleasure to be enjoyed in a few seconds time; for a lady, also naked, tall and fair haired, was moving across the room to join him where he lay. To guess what was in the mind of the King – if king he were – seemed at first sight easy enough, but closer examination revealed an unforeseen subtlety of expression. Proud, self-satisfied, thoughtful, more than a little amused, he seemed to be experiencing mixed emotions; feelings that went a long way beyond mere expectant sensuality. No doubt the King was ardent, not to say randy, in the mood for a romp; he was experiencing another relish too.

The lady – perhaps the Queen, perhaps a mistress – less intent on making love, anxious to augment pending pleasure by delicious delay, suddenly remembering her own neglect of some desirable adjunct, or necessary precaution, incident on what was about to take place, had paused. Her taut posture, arrested there in the middle of the bedchamber, immediately proposed to the mind these, and other possibilities; that she was utterly frigid, not at all looking forward to what lay ahead; that – like Pamela herself – she was frigid but wanted a lot of it all the same; that her excitement was no less than the King's, but her own attention had been suddenly deflected from the matter in hand by a disturbing sound or movement, heard, perceived, sensed, in the shadows of the room. She had scented danger. This last minute retardation in coming to bed had, at the same time, something of all women about it; the King's anticipatory complacence, something of all men.

The last possibility – that the lady had noticed an untoward happening in the background of the bedchamber – was the explanation. Her eyes were cast on the ground, while she seemed to contemplate looking back over her shoulder to scrutinize further whatever dismayed her. Had she glanced behind, she might, or might not, have been in time to mark down in the darkness the undoubted source of her uneasiness. A cloaked and helmeted personage was slipping swiftly, unostentatiously, away from the room towards a curtained doorway behind the pillars, presumably an emergency exit into the firmament beyond. At that end of the sky, an ominous storm was plainly blowing up, dark clouds already shot with coruscations of lightning and tongues of flame (as if an air-raid were in progress), their glare revealing, in the shadows of the bedchamber, an alcove, where this tall onlooker had undoubtedly lurked a moment beforehand. Whether or not the lady was categorically aware of an intruding presence threatening the privacy of sexual embrace, whether her suspicions had been only partially aroused, was undetermined. There was no doubt whatever some sort of apprehension had passed through her mind. That was all of which to be certain. The features of the cloaked man, now in retreat, were for the most part hidden by the jutting vizor of the plumed helmet he wore, so that his own emotions were invisible. The calmly classical treatment of the scene, breathtaking in opulence of shapes and colours, imposed at the same time a sense of awful tension, imminent tragedy not long to be delayed.

'I wonder whether the model was the painter's wife,' said Dr Brightman. 'She occurs so often in his pictures. I must look into that. If so, she was Guardi's sister. Gyges looks rather like the soldier in *The Agony in the Garden*, who so much resembles General Rommel.'

'I don't remember the story. Didn't Gyges possess a magic ring?'

'That was my strong conviction too,' said Glober.

Dr Brightman offered no apology for settling down to the comportment of a professional lecturer, one she fulfilled with distinction.

'Candaules was king of Lydia – capital, Sardis, of the New Testament – Gyges his chief officer and personal friend. Candaules was always boasting to Gyges of the beauty of his wife. Finding him, as the King thought, insufficiently impressed, Candaules suggested that Gyges should conceal himself in their bedroom in such a manner that he had opportunity to see the Queen naked. Gyges made some demur at that, public nakedness being a state the Lydians considered particularly scandalous.'

'The Lydians sound just full of small-town prejudices,' said Glober.

'On the contrary,' said Dr Brightman. 'The Greeks did not know what being rich meant until they came in contact with the Lydians, now thought to be ancestors of the Etruscans.'

I remembered the text, from the Book of Revelation, inscribed in gothic lettering on the walls of the chapel that had been the Company's barrack-room, when I first joined. Now it seemed particularly apt.

'Thou hast a few names even in Sardis which have

not defiled their garments, and they shall walk with me in white, for they are worthy.'

'Exactly,' said Dr Brightman. 'Gyges tried to be one of the worthy at first, but Candaules insisted, so he gave in, and was hidden in the royal bedchamber. Unfortunately for her husband, the Queen noticed the reluctant voyeur stealing away – we see her doing so above – and was understandably incensed. She sent for Gyges the following day, and presented him with two alternatives: either he could kill Candaules, and marry her *en secondes noces,* or – no doubt a simple undertaking in their respective circumstances at the Lydian court – she would arrange for Gyges himself to be done away with. In the latter event, familiarity with her unclothed beauty would die with him; in the former, become a perfectly proper aspect of a respectably married man's – or rather married king's – matrimonial relationship. Gyges chose the former course of action. His friend and sovereign, Candaules, was liquidated by him, he married the Queen, and ruled Lydia with credit for forty years.'

There was pause after Dr Brightman's terse recapitulation of the story. Everyone seemed to be thinking it over. Glober was the first to speak.

'Then the owner of the magic ring was another guy – another Gyges rather? Not the some Gyges that saw the lady nude?'

Dr Brightman gave the smile reserved for promising pupils.

'Versions vary in all such legends. According to Plato, Gyges descended into the earth, where he found a brazen horse, within which lay the body of a huge man wearing a brazen ring on his finger. Gyges took the ring, which had the property of rendering its wearer invisible. This attribute may well have facilitated the regicide. The Hollow Horse, you remember, is a widespread symbol of Death and Re-birth. You probably came across that in the works of Thomas Vaughan, the alchemist, Mr Jenkins, in the course of your Burton researches. The historical Gyges may well have excavated the remains of some Bronze Age chieftain, buried within a horse's skin or effigy. Think of the capture of Troy. I don't doubt they will find horses ritually buried round Sardis one of these days, where a pyramid tomb may still be seen, traditionally of Gyges — whose voyeurism brought him such good fortune.'

This was getting a long way from Tiepolo, but, seasoned in presentation of learning, Dr Brightman had dominated her audience. Even Pamela, who might have been expected to interrupt or walk away had listened with attention. So far from becoming restless or rebellious, she too showed signs of being impressed, in her own way stimulated, by the many striking features of the Candaules/Gyges story. Her cheeks had become less pale. Glober responded to the legend too, though in quite a different manner. He seemed almost cowed by its implications.

'That's a great tale,' he said. 'David and Uriah the other way round.'

'An excellent definition,' said Dr Brightman. 'You mean Candaules, by so to speak encouraging a Peeping Tom, put himself, without foreseeing that, in the forefront of the battle. One thinks of Vashti and Ahasuerus too, where much less was required. Nowadays such a treat would be in no way comparable. You need to go no further than the Lido to contemplate naked bodies — all but naked at least — but in Lydia, Judah too for that matter, the bikini would not have been tolerated.'

'There's a difference between a bikini, and nothing at all, Dr Brightman,' said Glober. 'You've got to grant that much.'

Pamela was full of contempt for such a comment.

94

Now she showed herself getting back to her more normal form.

'What are you talking about? What the King wanted was to be watched screwing.'

If she supposed that observation likely to discompose Dr Brightman, Pamela made a big mistake, though she was herself by then likely to be beyond such primitive essays in shocking. She had always spoken out exactly as she felt on any given occasion; at least exactly as it suited her to give public expression to whatever she wished to pass as her own feelings. In this particular case, she seemed genuinely interested in the true aim of Candaules, the theory put forward, a matter of psychological accuracy, rather than lubricious humour. Dr Brightman did not hesitate to take up the challenge.

'Others, as well as yourself, have supposed mere nakedness an insufficient motif, Lady Widmerpool. Gautier, in his conte written round the legend, characteristically adumbrates a melancholy artist-king, intoxicated by the beauty of his artist-model queen, whom he displays secretly to his friend Gyges, drawn as a French lieutenant of cavalry. Gide, on the other hand, takes quite a different view, somewhat reorganizing the story. Gide's Gyges is a poor fisherman, who delivers to the King's table a fish, in which the ring of invisibility is found. Candaules, a liberal, forward-looking, benevolent monarch – no less melancholy than Gautier's prince, though not, like him, a mere Ivory Tower aesthete – decides as a matter of social conscience to bestow on his impoverished subject, the fisherman, some of the privilege a king enjoys. Among such treats is the sight of the Queen naked. To this end, Candaules lends Gyges the ring. Gyges, once invisible, is master of the situation. He spends a night with the wife of Candaules, who thinks her husband in unusually high spirits. Naturally, Gyges slays his benefactor in the end, taking over Queen and Kingdom.'

'That taught His Majesty to brag about his luck,' said Glober. 'He went that much too far.'

Dr Brightman allowed such a point of view.

'Gide's political undertones insinuate that Candaules represents a too tolerant ruling class, over anxious to share personal advantages, some of which are perhaps better left unshared, anyway that sharing, in the case of Candaules, led to disaster. You must remember the play was written nearly half a century ago. I need hardly add that both Gautier and Gide treat the theme in essentially French terms, as if the particular events described could have taken place only in France.'

Pamela remained unsatisfied.

'That wasn't what I meant. I didn't say having an affair. I said watching – looking on, or being looked at.'

She spoke the words emphatically, in a clearer tone than that she was accustomed to use. Her attention had undoubtedly been captured. Dr Brightman, not in the least denying that to 'watch' was quite another matter, nodded again to show she fully grasped the disparity.

'You mean one facet of the legend links up with kingship in another guise? I agree. Sacrifice is almost implied. Public manifestation of himself as source of fertility might be required too, to forestall a successor from snatching that attribute of regality. You have made a good point, Lady Widmerpool. To speak less seriously, one cannot help recalling a local example here in Venice – or rather the island seclusion of Murano – of the practice to which you refer. I mean Casanova's divertissement with the two nuns under the eye of Cardinal de Bernis.'

Pamela, perhaps from ignorance of the Memoirs, appeared out-manoeuvred for the moment, at least attempted no comeback. The subject could already have begun to pall on her, though for once she was looking thoughtful rather than impatient. Moreland, too, was fond of talking about Casanova's threesome with the nuns.

'I've never myself been more than one of a pair,' Moreland said. 'How inexperienced one is, even though the best things in life are free. For the more venturesome, the song is not *How happy could I be with either*, but *How happy could I be with two girls.*'

By now the rest of the Conference had begun to infiltrate the Longhi room, the vanguard of oncoming intellectuals substantiating Dr Brightman's comparison with the sages, abbés, punchinellos, pictured on the white-and-gold walls. Gwinnett was among this advance party, which also included two other British representatives, Ada Leintwardine and Quentin Shuckerly. Both of these accommodated at an hotel on the Lido, I had done no more than exchange a few words with them. They were taking the Conference with great seriousness, from time to time addressing sessions, an obligation for which Gwinnett and myself had substituted contribution to the organ devoted to its 'dialogues'. Ada, not least because she retained some of the girlish good-looks of her twenties, had been warmly received in her observations regarding the necessity of assimilating European culture to that of Asia and Africa, delivered in primitive but daring French. Shuckerly, too, won applause by the artlessness and modesty with which he emphasized the many previous occasions on which he had made his now quite famous speech about culture being the scene-shifter to ring up the Iron Curtain.

Shuckerly was a great crony of Ada's. Tall, urbane, smiling, businesslike, with a complexion so richly tanned by the sun that his enemies (friends, too) hinted at artifice, he had by now begun almost to rival Mark Members himself as a notable figure at international congresses. In earlier days, both as intimate friend and committed poet, he had been closely associated with Malcolm Crowding. Bernard Shernmaker, always irked by even comparative success in others, had designated Shuckerly 'the air-hostess of English Letters' at some literary party. 'Better than the ad-man of french ones,' had been Shuckerly's retort, a slanting gloss on Shernmaker's recently published piece about Ferrand-Sénéschal. Ada and Shuckerly sat on the same committees, signed the same protests, seemed to share much the same temperament, except that Ada, so far as was known, required no analogous counterpoise to Shuckerly's alleged taste (Shernmaker again the authority) for being intermittently beaten-up.

Shernmaker had been malicious about Ada, too, in days of her first appearance as a novelist, though latterly, having in general somewhat lost his critical nerve, allowing her from time to time temperate praise. Some explained this unfriendly tone by rejected advances, at the period when Ada was new to London, and certainly Shernmaker remained always insistent that, in spite of marriage, Ada's emotional interests lay chiefly with her own sex. There may have been some truth in this assertion. If so, that had not prevented her from giving birth to twins soon after marriage to Quiggin, their identical, almost laughable, resemblance to their father scotching another of Shernmaker's disobliging innuendos. Quiggin did not by now at all mind his wife being a better known figure than himself. The sales of her books may even have played some part in his own evolvement, after Clapham's death, as chairman of the firm. In the delicate rôle – compared by Evadne Clapham to a troika – of publisher, husband, critic, Quiggin had judged his wife's first book, *I Stopped at a Chemist* (a tolerable film as *Sally Goes Shopping*), too short commercially. In consequence of this advice, Ada had written two long novels about domestic life, which threatened literary doldrums. She had extracted herself with *Bedsores* and *The Bitch Pack Meets on Wednesday*, since these never looked back as a successful writer. Ada's personality – what Members called her 'petits soins' – played a considerable part, too, in the Quiggins' notorious literary dinner parties.

As they advanced into the Tiepolo room, Shuckerly made for Dr Brightman, Ada for Pamela. She seemed very surprised to find her old friend in the Bragadin palace. As Ada passed him, Glober shot out an appraising glance, reminiscent of those Peter Templer used to give ladies he did not know, Glober's all-inclusive survey suggesting recognition of Ada's valuable qualities, additional to her good looks. Always a shade on the plump side (even when she had worked for Sillery), she was no thinner, but carried herself well, retaining that air of bright, blonde, efficient, self-possessed secretary, who knows the whereabouts of everything required in a properly run office, much too sensible to allow more than just the right minimum of flirtatious behaviour to pervade business hours. No doubt Ada had learnt a lot from contact with Sillery. At the ninetieth birthday celebrations mentioned by Dr Brightman, the names of both the Quiggins had appeared as present, Quiggin himself reported as having delivered one of the many speeches.

Ada hurried up to Pamela, and embraced her warmly. It looked as if they had not met for some time. Pamela's reception of this greeting was less obviously approving of reunion, though her accustomed coldness of manner was not to be constructed as pointer in one direction more than another. Ten years ago they had been on good terms. Since then they might well have quarrelled, moved apart, made friends again, never ceased to be friends. It was impossible to judge from outward signs. Pamela allowed herself to be kissed. She made no attempt to return the ardent flow of words from Ada that followed. No such display of sentiment was to be expected, even if Ada could claim, in the past, to have been Pamela's sole female friend and confidante. No doubt mere acceptance of Ada's continued devotion confirmed no rift had taken place.

'Pam, what are you doing here?. You're the last person I'd expected to see. You can't be a member of the Conference?'

Pamela made a face of disgust at the thought.

'What are you doing then?'

'I'm staying here.'

'In the Palazzo — with Mr Bragadin?'

'Of course.'

'Both of you?'

Ada allowed too much unconcealed curiosity to echo in that question for Pamela's taste. Her face hardened. She began to frown. As it turned out, that seemed more from contempt for Ada's crude inquisitiveness, than from displeasure at what she wanted to know. Whatever Pamela's feelings about her husband, she was not prepared to plunge into the heart-to-heart talk about him which Ada's question posed. Ada's tone sounded as if she too had heard Pamela's name connected with the Ferrand-Sénéschal affair. It was more than a conventional inquiry to a wife about her husband. The conventional assumption would in any case have been that Pamela was not accompanied by Widmerpool. Ada was no doubt dying to learn how he was taking this new scandal involving his wife's name; Pamela, perfectly grasping what her friend was after, not at all inclined, there and then, to make a present of the latest news. Instead, she gave Ada a look, hard, understanding, half-threatening in relation to more exciting items.

'He's arriving today.'

'In Venice?'

'Yes.'

This manner of stating Widmerpool's movements recalled the habit of referring always to 'him', rather than using a name. Ada's question was at least answered.

'That awful night-flight? I was a wreck when I arrived at four in the morning.'

Pamela laughed derisively.

'He wasn't man enough to take the night-flight this time. He's on a plane as far as Milan, from there by train.'

Ada was persistent.

'Is he feeling worried then?'

'Why should he be?'

'I don't know. I just wondered. He always has such a lot on his plate, as he himself always says. I must congratulate him on becoming a lord – and you too, darling.'

'Oh, that?'

'Aren't you pleased?'

Pamela did not bother to answer.

'I'm longing for a talk.'

Pamela did not answer that either. She began to frown again. It did not look as if she herself were longing for a talk at all. Her bearing suggested quite the contrary. In spite of such discouragement, Ada rattled on. She was, after all, used to Pamela and her ways. An affection of simplicity was simply part of Ada's tactic. She judged, probably rightly, that even if Pamela's prevailing aspect did not at present show a good disposition towards old acquaintance, that could in due course be overcome.

'How long are you both staying in Venice?'

'I don't know.'

'I've a story I must tell you.'

Ada lowered her voice. Gwinnett, finished with the Longhis, had proceeded on to examination of the Tiepolo. He was moving steadily in our direction. At any moment now opportunity would be offered for putting him in touch with Pamela. Obligation to effect an introduction, so that he could relate her to his work on Trapnel, was not to be ignored. On the other hand, was this the right moment? From Gwinnett's point of view the risk was considerable. Head-on presentation might – almost certainly would – result in one of Pamela's sudden capricious antagonisms, possibly aversion so keen that all further inquiry in her direction would be at an end. Nevertheless, in whatever manner Gwinnett were to approach her, that eventuality had to be faced. There was no way of guarding against their temperaments proving mutually antipathetic. This was as good a chance as likely to occur. In the case of flat refusal to co-operate, he would have to do the best he could. To bring them together in this neutral spot, even if Gwinnett did not, here and now, speak of Trapnel – an awkward subject to broach in the first few seconds after introduction – circumstances would at least allow him to absorb something of Pamela's personality, useful material for his book he might never secure again, if opportunity were missed. Before I could make up my mind how best to act, Glober, left on his own by Ada's monopoly of Pamela, Shuckerly's of Dr Brightman, began to speak of the ceiling again.

'The way the painter's contrived to illuminate those locations of dark pigmentation is just great. Dwell on that multi-coloured luminosity of cloud effect. To think I spent twenty-four hours in Jacky's Palazzo before stepping over to gaze.'

Continuous companionship, with the conversation that brought, was necessary to Glober all the time. His manner made one feel even momentary isolation of himself required ending instantly, if he were not to risk grave nervous strain. His words postponed need for decision about bringing together Gwinnett and Pamela, Gwinnett himself came up at that moment, and started off an inquiry of his own.

'Do you know the legend depicted up there? It's not familiar to me.'

Glober, recognizing another American, but taking charge probably more from instinct to speak authoritatively, than because a fellow-countryman had asked the question, stepped in with an answer.

'We've just been told the story by Dr Brightman. It's a great one.'

He proceeded to recapitulate, briefly and proficiently. Gwinnett listened with attention. I did not know whether he recognized Glober, nor, if so, whether he wanted to meet him. His own vague manner almost suggested unawareness that Glober and I had been talking together; that nothing was further from his mind than that Glober should reply to his question. At the same time, one never quite knew with Gwinnett; what he was thinking, how he would behave. That his action in approaching us at that moment was deliberate, premeditated, could not be entirely ruled out.

'Thanks a lot. That's an interesting story.'

Gwinnett evidently meant what he said. Although I was aware of hazards incident on introducing to each other nationals of the same country (Americans not least), without carefully reconnoitring the ground, no alternative was offered. I spoke their names, coupled with that of the college where Gwinnett taught English. He smiled faintly when this was done, but with an impassivity that gave nothing away, least of all any hint that he was already conversant with Glober's reputation. If interested in making this encounter, Gwinnett did not show it, holding his cards to his chest in a manner, to the popular European view, 'un-American'. Anyway, it was in contrast with Glober's exuberance, intact from younger days, tempered with that unnoisy manner which so well suited him. There was nothing in the least forced about Glober's friendliness, none of that sense of inadequacy sometimes noticeable after a gushing approach has lacked basic vitality to sustain its first impact. Glober possessed that inner strength. When he caught Gwinnett's two hands, the gesture managed to be warm, amusing, not at all reckless or overdone.

'One of the rarest signatures too,' he said.

Although he spoke in that quiet way, he might just as well have shouted, from the punch he put into this piece of banter, for, even if complimentary, banter was what it turned out to be. At the time, the bearing was obscure to me, unconnected with Dr Brightman's reference to the surname's link with a 'Signer' family; though I noted inwardly the odd coincidence of Gwinnett himself speaking ironically of Glober being 'able to sign his name'. The conjunction of phrase, a mere chance, made Gwinnett's reply seem the more enigmatic. Later, I wondered whether, in fact, he ever signed his own name without thinking of his ancestor. That was not impossible. At the moment he appeared a little put out, laughing in a deprecatory manner, as he tried to withdraw his fingers from Glober's grip.

'I take care my own signature's a rare one too,' he said. 'Anyway on cheques.'

There was a touch of reproof in this rather knockabout rejoinder. Gwinnett was probably flattered too. How much flattered was hard to assess, the incident not immediately explicable, its implications only subsequently revealed. Gwinnett was in any case, so it seemed to me, too good an American to persist, after all that, in his earlier, more distant air; to make absolutely unambiguous a preference for different, less overpowering, modes of address between strangers. There was no question of 'putting Glober in his place', an inclination that might easily have emerged in England from a personality of Gwinnett's type. At the same time, to the extent of showing the smallest spark of exuberance himself, he did not at all retreat from his own chosen position, just keeping a dead level of civility, to which exception could not possibly be taken.

In due course, Dr Brightman explained that, among endorsements of the Declaration of Independence, Button Gwinnett's signature happened to be much prized among collectors purposing to possess an example of each. In Gwinnett's light dismissal, as an individual, of Glober's commendatory teasing, in quite another form, something was reminiscent of Pamela's neutralization of Ada's affectionate embrace. Neutralization was the process Gwinnett's manner often called to mind. Pamela's exterior, to the uninformed observer, could have been interpreted as hostile. No hostility was present in Gwinnett's reply, just unspoken announcement of another way of life. If that were hostility, it was to be detected by only the most delicate instrument. Glober himself showed not the smallest awareness of even that antithesis. Constitutionally habituated, simply as a man, to being liked by people, he could have become insensitive to antipathy, unless explicit; alternatively, so intensely conscious of any attitude towards himself short of total surrender, that he was conditioned utterly to conceal any such awareness.

The dissimilarities of these two Americans seemed to put them into almost every direct opposition in relation to one another: Gwinnett, much the younger, a disturbed background, chancy fortunes, a small but appreciable stake in American history: Glober, of mature age, easy manner, worldly success, recent – not necessarily easy – family origins. One thought of the gladiator with the sword and shield; the one with the net and trident. No doubt gladiators too had in common the typical characteristics of their trade, and something bound Gwinnett and Glober together, perhaps merely their 'Americanness'. One struggled for a phrase to define this characteristic in common, if indeed it existed. An appropriate term warbled across the room from the lips of Quentin Shuckerly.

'So I told Bernard he was just like the lame boy in the Pied Piper, getting left behind as a critic, whenever a fashionable tune was played. I clinched my argument by using a word he didn't know – allotropic – a variation of properties that doesn't change the substance. My dear, the poor man was completely crushed.'

That seemed the term for Glober and Gwinnett, at least how they looked to one across the abyss of uncertainty that precluded definition, with any subtlety, of American types and ways. Meanwhile, the question of whether or not to introduce Gwinnett to Pamela, without saying some preliminary word first, was becoming more urgent than ever. Thinking about allotropy was no help. Then all at once, in a flash, the problem was solved, the Gordian Knot cut, possibly in interplay of that allotropic element. Personal responsibility was all at once removed. Glober, taking Gwinnett by the arm, broke in between Pamela and Ada.

'I want you to meet Professor Gwinnett, Pam. This is Lady Widmerpool, who's stopping in the Palazzo.'

Why Glober did that I could not guess at the time, have never since quite decided. The step may have been due to a compulsive, all-embracing need to arrange, in a manner satisfactory to himself, everyone within orbit – creating an instant court, as Dr Brightman might have said – the spirit in Glober that brought together the Mopsy Pontner dinner party. He may, on the other hand, having favourably marked down Ada, grasped that the simplest way to talk with her for a minute or two would be to occupy Pamela with Gwinnett. Alternatively, the consigning of Gwinnett to Pamela might have appealed to him as a delicate revenge for Gwinnett's latent superciliousness, at least refusal to fall in more amicably with Glober's own more effusive mood. To introduce Gwinnett to Pamela was as likely as not to cause a clash. That clash might be what Glober wished, not necessarily in a mood of retaliation, but with the object of bringing the two of them together for the spectacle, the sheer fun, mildly sadistic, of watching what was likely to be a 'scene' – any scene – in which Pamela was involved. What he certainly did not know was that Gwinnett's highest ambition at that moment was just what had taken place through Glober's own instrumentality.

If Glober sought drama, he was disappointed. At least he was disappointed if he wanted fireworks in the form of violent opposition or bad temper. In another sense – for anyone who knew the stakes for which Gwinnett was playing – the reception he received was intensely dramatic, more so than any brush-off could have been, however defiant. The mere fact that Gwinnett himself, not Pamela, took the offensive was in itself impressive.

'I'd hoped very much to meet you while I was in Venice, Lady Widmerpool. I didn't know I'd have this luck.'

He spoke very simply. Pamela gave him one of her blank stares. She did not speak. At that stage of their meeting it looked as if Gwinnett were going to get, if nothing worse, a characteristic rejection. She allowed him to take her hand, withdrawing it quickly.

'I'm writing a book on X. Trapnel,' Gwinnett said.

He paused. This frontal attack, taking over an active rôle, thrusting Pamela even momentarily into the passive, suggested something of Gwinnett's potential. He said the words quietly, quite a different quietness from Glober's, though suggesting something of the same muted strength. They were spoken almost casually, a statement just given for information, no more, before going on to speak of other things. There was no question of blurting out in an uncontrolled manner the nature of his 'project', what he wanted for it from her. To use such a tone was to tackle the approach in an effective, possibly the only effective, manner. It exhibited a fine appreciation of the fact that to gain Pamela's co-operation with regard to the biography was a matter of now or never. He must sink or swim. Gwinnett undoubtedly saw that. I admired him for attempting no compromise. There was again a parallel between Gwinnett's tone with Pamela, and the way he had replied to Glober, the one conveying only the merest atom of overt friendliness, just as the other conveyed possibly the reverse, difference between the two almost imperceptible. While this had been taking place, Glober had transferred his attention to Ada. They were chattering away together as if friends for years.

'I think you knew him,' said Gwinnet. 'Trapnel, I mean.'

Pamela, who had as usual registered no immediate outward reaction to his first statement, still remained silent. Gwinnett was silent too. In that, he showed his strength. After making the initial announcement of his position, he made no effort to develop the situation. They stood looking at each other. There was a long pause during which one felt anything might happen: Pamela walk away: burst out laughing: overwhelm Gwinnett with abuse: strike him in the face. After what seemed several minutes, but could only have been a second or two, Pamela spoke. Her voice was low.

'Poor X,' she said.

She sounded deeply moved, not far from tears. Gwinnett inclined his head a little. That movement was no more than a quiver, quick, awkward, at the same time reverential in its way, wholly without affectation. He too seemed to feel strong emotion. Something had been achieved between them.

'Yes – Trapnel wasn't always a lucky guy it seems.'

Now, it had become Trapnel's turn to join the dynasty

of Pamela's dead lovers. Emotional warmth in her was directed only towards the dead, men who had played some part in her life, but were no more there to do so. That was how it looked. The first time we had ever talked together, she had described herself as 'close' to her uncle, Charles Stringham, almost suggesting a sexual relationship. Stringham's circumstances made nothing more unlikely, in any physical form, although, in the last resort, close relationship of a sexual kind does not perhaps necessarily require such expression, something even undesired, except in infinitely sublimated shape. When, for example, Pamela had been racketing round during the war, with all sorts of lovers, from all sorts of nations, she had refused to give herself to Peter Templer (in his own words 'mad about her'); after he was killed calling him the 'nicest man I ever knew'.

Trapnel, whose rapid declension as a writer had been substantially accelerated by Pamela's own efforts, notably destruction of his manuscript, was now to be rehabilitated, memorialized, placed in historical perspective, among those loves with whom, but for unhappy chance, all might have been well. It was Death she liked. Mrs Erdleigh had hinted as much on the night of the flying-bombs. Would Gwinnett be able to offer her Death? At least, in managing to catch and hold the frail line cast to him, he had not made a bad beginning. There was hope for his book. Glober, after instigating the Gwinnett/Pamela conversation, must now have decided to put an end to it, having said all he wanted to say to Ada. Seeing out of the corner of his eye that Gwinnett's communion with Pamela produced no immediately lively incident, he may have judged it better to cut it short. Pamela herself anticipated anything he might be about to say.

'Why didn't you explain at first Professor Gwinnett was the man you need for the Trapnel film?'

Glober was not quite prepared for that question. It

opened up a new subject. Pamela turned to Gwinnett again.

'Louis wants to make a last film. I've told him it's to be based on the Trapnel novel that got destroyed. X himself said there was a film there. I've been telling Louis the best parts of the book, which I remember absolutely. He's not very quick about taking facts in, but he's got round to this as a proposition.'

Glober smiled, but made no effort to elaborate the subject put forward.

'Naturally I never read the last novel,' said Gwinnett. 'Did it have close bearing on Trapnel's own life.'

'Of course.'

Circumstances came to Glober's aid at that moment, in the manner they do with persons of adventurous temperament put in momentary difficulty. He brought an abrupt end to the matter being discussed by jerking his head towards the far side of the room.

'Here's Baby — with your husband.'

Two persons, without much ceremony, were forcing a channel between the dense accumulation of intellectuals, pottering about or gazing upward. One of these new arrivals was Widmerpool, the other a smartly dressed woman of about the same age-group. Widmerpool was undoubtedly seeking his wife. Even at a distance, symptoms of that condition were easily recognizable. They were a little different, a little more agitated, than any of his other outward displays of personal disturbance. As he pushed his way through the crowd, he had the look of a man who had not slept for several nights. No doubt the journey, even by train, had been tiring, but hardly trying enough to cause such an expression of worried annoyance, irritation merging into fear.

Thinner than in his younger days, Widmerpool was less bald than Glober, even if such hair as remained was sparse and grizzled. Rather absurdly, I was a little taken aback by this elderly appearance, physical changes in persons known for a long time always causing a certain inner uneasiness – Umfraville's sense of being let down by the rapidity with which friends and acquaintances decay, once the process has begun. Widmerpool's air of discomfort was by no means decreased by the heavy texture, in spite of the hot weather, of the dark suit he wore. Built for him when more bulky, it hung about his body in loose folds, like clothes on a scarecrow. He seemed to have come straight from the City; having regard to recent elevation in rank, more probably the House of Lords.

The woman with him was Baby Wentworth – or whatever she was now called. When last heard of, she had been married to an Italian. I remembered her beauty, sly look, short curly hair, thirty years before, when, supposedly mistress of Sir Magnus Donners, she had also been pursued, at different levels, by both Prince Theodoric and Barnby. Now in her fifties, Baby had not at all lost her smart appearance – she too wore trousers – but, if she looked less than her age, her features also registered considerable ups and downs of fortune. She made towards Glober, abandoned again by Pamela who had resumed talk with Gwinnett. Widmerpool went straight to his wife, inserting himself without apology between her and Gwinnett, in order to reduce delay in speaking to a minimum.

'Pam – I want a word in private at once.'

Gwinnett took a step back to allow Widmerpool easier passage. No doubt he guessed the relationship. Pamela, on the other hand, showed not the least recognition of the fact that her husband had just arrived. She took no notice of him whatsoever. Instead of offering any facility for speech, she quickly moved sideways and forward, again decreasing distance between Gwinnett and herself, blocking Widmerpool's way, so that she could continue a conversation, which, so far as could be judged, was going relatively well.

'Pam . . .'

Pamela threw him a glance. Her manner suggested that a man – a very unprepossessing man at that – was trying to pick her up in a public place; some uncouth sightseer, not even a member of the Conference, having gained access to the Palazzo because the door was open, was now going round accosting ladies encountered there. Widmerpool persisted.

'You must come with me. It's urgent.'

She answered now without turning her head.

'Do go away. I heard you the first time. Can't you take a hint? I'm being shown round the house by Louis Glober. You knew he was going to be staying with Jacky. At the moment I'm talking about a rather important matter to Professor Gwinnett.'

Widmerpool's reaction to this treatment was complex. On the one hand, he was obviously not at all surprised by blank refusal to co-operate; on the other, he could not be said to have received that refusal with anything like indifference. He paused for a moment, apparently analysing means of forcing his wife to obey; then he must have decided against any such attempt. His expression suggested the existence of one or two tricks up his sleeve, to be played when they were alone together. He was about to move away, return from wherever he had come, but, catching sight of me, stopped and nodded. Recognition evidently suggested more to him than the fact that we had not met since the night of the Election party. He went straight to the point, his manner confirming existence of some problem on his mind desperate to solve.

'Nicholas, how are you? Staying with Jacky Bragadin? No – then you are almost certainly a member of this

Conference going round? That is what I expected. Just the man I want to talk to.'

'Congratulations on the peerage.'

'Ah, yes. Thank you very much. Not very contemporary, such a designation sounds today, but it has its advantages. I didn't want to leave the Commons, no one less. 1955 may have been a moral victory – several of my constituents described my campaign as a greater *personal* triumph than the previous poll, when I was returned – but past efforts were forgotten in a fight that was not always a clean one. As I still have a lot of work in me, the Upper Chamber, so long as it hangs on, seemed as good a place to do that work as any other. As it happens, my normal activities are rather impeded at the moment by a number of irksome matters, indeed one domestic tragedy, since my mother passed away only a few days ago at her cottage in Kirkcudbrightshire, which she always spoke of as an ideal home for her declining years. She had reached a ripe age, so that the end was not unexpected. Unfortunately, it was quite impossible for me to take a journey as far as Scotland at this particular moment. I could not attempt it. At the same time, it was painful to leave a matter like my mother's burial in the hands of a secretary, competent as my own secretary happens to be. Something a little over and above routine competence is required at such a moment. None the less, that was what had to be done. I couldn't be in Kirkcudbrightshire and Venice at the same time, and, little as I like the place, I had to come to Venice.'

He stopped, overwhelmed by his troubles. I did not know why I was being told all this. Widmerpool's jaws worked up and down. He gave the impression of hesitation in asking some question. I enquired if he were in Venice on business, since he did not care for the city in other respects.

'Yes – no – not really. A slight rest. Pamela wanted a

short rest. To be quiet, out of things, just for a little. You may be able to help me, as a matter of fact, in something I want to know. Your Conference has been going on for a day or two?'

'Yes.'

'You meet and mix with the other members – the foreign ones, I mean?'

'Some of them.'

'I was hoping to kill two birds with one stone. Pamela was given an open invitation to stay in this imposing residence. The owner – Bragadin – is one of the smart international set, I understand, what the papers call café society, I'm told. All that sort of thing is a mystery to me. Distasteful too, in the highest degree. At the same time, it was convenient for Pamela to take a rest, even if in a style I myself cannot approve. But to get back to the Conference, am I right in supposing all these people round about are its members? I am. There chances to be one of them I am particularly anxious to meet, if here. It is a most lucky opportunity the two things coincided.'

'The Conference, and your visit?'

'Yes, yes. That is what I mean. Have you run across Dr Belkin? He is familiar to me only by name, through certain cultural societies to which I belong. By an unhappy mischance, we have never set eyes on each other, though we have corresponded – on cultural matters, of course. He was, incidentally, a mutual friend of poor Ferrand-Sénéschal. How sad that too. I am, of course, not sure that Dr Belkin will have been able to put in an appearance. He could have become too much occupied in the cultural affairs of his own country, in which he plays a central part. They may not have been able to spare him at the last moment. He is a busy man. Belkin? Dr Belkin? Have you heard anything of him, or seen him?'

I was about to answer that the name was unknown to me, when Pamela, overhearing Widmerpool's strained, eager tone, got her word in first. She turned from where she stood with Gwinnett, looked straight at her husband, and laughed outright. It was not a friendly laugh.

'You won't find your friend Belkin here.'

She spoke under her breath, almost in a hiss, still laughing. Widmerpool's face altered. He swallowed uneasily. When he replied he was quite calm.

'What do you mean?'

'What I say.'

'You only know about Belkin because you've heard me refer to him.'

'That's sufficient.'

'What information have you got regarding him then?'

'Just what you've told me. And a few small items I've picked up elsewhere.'

'But I haven't told you anything – I – that was what I wanted to talk to you about.'

'You don't have to.'

'Why should you think he won't be here? You don't know him personally any more than I do. Nothing I've said gave you any reason to draw that conclusion. Only quite a recent development makes me want to meet him rather urgently.'

'It wasn't what *you* said. It was what Léon-Joseph said.'

Considering the circumstances, Widmerpool took that comment stoically, though he was showing signs of strain. He seemed to want most to get to the bottom of Pamela's insinuation.

'He told you this before he . . .'

Widmerpool put the question composedly, as if what had happened to Ferrand-Sénéschal did not matter much, only out of respect he did not name it.

'No,' said Pamela, also speaking quietly. 'He told me after he'd died, of course – Léon-Joseph appeared to me as a ghost last night, and gave the information. He was gliding down the Grand Canal, walking on the water like Jesus, except that he was carrying his head under his arm like Mary Queen of Scots. I recognized the head by those blubber lips and rimless spectacles. The blubber lips spoke the words: "A cause de ses sentiments stalinistes, Belkin est foutu." '

Widmerpool appeared more disconcerted by the implications of Pamela's words than resentful of their ironic intonation. She said no more for the moment, returning to Gwinnett, who had politely moved a little to one side, when she broke off to take part in this last interchange. He must by then know for certain she was engaged with her husband. Opportunity was now more available than earlier to estimate Pamela's potentialities. This readiness of Gwinnett's to withdraw into the background showed comprehension. Widmerpool again thought things over for a moment. Then he made a step in his wife's direction. Once more Gwinnett moved away. Widmerpool was fairly angry now. Anger and fright seemed to make up his combined emotions.

'If this is true – Léon-Joseph really told you something of the kind before he died – why on earth didn't you pass it on?'

'Why should I?'

'*Why should you?*'

'Yes?'

Widmerpool, almost shaking now, was just able to control himself.

'You know its importance – if true . . . which I doubt . . . the whole point of making this contact . . . the consequences . . . you know perfectly well what I mean . . .'

It looked as if the consequences, whatever they were likely to be, remained too awesome to put into words. Pamela turned her head away, and upward. Resting lightly the tips of her fingers on her hips, she leant slowly back on her heels, revealing to advantage the slimness of her still immensely graceful neck. She tipped her head slightly to one side, apparently lost once more in fascination by the legend of Candaules and Gyges. Widmerpool could stand this treatment no longer. He burst out.

'What are you looking at? Answer my question. This is a serious matter, I tell you.'

Pamela did not reply at once. When she did so, she spoke in the absent strain of someone who had just made an absorbing discovery.

'There's a picture up there of a man exhibiting his naked wife to a friend. Have you inspected it yet?'

Widmerpool did not reply this time. His face was yellow. The look he gave her suggested that, of all things living, she was the most abhorrent to him. Pamela continued her soft, almost cooing commentary, a voice in complete contrast with her earlier sullenness.

'I know you can't tell one picture from another, haven't the slightest idea what those square, flat, brightly coloured surfaces are, which people put in frames, and hang on their walls, or why they hang them there. You probably think they conceal safes with money in them, or compromising documents, possibly dirty books and postcards. The favourite things you think it better to keep hidden away. All the same, the subject of this particular picture might catch your attention — for instance remind you of those photographs shut up in the secret drawer of that desk you sometimes forget to lock. I didn't know about them till the other day. I didn't even know you'd taken them. Wasn't that innocent of me? How Léon-Joseph laughed, when I told him. You were careless to forget about turning the key.'

Widmerpool had gone a pasty yellowish colour when his wife quoted Ferrand-Sénéschal's alleged conjecture about Dr Belkin's reasons for absenting himself from the Conference. Now the blood came back into his face, turning it brick red. He was furious. Even so, he must have grasped that whatever had to be said must wait for privacy. He made a powerful effort at self-control, which could not be concealed. Then he spoke quite soberly,

'You don't know how things stand, why it was necessary for me to come here. When you do, you will see you are being rather silly. There have been unfortunate developments certainly, absurd ones. Even if Belkin does not turn up, there will be a way out, but, if he is here, that will be easier. We'll have a talk later about the best way of handling matters. This may concern you as much as me, so please do not be frivolous about it.'

Pamela was uninterested.

'I haven't the least idea what matters need handling. Oh, yes – the picture on the ceiling? You mean that? You want more explanation? Well, the wife there, whose husband arranged for his chum to have a peep at her in that charming manner, handled things by getting the chum who'd enjoyed the eyeful to do the husband in.'

She looked about for Gwinnett again. He was on the other side of the room, in front of a highly coloured piece of Venetian eighteenth-century sculpture, torso of a Turk. Gwinnett was examining the elaborate folds of the marble turban. Pamela went to join him. There could be no doubt she was interested in Gwinnett. What had taken place between the Widmerpools had attracted no attention from surrounding members of the Conference, nor Bragadin guests. Gwinnett himself could hardly have failed to notice its earlier pungency, but may not have caught the drift. Pamela might well be on her way to give him an account of that. Perhaps his Trapnel studies had prepared him for something of the sort; perhaps he supposed this the manner English married couples normally behaved. Considering the things said, both Widmerpools could have appeared outwardly unruffled, the colour of Widmerpool's face reasonably attributable to the heat of the day, and texture of his clothes. He still seemed uncertain whether or not his wife had spoken with authority on the subject of Belkin. He looked at her questioningly for a second. When he turned to me again, his thoughts were far away.

'I wonder what's the best course to take about Belkin. The first thing to do is to make sure whether or not he's here. How can I find that out?'

'Ask one of the Executive Committee. Dr Brightman, over there, would know whom to tackle. She's talking to our host.'

Jacky Bragadin, not paying much attention to whatever Dr Brightman was saying to him, was casting anxious glances round the room. A few members of the Conference had begun to drift into the next gallery, by far the larger majority continuing to contemplate the Tiepolo. Jacky Bragadin seemed to fear the story of Candaules and Gyges had hynotized them, caused an aesthetic catalepsy to descend. Their state threatened to turn his home into a sort of Sleeping Beauty's Palace, rows of inert vertical figures of intellectuals, for ever straining sightless eyes upward towards the ceiling, impossible to eject from where they stood. He waved his hands.

'This way,' he cried. 'This way.'

He may have been merely regretful that his guests should exhaust so much appreciation on this single aspect, even if a highly prized one, of his treasures, anxious that should not be done to detriment of other splendid items. Most likely of all, he wanted to get us out of the place, hoped our sightseeing would be undertaken with all possible dispatch, leaving him and his guests in peace; or whatever passed for peace in such a house-party. One wondered how he could ever have been foolhardy enough to have presented Pamela with an open invitation to stay any time she liked. The cause, in his case, would not have been love. Possibly he had never done so. She had forced herself on him. It was waste of time to speculate how the Widmerpools had managed to install themselves in the Palazzo. Jacky Bragadin, like most rich people, was well able to attend to his own interests. He must have had his reasons.

'This way,' he repeated. 'This way.'

He tried to encourage the more obdurate loiterers with smiles and beckonings. They would not be persuaded. He gave it up for a moment. Dr Brightman pinned him down again. Glober reappeared beside Widmerpool and myself.

'Mr Jenkins, I want you and Signora Clarini to meet. Signora Clarini is stopping in the Palazzo too. Her husband's name you'll know, the celebrated Italian director.'

I explained Baby and I had already met, though contacts had been slight, ages before. In those days, soon after her own association with Sir Magnus Donners, the Italian husband had then been spoken of as satisfactory to herself, even if of dubious occupation. Now he was no longer dubious, he must also have become less satisfactory, because Baby seemed displeased at his name being dragged in. Glober, on hearing she and I had met, struck an amused pose, as always personal to himself, if to some extent drawn from that deep fund of American schematized humour, of which, in a more sparing and austere technique, Colonel Cobb had been something of a master. Glober was not at all displeased to find earlier knowledge of Baby would unequivocally demonstrate the sort of woman preparade to run after him; an undertaking on which she certainly seemed engaged.

'Baby, I believe you've met every man in the Eastern Hemisphere, and quite a few in the Western too.'

Possibly a small touch of malice was voiced. Baby may have thought that. She looked sulky. I remembered Barnby's passion for her, his comment how Sir Magnus never minded his girls having other commitments. That was hardly a subject to bridge our once slender acquaintance. Her manner, not outstandingly friendly, minimally accepted former meetings had taken place.

'Aren't you fed up with this heat?' she said. 'Everybody's dripping. Look at Louis. Isn't he a disgusting sight?'

Glober murmured consciously good-natured protests. 'Am I, Baby? But not everyone. Look at Lord Widmerpool, he's fresh as a daisy. I believe he's right to take that Milan route. I'll do the same myself next time.'

Drawing attention in this manner to Widmerpool's appearance was indication that Glober made no pretence of liking him. Baby did not even smile. Her demeanour wafted through the Tiepolo room a breath of the Nineteen-Twenties. Like one who hands on the torch of a past era of folk culture, she had somehow preserved intact, from ballroom and plage, golf course and hunting-field, a social technique fashionable then, even considered alluring. This rather unblissful breeze blowing across the years recalled a little Widmerpool's former fiancée, Mrs Haycock (Baby's distant cousin), though Baby herself had always been far the better-looking. She stopped a long way short of displaying the stigmata a lifetime of late parties and casual love affairs had bestowed on Mrs Haycock. Nevertheless, she had developed some of the same masculine hardening of the features, voice rising to a bark, elements veering in the direction of sex-change, threatened by too constant adjustment of husbands and lovers; comparable with the feminine characteristics acquired from too pertinacious womanizing.

'Are you hopping over to the Lido for a dip this evening, Louis? A bathe will do you good. Freshen you up. Then I'm going to visit Mrs Erdleigh, the famous clairvoyante, who's in Venice. Why don't you come there too? She'll tell your fortune.'

Glober shook his head glumly at the thought of looking into the future. He showed no great keenness to bathe either.

'I'll have to think about the Lido. Get my priorities straight.'

Widmerpool was becoming impatient again.

'Your Dr Brightman is talking for a very long time,' he said. 'Who is she?'

'A very distinguished scholar.'

'Oh.'

Jacky Bragadin was as eager to get away from Dr Brightman as Widmerpool to be put in contact with her. In Jacky Bragadin's efforts to escape, the two of them arrived beside us. Dr Brightman swept everyone in.

'I've been talking to our host about his Foundation. I thought something might be done for Russell Gwinnett. Where's he gone?'

'It must be on paper,' said Jacky Bragadin. 'Always on paper. The name sent to the Board. They look into such matters.'

He sounded desperate. Dr Brightman, pausing to explain that I wrote novels, ignored his misery. The information made Jacky Bragadin horribly uneasy, but at least resulted in a let-out from further discussion of his Foundation. I told Dr Brightman that Widmerpool wanted to meet one of the Executive Committee. At that she began to question Widmerpool too. Without great originality of subject matter, I spoke to Jacky Bragadin of the beauty of the ceiling.

'Nice colour,' he said, his heart not in the words.

'We were discussing the story – '

Jacky Bragadin's despair began rapidly to increase again at that. He laid his hand on my sleeve beseechingly.

'You must see the other rooms . . . They all must . . .'

He peered, without much hope, at Baby, still trying to persuade Glober to bathe. Widmerpool and Dr Brightman went off together, presumably to try and find a member of the Executive Committee. Most of the other members of the Conference, including Ada and Shuckerly, had begun to filter into the next room, a small backwash of Tiepolo enthusiasts from time to time borne back on an incoming current to take another look. Among these last was Gwinnett. Pamela was no longer to be seen. Gwinnett seemed by then rather dazed.

'How was it? You seemed to be making good going?'

'Lady Widmerpool's agreed to talk about Trapnel.'

'She has?'

'That's as I understand it.'

'Fine.'

'If she sticks to that. She's said some amazing things already.'

'You brought off quite a quick bit of work.'

'Do you think so?'

He appeared uncertain.

'At least we're going to meet again,' he said.

'What could be better than that?'

'Where do you think she's arranged to meet?'

'I can't guess.'

'Try.'

'Harry's Bar?'

Gwinnett shook his head.

'St Mark's.'

'In the Piazza?'

'In the Basilica.'

'Any particular place in the church?'

'She just said she'd be there at a certain time.'

'On, on . . .' pleaded Jacky Bragadin. 'On, on . . .'

# *THREE*

Daniel Tokenhouse rang up the following morning to acknowledge my notification of arrival in Venice. I was still in bed when he telephoned, though breakfast had been ordered. In keeping with an instinctive determination to hold the moral advantage, he made a point of ascertaining that I was not yet up. On the line, he sounded in tolerably good form, brisk, peremptory, as always. I had not expected him to be in the least senile, but the sharpness of his manner may have been amplified by some apprehension, shared by myself, that changes must have taken place in both of us during the last twenty years, which could prove mutually disenchanting.

'How are you, Dan?'

'In rude health. Working hard, as ever. Been up painting since half-past six this morning. Hate staying in bed. You'll find developments in my style. I shall be interested to hear what you think of them.'

Complete absorption in himself, and his own doings, always characterized Tokenhouse, a temperament that had served him pretty well in getting through what must have been, on the whole, rather a solitary life, especially of late years. He had in no way relaxed this solipsistic standpoint.

'When can your works be seen?'

'I've been thinking about that. Sunday morning would suit me best. You will not be in conference then, I trust, with your fellow intellectuals? I hope they are proving themselves worthy of their proud designation. Come about twelve o'clock midday – half-past eleven, if you prefer. That will give us more time. Do not fear. I shall not be attending matins.'

He gave his high, unamused laugh.

'How do I reach you, Dan?'

'I live, I am thankful to say, in a spot quite off the beaten track of that horrible fellow, the tourist. Among the people of Venice. The real people. I could not remain here an hour otherwise. My flat is in the quarter of the Arsenal, if you know where that is, a calle off the Via Garibaldi. You take an accelerato, then a short walk along the Riva Ca Di Dio and Riva Biagio. Let me explain the exact whereabouts, for it is not at all easy to find.'

He gave minute instructions, forcibly bringing back the years when I had worked under him, something establishing a relationship which can never wholly fade.

'Afterwards, I thought, we might walk as far as the Biennale together. I have not seen the latest Exhibition yet. I should like you to lunch with me at the restaurant in the Giardini.'

'I'll be with you, Dan, between half-past eleven and twelve on Sunday.'

'You may not care for the sort of work I am doing now. I warn you of that. Are you sure you know how to get here? Let me repeat my instructions.'

He went over the directions with that pedantic attention to detail natural to him, dilated by army training.

'Have you got it? Remember, an accelerato. When you disembark, turn to the right, walk straight on, then bear left, left again, then right – not left, remember – then right again. It's over a greengrocer's. Walk straight up.'

When Sunday morning came, the place turned out quite easy to find. It was a characteristic Tokenhouse abode, which, freedom from sound of traffic apart, might have been situated in an alley-way of some down-at-heel district of London, or anywhere else, all architectural and local emphasis as negative as possible; exceptional only insomuch as to discover — elect to inhabit — so featureless a location in Venice was in itself a shade impressive. I climbed the stairs and knocked. The door opened immediately, as if Tokenhouse had been already gripping the handle, impatiently awaiting someone to arrive.

'Hullo, Dan.'

'Come in, come in. Through here. This is the room where I paint.'

The windows faced on to a blank wall. Except for a pile of canvases, none of great size, stacked in one corner, the room showed no sign of being an artist's studio. It was scrupulously neat, suggesting for some perverse reason — possibly actual by-product of its owner's intense anti-clericalism — sense of arrival in the study of an urban vicarage or rectory, including an indefinably churchly smell.

'Did it take you long to get here? No? Not after my detailed instructions, I expect. They were necessary. How are you? What is your hotel like? I know it by name. I can't bear that fashionable end of the Canal. It gets worse every year. I continue to live in Venice only because I am used to the place by now. At my age it would be a great business to move. Besides, there are advantages. One can make oneself useful.'

He rapped his knuckles together several times, and nodded. In spite of the parsonic overtones of the sitting-room-studio, Tokenhouse himself did not look at all like a clergyman; nor even the very reasonably successful publisher of art books he had been in his time. Acquired erudition, heterodox opinions, expatriate domicile, none had done anything to alter deep dyed marks of the military profession, an appearance, one imagined, Tokenhouse would not have chosen. At the same time, if aware of looking like a retired soldier, even heartily disliking that, he would have considered dishonest any effort at diminishment brought about by artificial means, such as wearing relatively unconformist clothes. His clothes, in one sense, certainly were unconformist, but not at all with that object in view. Spare, wiry, very upright, he could be thought dried up, wizened, ascetic; considering his years, not particularly old. His body seemed made up of gristle, rather than flesh; grey hair, trimmed severely, almost *en brosse,* remaining thick. He peered alertly, rather peevishly, through gold-rimmed spectacles set well forward on a long thin reddish nose. An all-enveloping chilliness of manner hung about him, sense of being utterly cut off from the rest of the world, a personality, even physique, no sun could warm. Unlike Widmerpool, sweltering in his House of Lords suit, the ancient jacket Tokenhouse wore, good thick serviceable tweed, designed to keep out damp wind on the moors, his even older flannel trousers punctiliously pressed, seemed between them garments scarcely substantial enough to prevent him looking blue with cold, in spite of blazing Venetian sunlight outside.

'How are your family? You have children of your own almost grown up now, I believe? Is that not so?'

He spoke as if procreation of children were an extraordinary fate to overtake anyone, consequence of imprudence, if not worse. We talked for a time of things that had happened since our last meeting.

'Your father and I parted on bad terms. There was no other way. He could never see reason. An entirely unphilosophic mind. Childish view of politics. Now he is dead. Most of the people I used to know are dead. I don't find that makes much difference to me. I have learnt to be self-supporting. It is the only way. No good thinking about the past. The future is what matters. But you said you would like to see some of my work. Then we'll go to the Exhibition. The Gardens are within walking distance. The pictures aren't much good this year, I'm told, but let's look at my work first, if that is what you would like.'

Moving jerkily across the room, he returned once more with some of the unframed canvases, chosen from the pile that lay in the corner. He spread out several of these, propping them up against chairs.

'You've certainly changed your style, Dan.'

'True, O King.'

That had always been a favourite expression of Tokenhouse's, especially when not best pleased. I tried to think of something to say. The Camden Town Group had been wholly superseded, utterly swept away, so far as the art of Daniel Tokenhouse was concerned. What had taken its place was less easy to define; a sort of neo-primitivism. The light was bad for forming a judgment. So revolutionary was the transformation that a happy phrase to cover just what had happened did not come easily to mind. The new Tokenhouse style, in one of its expressions, suggested frescoes, frescoes on a very small scale; not at all in the manner of, say, Barnby's murals once decorating the entrance to the Donners-Brebner Building. After some minutes, Tokenhouse himself making no comment, I felt compelled to pronounce a judgment, however insipid.

'The garage scene has considerable force. Its colour emotive too, limiting yourself in that way to an almost regular monochrome, picked out with passages of flat heavy black.'

'You mean this study?'

'Both of those. Aren't they the same group from another angle?'

'Yes, this is another shot. Three in all. The subject is *Four priests rigging a miracle*. The rather larger version here, and its fellow, are less successful, I think. At the same time both have merit of a sort.'

'You always make several studies of the same subject nowadays?'

'I find that produces the best results. I work slowly.

That comes from lack of early training. My difficulty is usually to get the values correctly.'

'The browns, greys and blacks seem to create an effective recession.'

'Ah, you have misunderstood me. Having, so to speak, forged ahead politically myself, it is easy to forget other people remain content with old notions of painting, formalistic ones. I meant, of course, that it is not always plain sailing so far as political values are concerned. I am no longer interested in such purely technical achievements as correct recession, so called, or making a kind of pattern.'

'Still, incorrect recession can surely play havoc – unless, of course, deliberate distortion is in question. Was your change of technique gradual?'

Tokenhouse gave a restive intake of breath to show how wildly he had been misunderstood.

'One forgets, one forgets. Let me explain. I had begun to feel very impatient with Formalism, the sort of painting that derived from Impressionists and Post-Impressionists, not to mention their successors, such as the Surrealists – as I prefer to call them, Pseudo-Realists. I thought about it all a lot. I long pondered the phrase read somewhere: "A picture is an act of Socialism." I don't expect you're familiar with that approach. You may not agree anyway. Your dissent is immaterial to me. I made up my mind to embark on a fresh start. I began by taking a bus over the bridge to Mestre, and attempting some *plein air* studies. I set about one of those large installations there – hydro-electric, or whatever they are – a suitably functional conception. Absurd as that may seem, I created the impression of being engaged on some sort of industrial espionage. Nothing serious happened, but it was all rather tedious and discouraging. Much more important than the interfering attitude of the authorities was my own fear that Impressionist errors were creeping back, just as fallaciously as if I was one of the old ladies sitting on a camp-stool in front of the Salute. In short, I comprehended I was still hopelessly aesthetic.'

'I'd never call you an aesthete, Dan.'

Tokenhouse laughed shortly.

'Certainly not in the nineteenth-century use of the word. All the same, you have to watch yourself. We all have to. That was specially true of my next phase, when I thought I would try Political Symbolism. The effect was very mixed. I've painted-over quite a lot of them, wiped them out completely. This is one of the rather better efforts I preserved. It was completed quite soon after my breach with retrospection – accepting the past, I mean, simply as a point of departure. The important thing was I had learnt by then that Naturalism was not enough.'

'Like patriotism?'

Tokenhouse paid no attention, either because he never cared for flippancy, or, more likely, had passed beyond paying attention to most remarks made by other people. He had begun to speak quickly, excitedly, almost gabbling this account of his own development as a painter, reciting his painting creed like a lesson learnt by heart.

'I suddenly saw in a flash, a revelation, that I could not retain any remnant of self-respect, if I gave way to Formalism again in the slightest degree. I *must* satisfy my own conviction that a new ideological content had to be infused into painting, one free of all taints of neutrality. That was just as important for an amateur like myself, as for a professional painter of long standing and successful attainment.'

Like an onlooker dexterously exposing an attempt to deceive in manipulation of the Three-Card Trick, Tokenhouse seized the three studies of miracle-rigging priests, two in his right hand, one in his left, with incredible speed setting in their place a single example of his interim period. It was larger in size than earlier exhibits, brighter in colour. Most of his pictures, Formalist or Reformed, were apt to end up a superfluity of brownish-carmine tones. This latest canvas, vermilion and light cobalt, showed the origins of the fresco technique in representation of what were evidently factory workers, stripped to the waist, pushing over a precipice a disordered group of kings and bishops, easily recognizable by their crowns and mitres. Perhaps deliberately, treatment of posture and movement was a trifle wooden, but the painter had clearly taken a certain pleasure in depicting irresolute terror in the features of monarchs and ecclesiastics toppling into the abyss. The subject suggested, not for the first time in the character of Tokenhouse, a touch of muted sadism, revealed occasionally in conversation, otherwise kept, so far as one knew, in check.

'I found Politico-Symbolism, for a person of my limited imaginative faculties, a *cul de sac*. My aim latterly has been to depict social injustice in as straightforward a manner as possible, compatible with avoiding that too passive Realism of which I have spoken. My own constricted skill has prevented me from attempting some of the more ambitious subjects I have in mind, though I like to think there are signs of improvement. Ah-ha, you do too? I am glad. It is simply a question of documentation in the last resort. You meditate along the correct political lines, the picture almost paints itself. Look at this – and this.'

We inspected a representative collection of Tokenhouse's more recent work.

'I don't want to bore you with my efforts. Shall we set out for the Biennale? If you want to see more, we could look in again after lunch, but I expect you've had enough by now.'

He found an ashplant walking-stick, placed on his head a battered grey hat with a greenish-black ribbon, turned down the brim all round, opened the door of the flat. We set off for the Giardini, Tokenhouse at his habitual short rapid stride, a military quickstep, suggesting chronic fear of unpunctuality. He hurried along, hob-nailed shoes grinding the cobbles.

'I'm feeling rather pleased about a letter received this morning. I've been revising my will, terms that may surprise some people, among others making the lawyers agree to insert a clause for no religious ceremony at the funeral. They didn't like it. Don't like that sort of thing, even these days. I had my way. No nonsense of that sort. Well, tell me about your Conference. What do you all discuss? Plenty of nonsense talked there, I'll be bound.'

'The Philosophy of Engagement – Obligations of the Writer – the Arts in relation to World Government – all that sort of thing.'

'Ah-ha, yes. There can be serious sides to such questions, but they are rarely tackled. Now those attending your Conference, do any emigré writers from the USSR, or Balkan countries, turn up there? One would be interested to hear what such people are saying and thinking, especially the Russians. For example how they react to the "thaw", as people call it. I've been looking through a novel called *Dr Zhivago*. I expect you've heard of it. It's been given a good deal of publicity. I suppose that sort of book, purporting as it does to present the point of view of certain members of a generation very much on their way out, might give a certain amount of satisfaction to expatriate Russians? Those who've chosen to dissociate themselves from the great developments taking place in their country. It would gratify them, a book like that, by stilling their self-reproach. Have you come across instances of that? One would be interested to hear.'

'I haven't met any emigré Russians at the Conference. I couldn't swear none are there.'

'Which again reminds me. There's a certain Dr Belkin who might have turned up. He visits Venice from time to time. Usually lets me know at the last moment.'

'Not an emigré?'

'No, no. Far from it. A man of the soundest views in his own country. He informed me some little while ago he might be looking in on this congress, or one about this time. He enjoys coming to Venice, because he's devoted to painting. He's even kind enough to be interested in my own humble brush. Of course my sort of painting is practised comparatively little in Western Europe. Nice of him to include a novice like myself in his survey. He's been to visit me several times. Naturally we see eye to eye politically.'

'Somebody else was asking about him.'

'Belkin has many friends. I do what I can to keep him up to date about books and things. Hold them for him sometimes, if he's afraid they'll go astray in the post. That avoids delay in the long run. He admits his own impatience with some of the bureaucracy unavoidable in getting an entirely new system of government working, a revolutionary one. We all have to face that. There's quite a lot of stuff he prefers to collect personally when he turns up here.'

'Somebody said they thought he wouldn't be able to come to the Conference.'

'Very possibly not. It's of no great importance. I can hold his stuff for him. I always like to see Belkin. Such a cheerful fellow. Full of ideas. Where does this Conference of yours meet?'

'Over there on San Giorgio.'

A mist of heat hung over the dome and white campanile, beyond the glittering greenish stretch of water, across the surface of which needles of light perpetually flashed. It was so calm the halcyon's fabled nest seemed just to have floated by, subduing the faintest tremor of wind and wave. We reached the Gardens, and entered the cool of the lime trees. Tokenhouse made for the enclosure permanently consecrated to the cluster of strange little pavilions, which, every two years, house pictures and sculpture by which each country of the world chooses to be known to an international public.

'We'll look at everything. Just to get an idea how low the art of painting has fallen in these latter days of capitalism. You were speaking of the obligations of the artist. I hope someone has pointed out that art has been in the hands of snobs and speculators too long. Indeed, I can guarantee that the only sanctuary from subjectless bric-à-brac here will be in the national pavilions of what you no doubt term the Iron Curtain countries. We will visit the USSR first.'

The white pinnacled kiosk-like architecture of a small building, no doubt dating from pre-Revolutionary times, seemed by its outwardly church-like style to renew the ecclesiological atmosphere that pursued Tokenhouse throughout life. Within, total embargo on aesthetic abstraction proved his forecast correct. We loitered for a while over Black Sea mutineers and tractor-driving peasants. Never able wholly to control a taste for antagonism, even against his own recently voiced opinions, Tokenhouse shook his head more than once over these images of a way of life he approved, here found wanting in executive ability.

'Don't think I'm lapsing into aestheticism in complaining that some of these scenes from the Heroic Epoch seem a little lacking in inspiration. Not all of this expresses with conviction the Unity of the Masses. I shall return for a further assessment. Now we will marvel at the subjective inanities you probably much prefer.'

Tokenhouse showed no illwill in exploring the other national selections on view, my own presence giving excuse to examine what, alone, might have caused him to suffer guilt at inspecting at all.

'Absurd,' he kept muttering. 'Preposterous.'

In the French pavilion we came upon Ada Leintwardine and Louis Glober. They were standing before a massive work, seven or eight foot high, chiefly constructed from tin or zinc, horsehair, patent leather and cardboard. Ada was holding forth on its points, good and bad, Glober listening with a tolerant smile. Glober saw us first.

'Hi.'

As neither of them seemed attached to a party, it was to be supposed they had become sufficiently friendly at the Bragadin palace to arrange a visit to the Biennale together. There was the possibility, a remote one, that both had decided to spend Sunday morning at the Exhibition, run across each other by chance. Ada wore a skirt and carried a guidebook, outer marks of serious sightseeing, but the idea of Glober setting out on his own for such a trip was scarcely credible. Ada's immediate assumption of the exaggeratedly welcoming manner of one caught in compromising circumstances was not very convincing either. The Biennale was hardly the place for a secret assignation.

'Why, hullo,' she said. 'Everyone seems to have decided to come here today. What fun. We're having such an argument about the things on show, especially this one. Mr Glober sees African overtones, influenced by Ernst. To me the work's much more redolent of Samurai armour designed by Schwitters.'

To recognize a potential pivot of Conference gossip, a touch of piquancy, in detection of the pair of them together, was reasonable enough on Ada's part. Glober's greeting too, his serenely hearty manner always retaining a certain degree of irony, was seasoned this time with a small injection of deliberately roguish culpability. Nevertheless, their combined acceptance of giving cause for interesting speculation could not be taken at absolute face value. Pretence to an exciting vulnerability was more likely to be demanded by sexual prestige, an implied proposition that something was 'on', no more than mutual tribute to each other's status as 'attractive people'. That was to take a cool commonsense-inspired view. At the same time, the significance of so rapid a move towards association together was not to be altogether ignored, even if Glober, as playboy-tycoon, was no longer in his first youth; Ada, near-bestseller, mother of twins, alleged to prefer her own sex.

Ada's pronouncements on the subject of the artefact in front of us, extensive and well-informed, continued for some minutes, so there was no immediate opportunity to introduce Tokenhouse. He was contemplating the metal-and-leather framework with unconcealed dislike, dissatisfied, too, at prospect of meeting strangers, particularly an American, representing by his nationality all sorts of political and social attitudes to be disapproved. A pause in Ada's talk giving opportunity to tell him she was a well-known novelist, also active force in a publisher's office, so to speak, on the other side of the counter, he showed no awareness of her writing, but grudgingly muttered something about having heard of her husband. When, on the other hand, Glober's name was announced, Tokenhouse displayed an altogether unexpected remembrance of him. He seemed positively glad to meet Glober again after thirty years.

'You're the man who put up the idea of the Cubist series. Of course you are. I'm not in the least interested in Cubists now, with their ridiculous aesthetic ideas, but I thought them a good proposition at the time, and I haven't changed my mind about that. It was a good proposition then. I was quite right.'

This looked, at first, an altogether remarkable example of Glober's mastery of those attributes which impose their owner's personality for life; even after so trivial a business contact as that which had brought Tokenhouse and himself together. Then there turned out to exist a more tangible cause than Glober's charm, in itself, to stimulate Tokenhouse's memory. He began to chatter away in his rapid, assertive, disconnected manner, which, once under way, was impossible to check, however ill-adapted, or unintelligible, to his listeners.

'We made the blocks for the Cubist illustrations. They were never used. Your firm went out of business, but it wasn't due to that. Several American publishers went bust about that time. Some of the most active, as regards what were then new ideas. The whole thing was called off for quite other reasons. It was a great pity. I always held we could have made a success of things. I had a row with my board about it. They accused me of behaving in a high-handed manner. Very well, I said, if you think that, I'll pay for the blocks myself. I'll buy them at cost price. I'll stand the damage. They'll be my property. They could make no objection to that. So long as publishing remains in private hands, it might just as well be for my profit, as for that of any other speculator. I'd use them in my own good time. That was what happened. They've been in store ever since. I own them to this day. I stick to it that they would have made a good series in the light of what was being thought at the time.'

Tokenhouse was quite breathless by the end of his speech, excitement similar to that displayed by him when expatiating on what painting should be. Glober took in the situation at once. He grasped that he was dealing with an eccentric, one in a high class of his category, and roared with laughter. Glober may not have remembered much about Tokenhouse personally (he had shown no sign when I spoke of him earlier), but he appreciated that he was in the presence of an oddity, from whom amusement might, for the moment, be derived. Perhaps the notion of Tokenhouse buying the Cubists blocks appealed to Glober as, on however infinitesimal a scale, a touch of his own method, an element of playboy-tycoonery. That was in spite of Tokenhouse being, on the surface, about as far from a playboy as you could get, while his former status of tycoon, if ever to be so called, was an inconceivably modest one. Perhaps that was a misjudgment, however diluted, the characteristics being present in Tokenhouse too. The important fact was that, reunited with Glober, he was pleased to see him.

'Maybe we were men before our time, Mr Tokenhouse. Too ready to experiment with new ideas too early. I'm sorry it all ended that way. Not long after we met in London, I abandoned publishing for motion pictures. When I came back to publishing for a while, things had greatly changed. That was why I returned to the Coast.'

'Yes, yes.'

Tokenhouse spoke inattentively, still thinking about the blocks, certainly unapprised of 'the Coast', or why Glober should return there. This talk of publishing must have struck Ada as a useful opening. She had accepted without the least umbrage lack of acquaintance with herself as a novelist. The blocks offered as good, if not better, opportunity for impressing Glober with her own abilities.

'I should like to hear more about the Cubist blocks, Mr Tokenhouse. My husband's firm would certainly be glad to consider the question of taking them over from you, should you be interested in an advantageous price. In these days of steeply mounted production charges, they might find a place in our list.'

Tokenhouse, never much at ease with women, especially good-looking ones, approached this proposition with caution, but without open hostility. The incomparable training of having worked as Sillery's secretary behind her, Ada had made rather a speciality of handling the older generation of Quiggin & Craggs authors, becoming so accomplished in that respect that she might now be indulging in mere display of that dexterity for its own sake. Whether or not she wanted the blocks, Tokenhouse accepted the principle of a tender. He began to discuss a lot of not specially interesting technical particulars. Retirement from publishing, changed taste in art, revised ideological opinions, had none of them blunted a keen business sense. Ada showed no less briskness about the potential deal. Glober looked at his watch.

'Have you and Mr Tokenhouse any plans for luncheon? Mrs Quiggin and I – should I say Miss Leintwardine? – were going to the restaurant here. Why don't you both join us?'

Ada looked for a moment as if she might have preferred to keep Glober to herself, a natural enough instinct, then changed her mind, welcoming the suggestion.

'Do let's all lunch together – and call me Ada.'

Tokenhouse also hesitated for a moment at thus entangling himself with forms of social life against which he had openly declared war, but he had by no means finished what he had to say about the blocks. Having in any case planned to eat at the restaurant, refusal was difficult. Even if his reluctance, and Ada's, had been more determined, Glober's pressure to enlarge the party might have surmounted that too. To deny him would have required a lot of energy. If he had an ulterior motive, long or short term, nothing of the sort was apparent. As before in the Palazzo, he seemed to hope for no more than to collect round him as many persons as available. That was simply because collecting people round him (creating one of those rudimentary courts adumbrated by Dr Brightman) brought a sense of confidence in himself. Finally, everyone had by that time seen as much of the Exhibition as desired, whether to praise or blame. Art was abandoned. It was agreed the party should lunch together. We strolled across to the restaurant, finding a table to allow a good view of the water. Glober inquired about drinks.

'A nerone,' said Ada. 'With an urgent request for plenty of gin.'

Tokenhouse declared that he never took more than a single glass of wine in the middle of the day. Glober would not hear of that. So gently importunate was he about everyone having an aperitif that in the end Token-house, obstinate in his habits as a rule, surprisingly gave way, agreeing to begin with a 'punt è mes'. That was more of a triumph than Glober knew. He went on to make suggestions about what he should eat, judicious so far as that went, even if originating in a wish to impose the will. They were not acceptable to Ada. When Quiggin had married her, he had still taken pride in being an austere man – like most persons of that preten-sion, imposing frugality on his acquaintances, while making a lot of fuss himself, if food happened not to be absolutely to his own taste. Ada put an end to all that. Under her sway, Quiggin would now discuss bad wine, salad dressings, regional dishes, with the best. Such gastronomic ascendancy behind her, Ada was not likely to accept dictation from Glober.

Tokenhouse did not join in this chatter about food. He ordered spaghetti for himself, and sat back in silence. He would probably have liked to continue talking about blocks, but Ada must have decided nothing more could be settled about the matter until put before Quiggin. The fact was, Tokenhouse had lost the habit of this sort of party. In his publishing days he had gone out a good deal, possessing the reputation of an aggressive talker when the evening was well advanced, and he had taken a fair amount to drink. Even dead sober, he was usually prepared to shout down the rest of the party, if there were disagreements. Now he gave the impression of once more beginning to disapprove, earlier distrust of such company re-aroused in him. He was rather cross when Glober nodded for a repetition of the drinks, but swal-lowed the second glass of vermouth, also took several deep gulps of wine when it arrived. Ada switched her attention to him, now offering a clue to her own easy acceptance of breaking up a tête-à-tête with Glober.

'You never published any of St John Clarke's novels, Mr Tokenhouse, did you?'

Tokenhouse, who had been particularly irritated when St John Clarke failed to produce the promised Introduction to *The Art of Horace Isbister,* made some non-committal answer about his firm not dealing in fiction, which Ada must have known already. She pressed the subject, not, so it appeared, because Tokenhouse was likely to throw light on St John Clarke, as from some wish of her own to emphasize the almost forgotten novelist's unrecognized merits. Then her aim became clearer.

'Louis – I shall call you Louis, Mr Glober – has come to Europe to look for a story to film. Of course, I hoped he would want one of my own novels – in default of one of yours, Nick – but we've been talking together, and he was saying the moment must have arrived for something nostalgic, something Edwardian. Then I had the brilliant idea that St John Clarke was the answer.'

This was rather a different story from Pamela's statement that Glober was going to film something by Trapnel. What subject Glober should choose struck me at the time as a perfectly endurable topic, during luncheon in these fairly idyllic surroundings, not one to take for a moment seriously. The same applied to Pamela's earlier words on the matter, in that case easing the way for Gwinnett. Commercial deals like selling stories to film companies are more likely to emerge from tedious negotiation undertaken by agents in prosaic offices. Such was one's melancholy conclusion. Glober, if not a producer in the top class, had been quite a figure in Hollywood; he was therefore tough. No doubt his mood accorded with this sort of chit-chat. To conclude any true buyer's interest had been aroused would be to misconstrue the ways of film tycoons. All the same, to be too matter-of-fact about such possibilities could be wide of the mark, as to be too susceptive to pleasing possibilities. With businessmen, you can never tell; least of all when movies are in question. On Ada's part, this looked like declaration of war on Pamela. She sounded very sure of herself.

'Perhaps you don't know, Nick, that we control the St John Clarke rights now. Clapham got the lot before he died. Just for the sake of tidiness – but I forgot, you probably do know, because St John Clarke left the royalties to your Warminster brother-in-law, and of course they came back to Quiggin & Craggs in the Warminster Trust. JG secured our own interest before Craggs died.'

What Ada stated made sense. I had not known about the St John Clarke rights; at least never thought out that aspect. She was undoubtedly going to do her best to sell a St John Clarke novel to Glober.

'A strange man I used to know in the army was devoted to *Match Me Such Marvel*. He'd worked in a provincial theatre or cinema, so he might be the right pointer for popular success.'

Bithel's view, twenty years later, could represent the winning number. Ada was enthusiastic.

'*Match Me Such Marvel* is the one I suggested. There's a homosexual undercurrent. Of course, you Americans are so jumpy about homosexuality. It would be a great pity to leave that sequence out.'

'Who. says we're going to leave it out?' said Glober lazily. 'We Americans are getting round to hearing about all sorts of things of that kind these days. You don't do us justice. When were you last in the States, Ada?'

They were a well matched couple when it came to that sort of teasing, as cover for business negotiation. Tokenhouse, likely to disapprove of such levity, was ruminating on some matter of his own. Suddenly he joined in.

'St John Clarke was a vain fellow. I never cared for such novels of his as I read. He behaved in a most unsatisfactory manner dealing with my firm. It was only quite by chance I came across a pamphlet he had written in the latter part of his life dealing with an interest of my own, that is to say Socialist Realism in painting. That pamphlet was not without merit.'

Ada showed herself more than equal to this comment too. Her policy was, I think, to ventilate in a general way the claims of St John Clarke; get his name thoroughly into Glober's head, without bothering too much whether the impression was good or bad. When St John Clarke had sunk in as a personality, she would plug the book she wanted to be filmed. She showed warm appreciation of this new aspect of the novelist.

'Exactly, Mr Tokenhouse. St John Clarke is no back-number. His style may seem a little old-fashioned today, but there is nothing old-fashioned about his thought. He is full of compassion – compassion of his own sort, sometimes a little crudely expressed to the modern ear. I am most interested in what you say about his art criticism. I had missed that. Of course I know about Socialist Realism. I expect you used to read a magazine called *Fission*, which ran for a couple of years just after the war, and remember the instructive analysis Len Pugsley wrote there, called *Integral Foundations of a Fresh Approach to Art for the Masses.*'

Tokenhouse got out his pencil. Making Ada repeat the title of Pugsley's article, he wrote it on a paper table napkin. I recalled Bagshaw's editorial irritation at having to publish the piece.

'If we've got to print everything written by whoever's rogering Gypsy, we'll have to get a new paper allocation. Even our Commy subscribers don't want to read that stuff.'

Bagshaw's comment, partially disproved by Tokenhouse's interest, was borne out to the extent that Gypsy (retaining her name and style) had gone to live with Pugsley, when she became a widow. Tokenhouse now found himself assailed by Ada with an absolute barrage of expertise on his own subject. She began to reel off the names of what were evidently Socialist Realist painters.

'Svatogh? Gaponenko? Toidze? I can only remember a few of the ones Len mentioned. Of course you'll be familiar with all their pictures, and lots more. There is so much in art of which one remains so dreadfully ignorant. I must look into all that side of painting again, when I have a moment to spare.'

Tokenhouse, who had certainly begun luncheon in a mood of refusal to truckle to undue demands on making himself agreeable, could not fail to be impressed. I was impressed myself. In her days as employee at Quiggin & Craggs, the Left Wing bias of the firm had naturally demanded a smattering of Marxist vocabulary, but to retain enough political small talk of that period to meet Tokenhouse on his own Socialist Realist ground was no small achievement; not less because Quiggin himself, anyway commercially, had so far abrogated his own principles as to have lately scored a publishing bull's eye with the Memoirs of a Tory 'elder statesman'. Glober laughed quietly to himself.

'You two take me back to the Film Writers' Guild. Give me two minutes notice to beat it, before you throw the bomb.'

Seen closer, over a longer period, he was observable as a little tired, a little melancholy, amusing himself with mild jaunts such as this one, which made small demand on valuable reserves. He was husbanding his forces. To suppose that in no way implied a state of total exhaustion. You felt there was quite a lot left for future effort, even if requirement for everything to be played out in public, in a manner at once striking and elegant, increased need for exceptional energy. What did not happen in public had no reality for Glober at all. In spite of the quiet manner, there was no great suggestion of interior life. What was going on inside remained there only until it could be materially expressed as soon as possible. The tress of hair had to record the sexual conquest.

To unAmerican eyes, probing the mysteries of American comportment and observance, this seemed the antithesis of Gwinnett. Much going on in Gwinnett was never likely to find outward expression. That was how it looked. No doubt a European unfamiliarity heightened, rather than diminished, the contrast; even caricatured its salient features. That did not remove all substance, the core seeming to be the ease with which Glober manipulated the American way; Gwinnett's awkwardness in its employment. That was to put things crudely, possibly even wrongly, just consequence of meeting both in Europe. Glober, only recently sprung from the Continent, had about him something of the old fashioned Jamesian American, seeking new worlds to conquer. Gwinnett was not at all like that. With Gwinnett, everything was within himself. He had, so it seemed, come to Europe simply because he was passionately interested in Trapnel, obsessed by him, personally identified with him; again, one felt, inwardly, rather than outwardly.

Dr Brightman had called Gwinnett a 'gothic' American. What, in contrast, would she call Glober? She had invoked Classicism and Romanticism. Here again it was hard to apportion epithets. In one sense, Glober, the practical man, was also the 'romantic' – as often happens – Gwinnett, working on his own interior lines, the 'classical'. Gwinnett wanted to see things without their illusory trimmings; Glober forced things into his own picturesque mould. In doing that, Glober retained some humour. Could the same be said of Gwinnett? Would Gwinnett, for example, be capable of taking pleasure in Tokenhouse as a medium for amusement? Was the analogy to be found in quite other terms of reference: Don Juan for Glober, Gwinnett in Faust?

The wine, passing round rather rapidly, may have

played some part in these reflections. Tokenhouse was by now a little tight. Age, or abstinence, must have weakened his head. Perhaps solitude, sheer lack of opportunity to air his views, caused a few glasses to release the urgent need to hold forth again at a crowded table. He now proceeded to reproduce, in greatly extended form, the lecture he had given me earlier on the necessity for rejecting Formalism. In doing this, Tokenhouse passed all reasonable bounds of dialectical prosiness. Glober, showing American tolerance for persons outlining a favourite theme with searching thoroughness, did not interrupt him, but, when coffee came, Tokenhouse had gone too far in presuming on national forbearance in indicating to a compulsive talker that he has become a bore. By that time Tokenhouse had admitted he painted himself. Glober leant across the table.

'Now see here, Mr Tokenhouse. We're going to drink a glass of strega, then we're all coming back to your studio to admire your work.'

That took Tokenhouse so much by surprise that he scarcely demurred at the strega, protesting only briefly, as a matter of form. It was hard for an amateur painter – he kept on making a point of this status – to be other than flattered. It was agreed the party should make their way to the flat after leaving the restaurant. When the bill arrived, Glober insisted on paying. He swept aside energetic, if rambling, efforts on the part of Tokenhouse to prevent this on grounds that I was his guest. They argued for a time, Tokenhouse producing a ten-thousand-lire note, Glober thrusting it aside. We set off at last, Tokenhouse still talking hard. He was not drunk in any derogatory sense, had merely taken a little more than accustomed, which had transformed a prickly detachment into discursiveness not to be checked. He hurried along, the old grey hat jammed down on his head, swinging his stick, Glober taking long strides to keep up. Ada and I followed a short way behind.

'How on earth did you know the names of those painters, Ada? Are they Russian?'

Ada smiled, justifiably pleased with herself.

'Len Pugsley's at our Lido hotel. He'd brought the article with him, as basis of a speech he's going to make at the Conference. Getting something published in *Fission* was his first real step in life.'

'His last one too. Why hasn't he appeared?'

'Len's got a stomach upset. He's in bed. He wanted to rehearse his speech. He read it all to me. I say, I hear from Glober the Widmerpools have had a terrible row.'

'Isn't that a permanent state?'

'This one's worse than usual.'

Ada could offer no more at that moment, because Glober, fearing dispersal of his court, or that its courtiers were plotting against him, turned back to make sure we were included in whatever he was discussing with Tokenhouse. A few minutes later we entered the narrow calle in which the flat was situated. Tokenhouse led the way up the stairs. He opened the door, pointing ahead.

'Seat yourselves. I'm afraid there is nothing luxurious about my way of life. You must excuse that, take me as you find me, a humble amateur painter.'

He stumped off in the direction of the canvases in the corner.

Glober looked round the room.

'Mr Tokenhouse, you ought to advertise your studio as Annex to the Biennale Exposition.'

'I should, I should. I shall have to wait another two years now.'

Tokenhouse laughed excitedly, shuffling about arranging pictures at every angle. Glober's interest must have encouraged him to widen the scope of what he was prepared to display. In addition to those shown in the morning were others stacked in two cupboards.

'Do I detect the influence of Diego Rivera, Mr Tokenhouse?'

'Ah-ha, you may, you may.'

'Or is it José Clemente Orozco, who did those frescoes at Dartmouth? There is something of that artist too.'

Tokenhouse was in ecstasies, if such a word could be used of him at all.

'I would not deny influence of the former. I am less familiar with the work of the latter. I flatter myself in these experiments in style, now wholly abandoned, I have caught a small touch of Rivera's gift for speaking in a popular language. This, for instance – now who the devil can that be?'

A heavy knock had been given on the outside door. Tokenhouse set down the two pictures he was holding. He did not go to the door at once. Instead, he took a small diary from his pocket, and studied it. The knock came again. Tokenhouse, put out by this interruption, went into the passageway. The sound came of the door being opened, followed by muffled conversation. The caller's inquiry had not been audible. Tokenhouse's answer was testy, almost shrill.

'Yes, yes. Of course he mentioned your name to me. More than once in the past. I had no idea you were attending the Conference. You're not? Ah-ha, I see. Well, come in then. It's not very convenient, but now you're here, you'd better stay. I have some people looking at my pictures. Yes, my pictures, I said – but you can wait till they're gone. Then we can have a talk.'

He returned to the studio-room accompanied by Widmerpool.

'This is – did you say Lord – yes, Lord Widmerpool. Ah-ha, you know everybody. That makes things easier.'

Tokenhouse spoke the word 'Lord' with great contempt. Neither he, nor Widmerpool himself, looked in the least as if they believed the fact of 'knowing every-one' made things easier. Tokenhouse had spoken the words bitterly, ironically. In his own eyes nothing much worse could happen, now that his Private View had been interrupted, the chance of a lifetime mucked up; Widmerpool, armed with an introduction, arriving at this particular moment. Tokenhouse seemed to know in-stinctively that Widmerpool felt no interest whatever in pictures, good or bad.

'Take a seat.'

Widmerpool looked round. There was no very ob-vious place to do so. He was undoubtedly surprised at finding Glober, Ada, myself, here; not more so than I, that he should suppose it advantageous to visit Token-house. The connexion could hardly be publishing. By the time Widmerpool, in an advisory capacity, had been on the Quiggin & Craggs board, Tokenhouse's days as a publisher were over. Possibly some link went back to Widmerpool's time in a solicitor's office; his former firm perhaps that recording the ban on religious rites at the Tokenhouse obsequies. Widmerpool had plainly not been warned that painting was Tokenhouse's hobby. He stared rather wildly at the pictures propped up all over the room, then nodded to each of us in turn.

'Yes – we all know each other. How are you, Ada? We haven't met since *Fission,* I expect you're at the Conference, or come for the Film Festival?'

The last suggestion seemed to have struck him on the spur of the moment, probably on account of Glober's film connections. Ada pretended to be piqued.

'Didn't you notice me at the Bragadin palace, Ken-neth? I saw you. Pam and I talked away. I should have thought she'd have mentioned that to you.'

Widmerpool, discerning a probe for information, rather than expression of wounded feelings, gave nothing away. He smiled.

'Pam often forgets to tell me things. We think it best

not to live in each other's pockets. It makes married life easier. You would agree, wouldn't you, Louis?'

'I sure would.'

Glober laughed in his usual quiet friendly way, which did not at all conceal dislike. He also took the opportunity of stating his own situation.

'Mrs Quiggin and I were discussing the Biennale the time her Conference was looking over Jacky's place. We thought we'd take a look at the Biennale pictures together too. Who should we meet but Mr Jenkins and Mr Tokenhouse. Now we're admiring Mr Tokenhouse's pictures instead of those at the Biennale.'

That was brief, exact description of just what had happened. If Glober had designs on Pamela – it was hard to think otherwise – he might welcome opportunity of emphasizing to Widmerpool that he had 'picked up' Ada, accordingly was not to be taken as too serious a competitor for Pamela. Such was just a notion that occurred. If it displayed Glober's intention, Widmerpool showed no sign of appreciating the point.

'I see.'

He spoke flatly, staring round again at the rows of small canvases that cluttered the studio. Obviously they conveyed nothing to him. He appeared more than ever worried, but made an effort.

'Have you collected these over the years, Mr Tokenhouse?'

Tokenhouse looked furious.

'I painted them.'

He snapped out the answer.

'Yourself. I see. How clever.'

Widmerpool said that without the smallest irony.

'Merely a hobby. Not at all clever. The last thing they are – or I should wish them to be – is clever.'

Tokenhouse did not conceal his annoyance. Widmerpool had ruined the afternoon. Here were all his pictures spread out, a relatively sympathetic audience to whom he could preach his own theories of art, a unique occasion, in short, wrecked by the arrival of a self-important stranger – a 'lord' at that – with an introduction, presumably about some business matter. Again, it was hard to see what business interests Widmerpool and Tokenhouse could share, yet the connexion was clearly not a friendly one, some common acquaintance's suggestion that the two of them would get on well together. Although nettled, Tokenhouse did not seem exactly taken aback. Widmerpool, after whatever had been said at the door, must represent some burden liable to be shouldered sooner or later. The botheration was for such responsibility to have descended at this moment. Tokenhouse, accepting the party was over, like a child putting away its toys, began gloomily replacing the canvases in the nearer cupboard. Then one of Glober's gestures went some way towards saving the situation.

'Just a moment, Mr Tokenhouse. Don't be in such a hurry with those pictures of yours. Would you consider a sale? If you would – and don't tell me to hell with it – I'd like to know your price for the shipwreck scene.'

He pointed to one of the illustrations of social injustice, such it must be, seemingly enacted on the crowded deck of a boat, where several persons were in trouble. Tokenhouse paused in his tidying up. He visibly responded to the inquiry.

'Sell a picture?'

'That's what I hoped.'

Tokenhouse considered.

'I've only been asked that once before, apart from an occasion years ago – in my Formalist days – when requested to present a picture of mine to be raffled for a charity. It was one of those typical feckless efforts to bolster up the capitalist system – some parson at the bottom of it, of course – attempting to launch that sort of ameliorating endeavour, which I now recognize as worse, more deliberately harmful, than brutal indiff-

151

erence, and should now naturally refuse to have anything to do with. '

Tokenhouse turned to Widmerpool. He spoke rather spitefully.

'The only other occasion when I sold one of my pictures was to our mutual friend. The friend who sent you here. He very kindly bought one of my efforts.'

Widmerpool seemed further embarrassed. He started slightly. Then he made a movement of the hand to express appreciation.'

'Oh, yes. Did he, indeed? I didn't know he liked painting.'

'Of course he does. He bought one of the army incidents. I called it *Any Complaints?* A typical mess-room injustice about rations. To buy it was a charming return for a small service I had been able to perform for him. I had, of course, expected no such return, having acted entirely from principle.'

'I'm sorry I didn't know you were an artist,' said Widmerpool.

There was silence. Tokenhouse blew his nose. Glober returned to the question of buying a picture himself.

'Then I take it you will sell one, Mr Tokenhouse?'

'I see no reason why not, no reason at all.'

'The emigrant ship?'

'They are a poor family found travelling without a ticket on the vaporetto.'

'Better still. A souvenir of Venice. That's fine.'

Glober, certainly aware of Widmerpool's impatience to speak with Tokenhouse alone, was determined not to be hurried. Tokenhouse, equally recognizing Widmerpool's claim on him, whatever that was, also showed no scruple about keeping him waiting. He seemed almost to enjoy doing so. Glober inquired about terms. Widmerpool was getting increasingly restive. He fidgeted about. Glober began to argue that the sum Tokenhouse had named as price for his picture was altogether inadequate. A discussion now developed similar to that about paying the restaurant bill. At last Widmerpool could bear it no longer. He interrupted them.

'I expect you know our mutual friend was unable to come?'

He addressed himself to Tokenhouse, who took no notice of this comment.

'Our friend is not here,' Widmerpool repeated.

Although clear we should have to go soon, the strain of waiting for that moment was telling on him. Tokenhouse merely nodded, as much as to say he accepted that as regrettable, though of no great importance.

'He mentioned when I last saw him he might not be able to undertake the trip this time . . . Now, about wrappings. It will have to be newspaper. You must not mind it being a not very pro-American journal.'

Tokenhouse laughed quite heartily at his own joke. The all but unprecedented sale of a picture had for the moment quite altered him. He could not be bothered with Widmerpool's problems, however grave, until the negotiation was completed.

'It's all – well – a bit unfortunate,' said Widmerpool.

'Ah-ha, it is? I'm sorry . . . Now, string? Here we are. We'll have to unknot this. I think it good to have to make use of your hands from time to time. A bourgeois upbringing has given me no aptitude in that direction. I always tie granny knots. There we are. Not a very neat parcel, I fear, but people don't fuss about that sort of thing in this quarter of Venice. There we are. There we are.'

He handed Glober the picture, enclosed now in several sheets of *Unità*. Glober took it. Tokenhouse stood back.

'Luckily my pictures are a manageable size. Patrons of Veronese or Tiepolo would need more than the painter's morning paper to bring their purchases home wrapped up.'

The name of Tiepolo seemed to cause a moment's

faint embarrassment, not only to Widmerpool, but also, for some reason, to Ada and Glober. In any case, if we did not leave, Widmerpool was soon going to request our withdrawal in so many words. I could recognize the signs. Glober, too, seeing a showdown imminent, and deciding against a head-on clash at that moment, brought matters to a close, shaking hands with Tokenhouse. Tokenhouse saw us to the top of the stairs.

'I will get in touch with you again, Nick, before you leave Venice. There might be a small package I should like you to post for me in England. The mails are very uncertain here. Ah-ha, yes. Goodbye to you then, goodbye. I'm glad we had opportunity to meet again, Mr Glober. Yes, yes. I do my poor best. Ah-ha, ah-ha. I hope I may at least have acted as a signpost away from Formalism. Yes, do let me know about the blocks, Mrs Quiggin. I quite see your position. Goodbye, goodbye.'

We left him to Widmerpool, whatever dialogues lay ahead of them. After reaching the street, nothing was said for a minute or two. Then Glober spoke.

'That was a most interesting experience – and a superb addition to my collection of twentieth-century primitives.'

'I adored Mr Tokenhouse,' said Ada. 'Those blocks could be quite a snip, if he's prepared to consider a reasonable price. I remember JG talking of him now. I'm not sure JG didn't know the psychiatrist – a Party member – who treated Tokenhouse for his breakdown, anyway treated some ex-publisher for a breakdown. He used to treat a friend of Howard Craggs, an old girl called Milly Andriadis, who died in Paris last year.'

'I once went to a party given by Mrs Andriadis,' said Glober. 'That shows how old I am.'

Neither he nor Ada spoke of Widmerpool. There seemed something almost deliberate about their avoidance of his name. Then Glober stopped suddenly.

'Oh, hell.'

'What's happened?'

'I'd forgotten that contact man I was due to see at the Gritti.'

He looked at his watch.

'I'm going to be late. What's to be done in a town without taxis, and not a gondola in sight?'

Ada pointed.

'If you run, you'll catch the circolare. It's coming up. You could just about make it.'

Glober, with a shout that we must meet again soon, seemed delighted to show his mettle as a short-distance sprinter. Taking Tokenhouse's picture from under his arm, he bounded off. We saw him catch the boat, just as the rope was thrown across the rails. He turned and waved in our direction. We waved back.

'What energy.'

'All quite unnecessary too. He's surrounded by secretaries and hangers-on of one kind or another, who are only there to give an impression big business is being transacted. I'm going to make for the Lido. Have a rest, before going out this evening with Emily Brightman.'

We walked on towards the vaporetto stop.

'Who's this American called Gwinnett that Pam's taken a fancy to?'

'Has she taken a fancy to him? He's writing a book about our old friend X. Trapnel. If you don't deflect Glober's film interests to St John Clarke, Gwinnett might help in making a Trapnel film. Did she tell you she liked him?'

Ada laughed at such an idea.

'I was hearing about Gwinnett from Glober. Can you keep a secret? Glober wants to marry Pam, not just have an affair with her. Don't breathe a word to anyone. You won't, will you? He revealed that to me when he found I was her old friend. Only in the strictest confidence.'

'What does her husband think about that? He must have had plenty of opportunities to divorce her, if he wanted. Anyway, why should she herself decide to marry Glober?'

'I doubt if Kenneth knows yet. He just thinks Glober's one of her usuals. So far as Pam is concerned, the bait Glober holds out is the lead in this great film he's going to make.'

'Pamela? But she's never acted in her life, has she?'

Ada thought that a naive reaction.

'What does that matter? Besides, Pam's no fool. If she wants a thing, she'll force herself to do it. What Glober's worried about is this young American turning up, who's a Trapnel fan. He doesn't want Gwinnett sticking round, if he does a Trapnel film. That's why he's begun to look about for another book to make his picture from. There's a character just like Pam in *Match Me Such Marvel*. Of course, St John Clarke didn't know anything about women, but a competent script-writer could alter all that.'

'Why should she want to act at all?'

'Because Pam longs for fame.'

'You mean publicity?'

'Anything you like to call it. Nobody's ever heard of her. She doesn't care for that. For one thing, she isn't keen on nobody having heard of her, and quite a lot of people having heard of me.'

'Where did Glober meet her?'

'At her father's place in Montana. Cosmo Flitton married an American, and they run a dude ranch together. Wouldn't you adore to meet some dudes? Anyway, Pam went up there to stay, when she was in the States with Kenneth, and Louis Glober fell.'

'So Cosmo Flitton's still going?'

'Not only still going, but a highly regarded figure out there, with his one arm and reputation of an old hero. Everybody's mad about him. About Pam too,

Glober says. He also decribed a scene that took place last night at Jacky Bragadin's, which went rather far even for Pam. It all arose from the Tiepolo ceiling. That was why Kenneth Widmerpool winced when Tiepolo was mentioned by Mr Tokenhouse, just before we left. Do you know the subject of the picture? I was brought up on significant form, colour values, all that sort of thing, so I hadn't particularly noticed what was being illustrated. Unlike Mr Tokenhouse, and Len Pugsley, my family always rather looked down on people who thought a picture told a story. I know about Socialist Realism, but this is an Old Master. I just saw a classical subject, and left it at that. Apparently it's a man showing his naked wife to a friend.'

Ada spoke with clinical objectivity.

'Perfectly right.'

'For some reason Pam was determined to talk about that picture all through dinner. There were a lot of people there, Glober said. She was between a monsignore and a maharaja. You know how silent she is as a rule. That night she chattered incessantly. Went on and on. Nothing would stop her. She seemed to be doing this partly to get under the skin of a lady Glober knows, called Signora Clarini, the English wife of the Italian film director, but living apart. Apparently Signora Clarini was a girl-friend of Sir Magnus Donners years ago, and now wants to marry Glober. He conveyed that in his quiet way. Pam may decide not to marry him herself, she was going to make sure Signora Clarini didn't either. She kept on talking about Donners, implying he was a voyeur.'

'Pamela's hardly in a position to take a high moral line, if only after some of the things being said about her at the more sensational end of the French press.'

Ada had not heard about the Ferrand-Sénéschal revelations. She brushed them aside. Borrit, a War Office colleague, who had served in Africa, once spoke of the

Masai tribe holding, as a tenet of faith, that all cows in the world belong to them. Ada, in similar manner, arrogated to herself all the world's gossip, sources other than her own a presumption.

'Pam didn't take a high moral line. Quite the reverse. She spoke as if she and Signora Clarini were sister whores. That, according to Glober, was what made Signora Clarini so cross.'

'This was all in front of Widmerpool?'

'That's what Glober found so fascinating. Kenneth didn't attempt to shut her up. Of course he knows by now that's impossible, but Glober thought he was not only afraid of her – almost physically afraid – but got a kind of kick from what she was saying.'

'How did their host enjoy this small talk at his table?'

'Jacky Bragadin wasn't feeling well that evening, thought he was going to have one of his attacks, so wasn't bothering much. The monsignore was one of those worldly priests, who take anything in their stride, but the maharaja didn't know where to look. Louis Glober, to relieve the tension, persuaded the maharaja to teach him cricket. Jacky Bragadin found a Renaissance mace that belonged to some famous condottiere, and they used that for a bat. The maharaja bowled a peach, Glober hit it so hard he caught Kenneth on the jaw. That made further trouble.'

'Somebody once did that with a banana at school. His face must have a radar-like attraction for fruit. Glober still wants to marry Pamela in spite of all this?'

'I think so. He's quite tough. He says all his contemporaries have drunk themselves crazy, undergone major surgery, discharged both barrels with their big toe, dropped down dead on the set, and he's not going to fall for any of that. All the same, he's disturbed about Gwinnett. Pam asked Louis if Gwinnett was queer. That's what worried him. Her interest. Is he?'

'Homosexual?'

'Of course.'

'I don't think so. I don't think he's very normal either.'

'Will Gwinnett's book about Trapnel be good? Ought we to publish it? We'll talk about that later. Here's my vaporetto. See you at the *Men of Letters/Men of Science* session. I must polish up my speech. Don't breathe a word about anything I've said, will you?'

She boarded a vessel bound for the Lido. I waited for the next boat heading towards the Grand Canal. To present Sir Magnus Donners as Candaules at the Bragadin dinner party showed imagination on Pamela's part. Bob Duport had offered much the same solution as to what Sir Magnus 'liked'.

'Donners never minded people getting off with his girls. I've heard he's a voyeur.'

Barnby, without arriving at that logical conclusion, had expressed the same mild surprise at Sir Magnus's lack of jealousy. The subject, reduced to the crude medium of the peep-hole, recalled the visit to Stourwater, when, without warning, its owner had suddenly appeared through a concealed door, decorated with the spines of dummy books, just as if he had been waiting at an observation post. The principle could clearly be extended from a mere social occasion to one with intimate overtones. The power element in both uses was obvious enough.

'Peter may have developed special tastes too,' Duport said. 'Very intensive womanizing sometimes leads to that, and no one can say Peter hasn't been intensive.'

In days when Peter Templer had been pursuing Pamela, he might easily have talked to her about Sir Magnus, even taken her to see him, but not at Stourwater, the castle by then converted to wartime uses. The fact that his former home was now a girls' school, looked on as expensive, could hardly be unpleasing to the shade of Sir Magnus, if it walked there. The practices attributed to him, justly or not, had to be admitted as inescapably grotesque, humour never more patently the enemy of sex. Perhaps Gyges, too, had felt that; as king, living his next forty years in an atmosphere of meticulous sexual normality. I should have liked to discuss the whole matter with Moreland, but, although he was no longer married to Matilda, the habits of Sir Magnus and his mistresses remained a delicate one to broach. He was like that. Moreland was not well. In fact, things looked pretty bad. He would work for a time with energy, then fall into a lethargic condition. There had been financial strains too. One of his recordings becoming in a small way a popular hit, made that side easier lately. We rarely met. He and Audrey Maclintick – whom he had never married – lived, together with a black cat, Hardicanute, an obscure, secluded life.

At the hotel desk they handed out a letter from Isobel. I took it upstairs to read. Across the top of the page, an afterthought from personal things, that amorphous yet intense substance of which family life is made up, she had scribbled a casual postscript.

'Have you seen about Ferrand-Sénéschal? Probably not as you never read the papers abroad. Fascinating rumours about Pamela Widmerpool.'

I lay on the bed and dozed. It would have been wiser to have drunk less at lunch. I felt Glober was to blame. Quite a long time later the telephone buzzed, waking me.

'Hullo?'

'Is that Mr Jenkins?'

It was a man's voice, an American's.

'Speaking.'

'It's Russell Gwinnett.'

'Why, hullo?'

There was a pause at the other end of the line. I was

not sure we had not been cut off. Then Gwinnett cleared his throat.

'Can we have a talk?'

'Of course. When?'

He seemed undecided. While he was thinking, I looked to see the time. It was well after six.

'Now, if you like. We could have a drink somewhere.'

'I can't manage right now.'

There was another long pause. He seemed to regret having called. At least he sounded as if he required help in making up his mind whether or not to ring off. It looked as if he would do that, unless I could suggest an alternative. I had no plans for the evening. Dinner with Gwinnett would solve that problem. In an odd way, prospect of his company gave a sense of adventure.

'How about dining together?'

Gwinnett considered the proposal for some seconds. The idea seemed not greatly to appeal, but in the end he concurred.

'OK.'

He made it sound a concession.

'Where shall that be?'

'Not in the hotel, I guess.'

'I agree.'

Talk took place about restaurants. Gwinnett showed himself unexpectedly knowledgeable. In this, as in other matters, he was a dark horse. We fixed on one at last, arranging to meet at the table. He showed no immediate sign of getting off the line, but did not speak, nor appear, at that juncture, to have more to say.

'Eight o'clock then?'

'OK.'

'I'll be there.'

'OK.'

I hung up. He was not an easy man. All the same, I

liked him. Later, at the restaurant, he turned up punctually. The fact that I liked him was just as well, otherwise dinner, anyway at the start, would have been tedious. I had supposed, rather complacently, that Gwinnett wanted to talk about his assignation with Pamela; report on it, ask an opinion, perhaps discuss future tactics. As the meal progressed, he showed no sign of approaching that subject. The appointment might well have foundered. Nothing was more probable. The more one thought about it, the less likely seemed any possibility of Pamela having turned up. Gwinnett had almost certainly waited, perhaps for an hour or two, in the porch of the Basilica, then trudged back to the hotel. That was the picture. In any case, now we were together, he had to be allowed to approach the matter on his own terms. To force an issue would be fatal. Without going into details about Tokenhouse, I mentioned meeting Glober at the Biennale, lunching in his company. Gwinnett showed no interest. He talked of Conference matters. He was preparing a report for his College. The College, so it appeared, had arranged his attendance with that in view, the Venetian visit combined with London, for Trapnel research. He asked if I had known Dr Brightman for long.

'I met her for the first time here. I'd read some of her books.'

Gwinnett spoke highly of Dr Brightman, the good impression she had made on the Faculty, when exchange professor, her influence on his own way of looking at things. He said all that quite simply, in the manner Americans achieve, without self-consciousness or affectation, serious comment that, in English terms, would require – at least almost certainly receive – less direct unvarnished treatment. He let fall that his family had moved to New England after the Civil War. The impression was of an unusual, rather lonely young man, who had sustained a kind of intellectual nourishment from an older woman, with whom no sort of cross-currents of gender, not the slightest, were in question. I still wondered what was his trouble, the wound that had somehow maimed him. Dr Brightman must have been understanding about whatever that might be. Dinner was nearly at an end, when, quite suddenly, he turned to the subject of Pamela. This employment of two personalities in himself was possibly deliberate; voluntary or involuntary, characteristic of him.

'She showed up at San Marco.'

'She did?'

'Yes.'

Gwinnett's follow-up took so long to arrive that there were moments when it looked as if these words were all the information he proposed to give about the meeting.

'Is she likely to produce any usable Trapnel material?'

His silence extorted that. Gwinnett did not answer the question. Instead, he suggested we should leave the restaurant, drink more coffee elsewhere.

'All right.'

'Where shall we go?'

'Florian's?'

'OK.'

As soon as we were outside he began about Pamela. What he had to say may have seemed easier to express in comparative darkness of the street, rather than across the table at an over brightly lighted restaurant. Now he sounded thoroughly excited, not at all inert.

'I'm going to meet her in London.'

'That sounds all right.'

'I don't know.'

'Did she suggest that?'

'Yes – when she saw me in San Marco.'

'The interview there went off well?'

'She turned up on time.'

'That in itself must have been a surprise.'

Gwinnett laughed uneasily. He was evidently making a great effort, no doubt for the sake of his book, to be clear, uncomplicated, unlike how he usually felt, how at least he behaved.

'You know how dark it is in the Basilica? I was standing by the doors. I didn't recognize her for a moment, although I was thinking I must be careful not to miss her. She had dressed up all in black, a skirt, dark glasses, a kind of mantilla. She looked – I just don't know how to put it. I was almost scared. She didn't say a word. She took me by the hand, down one of those side aisles. It was the darkest part of the church. She stopped behind a pillar, a place she seemed to know already.'

Gwinnett was momentarily prevented from continuing his story by thickening of the crowd, as we approached the Piazza along a narrow street, necessitating our own advance in single file. Two nuns passed. Gwinnett turned back, indicating them.

'Do you know the first thing Lady Widmerpool said? She asked if the place we were in didn't make me want to turn to the religious life?'

'How did you answer that one?'

'I said it might be a good experience for some people. It wasn't one I felt drawn to myself. I asked if she herself was thinking of taking the veil.'

'Good for you.'

'I said her clothes looked more religious than in the Palazzo.'

'How did she take that?'

'She laughed. She said she often felt that way. I wasn't all that surprised. It fits in.'

The comment showed Gwinnett no beginner in female psychology. He and Pamela might be well matched. This was the first outward indication of a mystic side to her. Gwinnett for the moment had shaken off his own constraint.

'I began to speak of Trapnel. She listened, but didn't give much away. The next thing did startle me.'

He gave an embarrassed laugh.

'She grabbed hold of me,' he said.

'You mean —'

'Just that.'

'By the balls?'

'Yeah.'

'Literally?'

'Quite literally. Then she hinted the story about Ferrand-Sénéschal was true.'

Coming out from under the pillars, we entered the Piazza. The square was packed with people. They trailed rhythmically backwards and forwards like the huge chorus of an opera. One of the caffè orchestras was playing selections from *The Merry Widow*, Widmerpool's favourite waltz, he had said, just before Barbara Goring poured sugar over his head. The termination of the Pamela story had to be left in Gwinnett's discretion. It was not to be crudely probed.

'That was when she told me to call her up when I got to London. I just said I'd do that.'

'By that time she'd let go — or was she still holding on?'

He laughed. He seemed past embarrassment now.

'I'd disengaged her — told her to lay off.'

'How did she take that?'

'OK. She laughed the way she does. Then she took off.'

'To contemplate the religious life elsewhere?'

Gwinnett did not offer an opinion on that point.

'You heard no more from her about Trapnel?'

'Not a word.'

Most of the tables at Florian's seemed occupied. People from the Conference were scattered about among multitudes of tourists. Gwinnett and I moved this way or that through the crowded caffè, trying to find somewhere to sit. Then two chairs were vacated near the band. Making for them, we were about to settle down, when someone from the next table called out. They were a party of four, revealed to be Rosie Manasch – Rosie Stevens now for some years – her husband, Odo Stevens, and an American couple.

'Switch the chairs round and join us,' said Stevens. 'We've just finished a Greek cruise, staying in Venice a day or two to get our breath.'

Rosie introduced the Americans, middle-aged to elderly, immensely presentable. I played Gwinnett in return. It was more characteristic of Stevens than his wife that Gwinnett and I should not be allowed to sit by ourselves. Like Glober, he had a taste for forming courts. He was a little piqued, or pretended to be, at hearing about the Conference.

'Why do I never get asked to these international affairs? Not a grand enough writer, I suppose. Who's turned up? Mark Members? Quentin Shuckerly? The usual crowd?'

Now in his early forties, Odo Stevens, less unchanged than Rosie, had salvaged a fair amount of the bounce associated with his earlier days; Rosie, for her part, entirely retaining an intrinsic air of plump little queen of the harem. Having decided, possibly on sight, to marry Stevens, she seemed perfectly satisfied now the step was taken. So far as that went, so did Stevens. They had two or three children. There had been ups and downs during the years preceding marriage, but these had been survived, the chief discord when Matilda Donners had shown signs of wanting to capture Stevens for herself. Owing either to Matilda's tactical inferiority, or loss of interest in the prize, nothing had come of that, Rosie carrying Stevens off in the end. His temporary seizure by Matilda may have been planned more as a foray into her rival's territory – war considered as a mere extension of foreign policy – a sortie into the enemy's country, not intended as permanent advance beyond foremost defended localities, already recognized as such. At the time, Rosie took the aggression calmly, in that spirit preparing for withdrawal just as far as necessary, never losing her head. Matilda's punitive raid was, so to speak, driven off in due course, after admittedly inflicting a certain measure of casualty; both sides afterwards possessing some claim to have achieved their objective. During this little campaign, explosive while it lasted, Stevens was rumoured to have gone with Matilda to Ischia.

The battle over Stevens could claim a certain continuity from the past, Matilda and Rosie not only rivals at giving parties, but Rosie's first husband, Jock Udall, having belonged to a newspaper-owning family, traditionally opposed to Sir Magnus Donners and all his works. Some thought the pivot of the Ischia incident Stevens himself, bringing pressure on Rosie to force marriage. If so, the manoeuvre was successful. When his body was finally recovered from the battlefield, marriage took place, although only after a decent interval, to purge his contempt. The story that Stevens had given Rosie a black eye during these troubled times was never corroborated. After marriage, a greater docility was, on the contrary, evident in Stevens. He hovered about on the outskirts of the literary world, writing an occasional article, reviewing an occasional book. It was generally supposed he might have liked some regular occupation, but Rosie would not allow that, imposing idleness on her husband as a kind of eternal punishment for the brief scamper with Matilda. Stevens had never repeated the success of *Sad Majors,* a work distinguished, in its way, among examples of what its author called 'that dicey art-form, the war reminiscence'. The often promised book of verse – 'verse, not poetry', Stevens always insisted – had never appeared. I had heard it suggested that Stevens worked part-time for the Secret

Service War record, general abilities, way of life, none of them controverted that possibility, though equally the suggestion may have been quite groundless. When Rosie, and the two Americans, began to talk to Gwinnett, Stevens swivelled his chair round in my direction.

'Do you know who's in this town, Nick?'

'Who?'

'My old girl friend Pam Flitton, I saw her wandering across the Piazzetta soon after we arrived. She didn't see me.'

He spoke in a dramatically low voice. There was no doubt a touch of facetiousness in pretending his war-time affair with Pamela was a desperate secret from his wife, even if true he was more than a little in awe of Rosie.

'She's staying with someone called Jacky Bragadin. Both the Widmerpools are.'

'Somebody called Jacky Bragadin? Don't be so snob-bish, old cock. I know Jack Bragadin. Rosie's known him for years. He was a friend of her father's. He once came to a party of ours in London. Don't try and play down your smart friends, as if I was too dim to have heard of them. We were actually thinking of ringing Jacky up tomorrow, asking if we could come and see him.'

'Keep calm, Odo. He's not a friend of mine. I never met him before the Conference went over his Palazzo. That was how I knew the Widmerpools were staying with Jacky Bragadin.'

Rosie caught the name. She left the Americans to chat together with Gwinnett, who had assumed, with his compatriots, a blunt, matter-of-fact, all-purposes air.

'Did you mention Jacky Bragadin? How is he? His heart wasn't too good when I last saw him, also that trouble with his chest. We thought of getting into touch. Do you know who's staying there?'

'I was telling Odo – the Widmerpools, among others.'

'Good heavens, the Frog Footman, and that *ghastly* wife of his. What can Jacky be thinking of? Thank goodness you warned me. Who are the other unfortunates?'

'An American film tycoon called Louis Glober. Baby Clarini, who used to be Baby Wentworth. Those are the only ones I know about, in addition to the Widmerpools.'

Rosie made a face at the name of Baby Wentworth.

'Jacky certainly can take it on the chin, Baby and Pamela Widmerpool under the same roof. What about Louis Glober? I seem to know the name. Is he up to the weight of the others? I hope so.'

One of the Americans inquired about Glober.

'What's he up to now? Louis Glober hasn't made a picture in years. The last I heard of him was automobile racing, in fact saw him at the Indianapolis Speedway.'

They talked of Glober and his past exploits. Gwinnett remained silent. I had not caught the name of the Americans, indeed never found that out. The husband began to enlarge on the Glober legend.

'Did you ever hear of Glober's Montana caper?'

That looked a possibility as the story of Glober's meeting with Pamela, but turned out to have bearings of interest chiefly on Glober's many-sidedness. It explained, too, a Montana connection.

'One time Glober was in Hollywood, he went north with a cowboy actor – I'll think of the name – who was starring in a picture of Glober's. The Indians were bestowing some sort of a tribal honour on this actor, who'd invited Glober to accompany him, and watch the ceremony. Montana, it seems, went to Glober's head. That's how he is. He talked of starting life again up there, buying a defunct cattle business, refinancing Indian leases, that sort of stuff. He was crazy about it all.'

'Wouldn't mind that kind of life myself,' said Stevens. 'In the open all day.'

'Oh, darling?' said Rosie. 'Do you think so?'

'Glober stayed up there quite a while, talking of becoming a cattleman. All sorts of yarns came back to the Coast about his doings. There was supposed to have been a gun fight. A rancher found Glober in compromising circumstances with his wife. He pulled a gun, took a shot at Glober, and missed. Glober must have been prepared for trouble, because he had his own gun by him, blazed back, and missed too. They ran out of shells, or the lady herself intervened, so they settled to cut the cards for her. Glober lost, and returned to Hollywood.'

'His luck was in,' said Stevens.

The story suggested the *monde* in which Cosmo Flitton had come to rest. I caught Gwinnett's eye.

'That's all pure Trapnel – the sort of thing X would have loved, but never managed to bring off.'

Gwinnett nodded, without giving any indication whether or not he agreed.

'When the tale got back to Beverly Hills, Dorothy Parker said Glober planned to take the lead in his next picture himself. It was to be called *The Western of the Playboy World*.'

The American lady broke in.

'Louis Glober's got a fine side too. All that money he gave for the mental health research project, that institution for schizophrenics. It was all done on the quiet. Not a soul knew it was Glober, until – '

Stevens kicked me under the table. I lost track of the precise history of Glober's generous act, but caught enough to gather it had been brought about in deliberate secrecy, the teller of the story having happened quite by chance on the magnanimous part Glober had played. I could not at once understand whatever Stevens was signalling. His eyes stared fixedly in front of him. Glancing round in the direction towards which they were set, I was now able to observe Pamela Widmerpool moving between the closely packed tables and chairs. As usual she gave the impression almost of floating through the air. She was apparently looking for someone thought likely to be sitting at Florian's. At least that was the impression given. Possibly she was merely taking an evening walk, choosing to wander through the crowded caffè to give spice to a stroll, cause a little inconvenience, draw attention to herself. The people at the tables stared at her. As she wove her way amongst them, she paused from time to time to stare haughtily back. Stevens was rather rattled.

'She's bloody well making in our direction,' he muttered.

Pamela had hit him in the face the last time I had seen them together, but no doubt he feared her unhappy moral impact on his wife, rather than physical violence. The others had not noticed Pamela's onset. Rosie, always a great talker, had a conspicuous rival in the American lady. Gwinnett seemed resigned to the position in which he found himself. Pamela had marked down our table. She was steering for it, without the least hurry. The course unquestionably was intentional. She was still wearing her white trousers, carrying from her shoulder a bag hung from a gold chain. Stevens was surprisingly disturbed.

'Had this got to happen?'

Pamela halted behind the chair of the male American. He was unaware of her presence there.

'Have you seen Louis?'

'Glober?'

'No, Louis the Fourteenth.'

'I haven't seen either since lunch.'

'Did you lunch with Louis?'

'Yes, Glober – not the Roi Soleil.'

'I thought he was giving lunch to that old cow Ada. Do you know she put round a story that I left a picador in Spain because I found a basket-ball player twice his size?'

'Ada was there too.'

'Where?'

'The restaurant in the Giardini.'

'Did he take Ada back to screw her — if he can still manage that, or can't she face a man any longer?'

'So far as I knew Glober left for the Gritti Palace to meet a business acquaintance, and Ada returned to the Lido to work on a speech she's going to make at the Conference.'

'Louis's been seen at Cipriani's since he was at the Gritti.'

'Then I can't help.'

'I want some dope from him.'

Although the word might be reasonably used for any entity too much trouble to particularize, Pamela spoke as if she meant a drug, rather than, say, schedule of air-flights to London, programme of tomorrow's sightseeing, name of recommended restaurant. She sounded as if she felt a capricious desire for a narcotic Glober could supply, no breathless despairing longing, just what she wished at the moment. The possibility was not to be wholly dismissed as an aspect of Glober's courtship. The men of the party had risen, standing awkwardly beside their chairs, while this conversation proceeded, waiting for her to move on.

'How are you, Pam?' asked Stevens.

He still sounded nervous. She glanced at him, but gave no sign of having seen him before. Stevens himself may have hoped matters would rest there, that Pamela, failing to obtain the information she sought, would continue on her way without further acknowledgment. She remained, not speaking, looking coldly round, regarding Gwinnett with as chilly an eye as the rest. There was no suggestion they had met, far less touched on the religious life, shared some sort of physically sexual brush. Gwinnett himself was hardly more forthcoming. Absolutely poker-faced, his expression was that of a man determined not to fall below the standard of politeness required by convention towards an unknown woman pausing by the table at which he had been sitting, at the same time not unwilling that she should move on as quickly as possible to enable him to resume his seat. Pamela had no intention of moving on.

'I'm not going to drag the canals for Glober. I'll get the stuff from him tomorrow.'

She stepped forward to occupy the chair temporarily vacated by the American husband, thereby putting an end to any hope that she was not going to stay. The American managed to find another chair, then good-naturedly asked what she wanted to drink.

'A cappuccino.'

Stevens was forced into mumbling some sort of general introduction. Rosie, of course, knew perfectly well who Pamela was, but either the two of them, by some chance, had never met, or it suited the mood of both to pretend that. Gwinnett, without emphasis, allowed recognition of previous acquaintanceship of some sort by making a backward jerk of the head. Rosie, undoubtedly angry at Pamela imposing herself in this manner, was at the same time, unlike Stevens, quite unruffled in outward appearance.

'We heard you and your husband were staying with Jacky,' she said. 'How is he? Free from that catarrh of his, I hope?'

She expertly eyed Pamela's turn-out, letting the assessment pause for a second on what appeared to be a wine-stain, at closer range revealed, on the white trousers, which Pamela, in spite of other signs of grubbiness, had not bothered to change. Rosie also contemplated for a moment the crocodile-skin bag. Its heavy chain of gold looked rather an expensive item. This was all very cool on both sides, the sense of tension – though neither glanced at the other – between Pamela and Gwinnett, rather than Pamela and Rosie. When the cappuccino arrived, Pamela did not touch it. She sat there quietly, taking no notice of anyone. Then she seemed to decide to answer Rosie's question.

'Jacky's no worse than usual. Only worried about having a couple like us staying with him.'

'You and your husband?'

'Yes.'

Rosie laughed lightly.

'Why should he be worried by that?'

'One accused of murder, the other of spying.'

'Oh, really. Which of you did which?'

Still smiling, Rosie spoke quite evenly. Pamela allowed herself a faint smile too.

'The French papers are hinting I murdered Ferrand-Sénéschal.'

'The French writer?'

Rosie's tone suggested that to have murdered Ferrand-Sénéschal was an act, however thoughtless, anyone might easily have committed.

'They haven't said in so many words I did it yet.'

'Oh, good – and the spying?'

Pamela laughed.

'Only those in the know, like Jacky, are fussing about that at present.'

'I see.'

'Jacky thinks he'll get in wrong with one lot, or the other, through us. Jacky's got quite a lot of Communist chums, movie people, publishers, other rich people like himself. Some of them are Stalinists, and quarrelling with the new crowd. Jacky doesn't want a stink. It looks as if a stink's just what he's going to get. He didn't bargain for that when he said we could come and stay, though he wasn't too keen in the first place. I had to turn the heat on. He thought I'd keep an American called Louis Glober quiet, and we might both be useful in other ways. Now he wants to get rid of us. That may not be so easy.'

She laughed again. The joke had to be admitted as rather a good one, even if grimmish for Jacky Bragadin. Rosie smiled tolerantly. She did not pursue further inflexions of the story by asking more questions. She picked up the bag resting on the table, its long chain still looped round Pamela's shoulder.

'How pretty.'

'Do you think so? I hate the thing. This man Glober gave it me. He keeps saying he'll change it. He'll only get something worse, and I can't be bothered to spend hours in a shop with him.'

'Is Mr Glober over for the Film Festival?' asked one of the Americans.

'That's what he's put out. He probably wants to pick up some hints from the German film about the blackmailing whore.'

'I rather wish we were staying for the Film Festival,' said Rosie. 'I'd like to see Polly Duport in the Hardy picture. We know her. She's so nice, as well as being such a good actress.'

There was at lull in conversation. Stevens remarked that his new interest was in vintage cars. The Americans said they would have to be thinking of returning to their hotel soon. Rosie confirmed the view that it had been a tiring day. Stevens looked as if he might have liked to linger at Florian's, but any such intractability would clearly be inadvisable, if matrimonial routines were to operate harmoniously. He did not openly dissent. Within the limits of making no pretence she found the presence of Pamela welcome, Rosie had been perfectly polite. Stevens could count himself lucky the situation had not hardened into open discord. Retirement from the scene had something to offer. Pamela appeared indifferent to whether they stayed or went. Goodbyes were said. She nodded an almost imperceptible farewell and dismissal.

The Stevens party withdrew. They were enclosed almost immediately by the shadows of the Piazza. We sat for a minute or two in silence. The orchestra sawed away at *Tales of Hoffman*.

'What a shit Odo is,' said Pamela.

'Rosie is nice.'

It seemed best to make that statement right away, declare one's views on the subject, rather than wait for attack. That would be preferable to a follow-up defending Rosie, as a friend. Rather surprisingly, Pamela agreed.

'Yes, she's all right. I suppose she gets a kick out of keeping that little ponce.'

'You must admit his war record was good.'

'What's that to me?'

To stay longer at the table would be not only to prejudice Gwinnett's opportunity for further pursuit of Trapnel investigations, but also, if Pamela had taken a fancy to him, risk being told in uncompromising terms to leave them *à deux*.

'I'm off too.'

Pamela herself rose at that.

'I've had enough of this place,' she said.

That remark had all the appearance of being Gwinnett's cue, a chance not to be missed to take her elsewhere, to get out of her whatever he wanted. Florian's could reasonably be regarded as a distracting spot for serious discussion. Gwinnett himself stood up, but without putting forward any alternative proposal. There was a pause. As a matter of form, I offered to see Pamela back to the Bragadin palace. If Gwinnett did not want to settle immediately on another port of call, he could easily suggest the duty of taking her home should fall to him. He said nothing. Pamela herself categorically refused escort.

'Where's your hotel?'

I named it.

'Both of you?'

'Yes.'

She turned to Gwinnett.

'Are you going back too?'

'That was my intention.'

Pamela fully accepted the implication that he did not propose to take her on at that moment. She showed no resentment.

'I'll walk as far as your hotel, then decide what I want to do. I like wandering about Venice at night.'

Gwinnett was certainly showing himself capable of handling Pamela in his own manner. He seemed, at worst, to have accomplished a transformation of rôles, in which she stalked him, rather than he her. That might produce equally hazardous consequences, not least because Pamela herself showed positive taste for the re-adjustment. The hunter's pursuit was no doubt familiar to her from past experience, only exceptional, in this case, to the extent that Gwinnett was already in her power from need to acquire Trapnel material.

'OK,' he said.

The three of us set off together. Nothing much was said until we were quite close to the hotel. Then, on a little humped bridge crossing a narrow waterway, Pamela stopped. She went to the parapet of the bridge, leant over it, looking down towards the canal. Gwinnett and I stopped too. She stared at the water for some time without saying anything. Then she spoke in her low unaccentuated manner.

'I've thought of nothing but X since I've been in Venice. I see that manuscript of his floating away on every canal. You know Louis Glober wants to do it as a film, with that ending. It might have happened here. This place just below.'

Gwinnett seemed almost to have been waiting for her to make that speech.

'Why did you do it?'

He asked that quite bluntly.

'You think it was just to be bitchy.'

'I never said so.'

'But you think it.'

He did not answer. Pamela left the parapet of the bridge. She moved slowly towards him.

'I threw the book away because it wasn't worthy of X.'

'Then why do you want Glober to make a picture of something not worthy?'

'Because the best parts can be preserved in a film.'

I supposed by that she meant her own part, in whatever Trapnel had written, could be recorded that way; at least her version of it. Then Gwinnett played a trump. Considering contacts already made, he had shown characteristic self-control in withholding the information until now.

'Trapnel preserved the outline himself in his *Commonplace Book*.'

'What's that?'

'Something you don't know about.'

'Where is it?'

'I've got it.'

'He says there what he said in *Profiles in String*?'

'Some of it.'

'I'll destroy that too – if it isn't worthy of him.'

Gwinnett did not answer.

'You don't believe me?'

'I entirely believe you, Lady Widmerpool, but you don't have the *Commonplace Book*.'

In another mood she would certainly have shown contemptuous amusement for Gwinnett's prim formality of manner. Now she was working herself up into one of her rages.

'You won't take my word – that I threw the manuscript into the Canal because it wasn't good enough?'

'I take your word unreservedly, Lady Widmerpool.'

Gwinnett himself might have been quite angry by then. It was impossible to tell. As usual he spoke, like Pamela herself, in a low unemphatic tone.

'X himself knew it was a necessary sacrifice. He said so after. He liked to talk about that sort of thing. It was one side of him.'

What she stated about Trapnel was not at all untrue, if strange she had appreciated that aspect of him. She was an ideal instance of Barnby's pronouncement that, for a woman, being in love with a man does not necessarily imply behaving well to him. Some comment of Trapnel's about the destruction of the manuscript must have come to her ears later.

'That was why he threw away his swordstick too.'

This settled the fact of someone having given her an account of the incident. Not myself, unlikely to have been Bagshaw, the story had just travelled round.

'You knew that?'

She was insistent.

'I'd been told,' Gwinnett admitted.

He was stonewalling obstinately.

'You don't know what sacrifice is.'

Gwinnett gave an odd smile at that.

'What makes you think so?'

If Pamela were an uncomfortable person, so was he. The way he asked that question was dreadfully tortured. If she noticed that fact – as time went on one suspected she did not miss much – she gave no sign.

'I'll show you.'

She slipped from off her shoulder the bag Glober had given her, wound the chain quickly about it, forming a rough knot. Then, holding the shortened links of gold, whirled round the bundle in the air, like a sort of prayer-wheel, and tossed it over the side of the bridge. There was the gentlest of splashes. The crocodile-skin (returned to its natural element) bobbed about for a second or two on the surface of the water, the moonlight glinting on metal clasps, a moment later, weighed down by the weight of its chain, sinking into the dark currents of the little canal. Gwinnett still did not speak. Pamela returned from the parapet from which she had watched the bag disappear.

'That shows you what X did with something he valued.'

She had evidently intended to play out for Gwinnett's benefit a figurative representation of the offering up of both manuscript and swordstick. Gwinnett did not propose to allow that. He showed himself prepared for a tussle.

'You said just a short while back you didn't think all that of the purse.'

He stood there openly unimpressed. For the moment it looked as if Pamela were going to hit him in the face, register one of those backhand swings she had dealt Stevens in the past. She may have contemplated doing so, thought better of it. Instead, she took hold of his right arm with her left hand, and hammered on his chest with her fist. She must have hit him quite hard. He retreated a step or two from the force of the onset, laughing a little, still not speaking. Pamela ceasing to pound Gwinnett at last, stood back. She gave him a long searching look. Then she turned, and walked quickly away in the direction from which we had come. Gwinnett did nothing for a minute or two. Either a lot of breath had been knocked out of him, and he was recovering, or he remained lost in contemplation of the whole strange incident; probably both. Then at last he shook his head.

'I'd best go see what she's after.'

He too set off into the night. He did that at a more moderate speed than Pamela's. I left them to make whatever mutual co-ordination between them, physical or intellectual, seemed best in the light of whatever each required from the other. Even in the interests of getting a biography written about Trapnel, it was not for a third party to intervene further. Gwinnett had certainly entered the true Trapnel world in a manner no aspiring biographer could discount. It was like a supernatural story, a myth. If he wanted to avoid becoming the victim of sorcery, being himself turned into a toad, or something of that kind – in moral terms his dissertation follow *Profile in String* into the waters of the Styx – he would have to find the magic talisman, and do that pretty quickly. It might already be too late.

Dr Brightman was in the hall of the hotel. She too had just come in. The evening with Ada had been a great success.

'What a nice girl she is. I hear you both met at the Biennale. Russell Gwinnett suggested we should go there together. I must speak to him about it.'

'Russell Gwinnett's just been beaten up by Lady Widmerpool.'

Dr Brightman showed keen interest in the story of what had been happening. At the end she gave her verdict.

'Lady Widmerpool may be what Russell is looking for.'

'At least she could hardly be called a mother-substitute.'

'Mothers vary.'

'You called him gothic?'

'To avoid the word decadent, so dear to the American heart, especially when European failings are in question. It is rarely used with precision here either. Of course there were the *Décadents,* so designated by themselves, but think of the habits of Alexander the Great, or Julius Caesar, neither of whom can be regarded as exactly decadent personalities.'

'Are you implying sexual ambivalence in Gwinnett?'

'I think not. His life might have been easier had that been so. Of course he remains essentially American in believing all questions have answers, that there is an ideal life against which everyday life can be measured — but measured only in everyday terms, so that the ideal life would be another sort of everyday life. It is somewhere at that point Russell's difficulties lie.'

We said good night. I slept badly. Tokenhouse rang up early again the following morning. He brushed aside reference to the visit to his studio. He was, in his own terms, back to normal, comparative gaieties of the Glober luncheon obliterated entirely.

'I think you said you were going to be in Venice another day or two?'

I told him when the Conference broke up.

'In that case we shall not be able to meet again — and I shall not require the package, of which I spoke, posted in England. I find I am falling seriously behind in my work. Got to buckle down, not waste any more time with visitors, if the job is to be properly done. Of course I was glad to see you after so many years, hear your news. Painting is like everything else, it must be taken seriously. No good otherwise. That does not mean I was not pleased we fell in with each other. Let me know if you come to Venice again on a similar peregrination with your intellectual friends.'

'Did you clear up Widmerpool's problem?'

'Widmerpool?'

'The man who came in while we were looking at your pictures.'

'Widmerpool? Ah, yes, Lord Widmerpool. For the moment I could not place the name. Yes, yes. I did my best for him. Only a small matter. I don't know why he seemed so concerned about it. He simply wanted to ascertain the whereabouts of a friend we have in common. By the way, keep it to yourself, will you, that you met Lord Widmerpool at my studio. He asked me to say that. I have no idea why. He rather gave me to understand that he had offered some excuse, other than that he was coming to see me, to avoid some social engagement – I can sympathize with that – and did not want so flimsy a motive to be revealed. Well, I mustn't waste the whole morning coffee-housing on this vile instrument. Has your Conference settled anything by its coming together? No? I thought not. Goodbye to you, goodbye.'

He rang off. When I saw Gwinnett later in the morning before one of the sessions, I asked if he had caught up with Pamela. He replied so vaguely that it remained uncertain whether he had managed to find her; or found her, and been sent about his business. He said he was not packing up with the Conference, having decided to stay on for the Film Festival. Then he spoke as an afterthought.

'There's something I'd be glad for you to do for me when you get back to England – tell Trapnel's friend, Mr Bagshaw, whom you mentioned, I'll be calling him up. Just so he doesn't think I'm some crazy American dissertation-writer, and give me the brush-off.'

'He won't do that. Where are you staying in London?'

Gwinnett named an hotel in Bloomsbury, a former haunt of Trapnel's.

'That will be fairly spartan.'

'I'll get the atmosphere there. Later I might try some of the more rundown locations too.'

'You're going to do it in style.'

'Sure.'

I saw Gwinnett only once again, the day the Conference closed. He appeared carrying a small parcel, which looked like a paper-wrapped book. This he handed to me.

'It's Trapnel's *Commonplace Book*. You'll like to see it, though there isn't all that there.'

'Won't you need it? When will I be able to return it to you, and where?'

'You keep it for the next few weeks. I'd rather it

wasn't in my own hands for the time being. I'll get in touch when I want it back.'

That was all he would say, except also implying a preference not to be called up, otherwise contacted, at the hotel. Apart from the loan of the *Commonplace Book*, a generous one, our parting was as stiff as our meeting had been. Thinking over the unsolicited lending of the *Commonplace Book*, I could only surmise he felt the Trapnel notes, after what she had said, safer right away from Pamela. Did he not trust himself, or was it that he thought her capable of anything? Dr Brightman, not remaining for the Film Festival, was also delaying immediate return to England.

'It seemed a pity to be in this part of Italy, and not idle away a few days with the Ostrogoths and Lombards. The Venetian air overcomes one with dilettantism. That nice little Ada Leintwardine says she will join me for a night or two, when the Film Festival is over, at whatever place I have reached by then. Such an adventure to have met Lady Widmerpool. My colleagues will be green with envy.'

At that period, when one travelled to and from Venice direct by air (the route avoided by Widmerpool), a bus picked up, or set down, airport passengers in the Piazzale Roma. By night this happened at an uncomfortable hour. You waited in a caffè, the bus arriving about one o'clock in the morning. Ennui and dejection were to be associated with the small hours spent in that place. Even in daytime the Piazzale Roma, flanked by two garages of megalomaniac dimension, overspread with parked charabancs and trucks, crowded throughout the twenty-four hours with touts and loiterers, is a gloomy, dusty, untidy, rather sinister spot. These backblocks, raw underside of the incredible inviolate aqueous city, were no doubt regarded by Tokenhouse as the 'real Venice' — though one lot of human beings and their habitations cannot be less or more 'real' than another – purlieus that, in Casanova's day, would have teemed with swindlers, thieves, whores, pimps, police spies, flavours probably not wholly absent today.

Waiting for the airport bus, I watched gangs of young men circling the huge square again and again. They seemed to wander about there all night. As one of these clusters of itinerant corner-boys prowled past the caffè, a straggler from the group turned aside for a moment to utter the hissing accolade owed to any female passer-by not absolutely monstrous of feature.

'Bella! Bellissima!'

A confrère ahead of him looked round too, and the wolf-whistler, forgetting his own impassioned salutation of a moment before, entered into argument with his friend, quite evidently about another subject. They all trudged on, chattering together. Through the shadows, recurrently dispersed by flashing headlights of cars passing and repassing, a slim trousered figure receded through murky byways, slinking between shifting loafers and parked vehicles. It certainly looked like Pamela Widmerpool. She was alone, roving slowly, abstractedly, through the Venetian midnight.

# FOUR

Bagshaw was at once attentive to the idea of an American biographer of X. Trapnel seeking an interview with himself. In fact he pressed for a meeting to hear a fuller account of Gwinnett's needs. Television had made him more prolix than ever on the line. One was also increasingly aware that he was no longer Books-do-furnish-a-room Bagshaw of ancient days, but Lindsay Bagshaw, the Television 'personality', no towering magnate of that order, but, if only a minor scion, fully conscious of inspired status. He suggested a visit to his own house, something never before put forward. In the past, a pub would always have been proposed. Bagshaw himself was a little sheepish about the change. Complacent, he was also a trifle cowed. He attempted explanation.

'I like to get back as early as possible after work. May prefers that. There's always a lot to do at home.'

The idea of Bagshaw deferring, in this manner, to domesticity, owning, even renting, a house was an altogether unfamiliar one. In early life, married or single, his quarters had been kept secret. They were in a sense his only secret, everyone always knowing about his love affairs, political standpoint, prospects of changing his job, ups and downs of health. Where he lived was another matter. That was not revealed. One pictured him domiciled less vagrantly than Trapnel, all the same never in connexion with anything so portentous as a house. There was no reason why Bagshaw should not possess a house, nor in general be taken less seriously than other people. No doubt, for his purposes, he had done a good deal to encourage a view of himself as a grotesque figure, moving through a world of farce. Come to rest in relatively prosperous circumstances, he had now modified the rôle for which he had formerly typecast himself. Dynamic styles of life required one 'image'; static, another. How deep these changes went could not be judged. Bagshaw remained devious.

'We're a bit north of Primrose Hill. I got the lease on quite favourable terms during the property slump some years after the war, when I left *Fission*. I shall look forward to hearing all about Professor Gwinnett, when I see you.'

Bagshaw's house, larger than surmised, was of fairly dilapidated exterior. Waiting on the doorstep, I wondered whether the upper storeys were let off. Children's voices were to be heard above, one of them making rather a fuss. Children had never played a part in the Bagshaw field of operation. They seemed out of place there. I rang a couple of times, then knocked. The door was opened by a girl of about sixteen or seventeen. Rather vacant in expression, reasonably good-looking, she was not on sight identifiable as member of the family or hired retainer. The point could not be settled, because she turned away without speaking, and set off up some stairs. At first I supposed her a foreign 'au pair', speaking no English, possibly seeking an interpreter, but, as she disappeared, she could be heard complaining.

'All right, I'm coming. Don't make such a bloody row.'

The protest was a little hysterical as uttered. There was an impression, possibly due to a naturally tuberous figure, that she might be pregnant. That could easily have been a mistaken conclusion. I waited. Several doors could be explored, if no one appeared. I was about to experiment with one of these, when an elderly man, wearing a woollen dressing-gown, came slowly down the stairs up which the girl had departed. It was evident that he did not expect to find me in the hall. His arrival there would pose action of some sort, but, suddenly aware of my presence, he murmured some sort of apology, retreating up the stairs again. Even if Bagshaw's way of life had in certain respects altered, become more solid, a fundamental pattern of unconventionality remained. The problem of what to do next was solved by the appearance, from a door leading apparently to the basement, of Bagshaw himself.

'Ah, Nicholas. When did you arrive? How did you get in? Avril opened the door, I suppose. Where is she now? Gone off to quieten the kids, I expect. You haven't been here long, have you?'

'No, but a white-haired gentleman came down the stairs just now, apparently seeking help.'

Bagshaw dismissed that.

'Only my father. May didn't appear, did she? The gas-cooker's blown. Come in here, shall we?'

He had changed a good deal since last seen. At that period we did not have a television set, so I had never watched a Bagshaw programme. He looked not only much older, also much more untidy, which once would have seemed hard to achieve. The room we entered was even untidier than Bagshaw himself. The mess there was epic. It seemed half-study, half-nursery, in one corner a bookcase full of works on political theory, in another a large dolls' house, lacking its façade. The tables and floor were covered with typescripts, income-tax forms, newspapers, weeklies, mini-cars, children's bricks. Bagshaw made a space on the sofa, at the far end from that where the stuffing was bursting out.

'Now – a drink?'

'Who is Avril?'

'One of my stepdaughters.'

'I didn't know – '

'Three of them. Avril's not a bad girl. Not very

bright. A bit sub, to tell the truth. She's in rather a jam at the moment. Can't be helped.'

Bagshaw made a despairing, consciously theatrical gesture, no doubt developed from his professional life.

'Are the other stepchildren upstairs?'

He looked surprised. Certainly the ages seemed wrong, if anything were to be inferred from the noises being made.

'No, no. The ones upstairs are my own. The stepchildren are more or less grown-up. Getting into tangles with boyfriends all the time. You see I'm quite a family man now.'

Bagshaw said that in a whimsical, rather faraway voice, probably another echo of his programme. His whole demeanour had become more histrionic, at least histrionic in a different manner from formerly. He sat down without pouring himself out a drink, something not entirely without precedent, though unlikely to be linked now with curative abstinences of the past.

'Aren't you having anything?'

'I hardly drink at all these days. Find I feel better. Get through more work. Here's May. How's your migraine, dear? Have a drink, it may make you feel better. No? Too busy?'

Mrs Bagshaw, in her forties, with traces of the same blonde good-looks as her daughter, had the air of being dreadfully harassed. She was also rather lame. Evidently used to people coming to see her husband about matters connected with his work, perfectly polite, she obviously hoped to get out of the room as soon as possible, after giving some sort of a progress report about the cooking-stove crisis. This problem solved, or postponed, she excused herself and retired again. Bagshaw, who had listened gravely, replied with apparent good sense to his wife's statements and questions, clearly accepted this new incarnation of himself. In any case, it was no longer new to him. When Mrs Bagshaw had gone, he settled down again to his professionally avuncular manner.

'Where will this American friend of yours stay in London, Nicholas?'

'In one of those bleak hotels X used to frequent. He hopes to get the atmosphere first-hand. He really is very keen on doing the book well.'

'Which one?'

Bagshaw groaned at the name, and shook his head. To judge from the exterior of the place, that reaction was justified.

'I spent a night there myself once years ago – rather a sordid story I won't bore you with – in fact recommended the place to Trappy in the first instance. The bathroom accommodation doesn't exactly measure up to the highest mod. con. standards. You know how strongly Americans feel about these things.'

'Gwinnett wants the Trapnel ethos, not the best place in London to take a bath.'

'I see.'

That fact impressed Bagshaw. He thought about it for a moment.

'Look here, this idea occurred to me as soon as you mentioned your American. Why doesn't Professor Gwinnett – I mean only when he's completed his stint of Trapnel ports of call, not before – come and PG with us? The spare room's free at the moment. Our Japanese statistician went back to Osaka. I think we made him comfortable during his stay. At least he never complained. That may have been Zen, of course, overcoming of illusory dualisms. I got quite interested in Zen while he was with us.'

The idea of lodging with Bagshaw, a guest paying or non-paying, would once have seemed almost as extraordinary as the fact of his possessing a house. Even in the reformed state of his ménage there were disrecommendations. If anyone were to be 'lodger', Bagshaw himself had always appeared prototype of the kind, one of Nature's lodgers; coaxing the landlady, when behind with the rent, seducing her daughter, storing (in his revolutionary days) subversive pamphlets under the bed. He was imaginable in all such stylized circumstances; even meeting his death as a lodger – the Passing of the Third Floor Back, with Bagshaw as the body. Although that picture had to be revised, the thought of paying to live with Bagshaw was still to be accepted with some demur. That was what I felt as Bagshaw himself digressed on the subject.

'The Icelander, an economist, was rather a turgid fellow, the Eng. Lit. New Zealander, a charming boy. We're looking for a replacement just like your friend – and what could be better from his point of view, if he's writing a book about poor old Trappy? I'll tell you what, Nicholas, I'll send a line to Professor Gwinnett to await arrival, so that he can arrange to see me whenever it suits his purpose. We'll have a talk. If all goes well, I'll suggest he comes and beds down here. I'll put it this way, that he doesn't dream of doing any such thing until he's made an exhaustive study, in depth, of Trapnel haunts, thoroughly absorbed the Trapnel *Weltanschauung*. That should not take long. The essentials are not difficult to grasp.'

Gwinnett was, after all, well able to look after himself. He needed no surveillance, would resent anything of the sort. Besides, from Gwinnett's point of view, there was something to be said for hearing about Trapnel, while living side by side with Bagshaw. If he decided that to stay with the Bagshaws was convenient to his purpose, he would do so; if not, either refuse, or after brief trial withdraw. That was the situation. In any case, Gwinnett was not concerned with living a life of ease, but – something very different – living the life of Trapnel. To lodge with the Bagshaws would in no way run counter to that ambition, in spite of Trapnel himself never having undergone the experience. He must have done similar things. At that moment a girl, recognizable as sister of Avril, probably a year or so older, came into the room. She took no notice of us, but knelt down, and began hunting about in the bookcase. She, too, was fairly good-looking.

'What do you want, Felicity?'

'A book.'

'This is Mr Jenkins.'

'Hullo,' she said, without turning round.

'Where's Stella?' asked Bagshaw.

'God knows.'

She found her book, and went away, slamming the door after her. Bagshaw grimaced at the noise.

'That one's rather a worry too. Young people are nowadays. It's either Regan or Goneril. Look here, have you seen this? Only one paper reported the item.'

He searched about among the assortment of journals lying on the floor, indicating a short paragraph on the foreign news page, when he found the special one he wanted. Its subject was a recent state trial in one of the countries of Eastern Europe, action somewhat unexpected in an atmosphere, in general, of relaxed international tension. Representatives of an outgoing Government had been expelled from the Party, and a former police minister, with one or two others, imprisoned by the new administration taking over. No great prominence was being given by the London press to these proceedings, which appeared to be of a fairly stereotyped order in the People's Republic concerned. That morning a modest headline in my own paper had drawn attention to allegations that some of the accused had been in the pay of the British Secret Service. The three or four persons named as having set out to corrupt members of the fallen Government (together with certain officials and 'intellectuals') were all British Communists of some public standing, or at least prominent fellow-travellers, making little or no concealment of their political affiliations; in short, as little likely to be connected with the British Secret Service, as the accused of being in touch with that organization. An additional name, unintelligibly translated, had been put within inverted commas in Bagshaw's newspaper paragraph.

'Who is . . .?'

The row of consonants, unlinked by vowels, was not to be spoken aloud. Bagshaw was quite excited. He was no longer an oppressed family man, nor even a television 'personality'.

'Is it one of their own people?'

'You don't recognize the name?'

'Not at all.'

'Try speaking it.'

On the tongue the syllables were no more significant.

'An old friend.'

'Of yours?'

'Both of us.'

'A hanger-on of Gypsy's?'

That was just a shot at possibles.

'Once, I believe. A *Fission* connexion.'

'A foreigner?'

'Not at all.'

'You're not suggesting the name's "Widmerpool"?'

'What else could it be?'

'Denounced as — what amounts to being denounced as a Stalinist?'

'In fact, a Revisionist, I think.'

'But — '

'I always said he was at the game.'

'Does a certain Dr Belkin mean anything to you?'

Among the scores of such names proverbial to Bagshaw, Dr Belkin did not figure. That did not alter the conviction Bagshaw had already reached about Widmerpool.

'There have been some odd stories going round about both the Widmerpools since Ferrand-Sénéschal died.'

Bagshaw was not greatly interested in whatever part Pamela had played. It was the political angle he liked.

'That woman may have invented the whole tale about herself and Ferrand-Sénéschal. A sexual fantasy. It wouldn't surprise me at all. The denunciations at the trial are another matter. It's become a routine process. Nagy in Hungary, earlier in the year. Slansky in Czechoslovakia. I'd like to know just what happened about Widmerpool. He probably didn't move quite quick enough. Might be a double bluff. You can't tell. He himself could have felt he needed a little of that sort of attention to build up his reputation as an anti-Communist of the extreme Left. Make people think he's a safe man, because he's attacked from the Communist end. Pretend he's an enemy, when he's really a close friend.'

Bagshaw rambled on. Time came to leave. I was rather glad to go. The Bagshaw house was on the whole lowering to the spirit. Its other members did not appear again, but, when Bagshaw opened the front door, discordant sounds were still audible from the higher floors, together with the noise of loud hammering in the basement. Bagshaw came down the steps.

'Well, goodbye. I expect you're hard at work. I've been thinking a lot about Widmerpool. He's a very interesting political specimen.'

The Venetian trip, contrary to the promises of Mark Members, had not renewed energies for writing. All the same, established priorities, personal continuities, the confused scheme of things making up everyday life, all revived, routines proceeding much as before. The Conference settled down in the mind as a kind of dream, one of those dreams laden with the stuff of real life, stopping just the right side of nightmare, yet leaving disturbing undercurrents to haunt the daytime, clogging sources of imagination – whatever those may be – causing their enigmatic flow to ooze more sluggishly than ever, periodically cease entirely.

Gwinnett showed no sign of arrival in England. In the light of his general behaviour, changing moods, estrangement from social life, distaste for doing things in a humdrum fashion, that was not at all surprising. If still engaged in the unenviable labour of sampling first-hand former Trapnel anchorages, he might well judge that enterprise liable to prejudice from outside contacts. Some writers require complete segregation for getting down to a book. Gwinnett could be one of them. He was, in any case, under no obligation to keep me, or anyone else, informed of his movements. He might quite easily have decided that, so far as I was concerned, any crop of Trapnel memories had been sufficiently harvested by him in Venice. When it comes to recapitulation of what is known of a dead friend, for the benefit of a third party (whether or not writing a biography), remnants transmissible in a form at once lucid, unimpeded by subjective considerations, are astonishingly meagre.

I felt a little concerned by being left with the *Commonplace Book* on my hands, and would have liked opportunity to return it to Gwinnett. Scrappy, much abbreviated, lacking the usual neatness of Trapnel's holographs, its contents were not without interest to a professional writer, who had also known Trapnel. The notes gave an idea, quite a good idea, of what the novel destroyed by Pamela might have been like, had it ever been finished. Certain jottings, not always complimentary, had obvious reference to herself. Clearly obsessive, they were not always possible to interpret. If Pamela had her way, a film based on *Profiles in String* – more likely on Trapnel's own life – made by Glober, the *Commonplace Book* could be of assistance.

If Gwinnett wanted to 'understand' Trapnel, two aspects emerged, one general, the other peculiar to Trapnel himself. There was the larger question, why writers, with apparent reserves of energy and ideas, after making a good start, collapse, or fizzle out in inferior work. In Trapnel's case, that might have been inevitable. On the other hand, its consideration as an isolated instance unavoidably led to Pamela. Gwinnett's approach, not uncommon among biographers, seemed to be to see himself, at greater or lesser range, as projection of his subject. He aimed, anyway to some extent, at reconstructing in himself Trapnel's life, getting into Trapnel's skin, 'becoming' Trapnel. Accordingly, if, in the profoundest sense, he were to attempt to discover why Trapnel broke down, failed to surmount troubles, after all, not greatly worse than many other writers had borne – and mastered – the inference could not be dodged that Gwinnett himself must have some sort of a love affair with Pamela. So far as he had revealed his plans, Gwinnett appeared to aim at getting into Trapnel's skin, but not to that extent. In fact everything about Gwinnett suggested that he did not at all intend to have a love affair with Pamela. If he accepted the possibility, he was playing his cards with subtlety, holding them close to his chest. It was, of course, possible something of the sort had already taken place. Instinctively, one felt that had not happened.

This conjecture was endorsed – anyway in one sense – in an odd manner. To express how things fell out is to lean heavily on hearsay. That is unavoidable. Trapnel himself, speaking as a critic, used to insist that every novel must be told from a given point of view. An extension of that fact is that every story one hears has to be adjusted, in the mind of the listener, to prejudices of the teller in practice, most listeners increasing, reducing, discarding, much of what they have been told. In this case, the events have to be seen through the eyes of Bagshaw's father. What Bagshaw himself later related was not necessarily untrue. Bagshaw was in a position to get the first and best account. He must also have been the main channel to release details, even if other members of the household added to the story's volume. Nevertheless, Bagshaw's father, in his son's phrase 'the man on the spot', was the only human being who really knew the facts, he himself only some of them.

The first indication that Gwinnett had accepted Bagshaw's offer, gone to live in the house, was a story purporting to explain why he had left. This was towards Christmas. It looks as if the alleged happenings were broadcast to the world almost immediately after taking place, but only a long time later did I hear them from Bagshaw's own lips. Dating is possible, because, on that occasion, Bagshaw made a great point of the Christmas decorations being up, imparting a jovial grotesqueness to the scene. Knowledge of the Christmas decorations did certainly add something. Through thick and thin, Bagshaw always retained vestiges of a view of life suggesting a thwarted artist, no doubt the side that finally brought him where he was.

'My father enacted the whole curious incident under a sprig of mistletoe. In the middle of it all, some of the holly came down, with that curious scratchy noise holly makes.'

Although I had not expected Bagshaw's father to be descending the stairs in his dressing-gown, when I called at the house, I had, in the distant past, more than once heard Bagshaw speak of him. They were on good terms. Even in those days, that had seemed a matter of interest in the light of the manner Bragshaw himself used to go on. Bagshaw senior had been in the insurance business, not a notable success in his profession, being neither energetic nor ambitious, but with the valuable quality that he was prepared to put up in a good-natured spirit with his son's irregularities of conduct. On this account there was a certain justice in Bagshaw apparently more or less supporting his father in retirement.

Mr Bagshaw had risen in the night to relieve himself.

He was making his way to a bathroom in, or on the way down to, the basement. This fact at once raises questions as to the recesses of the Bagshaws' house, its interior architectural complications. An upper lavatory may not have existed, been out of order, possibly occupied, in view of what took place later. On the other hand, some preference or quirk may have brought him downstairs. He could have been making a similar journey, when I had seen him. Perhaps sleeping pills, digestive mixtures, medicaments of some sort, were deposited at this lower level. The essential thing was that Mr Bagshaw had to pass through the hall.

It seems to have been a mild night for the time of year. That did not prevent Mr Bagshaw from being surprised, even for a moment startled, when, turning on one of the lights, he saw a naked woman standing in the passage or hall. Here again the narrative lacks absolute positiveness. In a sense, the truth of its essential features is almost strengthened by the comparative unimportance adjudged to exact locality. Bagshaw's insistence on the mistletoe suggests the hall; other circumstances, a half-landing, or alcove, on the first-floor; not uncommon in a house of that date, possibly also offering a suitable nook or niche for mistletoe.

Bagshaw's father, short-sighted, had not brought his spectacles with him. His immediate assumption was that the dimly outlined female shape was one of his son's stepchildren, who, having taken a bath at a relatively unorthodox hour, had considered dressing not worth while for making the short transit required to her bedroom. Bagshaw, telling the story, admitted the girls behaved in a sufficiently unmethodical, not to say disordered manner, to make that possibility by no means out of the question. What seemed to have caused his father most surprise was not so much lack of clothing, but extinction of all movement. The naked lady was lost in thought, standing as if in silent vigil.

Mr Bagshaw made a conventional remark to the effect that she 'must not catch cold'. Then, probably owing to receiving no reply, grasped that he was not speaking to one of the family. He may also, in spite of his poor sight, have observed the lady's hair was grey, even if scarcely seeing well enough to appreciate threads of strawberry-pink caught by artificial light. Whatever he did or did not take in, one must concur in Bagshaw's praise of his father for showing good sense, in no manner panicking at this unforeseen eventuality. At one time or another, he had undoubtedly experienced testing incidents in the course of existence with Bagshaw as a son, but by then he was a man of a certain age, and, however happy-go-lucky the atmosphere of the household, this was exceptional. Speculation as to what Mr Bagshaw thought is really beside the point. What happened was that (as when I myself saw him) he muttered an apology, and moved on; his comportment model of what every elderly gentleman might hope to display in similar circumstances.

Whether or not he associated in his mind the midnight nymph with Gwinnett is another matter. Gwinnett by then had lived in the house some little time, probably a couple of months. Equally unknown is how Pamela, in the first instance, effected entry into the Bagshaw house. Even Bagshaw himself never claimed to be positive about that. His theory was she had somehow ascertained the whereabouts of Gwinnett's bedroom, then more or less broken in. That seems over-dramatic, if not infeasible. A more probable explanation, that one of the stepdaughters, the rather dotty, possibly pregnant one likeliest, had admitted her earlier in the evening, then denied doing so during subsequent investigations; Pamela finding Gwinnett in his room, or waiting there for his return. If the former, the two of them, Pamela and Gwinnett, had spent quite a long time, several hours, in the bedroom together, before Bagshaw's father encountered her, wherever he did, in an unclothed state.

She was no longer in the hall, or on the half-landing, when Mr Bagshaw reappeared on his return journey. He seems to have taken this as philosophically as he had earlier sight of her, simply retiring to bed again. If he hoped after that for a good night's rest, that hope was nullified by a further complication, a more ominous one. This development had taken place while he was himself down in the basement incommunicado. Bagshaw's other stepdaughter, Felicity, now played a part. Woken by the interchange, slight as that had been, between Pamela and Bagshaw's father, or (another possibility) herself cause of Mr Bagshaw's descent to the basement by excluding him from an upstairs retreat, perhaps noticing the light on, came down to see what was afoot. She was faced with the same spectacle, a slim grey-haired lady wearing no clothes. Bagshaw, when he spoke of the matter, added a gloss to the circumstances.

'The truth seems to be – I'd noticed it myself – Felicity had taken a fancy to Gwinnett. That was why she drew the obvious conclusions, and kicked up the hell of a row. So far as I know, Gwinnett hadn't made any sort of a pass at her. Perhaps that was what made her so keen on him. Before you could quote Proudhon's phrase about equilibrium of competition, her sister Stella heard the talking, and came down too. The whole lot were quarrelling like wild cats.'

Just what happened at this stage is not at all clear; nor at what moment were spoken the words to put in some sort of perspective subsequent events. Gwinnett, of course, himself appeared. He dealt as well as he could with Bagshaw's stepdaughters, while Pamela dressed and slipped away. Probably she retired on Gwinnett's arrival, leaving him to cope. She was not present by the time Bagshaw, made aware by the noise that something exceptional was taking place, joined the party. Mrs Bagshaw, like her father-in-law, assuming some comparatively minor domestic contingency in progress, still suffering from migraine, did not leave her bed. Avril, incurious or occupied with her own problems, also remained in her room. Bagshaw said that, insofar as it were possible to behave with dignity throughout the whole affair, Gwinnett contrived to do so.

'He didn't say much. Just offered some apologies. Of course, it was obviously Pamela Widmerpool's fault, not his. He didn't attempt to excuse himself on that account.'

The night's disturbances appear to have died down in a fairly banal family quarrel, nothing to do with Pamela or Gwinnett. In fact, the following day, Bagshaw — so far as I know, May Bagshaw too — was prepared for all to be forgiven and forgotten. On this point Bagshaw's father and stepdaughters do not seem to have been consulted. Gwinnett himself was firm that he must leave. He moved to a hotel (another of Trapnel's haunts) the same afternoon. Bagshaw said he was uncertain what he felt after Gwinnett had gone.

'I was sorry to lose him. At the same time I saw, from his own point of view, it would be difficult to stay on. The whole thing might happen again, if that woman knew he was still living with us. Of course, I thought they were having an affair, that she had come to the house to sleep with him. If so, I couldn't see why either of them needed to make all that to-do. Couldn't he have done whatever her other lovers do? That was how it looked at the moment.'

By the time Bagshaw told the story himself, a good deal had happened to give opportunity for improving its framework, accentuating highspots of the narrative. One could not be quite sure he had not seen things differently during the embroilment. For example, he spoke of words, possibly apocryphal, murmured by Pamela, as she withdrew (however that had happened) from the house. Bagshaw put this scarcely coherent sentence forward as key to what took place later, explanation, too, of the night's doings, or lack of them; for that matter, general relationship with Gwinnett.

Bagshaw could not swear to the exact phrase. It had something to do with 'dead woman' or 'death wish'. He also asserted that Gwinnett, while staying in the house, had spoken more than once of Pamela's conjunction with Ferrand-Sénéschal, bearing out Dr Brightman's theory that Gwinnett himself was more than a little taken up with mortality. Bagshaw gave other instances. At the time, naturally, emphasis immediately afterwards was laid on the question why Pamela had been wandering about without any clothes. Reflecting on similar instances in my own experience, there was the time (actually not witnessed) when the parlourmaid, Billson, had walked naked into the drawing-room at Stonehurst; more tangibly, when the front door of her flat had been opened to myself by Jean Duport in the same condition. Unlike Candaules's queen, these two had deliberately chosen to appear in that state, not, as the Queen – anyway vis-à-vis Gyges – involuntarily nude. Perhaps the Tiepolo picture had done something to disturb the balance of Pamela's mind, in the light of her reported behaviour at the Bragadin dinner party. The situation – just what had really caused the doings at the Bragshaws' – remained, at the end of that year, still obscure. Most people who took any interest in the matter simply assumed Pamela and Gwinnett had been 'having an affair', some row taken place, notable only for Pamela's incalculable manner of handling things.

About January or February, Gwinnett himself sent a line saying he would like to meet. He wished the *Commonplace Book* returned to him, unless I particularly needed to keep it longer. We arranged to lunch together on a day I was coming to London. Gwinnett had not remained unaffected by the months spent in England. Whether the change was due to odd experiences undergone, or simply because he felt a sense of release in making a start on his book, was impossible to say. The transformation itself was not easy to define. Not exactly loosened up, he gave at the same time an impression of being on better terms with himself. Here in London he looked more 'American' than in Venice. He still wore his light blue lenses, only just observably tinted against the sun. It was not the effect of these. The spectacles, thin filament of moustache, secretive manner, implied quite other origins. One thought, for some reason, of the Near East, though he was not in the least oriental. Perhaps his air was Mexican. The Americanism had something to do with the intense whiteness of his shirt, cut low in the neck, the light shade of the heavily welted rubber-soled shoes, almost yellow in colour. The shoes were the first thing you noticed about him. Ignorant still of just what had happened at the Bagshaws', I had no way of rationalizing to myself the slight, but apparent alteration. The *Commonplace Book*, was handed over. Gwinnett mentioned that he had stayed with the Bagshaws, then decided he would work more easily in another of Trapnel's hotels.

'How much of the book have you done?'

'I might have roughed out the first quarter.'

He spoke of some of his discoveries. From various sources, he had unearthed material about Trapnel's early life in Egypt. Perhaps concentrating on Egypt had given Gwinnett the Near East look. He could list, among other things, racehorses Trapnel's father had ridden, and their owners. There were striking facts about the schools Trapnel had attended, which were many and various. Gwinnett had worked hard.

'Have you traced any of the girls?'

'I have.'

Tessa, who had immediately preceded Pamela as

object of Trapnel's love, was doing extremely well. She was secretary, evidently a high-powered one, to the chairman of a noted firm of merchant bankers. Tessa had been helpful to Gwinnett in a straightforward way, giving him a clear, unvarnished account of Trapnel's daily life, its interior economy, seen from the point of view of an intelligent, capable mistress, who wanted her lover to become a success as a writer. Although retaining affectionate memories of Trapnel, she decided in due course, she said, that he lacked the necessary stamina. That was an interesting first-hand view. Gwinnett had appreciated its good points.

'Then there was Pat.'

Pat, now married to a don, Professor of Social Science, had been less willing to have her past dredged up. She had replied with a tactful letter saying she preferred not to see Gwinnett.

Sally was dead. That was all he had been able to find out about her.

'I'd have liked to know more – how and why she died.'

Jacqueline had married a journalist, and was living abroad, where her husband was foreign correspondent to a daily paper. Linda could not be traced.

'Did you know Pauline?'

'I never met her. I've heard Trapnel speak of her. He thought her depraved. Those were his words. They remained on good terms after parting.'

'I ran Pauline to earth.'

'What's she doing?'

'She's become a call-girl.'

'Trapnel said that was where Pauline would end.'

'Well, not much short of that, I'd say.'

Gwinnett seemed uncertain whether or not to qualify the description. He thought for a moment, then decided against amendment.

'I went to see her. She told me some facts.'

'Such as?'

'What some of her clients like.'

'Anything out of the usual run?'

'Not much, I guess.'

'I'd have thought Trapnel pretty normal.'

'She said he was.'

Gwinnett changed the subject. I thought he had abandoned it. I was wrong. He was choosing another conversational angle, one of his habits, at times effected in a manner a little disconcerting.

'Did Lindsay Bagshaw say there'd been some trouble at his place?'

'I haven't seen him, but I heard something of the sort. I knew you'd left.'

'You heard Lady Widmerpool kicked up a racket there?'

'Her name was mentioned.'

'As raising hell?'

'Well, yes.'

'If you run across Lady Widmerpool, do you mind not telling her my address?'

'OK.'

'You heard about Lord Widmerpool being denounced on the radio as a British agent? Lindsay Bagshaw talked his head off about it. I'm not that interested in politics, though I couldn't but be interested in such a thing happening. Just because of all the Trapnel tie-up with her. What do you think?'

'He might be in deep water. Hard to say, at this stage.'

Gwinnett hesitated, seeming, as he sometimes did, uncertain of the exact ground he wanted to occupy.

'Lady Widmerpool — Pamela — I wouldn't be in her husband's shoes, if she's left to decide his fate.'

'She's got it in for him?'

'That's how it looks.'

'You're avoiding her for the time being?'

That was a reasonable question in the circumstances. Gwinnett did not answer it. At the same time he accepted its inferences.

'Just to duck back to Pauline for a spell – she had dealings with Lord Widmerpool.'

'Professional ones, you mean?'

'Sure.'

'He picked her up somewhere? Answered an ad?'

'When his wife was living with Trapnel, Widmerpool, had her shadowed. As a former girl friend of Trapnel's, whom he saw once in a while, Pauline's name was given to Widmerpool.'

'And he went to see her?'

'They met somehow.'

'Continued to meet?'

'It seems arrangements were made satisfactory to both sides. Pauline later figured at several parties attended by Widmerpool – and the Frenchman, too, who died all that sudden, when Pamela was around.'

'Pauline told you that?'

Gwinnett nodded. He had a way with him when he sought information. At least information was what he acquired.

'Was Pamela herself included in these Pauline jaunts?'

'I don't know for certain. I don't believe so.'

Thought of Pamela seemed to depress Gwinnett. He fell into one of his glooms. Their relationship was an enigma. Perhaps he was in love with her, in spite of everything. We parted on good terms, the best. Gwinnett spoke as if we were likely to talk together again as a matter of course, do that quite soon. At the same time he parried any suggestion of coming to see us; even arranging another meeting in London. This determination that initiative should remain in his hands was a reminder of Trapnel methods. Possibly it was one of the ways in which Gwinnett was growing to resemble Trapnel.

During the next month or so, Gwinnett's problems receded in my mind as a matter of immediate interest, Widmerpool's too. Fresh information about the second of those came from two rather unexpected sources. These followed each other in quick succession, although quite unconnected.

For several years after the war, I had attended reunion dinners of one of the branches of the army in which I had served, usually deciding to do so at the last moment, even then never quite knowing what brought me there. Friends made in a military connexion were, on the whole, to be seen more conveniently, infinitely more agreeably, in settings of a less deliberate character, where former brother officers, now restored to civilian life in multitudinous shapes, had often passed into spheres with which it was hard to make conversational contact. Intermittent transactions in the past of forgotten military business provided only a frail link. All the same, when something momentous like a war has taken place, all existence turned upside down, personal life discarded, every relationship reorganized, there is a temptation, after all is over, to return to what remains of the machine, examine such paraphernalia as came one's way, pick about among the bent and rusting composite parts, assess merits and defects. Reunion dinners, to the point of morbidity, gave the chance of indulging in such reminiscent scrutinies. Not far from a vice, like most vices they began sooner or later to pall. Even the first revealed the gap, instantaneously come into being on demobilization, between what was; what, only a moment before, had been. On each subsequent occasion that hiatus widened perceptibly, moving in the direction of an all but impassable abyss.

There were, of course, windfalls. One evening, at such

an assemblage, my former Divisional Commander, General Liddament (by then promoted to the Army Council) turned up as guest of honour, making a lively speech about the country's military commitments 'round the map', ending with a recommendation that everyone present should read Trollope. That was an exceptional piece of luck. In the same way, an old colleague would sometimes appear; Hewetson, who had looked after the Belgians, now senior partner in a firm of solicitors: Slade, Pennistone's second-string with the Poles, head-master of a school in the Midlands: Dempster, retired from selling timber, settled in Norway, still telling his aunt's anecdotes about Ibsen. Finn, Commanding Officer of the Section, was dead. At the end of the war he had gone back briefly to his cosmetic business in Paris, soon after left, to end his days in contemplation of his past life and his VC, near Perpignan. Pennistone (mar-ried to a French girl, said to have taken an energetic part in the Resistance) had stepped into Finn's place in the firm. His letters reported good sales. He rarely came to England, spare time from the office taken up with writing a book on the philosophical ideas of Cyrano de Bergerac.

Usually there was less on offer, fewer, still fewer, even known by sight. That was especially true when the thinned ranks of branches, originally designed to be re-united on this particular occasion, were augmented by other elements. These, if remotely related in duties, had once been regarded with a certain professional suspicion, but their attendance too dwindled through death and inanition, requiring, as we did, bolstered numbers to make the party worth while. In short, feeling increas-ingly isolated, I lost the habit of attending these dinners. Then, a son likely to become liable for military service, it seemed wise to re-establish bearings in a current army world, find out what was happening, pick up any-thing to be known. I put down my name again, without much hope of seeing anyone with whom closer bonds were likely to be evoked than shared memory of whether or not some weapon, piece of equipment, had 'come off the security list' for release to the Allies, or by swopping stories about the shortcomings, as an officer and a man, of the unpopular brigadier.

That year the dinner was held on the premises of a club or association of vaguely patriotic intent, unfamiliar to myself both in membership and situation. The dining-room was decorated in a manner sober to the point of becoming sepulchral, drinks obtainable from a bar at one end. No one standing about there was an acquaintance. At the table assigned to my former Section, faces were equally unknown. Mutual introductions took place. My righthand neighbour, Lintot, fair, bald, running to fat, had looked after some of the Neutrals – a 'dismal crowd', he said – before Finn commanded, later posted to Censorship in the Middle East. He worked in a travel agency. We talked of the best places to take an autumn holiday abroad.

Macgivering, on the other side, also belonged to a War Office epoch earlier than my own. His duties had been in the Section handling in-coming telegrams, where he remembered the stunted middle-aged lieutenant, for ever polishing his Sam Browne belt. We had both forgotten his name. Macgivering himself, tall, spare, haggard, with a slight stutter, had been invalided out of the army, consequent on injury from enemy action, while in bed at his flat one early night of the blitz. We split a bottle of indifferent Médoc, and discussed car insurance, as he had some sort of public relations connection with the motor business.

Only towards the end of dinner did I notice Sunny Farebrother sitting at the end of a table on the far side of the room. During the war he had operated in several areas of army life, including at least one of those branches now joined to the increasingly disparate elements of this dinner. He had found himself a place at right angles to the 'high table', where more important members or guests sat. He was talking hard. His neighbour looked like a relatively senior officer, whom Farebrother appeared to be indoctrinating with some ideas of his own. Fare-brother looked in the best of form. He must be close on seventy, I thought. At the end of these dinners movement away from table places was customary, so that people could circulate. I decided to have a word with Farebrother at this interspersion. He was still in earnest conversation with the supposed general, when the time came. He could be pushing a share in which he was interested. I had not seen him at or near the bar on arrival. Probably he had deliberately turned up at the last moment to avoid threatened liability for buying a drink.

While I waited for a suitable moment to move across to Farebrother's table, a man with woolly grey hair and wire spectacles (the latter not yet a fashionable adjunct) came to speak with Lintot. Macgivering had already left, to make contact elsewhere in the room. I changed into his former seat, to allow the wire-spectacled man to talk in more comfort sitting next to Lintot. They appeared to know each other through civilian rather than army connexions. Lintot was astonished at the wire-spectacled man's presence at this dinner. His wonderment greatly pleased the other.

'Didn't expect to find your accountant here, did you, Mr Lintot? We can both of us forget the Inland Revenue for once, can't we? To tell the truth, I'm attending this dinner under rather false pretences. The fact is a friend of mine told me he was coming to London for this reunion. We wanted to talk together about certain matters, one thing and another, so as I'd gained a technical right to be deemed Intelligence personnel, I applied to the organizers of this "I" dinner. They said I could come. I always enjoy these get-togethers. My old mob have one. There's a POW one too. Why not roll up, I said to myself.'

'Never knew you were in the army. Of course we've always had a lot of other things to talk about, so that wasn't surprising.'

Lintot appeared rather at a loss what to say next. He drew me into the conversation, mentioning we had been in the same Section, though not in the War Office at the same period.

'This is – well, I've got to be formal, and call you Mr Cheesman, because I only know your initials – this is Mr Cheesman, whose accountancy firm acts for mine. For me personally too. We do our best against the taxman between us, don't we? I didn't expect to find him here. Never thought of Mr Cheesman as a military man somehow, though I never think of myself as one either, if it comes to that.'

'Yes, but you see my point. If I'm eligible, no reason why I shouldn't come to the dinner, is there?'

Cheesman was insistent. He was not in the least put out by Lintot's emphasis on the unmilitary impression he gave. What he was keen on, pedantically keen, consisted in establishing his, so to speak, legal right to be at the party. He spoke in a precise, measured tone, as if attendance at the dinner were a matter of logic, as much as free choice.

'Of course, of course. Glad to see you here. You're about the only man in the room I've met before.'

Lintot was quite uninterested in Cheesman's bona fides as 'I' personnel. Cheesman accepted that his point had been understood, even if unenthusiastically. Now, I remembered that manner, at once mild and aggressive. It brought back early days in the army – Bithel, Stringham, Widmerpool.

'Didn't you command the Mobile Laundry?'

I appended the number of General Liddament's Division to that question.

'You were there just for a short time, the Laundry only attached. Then it was posted to the Far East.'

Cheesman drew himself up slightly.

'Certainly I commanded that sub-unit. May I ask your name?'

I told him. It conveyed nothing. That was immaterial. Cheesman's own identity was the important factor.

'Surely you fetched up in Singapore?'

Cheesman nodded.

'In fact, you were a Jap POW?'

'Yes.'

Cheesman gave that answer perfectly composedly, but for a brief second, something much shorter than that, something scarcely measurable in time, there shot, like forked lightning, across his serious unornamental features that awful look, common to those who speak of that experience. I had seen it before. Cheesman's face re-verted – the word suggests too extended a duration of instantaneous, petrifying exposure of hidden feeling – to an habitual sedateness. I remembered his arrival at Div. HQ; showing him the Mobile Laundry quarters; making this new officer known to Sergeant-Major Ablett. Bithel had just been slung out. I had left Cheesman talking to the Sergeant-Major (who had the sub-unit well in hand), while I myself went off for a word with Stringham. One of Cheesman's peculiarities had been to wear a waistcoat under his service-dress tunic. He had been surprised at that garment provoking amused comment in mess.

'A waistcoat's always been part of any suit I wore. Why change just because I'm in the army? I've got to keep warm in the army, like anywhere else, haven't I?'

He did not give an inch, either, in adapting himself to military manners and speech, behaving to superiors as he would in a civilian firm, where he was paid to give the best advice he could in connexion with his own employment. He dressed nothing up in the forms and terms traditional to the military subordinate. Colonel Hogbourne-Johnson had been particularly irked by that side of Cheesman. He used to call him 'our Mr Cheesman', a phrase in which Cheesman himself would have found nothing derogatory. Thirty-nine when he joined the army at the beginning of the war, he wanted to 'command men'. He must be nearly sixty now. Except when that frightful look shot across his face, the features were scarcely more altered than Sunny Farebrother's.

'How the hell did you survive your Jap POW camp?' asked Lintot cheerfully.

Cheesman brushed the question aside.

'A bit of luck. The Nips were moving some of their prisoners in '44. Don't know where they were taking us. When we were at sea, the Nip transport was sunk by an American warship. No arrangements made for POWs, of course, when ship's company took to the boats, but the Americans rescued most of us – and a lot of the Nips too.'

'Don't expect you were feeling too good by that time?'

'Naturally I wasn't fit for normal duties for a month or two. When I was on my feet again, I got a change of job. They were short of Intelligence wallahs where I was. I'd picked up a few words of Japanese. It was thought better to make use of me in "I", rather than go back to Mobile Laundry duty, though I'd have liked to return to the job for which I'd been trained. That's why I'm allowed here, without being strictly speaking applicable. Funny meeting you, Mr Jenkins. I don't remember your face at all at that Div. HQ. The officer I recall is the DAAG, Major Widmerpool. He made quite an impression on me. Very efficient, I should say. A really good officer. You can always tell the type. I expect he's done well in civilian life too.'

'Do you remember a man in your sub-unit called Stringham?'

Cheesman looked surprised at the question.

'Of course I do. How did you know Stringham?'

'We were friends in civilian life.'

'You were?'

Cheesman found that statement hard to credit. He thought about it for a second or two. Stringham and I – that was the impression – seemed miles apart. He wrestled with the question inwardly. When at last he answered, it was as if prepared to accept my word, even then the claim scarcely believable.

'I see. I do recall now Stringham wasn't just the ordinary bloke you find in the ranks. I was taken aback at first when you said you'd known him. Of course, you get all sorts in a war. He was a superior type, an educated man. You could see that. All the same I never thought about it much. He never made any difficulties. I'd forgotten altogether. Just remember him in the jobs he used to do. I could never place him myself. What was his work in civilian life?'

That was a hard question to answer. What did Stringham do? Cheesman must be told something. What about the time when (with Bill Truscott as dominant colleague) he had been a sort of personal secretary to Sir Magnus Donners? I fell back on that. To be a secretary implied at least a measure of professional identity. That would serve the purposes of the moment.

'Stringham was private secretary to a business tycoon.'

'Oh, was he?'

Cheesman seemed at first more surprised than ever. He did not pursue the matter. His own job could well have brought him face to face with eccentric business tycoons. Either that struck him, or he decided to leave the question vague in solution.

'He was very fond of making jokes, but I always found him an excellent worker in my sub-unit.'

Cheesman said that without the least disapproval. He

spoke as one merely registering an unusual characteristic. So far as jokes were concerned, his own features proclaimed a state of intact virginity as to any experience or sense of them, immaculately so. Cheesman had never made a joke, never seen a joke, could live – and die – without jokes, even if he knew they existed. It did him credit to have so far rationalized Stringham's behaviour as to be capable of thus defining it. Stringham might have been worse typified.

'Stringham made jokes in the camp,' he added.

'He wasn't taken from Singapore too?'

'No.'

Again the ghastly forked lightning flashed, a flicker of Death's vision, reflected for a dreadful instant behind the wire spectacles' plates of glass. The flesh of Cheesman's face, softly wrinkled, made one think of those old servants of the past, who had worked unquestioningly for a lifetime in a single household. In Cheesman's case this unchanging interior had been, no doubt, his own austere, limited – one might reasonably say heroic – personality. There was the same self-assurance as Dan Tokenhouse, the same impression of having dispensed with sex. There was something else too.

'Stringham died in the camp. He behaved very well there.'

Cheesman thought for a moment after saying that.

'Very well. Yes. A good man. He wasn't too strong, you know. Fancy your having met him. They're odd these things. Sergeant-Major Ablett, you may remember him. He was rescued. He's quite prosperous now.'

The matter was better pressed no further. More information could easily become too much, too much anyway for one's peace of mind. Cheesman gave no sign that might be so. He also made no attempt to enlarge. Lintot, understandably, had not been much interested in these reminiscences. If Cheesman were his personal accountant, as well as his firm's, he may have felt he had a better right than myself to Cheesman's attention, even if he had brought us together again.

'Don't mind my talking shop for a moment, Mr Cheesman. It will save a letter. Now about Tax Reserve Certificates . . .'

By then Farebrother's senior officer had managed to get away, with or without buying the shares remained unknown. Farebrother himself was making preparations to leave the party, giving a final look round the room to make sure he had missed no one worthy of a few minutes' conversation. I went across to him. His friendliness was positively enormous. The powerful extrusion of Farebrother charm remained altogether undiminished by age. He was specially pleased about something, possibly success in whatever he had recommended his neighbour.

'There's an empty stretch of table over there, Nicholas. Let's sit at it. I don't feel like any more to drink, do you? Got to cut down on the pleasures of life nowadays. Something I want to ask you. What do you think of the latest development in the Widmerpool case?'

'I didn't know there was a case.'

'You haven't read the evening paper? The Question in the House? I think he's for it now.'

Farebrother was amazed anyone should have missed such a pleasure as that night's evening paper. His handsome greyhound profile, additionally distinguished with increased age, lighted up while he supplied a commentary. He made clear that, in his opinion, this news was going to offer no minor revenge. The Parliamentary Question had been on the subject of Widmerpool's commercial activities in Eastern Europe. To outward appearance worded in terms not at all sensational, they were, to an initiate in that form of attack, ominous in the extreme. The country concerned was the one where Widmerpool had been named in connexion with the State trial. Farebrother said he understood there had also been a denunciation on the air in one of their official broadcasts.

'The implications are of the most damaging order.'

'What's he really been up to?'

Farebrother, usually in the habit of cloaking his own imputations or reprisals in mild, vaguely expressed language, now made no bones about the disaster threatening his old enemy. He seemed to know more than was easily to be drawn from the mere wording of the Question, however much that were open to sophisticated interpretation. His war service (like that of Odo Stevens) had given Farebrother contacts from which such enlightenment might be derived. Someone in a position to 'know' could have dropped a hint. That was certainly the impression Farebrother himself, truly or not, hoped to give.

'Some underling on their side was accepting bribes, and has now defected, so I've heard said. That had been done with Widmerpool's connivance. He had been giving encouragement, too, by passing across little bits of information himself from time to time. How valuable that information was remains to be seen. In any case, I'm just putting two and two together. Most of it guesswork.'

'Will it come to arrest, a trial?'

'That depends what the employee reveals – if that story is true.'

'In any case that would be *in camera*?'

'You can't say. Some evidence probably.'

'The Question is just a ranging shot?'

'Not far from the target. Give him a jolt. I can tell you something else too.'

Farebrother looked about to make sure no one was sitting near us, who might overhear what he was going to say. Most of the diners were now congregated round the bar. Many had left, or were leaving. He put his arm over the back of my chair.

'I've just retired from one of the smaller merchant banks. We deal with European and overseas commercial activities and investments. Fascinating work.'

I toyed with the fantasy that Trapnel's former girl, Tessa, was going to abut on to what Farebrother had to say, then remembered Gwinnett had described her as working for the chairman of a large, rather than small, merchant bank.

'I don't mind telling you some of the Eastern European deals of our friend might be of interest from the taxation angle, if figures had to be produced in a court of law. Nothing to do with treasonable dealings, just bank statements. I make no accusations. Just of interest, I suggest.'

Farebrother smiled his charming smile. He settled back into his own chair. Then he looked at his watch.

'Good gracious me, I must be getting home. Geraldine and I are not at all late birds.'

'She is well, I hope.'

Farebrother snapped his fingers in the air to give some idea of his wife's overflowing health and spirits. He was in his gayest mood. The Parliamentary Question had made his day. It provided something far better, in a different class, from the occasion when Widmerpool's career had been threatened by nothing worse than the disapproval of General Liddament.

'We've found a nice little flat, not too expensive, well appointed as you could wish. Geraldine has a wonderful instinct for the right sort of economies, so we don't have to be thinking about the pennies all the time now. In fact we find we can run a country cottage too. Roses are my interest these days. I don't mind telling you, Nicholas, I'm rather proud of my roses. You and your wife must look us up, if you're ever passing. We can't always manage luncheon. Tea certainly. Well, it's been a most enjoyable evening. I heard Ivo Deanery was to be present as a guest – can't remember if you know him, he's a major-general now – and we settled some useful matters. Don't forget that invitation – preferably when the roses are in bloom.'

He repeated the address of the cottage, waved one of his genial goodbyes, was gone. The following day, the Parliamentary Question was brought up again at another party, in very different circumstances. This occasion owed something to the diplomatic détente of which Bagshaw had spoken. The so-called 'thaw' had been reflected, in a minor manner, by the tour through some of the European capitals of a well-known Russian author, bestseller in his own country. To give a few of our own literary world opportunity to meet a confrère not in general encountered in the West, a luncheon, to which I found myself invited, was given at the Soviet Embassy.

At this gathering, a foreseen profusion of literary figures had been perceptibly infused with a sprinkling of MPs, other notabilities, official and semi-official, either with a view to imparting additional robustness of texture to the party, or, more probably, simply to work off individuals, whose names were listed for entertainment, sooner or later, on the ambassadorial roster. Including our hosts of the Embassy staff, a large number of whom were present, about forty or fifty persons were drinking vodka, sampling zakuski, sitting in small groups scattered about a long, austerely decorated drawing-room. There was a faint atmosphere of constraint, as if someone or something essential to the party had not yet been manifested, but that would happen in a moment, when, from then on, all would be well, much easier, more relaxed.

The invitation had not included wives of writers asked as guests, but both the Quiggins were there, Quiggin's status as a publisher no doubt judged of sufficient eminence to be considered out of context, permitting accompaniment of his novelist consort. Alaric Kydd – to use a favourite phrase of Uncle Giles's – was behaving as if he owned the place. Other writers included L. O. Salvidge, Bernard Shernmaker, Quentin Shuckerly, a lot more, men greatly predominating in numbers over women. Mark Members was absent, known to be ill; Len Pugsley, not important enough, or considered too closely 'committed' to be asked to a purely social party. Evadne Clapham had also been overlooked, more probably barred from acceptance by a too relentless social programme of her own. Dr Brightman, sprucely dressed in a fur cap and high fur collar, revealing a rather chilly manner to Ada Leintwardine, passed her with a smile, moving on to where L. O. Salvidge and I were chatting to one of the secretaries of embassy.

'I hope you don't think my clothes too *voulu*?'

The secretary nodded, and laughed. He was a tall fair young man, of surface indistinguishable from any other member of London's diplomatic corps of similar age and seniority. We discussed signs of spring in the London parks. The young secretary moved away for a moment to receive incoming guests. Salvidge caught my eye. His silent lips formed the words 'KGB'. The secretary returned before any sort of secretly uttered return comment was possible. Dr Brightman shared none of Salvidge's trepidation about our surroundings.

'Have you seen anything of Russell Gwinnett? I've quite lost touch with him. He was staying at one moment with some people called Bagshaw. He wrote to me from their house. Rather a depressed letter. I hear he left after some sort of trouble. The most extraordinary story I was told.'

Salvidge must have thought this subject dangerously controversial, perhaps because Gwinnett was American. He showed disquiet. At the same time he did not want to appear excluded from the circles of which Dr Brightman spoke.

'Gwinnett came to see me. We had a talk. A nice

young man. Not very exciting. I was not sure he was up to tackling so picturesque a figure as Trapnel.'

Salvidge turned to the secretary to explain what he was talking about.

'This is a young writer called Gwinnett – G-W-I-N-N-E-T-T – who is writing a book about a novelist, now dead, called Trapnel – T-R-A-P-N-E-L – a good writer. One of our best.'

'Yes?'

Salvidge must have thought this the moment to change the subject, probably what he had been leading up to.

'Dr Brightman here, you know, is writing a book about Boethius – B-O-E-no diphthong – '

The secretary nodded politely, but cut Salvidge off.

'See, we must go into luncheon.'

We were firmly shepherded into the dining-rom. So far as Salvidge was concerned, not a moment too soon. Here again was a faint sense of austerity, an impression of off-white walls sparsely decorated with pictures, landscapes light in tone – the steppe – birch trees – sunset on snow – nothing in the least reminiscent of Tokenhouse and his school. My place at table was between another secretary, possibly counsellor, somewhat older than the first, equally trimmed to outward diplomatic convention; on the other side, a personage not encountered for years, Bill Truscott.

Tipped, as a young man, for at least a place in the Cabinet, even if by some mischance he failed to become Prime Minister, Truscott, after a promising start at Donners-Brebner, had come to rest in some governmental corporation, possibly the Coal Board. The Russian engaged with his other neighbour when I sat down, Truscott and I went through the process of recalling where we had last met. He still carried some of his old, rather distinguished style, a touch, too, of the old underlying toughness that had made people think he would forge ahead. Fresh from observing Farebrother as a professional charmer, one could not help feeling Truscott, at least ten years younger, had worn worse. His manner dated. If he had become the 'great man' predicted, no doubt it would have been perfectly serviceable As he was, the demeanour was a trifle laboured, ponderous.

I thought of my undergraduate days, when Truscott had been not merely an imposing, but positively frightening figure, setting up, by his flow of talk, standards of sophistication never to be contemplated as attainable. This brilliance of exterior, again, had been of quite a different sort from Glober's. Even in those days, Truscott had been far less lively. There could be no great difference in age, even if the advantage was slightly on Truscott's side. Unlike Glober, he had remained a bachelor. I spoke of Sillery's ninetieth birthday party. It appeared Truscott had not been invited. He showed a little bitterness about that. It was true he had been one of the staunchest vassals of Sillery's court. He should not have been forgotten. He asked if I often found myself in this embassy.

'My first visit – and you?'

'I'm asked from time to time. I'm afraid I'm not at all conversant with the current work of the guest of honour. I never read novels nowadays . . .'

Possibly thinking that admission, for more than one reason, suggested a too headlong falling-off from what had once been an all embracing intellectual coverage, Truscott corrected himself. He gave one of his winning smiles.

'That is, you understand, I don't find much time, with so many things going on – as we all have – of course I fully intend . . . and naturally . . .'

I told him what I had heard about Stringham, once his fellow secretary. Truscott showed interest.

'Very sad. Poor Charles. He was a pleasant companion. One of the nicer people round Donners.'

Thought of his days working for Sir Magnus must have brought Widmerpool to mind; more specifically, as agent of his own sacking from Donners-Brebner. He lowered his voice.

'Hardly a subject for discussion here, but one cannot help being a little intrigued by the embarrassments, at the moment, of another protégé of Sir Magnus of that period.'

'What's going to happen to him?'

By that time, having read the morning paper, I saw what Farebrother meant by speaking of Widmerpool's position as insecure. Truscott certainly thought the same. He coughed, in a semi-official manner.

'I should expect various enquiries of a – well, not exactly public nature – not immediately public, I mean – likely to be set on foot.'

'You think it pretty serious?'

'That would certainly be . . .'

'Might come to a trial?'

'One cannot tell. I – '

Massive middle-aged waitresses had been bustling about the room, snapping out a sharp commentary to each other in their own language, as they clattered with the plates. Now, one of them interposed a large dish of fish between Truscott and myself, severing our connexion. At the same moment, my Russian neighbour began a conversation. Soon, by natural processes, we were discussing Russian writers. After Lermontov and Pushkin, Gogol and Gontcharov, Tchekov and Tolstoy, Dostoevsky's name cropped up. Pennistone – who would never allow intellectual standards to be lowered, just because he was in the army, a war on – had complained that, when he spoke of Dostoevsky's Grand Inquisitor to General Lebedev, the Soviet military attaché (unconvincing as a regular soldier) had recommended Nekrasov's truer picture of Russian life. In short, Dostoevsky, impossible to ignore, equally impossible to assimilate into Communist life, a monolithic embarrassment to his countrymen, was a tendentious subject for the present luncheon party, however unequivocally political the tradition of the Russian novel. Remembering Trapnel once speculated on the meaning of the surname 'Karamazov', I put the question.

'Am I right in thinking "kara" has some implication of blackness? The former Serbian royal house, Karageorgevitch, was not that founded by Black George? But "mazov"? How would that be translated into English?'

My Russian neighbour laughed. He seemed very willing that a Dostoevskian commentary should move into etymological channels, away from potentially political ones. The idea of giving The Brothers an English surname pleased him.

'I shall consult a colleague.'

He spoke quickly in his own language across the table. There was a short discussion. He returned to me.

'He says "kara" means "black" in Turkish. There is a Russian adjective "chernomazy" — do you say "swarthy"? Then "maz", it is "grease", the verb, to smear or to oil. Would that be "varnish" in English?'

Dr Brightman, sitting next to the informant on the other side of the table, was not to be left out of a discussion of this nature. She showed interest at once.

'*The Brothers Blackvarnish?* No, that would hardly do, I think. We must find something better than that.'

She shook her head, giving the matter her full attention.

'How would *The Blacklacquer Brothers* be?'

We discussed the question. While we did so, I reflected how this was all based on Trapnel's meditation on the meaning of the name, his argument with Bagshaw in that dreary pub came back, Trapnel's contention that there was no such thing as Naturalism in novel writing, one of his favourite themes.

'Reading novels needs almost as much talent as writing them,' he used to say.

The occasion had been just before Bagshaw and I had taken him home, on the way found that Pamela had thrown his manuscript into the Regent Canal. Trapnel had said something else that evening too. Now the words came back, in the way spoken words do, with quite a new meaning.

'Call Hemingway's impotent good guy naturalistic? Think of what Dostoevsky would have made of him? After all, Dostoevsky did deal with an impotent good guy in love with a bitch.'

Was that the answer? Was he a good guy? Was he in love? Was the condition only released by Death? The train of thought was interrupted by Dr Brightman offering a new suggestion.

'Simply making use of the connection with linseed oil — *The Linseed Brothers*?'

'That omits the element of blackness, of darkness, which obviously broods over the story, and must be conveyed by the name.'

When it was time to thank for the party, leave, Truscott, who was by then talking with the Ambassador, gave a smile that indicated he had hopes of the very worst for Widmerpool. Coming down the steps of the Embassy, I found myself with the Quiggins. We walked along Kensington Palace Gardens together, moving south towards the High Street. I asked Ada if any progress had been made in deciding what was to be Glober's last great film.

'Do you mean to say you don't know? Louis is coming over next month. Everything is arranged.'

'What's it to be?'

'*Match Me Such Marvel*, of course. I'm sure it's going to make a box-office record. I can't wait.'

'So Trapnel's off?'

Ada showed more pity than astonishment.

'Trapnel?'

'Glober was going to do a Trapnel film when we were in Venice. Probably a kind of life of Trapnel, with Pamela Widmerpool in the lead. You'd only just begun to make St John Clarke propaganda with him.'

'He saw at once the St John Clarke novel was a much better idea.'

'Is Pamela equally happy?'

Quiggin cut in.

'I'm bored to death with this film of Glober's. I don't believe we're really going to make any money out of it, even if he does it. You never know with these people. Set against Ada's time writing her own novels, or working in the firm, I've always doubted whether it's worth while.'

'Oh, shut up,' said Ada.

She turned to me again.

'Do you really not know about Louis deciding on another girl for his leading lady, as well as ditching the Trapnel idea? That was all settled months ago.'

'Glober found Pamela too much in the end?'

'He fell for someone else.'

Quiggin continued to show irritation about the film.

'Do let's discuss another subject. The food at lunch wasn't too bad. I'm never sure Caucasian wine suits me. I thought he seemed rather a sulky little man, when I had a word with him through the interpreter.'

'Who's Glober fallen for now?'

'Why, Polly Duport, of course. You must live absolutely out of the world not to know that. He saw her in the Hardy film at the Venice Festival. She turned up there herself. It was an instantaneous click.'

'Didn't that cause trouble?'

'With Pam?'

'Yes.'

'I don't think Pam really cared by then, even if she cared much before. She was already mad about that other American, what was he called – Russell Gwinnett. She still is. Haven't you heard about what happened at the Bagshaws'?'

'I know about that, more or less, but not about Polly Duport.'

'You remember how horrid Pam was to me in Venice, considering what friends we'd been. She's been ringing me up almost daily lately, trying to find out what's become of Gwinnett. How should I know? I barely met him. The most I did was to ask for us to be allowed to consider his book on X. Trapnel, when it's finished.'

This upset Quiggin again.

'A book on X. Trapnel is never going to sell. Why get us involved in it at all. It would only mean more money down the drain.'

'So any question of Pamela marrying Glober is at an end?'

'Why should she marry Glober?'

'You said he wanted to marry her – not just have an affair with her.'

'I did?'

'Yes.'

'I'm sure I didn't. Anyway, if I did, I shouldn't have done so. Forget about it. Of course, it's all off. How could it be anything else? Louis's terribly sweet and kind, but you never know what he's going to do next.'

'That's just what I've already stated,' said Quiggin.

'All film people go on like that. Never mind. I do think he really is keen on *Match Me Such Marvel*. Of course it's not going to be called that. We haven't decided on the best title yet. Polly is a marvellous girl too. Not only glamorous, but a real professional.'

'What I can't believe is Pamela making no row.'

'Even Pam realized she'd never get the part once Louis began taking Polly out to dinner.'

'Did Pamela meet Polly Duport?'

'I didn't think so. The Widmerpools went back to England halfway through the Film Festival. It was Pam's thing about Gwinnett, as much as anything else, that caused Louis to give her up. It serves Pam right. I believe she really did think she was going to become famous.'

'Why did Glober object so much? Gwinnett was positively running away from the situation, so far as anything Glober might object to. He still is. Even in the early stages, he only wanted Trapnel information.'

'Louis didn't think so. Anyway there was Pam. Perhaps it was because he was another American.'

'Is Glober going to marry Polly Duport now?'

'Isn't she married already, to an actor, though they're living apart? She was on her own when she came to Venice. Perhaps he will.'

'What does Widmerpool think about it all? His feelings don't seem to have been considered much, whether Pam leaves him or stays. Your idea was that he would be quite glad to get her taken off his hands. Now, if he goes to prison for spying, she'll be able to visit him in the Scrubs or Dartmoor, wherever he's sent — give him additional hell.'

Quiggin was outraged.

'You think that a matter to joke about?'

'Isn't that what it looks like?'

'That Parliamentary Question was disgraceful. Our own particular form of McCarthyism. All very gentlemanly, of course, none the less smearingly vindictive.'

'You think he'll emerge without a stain on his character?'

Quiggin was prepared to be less severe on that point.

'Haven't we all sins to forgive? Sins of over-enthusiasm, I mean. Look, Ada, there's our bus.'

# FIVE

Each recriminative decade poses new riddles, how best to live, how best to write. One's fifties, in principle less acceptable than one's forties, at least confirm most worst suspicions about life, thereby disposing of an appreciable tract of vain expectation, standardized fantasy, obstructive to writing, as to living. The quinquagenarian may not be master of himself, he is, notwithstanding, master of a passable miscellany of experience on which to draw when forming opinions, distorted or the reverse, at least up to a point his own. After passing the half-century, one unavoidable conclusion is that many things seeming incredible on starting out, are, in fact, by no means to be located in an area beyond belief. The 'Widmerpool case' fell into that category. It remained enigmatic so far as the public were concerned. People who liked to regard themselves as 'in the know' were not much better off, one rumour contradicting another, what exactly Widmerpool had done to put himself in such an awkward spot remaining undefined. One extraneous item came my own way, which, as purely negative evidence, could have been added to material sifted by whatever official body was undertaking an enquiry. It was expressed in the form of a picture postcard of the Doge's Palace.

'Have to date heard nothing from your friend about blocks. Weather here good. D. McN. T.'

That, at least, indicated none of the disaster, threatening Widmerpool on account of Dr Belkin's absence from the Conference, had resulted in Tokenhouse suffering comparable repercussions. I had intended to ask the

Quiggins about the blocks for the Cubist series, when walking with them after luncheon at the Soviet Embassy. More personally engrossing matters had intervened. The blocks remained forgotten. I sent Tokenhouse a postcard of Nelson's Column, saying (in army parlance) the matter would be looked into, a report forwarded.

In early summer, Isobel and I went by chance to a musical party organized by Rosie and Odo Stevens. It was a charity affair, our inclusion nothing to do with the meeting in Venice. In fact, the people who brought us knew the Stevenses hardly at all. I make this point to emphasize that guests present at this particular entertainment were not handpicked. No doubt everyone who received an invitation, in the first instance, was an acquaintance of some sort. Beyond such intermediaries stretched a relatively anonymous conflux of persons, whose passport to the house lay only in willingness to buy a ticket. Had things been otherwise, the evening might have turned out differently; possibly not certain other events that followed.

The Stevens house in Regent's Park, not large by the standards of Rosie's parents, though done up inside with a touch of the old Manasch resplendence, had room for a marquee to be built out on to a flat roof at the back to create an improvised auditorium, accommodating a respectable number of persons. Rosie had inherited two or three very acceptable pictures, and pieces of furniture, which Hugo Tolland, speaking from an antique dealer's point of view, regarded with respect. He had sold her two French commodes from his own shop, so they had not been acquired cheaply. Offering this sort of show for a charitable purpose was, on Rosie's part, a pious memento of the days when Sir Herbert and Lady Manasch, great patrons of the arts, had mounted similar projects. Stevens himself, claiming musical enthusiasms, as well as a strong taste for parties, may on this occasion have been at least as responsible as his wife. The 'good cause' was connected with one or more of the emergent African countries; the piece to be performed, Mozart's *Die Entführung aus dem Serail* – the *'Seraglio'*. The price of a ticket included supper after the opera had been performed.

Like the Soviet luncheon party – some of the same guests – there was a distinctly political flavour about the people collected, before the performance, in the Stevens drawing-room, MPs from both sides of the house, some African diplomatic representatives. This time the musical world, Rosie always maintaining links there, took the place of writers. Many of those present were unknown to myself. I recognized a Tory Cabinet Minister, and a female member of the Labour Shadow Cabinet, from pictures in the press. The music critic, Gossage, and Norman Chandler, who directed now, rather than dancing or acting, had come together. Gossage, a trifle more dried up and toothy than formerly, had exchanged his former pince-nez for rimless spectacles. His little moustache had gone white. Chandler, slightly filled out from the skeletal thinness of his younger days, retained a marionette-like appearance, a marionette now of a certain age. Living in one of the Ted Jeavons flats, Chandler had developed into rather a crony of Jeavons. They used to watch television together.

'Don't think there's much fear I'll be suspected,' Jeavons said. 'All the same, you never know what people will say behind your back.'

On arrival, Isobel had paused to talk with Rosie, who had been a former friend of Molly Jeavons. Moving through the crowd, I came on Audrey Maclintick. She announced the unforeseen fact that Moreland had advised on the *Seraglio*'s production. Quite apart from his poor health, that was unexpected. Moreland had always set his face against charity performances, although there had been occasions in the past when he had been more or less forced to take part in them. Audrey Maclintick agreed their presence was unlooked for. She added that it was not at all the sort of party she was used to. She had said just the same thing when Mrs Foxe had given a party for Moreland's Symphony, more than twenty years before. She herself was not much altered from then, even to the extent of still wearing a version, modified into a more contemporary style, of the dress which, at Mrs Foxe's, had caused Stringham to address her as 'Little Bo-Peep.'

'Hugh's name isn't on the programme?'

'He didn't want it there. The word "Africa" did it. Moreland's cracked about Africa. Always has been, always will be, I suppose. Goes off on the quiet to the British Museum to gaze on the African idols there. Mrs Stevens only had to say the money was going to Africa for Moreland to knock off all his other work, and set about the Mozart. Doesn't matter what worry it causes me. Of course, Moreland knew Mrs Stevens in what he loves to call The Old Days, so The Old Days might have been sufficient anyway, without being clinched by Africa. Whatever I said wasn't going to make any difference.'

Moreland, it was true, had always responded strongly to things African, rather as fountainhead of fetish and voodoo, than aspects of the African continent likely to be benefited by funds raised that night. The fascination exercised on his imagination by such incantatory cults was not unlike Bagshaw's unquenched curiosity about the ritual and dogma of Marxism, neither believers, both enthralled. Once Moreland's attention had been imaginatively aroused, he would find no difficulty in ignoring the fact that witch-doctors, zombies, cults of the dead, might not greatly profit from his help. Moreland himself came up at that moment. Audrey Maclintick did not give him time to speak.

'I expect you've seen who's here tonight – Lady Donners. That was bound to happen. Just her sort of party.

I don't expect she wants to see me, any more than I do her. Well, I'll leave you two together to have a talk about The Old Days, which I've no doubt you'll start off on at once. Don't let Moreland have another drink before the curtain goes up. It isn't good for him. He ought to be in bed in any case, not mooning about at a place like this.'

She made off. So far as Moreland having another drink, she was probably right. He did not look at all well. Once, he would have been put out by such an injunction from wife, mistress, anyone else, made a great fuss about being treated as if not able to look after himself. Now, he was not at all concerned, taking the admonition as a matter of course, almost a demonstration of affection, which no doubt in a sense it was. Audrey Maclintick was said to look after him well, in what were not always easy circumstances. Moreland, too, showed signs of accepting her view that his own presence in the Stevens house required excuse.

'Never again. Not after what I've been through with the *Seraglio* committee ladies. Valmont's valet remarked the big difference between persuading a woman to sleep with you, which she really wants to do – though personally I've often found to the contrary – and inducing her to agree to something that offers no comparable satisfaction. My God, he was right.

                                    Put me
          To yoking foxes, milking of he-goats,
          Gathering all the leaves fall'n this autumn.
          Drawing farts from dead bodies,
          Mustering of ants and numbering of atoms,
          There is no hell to a lady of fashion.

I don't mean Rosie. She's all right. It was the rest of them. They expected me to do just the very things I've mentioned – every one of them.'

233

'You've been saying for years you live beyond the pleasure principle. Why boggle at ladies of fashion? Do they still exist?'

'Believe me they do. Matty's one now. I've just been having a word with her. Almost the first since we were husband and wife, beyond saying hullo, when we saw each other at the Ballet or the Opera. She seems to have supported the death of the Great Industrialist remarkably well.'

Matilda Donners was standing on the far side of the room. I had the impression Moreland had never managed to fall entirely out of love with her.

'I got her to introduce me to Polly Duport, whom she's talking to now. I've always been rather a fan. What I mean about Matty's social manner is that, having brought Polly Duport and myself together, she then had to suggest that I do the musical settings for some film Polly Duport's going to play the lead in. It's made from a St John Clarke novel, if you can imagine anything more grotesque. I remember my aunt thinking me too young to read *Fields of Amaranth,* but it isn't that one, and that isn't my objection. The producer, an American called Glober, was also pressed on me by Matty. He's that tall, bald, melodramatic character, talking to her now, looking as if he's going to play Long John Silver in a Christmas production of *Treasure Island.*'

'You've met Glober before.'

I recalled to Moreland the Mopsy Pontner dinner party. The effect was almost startling. The blood came rushing into his face as if he were about to have apoplexy. He began to laugh uncontrollably, quite in the old manner. Then, with an effort, he stopped. He was almost breathless, coughing hard. At the end of this near paroxysm he looked less ill, more exhausted. The information had greatly cheered him.

'No, really, that's too much. Am I to be suffocated

by nostalgia? Will that be my end? I should not be at all surprised. I can see the headline:

MUSICIAN DIES OF NOSTALGIA

They'd put someone like Gossage on to the obit. "Mr Hugh Moreland – probably just Hugh Moreland these days – (writes our Music Critic), at a fashionable gathering last night – I'm sure Gossage still talks about fashionable gatherings – succumbed to an acute attack of nostalgia, a malady to which he had been a martyr for years. His best known works, etc., etc. . . ." Are you aware, quite apart from Matty turning up here tonight, there hangs on the stairs of this very house Barnby's drawing – in his naturalistic manner, I'm glad to say – of Norma, that little waitress at Casanova's Chinese Restaurant? All this, and Mopsy Pontner too. I can't bear it. I shall mount the stage, and announce that, instead of Mozart tonight, I am myself going to entertain the company with a potpourri of nostalgic melodies.'

Moreland paused. He stepped back, clasping his hands, intoned gently:

> 'Dearest, our day is over,
> Ended the dream divine.
> You must go back to your life,
> I must go back to mine.

Nothing short of some such outward expression of my own nostalgic feelings would be at all adequate. You shouldn't have told me about Mopsy Pontner. It wasn't the act of a friend.'

Although still laughing, Moreland, as before sometimes in such moods, had stirred himself emotionally by his own irony, his eyes filling with tears. Stevens came up to us.

'Look, Hugh, the curtain isn't going to rise absolutely

on time. One of the Violins was a minute or two late. The regular player went down with flu at the last moment, and a substitute had to be found at short notice. We've been assured he's all right. He's upstairs peeing at the moment, but he'll be along when he's finished, and start fiddling away. Don't get worked up about the delay.'

'You speak as if I was a temperamental impresario about to throw a scene. It's no affair of mine when the curtain goes up. I'd much rather have another drink, which the delay gives me the right to do, whatever Audrey says.'

It was remarkable he should admit to being defiant about what she said. Moreland went off. There was no means of putting a veto on drink into operation. He moved as if his joints were rather stiff these days. Stevens laughed.

'Isn't Hugh splendid? Rosie thought he wasn't well, but he seems perfectly all right to me. I say, who do you think have turned up tonight? The Widmerpools. I suppose he's celebrating.'

'What's he got to celebrate about? I thought he was going to be sent to the Tower, hanged, drawn and quartered.'

'Not now. It's been found "not in the public interest" to proceed with the case. I was hearing about it earlier in the day. A journalist I know told me some quite interesting things. Widmerpool was damned lucky. You can take it from me he was in a tight corner. I suppose he thought this a good opportunity to show himself in public. You can't exactly say with an untarnished reputation, but at least not serving twenty-five years for espionage.'

'Did he apply to you for a ticket, as a once close friend of his wife's?'

'The Widmerpools, old cock, were brought by a friend of Rosie's, Sir Leonard Short, a civil servant with musical leanings, who use to frequent her parents' house. As luck will have it, Tompsitt's here too, our ambassador in the place where Widmerpool was having his trouble. They'll be able to dish it up together. All very respectable.'

'Is the large grim lady Tompsitt's wife?'

'She's rather rich. Schweizer Deutsch. Been married before. Ah, things are moving quicker now. I see Rosie is making signs. Do you and Isobel know where your seats are? I want to talk to Isobel. I haven't seen her for ages.'

He obviously had no idea how much Isobel disliked him. We all passed into the marquee. The Widmerpools, with Short (knighted at the last Birthday Honours), were several rows in front. Short, although his prim buttoned-up exterior allowed few inner doubts to be observed, looked less happy than the occasion seemed to demand, if what Stevens reported about Widmerpool were true. Pressure had perhaps been put on him to arrange this public appearance signalizing exculpation. Less dramatically than that, Widmerpool could simply have wished to hear the opera performed because he hoped to be identified with this particular charity. Love of music was unlikely to have brought him, whatever other reason. He, too, was looking more aggrieved than triumphant. Short's apparent uneasiness – Widmerpool's too, for that matter – may have been due to discovering that Pamela was far from popular with her hostess. If it came to that, Short was not at all well disposed to Pamela himself. She sat beside him, a look of utter contempt on her face, at the same time, rare with her, smiling faintly. She had got herself up in her smartest manner. Only those who knew her reputation might have reflected that, in another, more perverse mood, she might easily have turned up to watch the *Seraglio* wearing an old pair of jeans.

Rosie, Stevens, the Tory Cabinet Minister, his wife,

Matilda Donners (who seemed to have brought the last two), were all sitting rather to the side of the front row. Their group, which included Polly Duport and Glober, had probably dined together. Behind the Widmerpools sat the Tompsitts, whom I had noticed on arrival. I had not set eyes on Tompsitt since hearing him, at the close of some interservice committee, deplore, with Widmerpool, the Poles' lack of circumspection in making representation about Katyn to the International Red Cross. The air of disorder, marking out Tompsitt in his early days as a young diplomatist free from the conventionality ascribed to his kind, had settled down to a middle-aged unkemptness, implying chronic irritability, as much as a free spirit. The exceptionally peevish expression on his face at that moment could be attributed to Widmerpool himself, who, leaning back in a manner threatening to repeat his wife's chair-breaking incident at the French Embassy, showed no sign of ceasing to talk, in deference to the opening notes of the Overture. Finally, Tompsitt's wife raised her programme menacingly. Widmerpool, bowing to force, turned away from them. The curtain rose revealing the Pasha's palace.

During the first interval, on the way out of the marquee, we came on Glober. He was holding Polly Duport lightly by the arm.

'Why, hullo, Nick. Fancy meeting you here. What a hell of a good time we all had in Venice. I'm not going to forget your Major Tokenhouse in years. I had that picture of his packaged, and sent back to the States, where it's to become one of the treasures of the Glober collection of twentieth-century primitives. Why didn't you stop over for the Film Festival, and meet Polly here?'

In saying all this Glober managed also to convey an odd sense of added remoteness, not only in speaking of our Venetian meeting, also somehow in relation to himself. He was not in the least unfriendly, absolutely the reverse, still enormously cordial, at the same time in a manner that set him at a distance, put a cordon round him, entrenched his position. It was a little like the rays people seem to emit when they have promised a job, promotion, invitation, satisfaction of one sort or another, then withdrawn the offer. He continued to speak for a minute or two about the Tokenhouse picture, imprisoning all around him within the net of his own social technique, moving on to the Film Festival, then the St John Clarke novel. He was not quite prepared for Isobel's knowledge (in certain areas rivalling Trapnel's) of obscure or forgotten fiction.

'How will you handle the scene where Phyllida and Prosper get lost in the mist on the glacier at Schwarenbach?'

While Glober dealt with that question, I reminded Polly Duport of our drive back from the St Paul's service, with her mother and stepfather. Undeniably a beauty, less remarkably so off the stage, she had now, I thought, come to resemble Duport more than Jean. She had her father's cool, wary scepticism, as well as Jean's figure and grey eyes. In her thirties, already well known, she had in the film at Venice somehow achieved this additional prestige, a flowering which had instinctively caught Glober's fancy, aroused his untiring interest in the immediate.

'I remember an English officer joining us. So that was you? I suppose you were keeping an eye on my stepfather, making sure he behaved properly in church?'

The comment recalled her mother.

'How is Colonel Flores?'

'Very well indeed. He's a general now, but more or less retired from the army, and in politics.'

'And your mother?'

'She's all right. Fine, in fact. Carlos's new job suits her. You see he's Head of the Government.'

'I didn't know that.'

'For a year now.'

'Dictator?'

'We don't call it that.'

'Your mother must enjoy being Dictatress – Dictatrix, more correctly.'

Polly Duport laughed. She was charming, in spite of resemblance to her father, much 'nicer', one felt, than her mother, but without, so far as I was myself concerned, any of her mother's former bowling-over endowments. Glober must have felt the reverse. Her professionalism of the Theatre, a seriousness her mother could never have achieved, in the Theatre, or any other of the arts, possibly exerting some of that effect on him.

'I think Mama would certainly rather do the job herself.'

'And your father?'

'Do you know him too? You are well up in our family. Papa's in the crude still.'

'The crude?'

This seemed an enormously suitable calling, whatever it was, for Duport to follow, but one could not in the least imagine financial or administrative shape taken by such employment.

'Crude oil. That's how it's known in the trade. His business is mixed up with importing into Canada for processing. He doesn't do too badly. That's his life. Has been for quite a long time now. He's rather crotchety these days. Trouble with his inside. He never really recovered from that upset in the war. Still, Papa has his moments.'

The way she said that recalled Jean again. Glober, who had been explaining to Isobel how he was going to shoot *Match Me Such Marvel* in Spain, returned to holding Polly Duport's arm.

'More Mozart now. We'll see you at the next intermission.'

The Widmerpools, Tompsitts, and Short, were standing not far away, the men discussing something in an undertone. Mrs Tompsitt, no beauty, looked less than pleased. As Stevens remarked, she had the air of being rich. She and Pamela were not talking together. Pamela's eye was on us. She was still smiling a little to herself. Glober glanced in her direction, raising his hand slightly in greeting. From the gesture, they appeared not to have met earlier that evening. Pamela made no sign in return, not altering her faint smile. If Glober felt himself in a delicate position, he gave no outward evidence of that. As he strolled away, hand on Polly Duport's elbow, he was perfectly at ease.

'That was the American who planned to run away with Lady Widmerpool, but is to do so no longer?'

'That's the one.'

'She's looking rather frightening tonight.'

Isobel's comment, although it could not possibly have been heard by Pamela at that range, appeared in some manner to react on her. As we approached the marquee again, she broke off from the Tompsitt group, and came towards us. We said good evening.

'I've just this afternoon found where Gwinnett's staying.'

Pamela spoke that like a comment on something we had already discussed together.

'You have?'

'He's been in hiding.'

She laughed. The laugh sounded a little mad.

'You'll never guess who gave me the address.'

'I'm sure I can't.'

'A tart.'

'Indeed?'

'Does it surprise you, him knowing a tart?'

'I'll have to think about the answer to that.'

'Perhaps you know her too?'

'I've no reason to suppose so.'

'She's called Pauline.'

'As it happens, I never met her.'

'A girl of X's.'

'Of course.'

'So it's all above board, so far as Gwinnett's concerned.'

'I agree.'

The music began. She laughed again, and turned away. We found our seats. The Second Act took place, the drunken scenes, the setting to rest of fears that the girls might join the Pasha's harem. When we came out for the second interval, Moreland reappeared. Gossage and Chandler came up.

'I'm always fond of the English maid, Blonde,' Moreland said. 'Unlike the Pasha's gardener, I find that vixenish touch sympathetic.'

'I'm mad about Osmin,' said Chandler.

Gossage giggled nervously, a giggle unaltered by increased age. He brought conversation back to more serious criticism.

'The man's more of a baritone than a bass. Some cardinal appoggiaturas went west in the last Act, I'm afraid. No harm in subordinating virtuosity to dramatic expression once in a way. Not least in a work of this kind. We can't deny a lyrical tenderness, can we? I expect you agree with that, Mrs . . .'

Hesitating to call her 'Mrs Maclintick', after all these years of living with Moreland, at the same time, never having graduated to addressing her as 'Audrey', Gossage's voice trailed gently away. Audrey Maclintick took no notice of him. She spoke quietly, but there was a rasp in her tone.

'Have you seen the substitute Violin, Moreland?'

Moreland guessed from her manner of speaking trouble was on the way. He was plainly without a clue what form that might take, why she had asked the question.

'Has he arrived tight, or something? I've conducted unshaved myself before now. One mustn't be too critical.

This one's a substitute for the regular man, who's ill. The orchestra wasn't too bad. Allowing for Gossage's just strictures on the subject of appoggiaturas.'

'You haven't noticed one of the Violins, Moreland?'

'No, should I? Has he got two heads, or a forked tail emerging from the seat of his trousers?'

Moreland said that in a conciliatory manner, one he used often to employ with Matilda. Audrey Maclintick brought out of the answer through her teeth.

'It's Carolo.'

Moreland was not at all prepared for that. It was not a contingency anyone was likely to foretell; at the same time, the musical world being what it was, one not in the least unheard of in the circumstances. At first Moreland looked dreadfully upset. Then, seeing the matter in clearer proportion, his face cleared. There were signs that he was going to laugh. He successfully managed not to do so, his mouth trembling so much in the effort that it looked for a second as if he might burst into an almost hysterical peal, similar to that brought on by news of Glober's identity. Audrey Maclintick, for her part, showed no sign of seeing anything funny in the presence of her former lover – the man for whom she had left Maclintick – turning up in the *Seraglio* orchestra. Her demeanour almost suggested suspicion that Moreland himself had deliberately engineered transposition of violinists, just to disturb her own feelings. Seeing she was thoroughly agitated about what seemed to himself merely comic – another nostalgic enrichment of the Stevens party – he pulled himself together, plainly with an effort, and spoke soothingly.

'Is this really true? Are you sure it's Carolo? Musical types often resemble each other facially, especially violinists. I've noticed when conducting.'

Audrey Maclintick would have none of that.

'I lived with the man for three years, didn't I? Why should I say he was substitute Violin, if he wasn't? I

243

got to know him by sight, even if he didn't spend much time in the house.

Her fluster about the matter was unforeseen. On the whole, one would have been much more prepared for complete indifference. Objecting to the presence of Matilda was another matter. The intensity of feeling that bound Audrey Maclintick to Moreland was all at once momentarily revealed. Moreland made a face in my direction. He must have been wondering whether Matilda – actually married to Carolo for a short period in her early life – had also noticed the presence of her former husband. All this talk caused Gossage to suffer one of his most severe conjunctions of embarrassment. Like a man playing an invisible piano, he made wriggling movements in the air with fingers of both hands, while he mused aloud in a kind of aside.

'I did hear Carolo was not so very prosperous some years ago. No reason why he shouldn't have substituted tonight, prosperous or not. Did it to oblige, I expect.'

Chandler disagreed.

'Who ever heard of Carolo being obliging, since the days when he was fiddling away at Vieuxtemps, in a black velvet suit and lace collar? He's not dressed like that tonight, is he? Now that we're none of us so young, I'm wearing quieter clothes myself.'

That gave Moreland a chance to deflect the conversation.

'Nonsense, Norman, you're known as London's most eminent Teddy Boy.'

The measure was successful so far as putting an end to further discussion about Carolo, until time to return to the marquee. On the way there, Gossage was still muttering to himself.

'They've got polish. Vivacity.'

That was safely to relegate Carolo to a collective group. The orchestra could not be seen from where we sat. So far as I know, direct contact was never made during the further course of the evening between Carolo and his former ladies, but, at the termination of the opera, expression was given to a kind of apotheosis of the situation. This juncture, brief but striking, to be appreciated only by those conversant with Carolo's earlier fame, was too dramatic, too trite, to be altogether good art. Nevertheless, it had its certain splendour, however banal. This happened when, praise of the Pasha's renunciation of revenge chanted to a close, the curtain fell to much applause; then rose again for the reappearance of the cast. The audience was enthusiastic. The curtain rose, fell again, several times. The cast bowed their way off. It was the turn of the orchestral players. They trooped on to the stage.

'Which is Carolo?' whispered Isobel.

I was not sure I should have recognized him among the Violins without prompting. That was not because Carolo's appearance had become in any manner less picturesque than when younger. On the contrary the romantic raven locks, now snow white, had been allowed to grow comparatively long, in the manner of Liszt, to whom Carolo bore some slight resemblance. His whole being continued to proclaim the sufferings of the artist, just as in days gone by, in the basement dining-room of the Maclinticks. He bowed repeatedly (without the warmth of the old singer in Venice) to the charity-performance guests, with his colleagues, the general acknowledgment of the orchestra.

Then the orchestral players turned, in unison, towards the side of the auditorium, where Rosie and Stevens sat, together with Matilda, the Cabinet Minister and his wife. To these, as begetters of the show, Carolo and his fellows now made a personal tribute, Matilda, of necessity, included in this profound obeisance. The faint smile she gave, while she clapped, was not, I think, illusory. It marked her recognition that rôles had changed since Carolo, young and promising musician, had picked up, married, a little girl from the provinces, just managing to keep afloat as an actress. Matilda's attitude, more philosophic that Audrey Maclintick's, had not been of the temperament to remain married to Moreland. A few minutes later, illustration was provided of unlikely ties that can, on the other hand, keep a couple together, without marriage, probably without sexual relationship. This took place on the way to the supper-room. Odo Stevens came up with two people for whom he wanted to find a place.

'Do you remember, when you and I lived in that block of flats during the war – just before I went off with my Partisans? Of course you do. Here's Myra Erdleigh, who was there too, and this is Mr Stripling. Jimmy Stripling is teaching me a lot about my new passion I was talking about in Venice, vintage cars. Let's find a table.'

Age – goodness knows how old she was – had exalted Mrs Erdleigh's unsubstantiality. She looked very old indeed, yet old in an intangible, rather than corporeal sense. Lighter than air, disembodied from a material world, the swirl of capes, hoods, stoles, scarves, veils, as usual encompassed her from head to foot, all seeming of so light a texture that, far from bringing an impression of accretion, their blurring of hard outlines produced a positively spectral effect, a Whistlerian nocturne in portraiture, sage greens, sombre blues, almost frivolous greys, sprinkled with gold.

Jimmy Stripling, certainly a lot younger than Mrs Erdleigh, had become old in a different, more conventional genre. Tall, shambling, what remained of his hair grey, rather greasy, his bulky figure, which took up more room than ever, was shapeless and bent. Even so, he seemed in certain respects less broken down, morally speaking, than in his middle period. To be old suited him better, gave excuse to a bemused demeanour, pulled it together. Stevens was delighted with both of them.

'Myra and I met again in Venice. That was after you'd left. We talked a lot about those wartime flats, and the people who lived there. All those Belgians. Myra told my fortune then. She predicted a *belle guerre* for me. I didn't have too bad a one, so she prophesied right.'

Mrs Erdleigh took my hand. As in the past, her touch brought a sense of intercommunication, one conveyed by vibrations that imposed themselves almost more by not-being, than by being. They emphasized the inexistence of the flesh, rather than, by direct contact, extending its pressures and undercurrents.

'We have not met since that night of dangers.'

She smiled her otherworldly smile, misted hazel eyes roaming over past and future, apportioning to each their substance and shadow, elements to herself one and indivisible. I asked if she had been staying at the Bragadin palace. She shook her head in a faraway manner.

'I went only a few times to see Baby Clarini. She is a very old friend. Under Scorpio, like that other lady at the Palazzo, who is here tonight. Baby has had a sad life. She has never delved down to those eternal foundations, of which Thomas Vaughan speaks — Eugenius Philalethes, as we know him — that transform the hard stubborn flints of the world into chrysolites and jasper.'

She did not seem at all surprised when I told her Dr Brightman had also, speaking of *Borage and Hellebore,* invoked the name of Thomas Vaughan in Venice.

'His spirit was moving there. The Lion of St Mark could symbolize that green lion he calls the body, the magical entity that must clip the wings of the eagle. Do you remember planchette on that dark afternoon in the country? It was Baby's planchette that had been borrowed.'

I had forgotten that fact. The occasion, in any case, was not one desirable for resurrection at that moment. Better reminiscence should stop there. Mrs Erdleigh, who had perhaps been teasing, allowed that view to prevail. I followed up her astrological connotation of Baby Clarini by drawing attention to Isobel's horoscope.

'My wife is under Pisces. She rebels against that.'

Isobel made some complaint about the trials to which Piscians are subject. Mrs Erdleigh turned on to her a soothsayer's gaze, friendly but all-seeing.

'Remember always. The Fishes are ruled by Jupiter – give no credence to Neptune. There is the safeguard. When first I put out the cards for your husband, I told him you two would meet, and all would be well.'

If my acknowledgment fell short of absolute agreement that Mrs Erdleigh had seen so far ahead, it also fell much farther short of truthful denial that she had said anything of the sort. Sorceresses, more than most, are safer allowed their professional *amour propre*. Stripling leant across the table. He had sat down opposite, next to Stevens. He was probably under permanent orders to remain directly within Mrs Erdleigh's eye.

'Are you one of these musical people? I expect so. I don't know a thing about Mozart opera, or anyone else's, but Myra wanted to come. Myra and I have been friends for years. I have to do what she wants. She's such a wonderful person. What she knows is uncanny, far more than that. No, it is, Myra, I mean it.'

Mrs Erdleigh had made no attempt to deny omniscience, but Stripling may have felt the whole speech necessary to establish his own standing. I attempted some remark about having met him at the Templers' years before.

'Of course, of course. Poor old Peter.'

Stripling did not seem very capable of taking in chronological bearings about people any longer, only motor-cars, as it turned out a moment later, when I told him about seeing Sunny Farebrother some months before. Farebrother, too, then a butt of Stripling's derision, had been at the Templer house when we first met.

'Sunny Farebrother? Do you know I was thinking of Sunny the other day. He used to own an old Ford car years ago – thirty or forty, old even then – so much so, people like me ragged him about it. No hope he's kept it, I suppose? He's always been a very economical man, but I don't expect there's any hope of that. I'd give a lot to possess that car. Cars are the only things I know about. Are you interested in cars?'

'I possess one, so I have to be to that extent.'

Stripling shook his head. That was not enough.

'I've loved cars all my life. Love's the only word. Passionate love. Some feel like that about them. Probably why my marriage wasn't a success. I loved cars over well. I'm too old to race them now, but I study them, and collect them. Not a rally, not a *concours d'élégance*, I miss. You know Odo's got very keen on vintage cars too.'

When people speak of a subject close to them, they can look transformed. Almost as mystically absorbed in car lore as Mrs Erdleigh in a transcendental vision, Stripling suddenly changed from his dreamy state to one of intense excitement. He had just thought of something he could not wait to communicate to Stevens, something of paramount importance to both of them.

'I say, Odo, do you know there's an American at this party who's keen on vintage cars? A fellow called Glober. Told me quite by chance a minute before the opera started. It's just come back to me. I'd mentioned I owned two Armstrong Siddeleys, '26 and '27, which both still go like smoke. Powerful as dreadnoughts, the pair of them. He was as keen as mustard at once. They're 14 h.p., o.h.v., four-cylinder, sparely raked windscreens, both absolute treasures the way they pound along. What do you think Glober told me? He owns a

4½ litre supercharged '31 Bentley, which he's got here tonight. Only bought her last week. Of course, he wanted to see the Armstrong Siddeleys, when he's got a chance to let up on the film he's making – he's a film producer – and he's going to show me the Bentley when we leave. He's pondering a Bugatti 35.'

Stevens took charge of Stripling at this stage.

'Of course I know Louis Glober's in the vintage market, Jimmy. What are you thinking about? But, look here, tell me again what you were saying the other day about the 1902, 5 h.p., Renault Voiturette. It's the big stuff I'm getting interested in now. There was also a 1903 Panhard et Levassor, 10 h.p. tonneau, I wanted to discuss.'

They settled down to the subject.

'Though many desire these treasures, none enter but he who knows the key and how to use it.'

For a moment, Mrs Erdleigh sounded as if she, too, had embarked on the subject of vintage cars, but occult practices were still her theme.

'I remember Dr Trelawney saying much the same not long before he – '

I stopped just in time, at the last minute remembering no one, least of all a mage like Dr Trelawney, should be disparaged by the statement that Death had overtaken him. Providential suspension on my lips of that misnomer was barely accepted by Mrs Erdleigh. She had already begun to shake her head at such a near lapse, congenital lack of insight, all but openly displayed.

'You mean not long before he achieved the Eighth Sphere to which Trismegistus refers?'

'Exactly.'

'Where, as again Vaughan writes, the liberated soul ascends, looking at the sunset towards the west wind, and hearing secret harmonies. He calls this world, where we are now, an outdoor theatre, in whose wings the Dead wait their cue for return to the stage – an image from the *opèra bouffe* we have just witnessed. In a short space now, I too shall leave for the wings. Perhaps before the drama is played out, of which the opening Act was in the Bragadin palace. The rumble of wheels sounds. Once set in motion, the chariot of the soul does not long linger.'

'What was begun at Jacky Bragadin's?'

'Much to disorder the hierarchy of being. Elsewhere too. Pluto disports himself in the Eighth House.'

I should have liked to continue, try to persuade Mrs Erdleigh to show herself a little more explicit, but her attention was distracted by a young Labour MP, politely sceptical, also anxious to enquire into his own astrological nativity. Mrs Erdleigh's engagement in this, other similar interrogations, took up the rest of supper. After we had moved away from the table, further opportunity came to talk to Stevens, who had for the moment renounced vintage cars, about Widmerpool, what had taken place to extricate him from his embarrassments. Stevens himself was greatly preoccupied with this question.

'It's been suggested he wrote an indiscreet letter. Realized he'd gone too far, then tried to withdraw. That might have been in office hours, or when he was being cultured in Eastern Europe. You can't tell. It's not denied now he's a close sympathizer. Even so, he didn't want to get in trouble with his own security authorities. A spot of blackmail seems to have been the result. I know the form. One of my own mob found himself in a tangle that way. Thought it all in the interests of "international goodwill" to hand over one or two quite important little items. They asked for more, he stalled — got cold feet — they gave him away to us.'

'Somebody said there was a defection on their side.'

Stevens gave a sharp look.

'Perhaps there was. Whatever happened, he's got away with it.'

Stevens moved at ease through the world of secret traffickings of this kind. He was about to continue an exposition of what happened to such suspects, when – when not – convenient to prosecute, but was interrupted by Rosie. She came up in a state of some disquiet. Her little black eyes were popping out of her head with agitation.

'Odo, come at once. Something rather worrying has happened.'

Stevens went off with her. Rosie's anxiety might have any cause, the house on fire, an undesired invitation she wanted help in refusing, one of the children been sick, the degree of seriousness could not be estimated. Stevens's comments had interest. What dreams of power, practical or phantasmic had long tantalized Widmerpool's heart, what plans meditated to put them into effect? Stevens had spoken ironically of betrayals in the interest of 'international goodwill'; Bagshaw, speculating on less highflown motives, satisfaction of a taste for wholesale destruction, vicarious individual revenge against society. Neither Bagshaw nor Stevens spoke without experience. Perhaps, in Widmerpool's case, both aspects managed to coalesce. Chandler and Gossage passed. They said goodnight.

'A nice turn of power in the middle notes, didn't you think?' said Gossage. 'A fine sensibility of phrase?'

'Hugh didn't look too well,' said Chandler. 'I hope he's all right. I hadn't seen him for an age.'

They passed on. It was time to leave. I began to look about for Isobel. Before I found her, Stevens returned to the room. I took this opportunity of saying goodbye, as he seemed on his way somewhere. He confirmed, as it were, the words spoken a minute before by Chandler.

'Hugh Moreland's not very well. He's gone to lie down in the study. I'm on my way to get the car. I can run them home.'

Stevens, many of his characteristics uncommendable,

was good at taking charge when certain kinds of awkward situation arose.

'Is Hugh bad?'

'Doesn't look too good. He had a blackout, and fell. He's all right now, all right in the sense that he doesn't want to leave, because he says there are a lot of things about the *Seraglio* he still wants to discuss. We've persuaded him to take it easy for the moment. He'll be better when he gets to bed.'

'Can one see him?'

'Yes, do go up. Might keep him quiet. Don't bring a crowd with you. The room's the little study on the second floor, to the left.'

I found Isobel, and we both went upstairs. Moreland was lying on a small sofa, Rosie and Audrey Maclintick standing over him. The sofa was not big enough to contain his body comfortably at full length. He was drinking a glass of water, something I had never before seen him do, except after a heavy evening the night before. As Chandler had said, he did not look at all well. He was refusing to compromise with his own situation further than agreement to be driven home, when Stevens returned. Audrey Maclintick was trying to persuade him to rest quietly, until the car was announced as at the front door. When he saw us, he began to laugh in his old way.

'I told you nostalgia would get me. It did. Absolutely spun me over like a ninepin. It was Carolo put the finishing touch. I can't take it as I used. They say you lose your head for nostalgia, as you get older. That's also the time when waves of it come sweeping down without warning. You have to ration yourself, or a sudden dose knocks you out, as it did me.'

'You stop talking so much, and take it easy,' said Audrey Maclintick. 'I'm going to get that precious doctor of yours round as soon as you're in bed, no matter what the time is, and how much he's had to

253

drink, if he hasn't passed out cold. Even he told you to be careful, the last time he looked you over. You're going to stay in bed for a week or two now, if I have anything to do with it.'

Moreland did not listen. In spite of Rosie's added protest that he would be wiser to remain quiet, he continued to insist he would be perfectly recovered the following day. He also kept on returning to what had been happening that evening.

'There were a lot of people near me talking about vintage cars. There's nostalgia, if you like.

> For some we loved, the loveliest and the best,
> That from his vintage rolling Time hath pressed.

That's a striking image. I remember, years ago, a man who kept on quoting Omar at that party of Mrs Foxe's, after my Symphony. I've only just grasped that the verse refers to a car. Life's vintage car, in which we're all travelling. Better than Trapnel's Camel, more Hegelian too. Then you're suddenly told to get out and walk – pressed to, as the poet truly says.'

There was nothing to be done until Stevens returned. Staying with Moreland was only to encourage running on like this, tiring himself, so Isobel and I spoke a word or two, then said goodnight. It was not quite clear what sort of a fall he had suffered. He seemed to have lost his senses for a minute or so, afterwards felt no worse than a little dazed.

'I was pretty normal when I got up from the floor. If one could ever truthfully say that about oneself.'

A large proportion of the guests had already left when we arrived downstairs again.

'Poor Hugh,' said Isobel. 'He didn't look at all well to me.'

'Nor me.'

Outside, the night was dark. There was no moon. A

breeze, fresh, almost country-scented, blew in from the Park's tall clusters of trees. We were aiming to cut through from the terrace, where the Stevens house stood, making for a street beyond, which ran parallel, where a taxi could be picked up. A few doors away from the Stevens entrance, two or three persons, standing against the railings, were having some sort of argument. Having attended the party, they seemed now to be squabbling. Numbers and sex were not at first distinguishable in the gloom, but turned out as a woman, two men, in fact the Widmerpools and Short. Widmerpool was giving Short a dressing-down. He was very angry. Short was defending himself mildly, but with bureaucratic obstinacy. He could be heard maintaining that administrative breakdowns were from time to time unavoidable.

'I've already told you, Kenneth, that I quite plainly instructed the car to be outside waiting. The driver must have mistaken the address. If so, he will be along in a minute or two.'

As we went by, Widmerpool recognized us.

'Have you by any chance got a car? Our hired vehicle hasn't turned up. Leonard has made some sort of muddle. I suppose you couldn't give us a lift?'

'We're on our way to pick up a taxi.'

'Oh.'

'Why not do the same? They come down fairly frequently in the street behind here.'

'Pam doesn't want to walk that far. Oh, hell and blast. Why must this have happened?'

Widmerpool was not merely cross, put out by the car not being on time, but wrought up to an extent almost resembling drunkenness. Drink, which he hardly touched as a rule, was unlikely to have played any part in this highly strung state, unless, quite exceptionally, he had felt the *Seraglio* an occasion to swallow a few glasses, more to impress others with his own improved situation, than because he enjoyed their effect. Apart from threat of prosecution, he could have been suffering more than usual domestic strain, Pamela's design to leave him — if all alleged about Glober were true — now suddenly put into reverse gear. Even if Widmerpool did not know the reason, her change of plans, involvement with Gwinnett, might well have caused more than usually uncomfortable repercussions at home. The fact that she would not walk the few yards necessary to find a taxi showed her mood. Widmerpool stamped his feet. Short addressed us in a more temperate manner.

'If you should see anything looking like a hired car waiting round the corner, please ask the chauffeur if he's booked in the name of Sir Leonard Short, will you? He may have mistaken the address. If so, just send him along here.'

We said we would do that.

'Goodnight.'

'Goodnight.'

The only answer was Short's.

'I told you Lady Widmerpool was looking frightening,' said Isobel.

'Will they wait there all night?'

'I think she's planning something. That was how she looked to me.'

By that time we had reached the main road. A taxi cruised by. So far as we were both concerned, that closed the *Seraglio* evening.

As with stories of Trapnel's last hours, others in connection with Gwinnett's decampment from the Bagshaws', what followed, outside the Stevens house in Regent's Park, appeared afterwards in various versions. One hears about life, all the time, from different people, with very different narrative gifts. Accordingly, not only are many episodes, in which you may even have played a part yourself, hard enough to assess; a lot more must be judged from haphazard accounts given by others. Even if reported in good faith, some choose one aspect on which to concentrate, some another. This truth, obvious enough, was particularly applicable to the events following the *Seraglio* party. Even so, essential facts were scarcely in question. My own informants were Moreland and Stevens.

There was no irreplaceable divergence between these two accounts, although, when it came to telling a story in which veracity had to be measured against picturesque detail, neither could be called pedantically veracious; Moreland, in this respect the more reliable, being, if the more imaginative, the one who also best appreciated the graphic power of fact. Moreland talked about the scene right up to the end. He never tired of it. There can be no doubt it cheered his last months, added, as he himself said, to the richness of his own experience. His powerful gift of creative imagery led him, over and over again, to reconstruct the incidents, whenever anyone came to visit him.

Stevens, in principle to be thought of as a type used to violent scenes, was in a sense more taken by surprise, worse shocked, than Moreland. Marriage may have enervated Stevens, accustomed him by then to sedate, well-behaved routines. The rational, utilitarian, unruffled point of view, tempered with toughness, that directed most of his life – had so directed it in the past – could mislead, as well as stimulate. Like many persons who had enjoyed a comparatively adventurous career, knocked about the world a good deal, he retained a strain of naivety, naivety penetrating just the areas of the mind which, in Moreland's case, were quite free from any such inhibition. Indeed, Moreland used to complain himself that 'naivety in short supply' could be a disadvantage in practising the arts, where it is often necessary to see one thing only, that particular thing with supreme clarity In fact, when it came to giving a convincing description of what took place that night, the details Stevens produced, except for a few useful appendices, were little more than confirmation of Moreland's epic account. Stevens himself excused the scrappiness of his own narration.

'It was so bloody dark, and I was worrying all the time about getting Hugh home, before he had another fit, or whatever it was.'

The Stevens garage was in a mews behind the house. When Stevens drove the car back towards his own front door, he noticed figures talking together a few yards up the terrace. He did not identify them, merely supposing they were guests having a final musical dispute before parting on their separate ways. Moreland, Audrey Maclintick, several others, were by then chatting with Rosie in the hall, Moreland having become so restless lying on the sofa that it seemed best to come downstairs to wait for the car. There they found Mrs Erdleigh, Stripling, Glober, Polly Duport, all about to leave. Moreland at once recognized the potentialities of Mrs Erdleigh, whom he had not met earlier that evening. Within a matter of minutes – as he himself admitted – they were discussing together the magical writings of Cornelius Agrippa. Moreland and Mrs Erdleigh had already reached the Book of Abramelin the Mage, spells for surrounding an enemy with a vision of trellis-work, others for causing the Pope to fall in love with you, when Stevens came up the steps. Meanwhile Glober and Stripling had returned to vintage cars.

'Now we'll take a look at the Bentley, Mr Stripling. My automobile's parked at the end of the block.'

Stripling must already have obtained permission from Mrs Erdleigh to inspect the Bentley, before restoring her to whatever witch's lair she inhabited, but there is some uncertainty as to how exactly the outgoing party came on the Widmerpools and Short, still hanging about in the terrace, waiting for their car. It seems possible that Moreland refused to enter the Stevens car before he had finished his occult conversation with Mrs Erdleigh. Alternatively, his interest by now aroused in vintage cars, he too could have wanted to inspect Glober's vehicle. Moreland seems to have been strolling with Mrs Erdleigh; Stevens and Audrey behind; Stripling, Glober, Polly Duport, a short way ahead. The talk of cars may have been carried to the ears of Short, who (having made contact with Glober at supper on the subject of the French political situation vis-à-vis Algeria) now repeated a request for a 'lift'. Polly Duport was alleged to have thrown back a comment to the effect that the '31 Bentley was the 'size of a bus', thereby raising Short's hopes. Another possibility is that Pamela had intended that something of this sort should happen. She had been waiting for a chance at the party. That had not arisen. She could hardly have foreseen the lateness of the hired car, but might have grasped that Glober, still in the Stevens house, was bound sooner or later to pass that way. Short, having no reason to connect Glober with the Widmerpools, stepped forward, and made a little speech.

'If your car is really so commodious, Mr Glober, I wonder whether you could include in it a party of three — for our own hired vehicle does not seem to have turned up. It would be too kind were you able to manage that good office. We all live in the Westminster direction, if you happened to be going that way. It ill becomes a native of this country to seek transport from a transatlantic visitor, guest to our shores, but, not for the first time in recent years, we must needs throw ourselves upon the goodwill of American resources.'

Uncertainty prevails whether or not, at this stage, Glober immediately grasped that the other applicants for help were the Widmerpools. On the whole, it seems likely he did not. In the dark, there was no reason why he should recognize them. At the same time, Glober, out of sheer love of living dangerously, may have accepted this as a challenge. Moreland was ignorant of

Glober's former affiliations with Pamela, of whom he knew little or nothing at that time. Stevens, too, had not kept up with Pamela's ever varying situation, by then of no particular interest to him, provided his own married life was not embarrassed by it. In Venice, he had no doubt thought of the Widmerpools as guests of Jacky Bragadin, rather than connecting either of them with Glober; Pamela's own references to Glober giving no reason to convey the comparative seriousness of her relationship with him.

'I'd just love to give you all a ride in my new automobile. Come with us.'

Only after Glober had made that statement, so it appears, did Widmerpool join the group. Pamela still remained a little apart.

'This is very kind,' said Widmerpool. 'We have not seen each other since Venice.'

That indicated he and Glober had exchanged no word at the party. Glober bowed.

'You're welcome.'

Glober then introduced Mrs Erdleigh, Jimmy Stripling, Moreland, and Audrey Maclintick. If Widmerpool was to make a convenience of his car, Glober was determined to have some amusement too. Audrey Maclintick, of course, wanted to get Moreland into the Stevens car — and home — but for once does not seem to have succeeded in making her voice heard. Moreland, telling the story, emphasized the formality of Glober's introductions. That was the moment when Pamela joined the group. She came towards them hesitantly, as if she wanted to be introduced too. Her arrival impressed Moreland, not on account of any foreseeable disharmony that might include Glober, but because of the look given her by Mrs Erdleigh, more precisely rays of mystic disapproval trajected with force noticeable even in the dark. That perception was characteristic of Moreland. Mrs Erdleigh had made a deep impression on him.

'The Sorceress seemed to know Lady Widmerpool already. At least she gave her extraordinary smile – one I would rather not have played on myself.'

Pamela had smiled in return. She took no other notice of Mrs Erdleigh, nor the rest of them. The person to whom she addressed herself was Polly Duport. Pamela did not come close, but it was plain to whom she was speaking.

'I hear you're going to be the star in Louis's new film.'

Pamela said that very gently, barely audibly. Her tone almost suggested she was shy of mentioning the matter at all, though beyond words delighted at hearing such a rumour. All she wanted was to have the good news confirmed. Both Moreland and Stevens agreed there was not the smallest hint of unfriendliness in Pamela's voice. At the same time, Stevens, knowing Pamela to the extent of having lived with her for at least a few weeks, had no doubt something ominous was brewing. Moreland, it seemed, had not bothered to categorize Pamela at all; so far as he was concerned, another 'lady of fashion', full of every sort of nonsense about music, to be avoided at all costs. He admitted to having been struck by her looks, when he came to examine her.

Polly Duport, whether she knew much or little about Pamela, can have had few illusions as to friendliness. She could hardly have failed to hear of Glober's comparatively recent intention to cast Pamela for the lead she herself – anyway for the moment – was intended by him to play. Beyond that knowledge, of a purely business sort, the extent of her awareness of Pamela's character, even nature of relationship with Glober, could well be over-estimated. The segregated life of the Theatre, separated by its nature from so much going on round about, might easily have prevented her from hearing more than essential; so to speak, her own cue in taking Pamela's place. Polly Duport herself may not have been, over and above that, at all interested. She would know that Pamela, not a professional actress, had been in the running as 'star' of Glober's film, had probably experienced some sort of love affair with him. That was not necessarily significant. There was no reason for her to guess Glober had planned to marry Pamela.

Polly Duport, replying to Pamela's question, seems to have let fall a scrap of stylized stage banter adapted to such an inquiry, one of those conventional sets of phrase, existing in every professional world, in this case designed for use in counteracting another player, complimentary, spiteful, a mixture of both; clichés probably often in demand throughout the give-and-take of life in the Theatre. Moreland could not remember the actual comeback employed. He suggested several known to himself from his own backstage undertakings. Whatever form Polly Duport's answer presented was amicably accepted by Pamela, but she did not abandon the subject.

'I'm sure you'll like working with Louis.'

'Who could doubt that?' said Polly Duport.

She spoke lightly, of course. Pamela was behaving as if so pleased about the whole arrangement, that she was even a little anxious that it might not all go as well as deserved.

'You mean because all women love Louis?'

'All the world, surely?'

That was a neat reply. Pamela recognized it as such. She smiled, rather sadly, even though the idea seemed to please her. There was an instant's pause. Moreland said this was the point when the atmosphere became very highly charged. One of the elements causing him to notice that was Stripling suddenly ceasing to reel off names and dates of vintage cars, which, until this tenseness made itself felt, he had, up to the last possible moment, continued to recite to Glober. Pamela spoke again, this time reflectively.

'Quite a lot of people have loved Louis.'

'They couldn't help it,' said Polly Duport.

Pamela laughed softly.

'I expect you know,' she said. 'Louis's stuffed a charming little cushion with hair snipped from the pussies of ladies he's had?'

Stevens said afterwards that he 'recognized that inquiry as signal for trouble starting'. Both he and Moreland, in whatever other respects their stories differed, stood shoulder to shoulder as regards those precise words of Pamela's. Where they disagreed was as to the manner in which Polly Duport took them. Stevens thought her outraged. Moreland's view was of her merely raising an eyebrow, so to speak, at the crudeness of phrasing. She was not in the least disconcerted by the eccentricity of the practice. Moreland was absolutely firm on that.

'Miss Duport showed not the slightest sign of wilting.'

He agreed with Stevens that she made no comment. No one else made any comment either. They just stood, 'as if hypnotized', Moreland said. Pamela laughed quietly to herself, giving the impression that thought of Glober's whim amused her. She turned towards him.

'You have, haven't you, Louis?'

'Have what, honey?'

Glober was absolutely relaxed. Stevens, again fancying other people as scandalized as himself, supposed him taken aback a moment before. If so, Glober was now completely recovered.

'Stuffed a cushion?'

'Sure.'

'As well as the ladies themselves?'

'Correct.'

Glober remained unrattled. Pamela laughed this time shrilly. She was working herself up to a climax, possibly a sexual one. Stevens said her behaviour reminded him of a scene made at a black-market night-club during the war, when she had started a sudden row, calling out to the people at the next table that he was impotent. Stevens never minded telling that sort of story about himself. It was one of his good points. In any case, even if at one time or another he had failed to satisfy Pamela, the charge was hard to substantiate, in her case not a specially damaging one. As Barnby used to say in that connexion, 'There's a boomerang aspect.' Glober remained equally undisturbed. His conversational tone matched Pamela's.

'I thought Miss Duport would just like to know what's expected. Perhaps you've been at work with the nail-scissors already, Louis? Anyway, it's a cheaper hobby than his.'

She pointed at Widmerpool. At this stage of the proceedings, Mrs Erdleigh seems to have taken charge. One imagines that, in her own incorporeal manner, she floated from the exterior of the group to its moral centre, wherever that might be. She appears to have laid a hand on Pamela's arm, a movement to suggest restraint. This was the interlude Moreland most enjoyed describing, what he called 'the Sorceress in the ascendant, Lady Widmerpool afflicted'. He said that Pamela, at contact of Mrs Erdleigh's fingers, shot out a look of intense malevolence, hesitating for a second in whatever she was about to say.

'My dear, beware. You are near the abyss. You stand at its utmost edge. Do not forget the warning I gave when you showed me your palm on that dread night.'

Stevens took the line later that neither second-sight nor magical powers were required to foretell the way things were moving. He may have been right. At the same time, however obscurely phrased, Mrs Erdleigh's presentiments were near the mark.

'The vessels of Saturn must not be shed to their dregs.'

Stevens, incapable himself of reproducing cabalistic

dialectic, was no less impressed than Moreland, in whose repetition such specialized language lost none of its singularity. The unwonted nature of Mrs Erdleigh's invocations did not so much in themselves bewilder Stevens as in their practical effect on Pamela.

'The extraordinary thing was Pam more or less understood the stuff. That was how it looked. At least she stopped in her tracks for a second or two. I've never seen anything like it.'

Stevens was certainly taken aback, but the spell, as it turned out, was short lasting. Briefly quelled, Pamela recovered herself.

'Then you know?'

'Time yet remains to evade the ghastly cataract.'

'But you know?'

'Knowledge is the treasure of our unsealed fountains.'

Pamela gave what Stevens, in his flamboyant manner, called a 'terrible laugh'. Moreland admitted he, too, had found that laugh uncomfortable.

'Then I'll unseal them – and him.'

Mrs Erdleigh made some sort of motion with her hand, one of her mystic passes, conceivably no more than an emotional gesture, at which Pamela drew herself away, Moreland said, 'like a serpent'. Mrs Erdleigh issued her final warning.

'Court at your peril those spirits that dabble lasciviously with primeval matter, horrid substances, sperm of the world, producing monsters and fantastic things, as it is written, so that the toad, this leprous earth, eats up the eagle.'

Then Pamela began to scream with laughter again, shriller even than before.

'You know, you know, you know. You're a wonderful old girl. You don't have to be told Léon-Joseph croaked in bed with me. You know already. You know it's true, what nobody else quite believes.'

To what extent that plain statement was at once comprehended by those standing round remains uncertain. Probably the words did not wholly sink in until later. At moment of utterance they could have sounded all part of this extraordinary interchange, at once metaphorical and coarsely earthy. Some doubt existed, in repetition, as to the exact phrases Pamela used. Whatever they were, positiveness of assertion was in no way diminished. She turned to Widmerpool again.

'You tell them about it. After all, you were there.'

She pointed at him, now speaking to the others.

'He thought I didn't spot he was watching through the curtain.'

Up to this stage of things, it appears, no one except Mrs Erdleigh had attempted to tackle Pamela. Mrs Erdleigh, so far as it went, having done that with success, spoken her warning, withdrew into the shadows. Widmerpool had remained all the time silent. Even now he did not at once answer this imputation on himself. He heard it to the end without speaking. Glober, uncharacteristically at a loss for the inspired wisecrack to ease the situation, was equally mute. After that, from the moment Pamela voiced these revelations, there is difficulty in pinpointing order of events, reliable continuity almost impossible to establish. Accounts given by Moreland and Stevens were at odds with each other. What appears to have taken place is that Pamela, dissatisfied at her words being received with comparative calm, at best so stunning that her hearers lacked reaction, chose another line of attack. It is no less possible she was building up, in any case, to that. Stevens, more at home this time with plain statements, rather than Mrs Erdleigh's oracular sayings, gave a convincing imitation of Pamela's hissing denunciation.

'You might think that enough. Watching your wife being screwed. Naturally it wasn't the first time. It was just the first time with a blubber-lipped Frenchman, who couldn't do it, then popped off. Of course he had arranged it all with Léon-Joseph beforehand – except the popping off – and in some ways it made things easier to have two of us to explain to the hotel people that Monsieur Ferrand-Sénéschal had just passed away, while we were visiting him. Then there's a tart called Pauline he has games with. He used to photograph her. I found the photographs. He didn't guess I'd meet Pauline too.'

Even then Widmerpool seems to have made no active protest. What really upset him was Pamela's next item.

'He's been telling everybody that he hasn't the slightest idea why they thought he was spying. I can explain that too, all his little under-the-counter Communist games. How he's got out of his trouble, in spite of their holding an interesting little note in his own handwriting. He's given the show away as often, and as far, as he dares. Unfortunately, he gave it away to his old pals, the Stalinists. The lot who are in now want to discredit some of those old pals. That's where Léon-Joseph comes in again. Poor old Ferrand-Sénéschal was playing just the same sort of game – as well as an occasional orgy, when he felt up to it. So what he did was to hand over all the information he possessed about Ferrand-Sénéschal, some of that quite spicy. That's why he was let off this time with a caution.'

Stevens, his mind, as I have said, adjusted to secret traffickings, his nature to physical violence, reported Pamela's words as cut short at Widmerpool seizing her by the throat. Moreland disagreed that anything so forcible had happened, at least immediately. Moreland thought Widmerpool had simply caught her arm, possibly struck her on the arm, attempting to silence his wife. The scene partook, in far more savage temper, of that enacted at the Huntercombes' ball, when, after Barbara Goring had cut his dance, Widmerpool grasped her wrist. The upshot then had been Barbara pouring sugar over his head. Widmerpool's onslaught this time might be additionally menacing, stakes of the game, so to speak, immensely higher; the physical protest was the same, final exasperation of nerves kept by a woman too long on edge. Another analogy with this earlier grapple was Pamela, no more daunted at the assault than Barbara by her clutched wrist, dragged herself away, screaming with laughter. The scene was not without its horrifying, morally upsetting, side. Moreland emphasized that; Stevens, too, in his own terms.

'In fact, I thought I was going to be sick,' Moreland said. 'Nausea might have been caused by my recent *crise*. If I had vomited, that would scarcely have added at all to other gruesome aspects.'

In emerging from this hand-to-hand affray with Pamela, possibly beaten off by her own counter-attack, Widmerpool seems to have stepped back without warning, retreating heavily on to Glober, who may himself have moved forward with an idea of separating husband and wife. Stevens thought Stripling had made some ponderous, ineffectual attempt to intervene. That is to some extent controverted by subsequent evidence. The view of Stevens was that Stripling had tried to catch Widmerpool round the waist, with the idea of restraining him, an act misattributed by Widmerpool to Glober. Both Moreland and Stevens agreed that, in the early stages of the Widmerpools' clinch, Glober took no special initiative. Perhaps, for once, he felt a certain diffidence, owing to the intricacies of his own position. Possibly, too, he was not unwilling to watch them fight it out on their own. There is some corroboration of Stripling playing a comparatively active part at this stage, but things moving so quickly, it was hard to know what he did, how long remained present.

What does seem fairly certain is that Widmerpool, stepping backwards, immediately supposed himself to have been in some manner curbed or coerced. Simultaneously, Mrs Erdleigh, foreseeing trouble when Stripling laid a hand on Widmerpool, may at once have spirited Stripling away by more or less occult means. That would to some extent explain why Widmerpool, finding Glober, rather than Stripling, made an angry, presumably derogatory comment. It is possible, of course, Glober had indeed taken hold of him. They faced one another. That was when Glober hit Widmerpool.

'It's never a KO on these occasions,' said Stevens. 'I've seen it happen before, though not with men of quite that age. Widmerpool just staggered a bit, and put his hand up to his face. No question of dropping like a sack of potatoes, being out for the count, floored by a straight left, or right hook. That only happens professionally, or in the movies. The chief damage was his spectacles. They were knocked off his nose, and broke, so the midnight match had to be called off.'

No one watching denied the light had been too bad for the fracas to be critically assessed blow by blow. For this latter stage of the story, Stevens was probably the better equipped reporter. Moreland, his own nervous tensions by this time strongly reacting, not to mention the recent collapse he had suffered, was by now partly repelled by what was happening, partly lost in a fantastic world of his own, in which he seemed to be dreaming, rather than observing. He admitted that. Stevens, more down to earth in affecting to regret unachieved refinements of the boxing-ring, seems also to have been a little shocked, a condition vacillatingly induced, in this case, by the age of the antagonists. It is impossible to say how matters would have developed had not interruption taken place from outside. A large car drove jerkily down the terrace, the chauffeur slowing up from time to time, while he looked out of its window to ascertain the number of each house as he passed. He drew up just beside the spot where everyone was standing.

'None of you gentlemen Sir Leonard Short by any chance?'

Short stepped forward. Until then he had been inactive. He may have withdrawn completely, while the imbroglio was at its worst. Now he entered the limelight.

'Yes. I am Sir Leonard Short. I should like some explanation. I cannot in the least understand why this car should be so late.'

'I am a trifle after time, sir. Sorry about that. Went to the wrong address. There's a Terrace, and a Place, and a Gate. Very confusing.'

'This unpunctuality is not at all satisfactory. I shall take the matter up.'

Short opened the door of the car with a consciously angry jerk. He brusquely indicated to Widmerpool that he was to get in, do that quickly. Short was in command. Stevens said one saw what he could be like in the Ministry. Widmerpool, who had already picked up the remains of his spectacles from the pavement, obeyed. Short followed, slamming the door. The car drove slowly down the terrace. Moreland said it was a good, an effective exit.

'When I looked round, the three of us – Audrey, Odo, myself – were alone. It was like a fairy story. The Sorceress was gone, taking off, no doubt, on her broomstick, the tall elderly vintage-car-bore riding pillion. Lady Widmerpool was gone too. That was the most mysterious. I have the impression she made some parting shot to the effect that none of us would see her again. The American tycoon and Polly Duport were almost out of sight, heading for the far end of the terrace. I don't exactly know how any of them faded away. I was feeling I might pass out again by then. Much relieved when Odo drove us home.'

# SIX

Gwinnett wrote me a longish letter about a year later. By then he was living in the south of Spain. He referred only indirectly to the embarrassments ('to use no harsher term') suffered during the latter period of his London visit. He said he wrote chiefly to confirm details I had given him in Venice concerning Trapnel's habits, dress, turns of phrase. The notes he had then made seemed to conflict, in certain minor respects, with other sources of research. Apart from checking this Trapnel information, he just touched on the comparatively smooth manner in which dealings with the police, other persons more or less officially concerned, had passed off, including journalists. The briefness, relatively unsensational nature of the inevitable publicity, had impressed him too.

Pamela's name did not occur in the letter. At the same time, Gwinnett's emphasis on Trapnel, in what he wrote, may have been a formality, something to supply basis for communication, felt to be needed, of necessity delicate to express. The Trapnel inquiries were plainly not urgent. In their connection, Gwinnett spoke of returning to his critical biography only after sufficient time had elapsed to ensure the dissertation's approach remained objective, ran no risk of being too much coloured by events that concerned himself, rather than his subject. Characteristically, he added that he still believed in 'aiming at objectivity, however much that method may be currently under fire'. As well as reducing immediate attention to the Trapnel book – though not his own fundamental interest in Trapnel himself –

Gwinnett had abandoned academic life as a formal profession for the time being. He might return to the campus one of these days, he said, at the moment he only wanted to ruminate on that possibility. His new job, also teaching, was of quite a different order. He had become instructor of water-skiing at one of the Mediterranean seaside resorts of the Spanish coast. He said he liked the work pretty well.

Gwinnett also touched on Glober's death. The accident (on the Moyenne Corniche) had been one of those reflecting no marked blame on anyone, except that the car had been travelling at an unusually high speed. A friend of Glober's, a well-known French racing-driver, had been at the wheel. The story received very thorough press coverage. It was the sort of end Glober himself would have approved. Although the last time I saw him – of which I will speak later – he was with Polly Duport, *Match Me Such Marvel,* was soon after abandoned as a project. No one seemed to know how far things had gone between them in personal relationship. The general view was that her profession, rather than love affairs, came first in her life. She may have been well out of the Glober assignment, because, about a month before Glober died, she acquired a good part (not the lead, one in some ways preferable to that) in a big 'international' film made by Clarini, Baby Wentworth's estranged husband.

I had the impression that Gwinnett and Glober had never much cared for one another. Beyond appreciating the obvious fact of their differing circumstances, I had no well defined comprehension of how they would have mutually reacted in their own country. In his letter, Gwinnett – like Gwinnett in the flesh – remained enigmatic, but he did comment on the way Death (he gave the capital letter) had been in evidence all round. There was nothing in the least obsessive in the manner he treated the subject. He did not, of course, disclose whether he had 'known' Pamela's condition before she came to the hotel. How could he disclose that?

The fact is, Gwinnett must have known. Otherwise there would have been no point in Pamela making the sacrifice of herself. Her act could only be looked upon as a sacrifice – of herself, to herself. So far as sacrifice went, Gwinnett could accept Pamela's, as much as Iphigenia's. The sole matter for doubt, in the light of inhibitions existing, not on one side only, was whether, at such a cost, all had been achieved. One hoped so. I wrote a letter back to Gwinnett. I told him how I had seen Glober, without having opportunity to speak with him, in the autumn of the previous year. I did not mention I had seen Widmerpool too on that occasion. It seemed better not. I always liked Gwinnett. I liked Glober too.

During the months that remained to Moreland, after the *Seraglio* party, we often used to talk about the story of Candaules and Gyges. He had never heard of the Jacky Bragadin Tiepolo. The hospital was on the south bank of the River.

'One might really have considered the legend as a theme for opera,' Moreland said. 'I mean, if other things had been equal.'

He lay in bed with an enormous pile of books beside him, books all over the bed too. He would quote from these from time to time. He was very taken with the idea of the comparison Pamela herself had made.

'Candaules can obviously be better paralleled than Gyges. Most men have a bit of Candaules in them. Your friend Widmerpool seems to have quite a lot, if he really liked exhibiting his wife. She was the Queen all right, if she's to be believed as being put on show. Also, in knowing that, herself intended to kill the King. Not necessarily physical killing, but revenge. Who was Gyges?'

'Hardly Ferrand-Sénéschal. In any case, through no fault of his own, he failed in that rôle. Others seemed to have enjoyed his Gyges-like privileges without dethroning the King. Candaules-Widmerpool continues to reign.'

'No, it doesn't really work,' said Moreland. 'All the same, it's a splendid fable of Love and Friendship — what you're liable to get from both — but the bearings are more general than particular, in spite of certain striking resemblances in this case. You really think she took the overdose, told him, then . . .'

'What else could have happened?'

'Literally dying for love.'

'Death happened to be the price. The sole price.'

'All other people's sexual relations are hard to imagine. The more staid the people, the more inconceivable their sexual relations. For some, the orgy is the most natural. On that night after the *Seraglio,* I was very struck by the goings-on with which Lady Widmerpool taxed her husband. I've next to no voyeurist tastes myself. I lack the love of power that makes the true voyeur. When I was in Marseilles, years ago, working on *Vieux Port,* there was a brothel, where, allegedly unknown to the occupants, you could look through to a room used by other clients. I never felt the smallest urge to buy a ticket. It was Donners's thing, you know.'

Moreland reflected a moment on what he had said. While still married to Matilda, he had, rather naturally, always avoided reference to that side of Sir Magnus's life. This was the first time, to my own knowledge, he had ever brought up the subject.

'Did I ever tell you how the Great Industrialist once confided to me that, when a young man — already doing pretty well financially — the doctors told him he had only a year to live? Of course that now seems the hell of a long time, in the light of one's own medical adviser's admonitions — not that I'm greatly concerned about keeping the old hulk afloat for another voyage or two, in the increasingly stormy seas of contemporary life, especially by drastic cutting down of the rum ration, and confining oneself to ship's biscuit, the régime recommended. That's by the way. The point is, I now find myself in a stronger position than in those days for vividly imagining what it felt like to be the man in the van Gogh picture, so to speak Donners-on-the-brink-of-Eternity. Do you know what action Donners took? I'll tell you in his own words.'

Moreland adopted the flat lugubrious voice, conventionally used by those who knew Sir Magnus, to imitate – never very effectively, because inimitable – his manner of talking.

'I rented a little cottage in The Weald, gem of a place that brought a lump to the throat by its charm. There I settled down to read the best – only the best – of all literatures, English, French, German, Italian, Scandinavian.'

Moreland paused.

'I don't know why Spanish was left out. Perhaps it was included, and I've forgotten. Between these injections of the best literature, Donners listened to recordings of the best – only the best – music.'

'Interrupted by meals composed of the best food and the best wine?'

'Donners, as you must remember to your cost, like most power maniacs, was not at all interested in food and drink. Although far more in his line, I presume the best sexual sensations were also omitted. That would be not so much because their physical expression might hasten ringing down the curtain, as on account of the apodictic intention. Is "apodictic" the right word? I once used it with effect in an article attacking Honegger. The *villeggiatura* was very specifically designed to rise above coarser manifestations of the senses.'

'In the end did all this culture bring about a cure?'

'It wasn't the culture. The medicos made a mistake.

They'd got the slides mixed, or the doctrine changed as to whatever Donners was suffering from being fatal. Something of the sort. Anyway they guessed wrong. Everything with Donners was right as rain. After spending a month or two at his dream cottage, he went back to making money, governing the country, achieving all-time records in utterance of conversational clichés, diverting himself in his own odd ways, all the many activities for which we used to know and love him. That went on until he was gathered in at whatever ripe old age he reached – not far short of eighty, so far as I remember.'

'Also, if one may say so, without showing much outward sign of having concentrated on the best literature of half-a-dozen nations.'

'Not the smallest. I was thinking that the other day while reading a translation of *I Promessi Sposi*. It sounds as if I were modelling myself on Donners, but I've got a lot of detective stories too. There was a special reason why *I Promessi Sposi* made me think of Donners, wonder whether it figured on his list, when he put on that final spurt to become cultured before *rigor mortis* set in. Like so many romantic novels, the story turns to some extent on the Villain upsetting the Hero by abducting the Heroine, unwilling victim threatened by the former's lust. That particular theme always misses the main point in the tribulations of Heroes in real life, where the trouble is that the Heroine, once abducted, is likely to be only too anxious to suffer a fate worse than death.'

'You mean Sir Magnus and his girls?'

For the moment I had not thought of Matilda.

'I meant when he abducted Matty, and married her. Not exactly a precise parallel with Manzoni, I admit, but you'll see what I mean.'

I did not know what to answer. This was the first time Moreland had ever spoken in such terms of Matilda leaving him for Sir Magnus Donners. He sighed, then laughed.

'I suppose she liked being married to him. She remained in that state without apparent stress. She knew him, of course, from their first round together. In his odd way, he must have been attached to her too. All the same, I believe her when she said – consistently said – that she herself always refused to play his games, the way some – presumably most – of his girls did. I mean his taste, like your friend Lord Widmerpool's, for watching other people make love.'

'He was a friend of Donners too, but I don't think Widmerpool got the habit there. What you say was certainly one of the things alleged. So it was true?'

'Let's approach the matter in the narrative technique of *The Arabian Nights* – the world where Donners really belonged – with a story. In fact, two stories. You must be familiar with both, favourite tales of my youth. To tell the truth, I've heard neither of them since the war. I've no doubt they survive in renovated shape.'

Moreland sighed again.

'The first yarn is of a man making his way home late one night in London. He finds two ladies whose car has broken down. It is in the small hours, not a soul abroad. The earliest version ever told me represented the two ladies – one young and beautiful, the other older, but very distinguished – as having failed to crank their car with the starting-handle. Thought of this vintage jewel would make the mouths water of those vintage-hounds at the *Seraglio,* and shows the antiquity of the legend. No doubt the help required was later adapted to more up-to-date mechanics. In yet earlier days, the horses of their phaeton were probably restive, or the carriage immobilized for some other contemporary reason. Anyway, the man gets the engine humming. The ladies are grateful, so much so, they ask him back to their home for a drink. He accepts. After placing the glass to his lips, he remembers no more. He is found the following day, unconscious, in the gutter of some alley in a deserted neighbourhood. He has been castrated.'

'A favourite anecdote of my father's.'

'Of all that generation. The other story concerns a man – I like to think the same man, before he was so cruelly incapacitated – who is accosted by a beautiful girl, again late at night, no one about. He thinks her a tart, though her manner does not suggest that. She says she wants not money, but love. At first he declines, but is at last persuaded by assurances that something about him attracted her. They adjourn to her flat, conveniently near. The girl leads the way up some stairs into a room, unexpectedly large, hung with dark curtains up to the ceiling. Set in the middle of the floor is a divan or bed. On it, in one form or another, perhaps several, they execute together the sexual act. When all is ended, the man, still incredulous, makes attempt to offer payment. The girl again refuses, saying the pleasure was its own reward. The man is so bewildered that, when he leaves, he forgets something – umbrella, hat, overcoat. Whatever it is, he remembers at the foot of the stairs. He remounts them. The door of the curtained room is shut – locked. Within, he can hear the babble of voices. A crowd of people must have emerged from behind the curtains. His sexual activities – possibly deviations – have been object of gratification for a concealed clientèle.'

'I've heard that one too.'

'We all have. It's gone the round for years. Just within the bounds of possibility, do you think?'

'Why was the situation complicated by refusal of payment?'

'To make sure he agreed. The appeal to male vanity may have added to the audience's fun. If he swallowed the declaration that she thought him so attractive, the display would not be over too quickly. Do you suppose Sir Magnus was behind the curtain?'

'He may have watched the castration too.'

'Some of his ladies would have been well qualified as surgeons,' said Moreland.

He lay back in the bed. I suppose he meant Matilda. Then he took a book from the stack of works of every sort piled up on the table beside him.

'I always enjoy this title – *Cambises, King of Percia: a Lamentable Tragedy mixed full of Pleasant Mirth.*'

'What's it like?'

'Not particularly exciting, but does summarize life.'

One day in November, having a lot of things to do in London, before returning to the country that afternoon, I went to see Moreland earlier than usual. It was bleak, rainy weather. When I crossed the River, by Westminster Bridge, two vintage cars were approaching the Houses of Parliament. Another passed before I reached the hospital. Some sort of rally was in progress, for others appeared. I watched them go over the bridge, then went on. Moreland had no one with him. Audrey Maclintick would turn up later in the morning, possibly someone else drop in. Usually these friends were musical acquaintances, unknown to myself. I reported that droves of vintage cars were traversing the Thames in convoy. Moreland reached out for one of the books again.

'I've been researching the subject, since quoting to you the Khayyám reference. Keats was an addict too.

> Like to a moving vintage down they came,
> Crowned with green leaves, and faces all on
>   flame . . .
> Within his car, aloft, young Bacchus stood . . .

What could be more specific than that? Interesting that you stood upright to drive those early models. One presumes the vintage, where the Grapes of Wrath were stored, was a tradesman's van of Edwardian date or earlier.'

He threw the book down, and chose another. He was full of nervous energy. The impression one derived of his state was not a good one.

'I've been haunted by the story of Lady Widmerpool. Have you ever read *The Dutch Courtezan*? Listen to her song – forgive me quoting so much verse. Things one reads become obsessional, while one lies here.

> The darke is my delight,
> So 'tis the nightingale's.
> My musicke's in the night,
> So is the nightingale's.
> My body is but little,
> So is the nightingale's.
> I love to sleep next prickle
> So doth the nightingale.

It makes her sound nice, but she wasn't really a very nice girl.'

'The Dutch Courtezan, or Pamela Widmerpool?'

'I meant the former. Lady Widmerpool had her failings too, if that evening was anything to go by. Still, it's impressive what she did. How some men get girls hotted up. No, what I was going to say about the Dutch Courtezan was – if there'd been time to spare – I might have toyed with doing a setting for her song, whatever she was like. One could have brought it into the opera about Candaules and Gyges perhaps. That would have made Gossage sit up.'

He sighed, more exhaustedly than regretfully, I thought. That morning was the last time I saw Moreland. It was also the last time I had, with anyone, the sort of talk we used to have together. Things drawing to a close, even quite suddenly, was hardly a surprise. The look Moreland had was the one people take on when a stage has been reached quite different from just being ill.

'I'll have to think about that song,' he said.

Drizzle was coming down fairly hard outside. I walked back over the bridge. Vintage cars still penetrated the traffic moving south. They advanced in small groups, separated from each other by a few minutes. More exaggerated in style, some of the period costumes assumed by drivers and passengers recalled the deerstalker cap, check ulster, General Conyers had worn, when, on the eve of the 'first' war, he had mastered the hill leading to Stonehurst, in his fabled motor-car. I wondered if the Conyers car had survived, to become a collector's piece of incalculable value to people like Jimmy Stripling. Here and there, from open hoodless vehicles, protruded an umbrella, sometimes of burlesque size or colour. I paused to watch them by the statue of Boadicea — Budicca, one would name her, if speaking with Dr Brightman — in the chariot. The chariot horses recalled what a squalid part the philosopher, Seneca, with his shady horse-dealing, had played in that affair. Below was inscribed the pay-off for the Romans.

> Regions Caesar never knew
> Thy posterity shall sway.

Whatever else might be thought of that observation, the Queen was obviously driving the ultimate in British vintage makes. A liability suddenly presented itself, bringing such musings sharply to a close, demanding rapid decisions. Widmerpool, approaching from right angles, was walking along the Embankment in the direction of Parliament. It might have been possible to avoid him by crossing quickly in front, because, as usual when alone, his mind seemed bent on a problem. At that moment something happened to cause the attention of both of us to be concentrated all at once in the same direction. This was the loud, prolonged hooting of one of the vintage cars, which, having crossed Parliament Square, was approaching Westminster Bridge.

Widmerpool stopped dead. He stared for a second with irritated contempt. Then his face took on a look of enraged surprise. The very sight of the vintage cars appeared to stir in him feelings of the deepest disgust, uncontrollable resentment. That would not be altogether out of character. His deep absorption in whatever he was regarding gave opportunity to avoid him. Instead, I myself tried to trace the screeching noises to their source. They were issuing from the horn, whimsically shaped like a dragon's head, of a vintage car driven by a man wearing neo-Edwardian outfit, beside whom sat a young woman in normal dress for an outing. The reason for Widmerpool's outraged expression became clear, even then not immediately. I am not sure I should have recognized Glober, in his near-fancy-dress, had not Polly Duport been there too. My first thought, complacently self-regarding, had been to suppose they had seen me, hooted, if not in a mere friendly gesture, at least to signalize Glober's own glorious vintage progress. A similar explanation of why the horn had sounded offered itself to Widmerpool. He, too, thought they had hooted at him. He took for granted that Glober was hooting in derision.

The doubtful taste of such an act – given all the circumstances – had time to strike me, slightly appal me, before I became aware that the imputation was altogether unjust. Glober had noticed neither Widmerpool, nor myself. The crescendo of resonances on the dragonhorn had been prompted by Odo Stevens, with Jimmy Stripling, at that moment passing Glober's Boadicean machine, in one of similar date, though without a hood. Stevens, clad even more exotically than Glober, was driving; Stripling, wearing a simple cap and mackintosh, holding a large green umbrella over their heads. Widmerpool turned away from contemplation of the scene. He was red with anger. There could be no doubt he supposed himself the object of ridicule. All this had taken a moment or two to absorb. Escape was now out of the question. We were only a few yards apart. He could not fail to see me. I spoke first, as the best form of defence.

'I'm glad I'm not driving a long distance on a day like this in a car liable to break down.'

That was not a particularly interesting nor profound observation. Nothing better came to mind to bridge the moments before mutation of the traffic lights allowed evasion by crossing the road. Widmerpool accepted this opening by giving an equally flat reply.

'I'm on my way to the House of Lords.'

The statement carried conviction. The block of flats in which he lived was only a few minutes walk from where we stood. Riverside approach to Parliament would be preferable to the Whitehall route. He showed outward mark of the stresses endured. His body was thinner, the flesh of his face hanging in sallow pouches. So deeply, so all envelopingly, was he dressed in black, that he looked almost ecclesiastical.

'After what I've been through, I think it my duty to show I can rise above personal attack – and, I might add, personal misfortune.'

I made some acknowledgment, one not conspicuously glowing, of these sentiments. Short of turning on one's heel, which would have been overdramatic, it was still impossible to get away. Widmerpool, for his part, appeared quite pleased at this opportunity for uttering a short address on his own situation, possibly some sort of informal rehearsal of material later to be used in a speech.

'I do not propose for one moment to abandon the cause of genuine internationalism. It has been said that a presumption of innocence is a peculiarity of bourgeois liberal law. My own experience of bourgeois liberal law is the reverse. From the first, in my own case, there was a presumption of culpability. Fortunately, I was in a position to rebut my accusers. In the Upper House, wherever else I am called upon to serve the purposes of political truth, I shall continue to assail the limitations of contemporary empiricism, and expose the bankruptcy of cold-war propagandists.'

He sounded more than a little unhinged. Widmerpool had not finished. Without altering his tone, he changed the subject.

'The squalor – the squalor of that hotel.'

Traffic, beginning to slow up at the amber, came at last to a halt at red. Grinding noises provided exemption from need to produce an audible reply. Widmerpool showed no sign of expecting anything of the sort.

'The sheer ingratitude,' he said.

'I must be getting on. There's a lot to do. I want to get home before dark.'

He was never greatly interested in other people's doings. I added some platitude about the evenings drawing in. Widmerpool did not question the notation of the days. He turned to wait for the other lights to change, enabling him to proceed towards his destination. I crossed Whitehall swiftly. Another burst of vintage cars was advancing towards the bridge.

# Anthony Powell

### *A Dance to the Music of Time*

'The most significant work of fiction produced in England
since the last war' *Clive James*

**FLAMINGO**

# Russian Novels

**The First Circle** Alexander Solzhenitsyn      £3.95

The unforgettable novel of Stalin's post-war Terror.

'An unqualified masterpiece – this immense epic of the dark side of Soviet life.' *Observer*

'At once classic and contemporary . . . future generations will read it with wonder and awe.' *New York Times*


**The White Guard** Mikhail Bulgakov      £2.95

'A powerful reverie . . . the city is so vivid to the eye that it is the real hero of the book.' V. S. Pritchett, *New Statesman*

'Set in Kiev in 1918 . . . the tumultuous atmosphere of the Ukrainian capital in revolution and civil war is brilliantly evoked.' *Daily Telegraph*

FLAMINGO

# SIMONE DE BEAUVOIR

**She Came to Stay**  £3.50
The passionately eloquent and ironic novel she wrote as
an act of revenge against the woman who so nearly
destroyed her life with the philosopher Sartre. 'A writer
whose tears for her characters freeze as they drop.'
*Sunday Times*

**The Mandarins**  £3.95
'A magnificent satire by the author of *The Second Sex*.
*The Mandarins* gives us a brilliant survey of the post-war
French intellectual . . . a dazzling panorama.' *New
Statesman*. 'A superb document . . . a remarkable novel.'
*Sunday Times*

**When Things of the Spirit Come First**  £1.95
The five women at the centre of this novel are all
enmeshed in the moral and social demands of middle-class
society. Even those among them who try to be rebels
themselves are hobbled by their upbringing and their
self-deception.

'It is because of women like Simone de Beauvoir that the
prejudice and repression of which she writes no longer
has such effect.' *Over 21*

FLAMINGO

**FLAMINGO**

Flamingo is a new, quality imprint publishing both fiction and non-fiction. Below are some recent titles.

**Fiction**
- [ ] A Chain of Voices *André Brink* £2.95
- [ ] An Instant in the Wind *André Brink* £2.50
- [ ] New Worlds: an Anthology *Michael Moorcock* (ed.) £3.50
- [ ] A Question of Upbringing *Anthony Powell* £2.50
- [ ] The Acceptance World *Anthony Powell* £2.50
- [ ] A Buyer's Market *Anthony Powell* £2.95
- [ ] The White Guard *Mikhail Bulgakov* £2.95

**Non-fiction**
- [ ] Old Glory *Jonathan Raban* £2.95
- [ ] The Turning Point *Fritjof Capra* £3.50
- [ ] Keywords (new edition) *Raymond Williams* £2.95
- [ ] Arabia Through the Looking Glass *Jonathan Raban* £2.95
- [ ] The Tao of Physics (new edition) *Fritjof Capra* £2.95
- [ ] The First Three Minutes (new edition) *Steven Weinberg* £2.50
- [ ] The Letters of Vincent van Gogh *Mark Roskill* (ed.) £3.50

You can buy Flamingo paperbacks at your local bookshop or newsagent. Or you can order them from Fontana Paperbacks, Cash Sales Department, Box 29, Douglas, Isle of Man. Please send a cheque, postal or money order (not currency) worth the purchase price plus 10p per book (or plus 12p per book if outside the UK).

NAME (Block letters) _____

ADDRESS _____

_____

_____